HIS FATHER'S HOUSE

HIS FATHER'S HOUSE

A Novel

D. J. MEADOR

PELICAN PUBLISHING COMPANY
Gretna 1994

Library of Congress Cataloging-in-Publication Data
Meador, Daniel John.
His father's house / D.J. Meador
p. cm.
ISBN 1-56554-032-8
1. Fathers and sons—Alabama—Fiction. 2. Germany—Fiction.
I. Title.
PS3563.E1687 1994
813′.54—dc20 93-37982
CIP

Manufactured in the United States of America

Published by Pelican Publishing Company, Inc.
1101 Monroe Street, Gretna, Louisiana 70053

Dedicated to the memory
of my father and mother:

Daniel John Meador, Jr.
of Myrtlewood, Marengo County, Alabama
1888-1965

Mabel Kirkpatrick Meador
of Cahaba, Dallas County, Alabama
1896-1945

The wind goeth toward the south, and turneth about unto the north; it whirleth about continually, and the wind returneth again according to his circuits.

All the rivers run into the sea; yet the sea is not full; unto the place from whence the rivers come, thither they return again. . . .

The thing that hath been, it is that which shall be; and that which is done is that which shall be done.

Eccles. 1:6-7, 9
(King James Version)

Wir sehen jetzt durch einen Spiegel in einem dunkeln Wort; dann aber von Angesicht zu Angesicht. Jetzt erkenne ich stückweise; dann aber werde ich erkennen, gleichwie ich erkannt bin.

1 Cor. 13:12
(Martin Luther Translation)

CONTENTS

Part One – Remberton 9

Part Two – Germany 35

Part Three – Virginia 273

Part Four – Prinzenheim 317

Epilogue..379

PART ONE
Remberton

Chapter 1

THE LATE AFTERNOON IN JUNE was unusually hot and humid for an Alabama day so early in the summer. Robert Trepnitz Kirkman sat slouched in an old white wicker chair on the screened porch of his late father's house. Attic and closet dust, mingled with a day-long accumulation of perspiration, besmirched his white tennis shirt and green bermuda shorts. He slipped off his well-worn loafers to let his bare feet catch the gentle breeze from the steadily clicking ceiling fan.

On the straw rug in front of him sat a battered brown footlocker with its hinged top standing open. It emitted the pleasant aroma of long pent-up mothballs. Beside it in a jumbled pile lay a high-necked olive drab tunic, a russet leather Sam Browne belt, and a pair of khaki britches cut for riding boots.

For some minutes he had been looking with perplexed fascination at a small photograph and a letter handwritten in German. Staring back at him from the yellowed photograph was an attractive young woman with a thin face, high cheek bones, and light-colored hair shaped in the style of the First World War. Standing beside her was a small boy, probably no more than two or three years old. On her lap she held an even younger child.

As he puzzled over who this woman could be and where the photograph could have come from, he heard the low rumbling of thunder in the west, signaling the approach of a late afternoon thunderstorm. He looked forward to its climax of thunder, lightning, wind, and lashing rain. However, judging from the still-distant mutterings, he had a while to savor the gradual build-up to that ferocious display, which would break the heat, leaving a cool and delicious summer twilight.

A car swished by on the quiet street in front of the house, headed toward the center of town. Numerous times, he had tried to describe Remberton to his northern classmates at the University of Virginia Law

School and to friends he had made later in New York, but he always felt unsuccessful in conveying the ambience and realities of the scene.

As he used to explain, Remberton is a county seat of fewer than eight thousand souls—more than a third of them black. The town sits on the southern edge of the Alabama Black Belt, a name derived from the rich black topsoil and not—as his northern friends were prone to assume—from the color of its inhabitants. It is an imprint of an ancient sea, a great crescent-shaped body of water which began at Columbus, Mississippi, then widened to the south, swinging eastward across the middle of Alabama, never more than fifty miles wide, and tapering off before reaching the Chattahoochee River. This ancient sea bed, crisscrossed by rivers with names redolent of former Indian inhabitants—Cahaba, Alabama, Tombigbee, and Black Warrior—was fertile and gently rolling land, flat in many stretches. Into it in the early nineteenth century poured the bold seekers of new cotton country, chiefly people from South Carolina and Virginia.

To the north and west of Remberton run the rich rolling pasture lands, once planted in cotton. Sprinkled with oaks and cedars and occasional patches of pines, this land extends all the way to the Alabama River, once the major artery of commerce but now a lonely, muddy band of water, seemingly peaceful yet powerful, flowing southward to Mobile and the Gulf.

Just south of the town the land changes; the soil becomes thin and sandy, and pine trees abound. Here one will find no relics of the antebellum South and few families of venerable lineage. Until the prosperity of the mid-twentieth century, this was a land of poor whites eking a living out of the infertile piney woods. At the border of these contrasting regions and cultures, Remberton is a blend of both. Thus, as Robert Kirkman had tried to explain in late night bull sessions on the travails of the South, there were—he could testify from his own experience—at least two Souths, strikingly different from each other.

His genealogical and spiritual roots ran toward the river to the north and west of Remberton. His father, Robert Edward Kirkman, known as Mr. Ed, was born and reared some thirty miles to the northwest, the son of a landed family with holdings of several thousand acres along the river. All except a few fragments had been lost by the family during the Depression.

Despite his rearing, Mr. Ed had not been attracted to agricultural pursuits. Instead, he moved to Remberton and entered the practice of law. There he met and married Rob's mother, a literary and strong-minded woman named Emily Shepperson. Her family were townspeople and had been in Remberton for decades, rising to a position of affluence from mercantile pursuits. Her father, Noble Shepperson, owned the cotton gin and warehouse, as well as one of the town's two wholesale grocery companies. All that, too, disappeared in the Depression. Thus it was that young Rob Kirkman, who would have been heir to lands and mercantile interests of impressive value, found himself growing up in relatively modest circumstances.

Rob was very much aware that the house where he sat on this June afternoon, four decades after those economic traumas, was about all, in a tangible way, that remained of a vanished legacy. It was originally the house of his grandfather, Noble Shepperson, dead now for many years. It was also the house where Rob's mother, Miss Em, was born and where he himself had been reared.

With his mother and father both gone, the roomy, one-story Victorian house now belonged to Rob. He had come home in this summer of 1973 to sort out his father's effects and to decide what to do with the place. For three days, he had been cleaning out closets and the attic, hauling clothes down to the thrift shop or giving them to the yard man and anybody else chancing to come by. Today, however, he was concentrating on books, papers, and assorted artifacts that had accumulated in his father's study and attic for fifty years. It had been an emotional day, mixed with sadness, amusement, warm memories and pain over the loss of his father just three months before. At this moment, though, he was overcome with curiosity about the photograph and letter he held in his hand.

The thunder was growing louder, like distant artillery moving closer. The dark clouds in the west had not yet obscured the sun, but the leaves of the pecan trees surrounding the house were beginning to stir in the faint breeze, a prelude to the coming storm.

As Rob read the handwritten letter for the second time, he inwardly congratulated himself on the proficiency he had achieved in German. He had been listening to German cassettes for the last several months to brush up on his grammar in preparation for a conference he was scheduled to attend in Marburg in July.

The letter was on delicate paper, engraved at the top with the name Martina Baroness von Egloffsberg. On the next line were the words *Schloss Bachdorf.* The word *schloss,* he mused, was always ambiguous in English translation. He took it to mean a residence of considerable pretentions, possibly a large manor house, not necessarily a castle, although it certainly could be. The letter was dated 6 October 1918. By his translation, it read:

My dearest Bruno,

Although I wrote you all of our news only two days ago, I am writing now because I have just received the photograph of the two boys and me that was taken on our recent visit to Leipzig. I did not want to delay in sending one to you. Everyone says that your sons look like you, and I think that we must agree that it can be seen in this picture.

We are receiving news of a new offensive by the Americans, but we do not know what is really happening. Surely after four years, there must be a way to bring this dreadful war to an end.

Your father is feeling a little better today, but he is still weak. We pray that you will come safely through the events now unfolding and will be home with us again soon.

With heartfelt love,
Martina

Rob studied again the faces in the faded picture. The light-haired woman appeared to be no older than twenty-one or twenty-two. There was an aura of elegance about her. On the back of the picture was the stamp of a Leipzig photographic studio.

The First World War had been part of Rob Kirkman's childhood. He had been gripped by the pictures in a *Big Little Book* of the debased landscapes of France and Belgium, with the tangled barbed wire, shell holes, and stark tree trunks. He could envision those scenes clearly now, especially those that showed men going over the top and advancing across no-man's-land. As a teenager, he had quizzed his father about his wartime experiences, but his father would give him only sketchy accounts. He did not relive the war and did not seem to be interested in talking much about it. Rob knew that his father, an infantry lieutenant, had been in the last great American push through the Argonne in October of 1918. At various times in the past, he had seen the uniforms that were now piled on the porch floor, but he realized now that he had never gotten many details. He was certain that he had never seen nor heard of the German letter and picture that he now held in his hand. He was overcome with remorse at not having talked more with his father about a lifetime of rich and varied experiences, experiences now closed to him forever.

Rob now sensed the depth of his love for his father, that soft-spoken man who had obviously been devoted to his well-being, living alone in the twilight years, reading books on gardening, hunting, and fishing more than law books, and sending his son news clippings on local history, achievements of great men, and the sad condition of state politics.

He saw himself standing beside the open grave in the coolish warmth of early spring, a light breeze rattling the hard leaves of the magnolia trees lining the lanes of the cemetery. He heard the minister reciting the familiar words: "In my father's house are many rooms. If it were not so I would have told you. I go to prepare a place for you." He remembered now how he struggled to retain his composure.

The approaching thunderstorm was gaining momentum. It was only five in the afternoon, but the sun had gone and the sky was an angry gray. The thunder had grown to a continuous, crashing rumble. "Giants are rolling barrels across the sky," he had been told in his childhood. From somewhere far off, there rose a sound like the distant roar of ocean surf. Then, as if some mighty hand had thrown a switch, the wind bent the limbs of the trees. It hit him as though he had stepped in front of one of those large electric fans that stood by the front doors of unairconditioned stores in summer. He heard doors slamming in the house as the wind rushed through. Lightning flashed close by; thunder crashed directly overhead. If she were here, his mother would tell him that he should come in from the porch. But he reveled in this magnificent unleashing of the elements.

Indeed, since his early years, he associated these late afternoon summer thunderstorms with the end of the world or with that day when he too would cross the great divide. He had often imagined that day. He would be walking along a deserted country road, a gradually rising road that he remembered from childhood on his grandmother's place at Trepnitz Hills. The wind would be rising and the thunder growing louder. He would begin to run forward into the wind as he saw ahead a throng of people coming to meet him. In the lead he would see his mother, his grandparents, and long-dead aunts and uncles. Now he added his father to this assemblage welcoming him.

The first splats of rain hit the porch steps, at first singly here and there, then the advancing wall of water came roaring through the trees. The deluge slammed across the lawn and engulfed the house. Spray whipped across the porch.

Rob remained slumped in the wicker chair. The loneliness of his situation struck him with the force of the thunderstorm raging all around. Here he was, past forty, unmarried, father and mother gone, and no brothers and sisters. Where would he go from here? He had a vague feeling that he was at a fork in the road.

Rob was brought back to reality as he became aware that the door bell was ringing. The thunderstorm had passed. The rain had stopped, but there was a heavy dripping from the pecan trees. The sun was struggling through the clouds in the western sky, casting a strange rosy gray glow—the post-thunderstorm prelude to sunset and darkness.

The door bell rang again, and he sprang to his feet and pulled on his loafers. He passed through the parlor and into the hall. As he opened the solid wooden door, a warm voice exclaimed, "Robby!"

He knew he was home. Robby was his Remberton name. It was a sure sign that the speaker was a lifelong acquaintance. Nobody who came to know him in college, law school, or ever after had called him anything but Rob. But in Remberton he will be Robby until judgment day.

"Robby," she said, "Why haven't you let anyone know you were here?" She was reaching for the handle on the screened door at the same time that he was pushing it open.

"Pookie, my goodness, what a pleasant surprise." They hugged with genuine warmth. "How's Richard?"

"He's fine as usual. Gone to Montgomery this afternoon and probably won't be home for supper 'til late. I meant to come by earlier, but the lightning and rain held me up."

He felt embarrassed and grimy. She was fresh, scrubbed, and smelling of some flowery perfume. From their childhood she had reminded him of Shirley Temple.

"Why don't we go on back to the kitchen and get a drink?" he said, pulling her by the elbow toward the rear of the hall. "This house is all torn up. I've been here for three days digging out old clothes and everything you can think of. Uncle Noble has had Lucy come by a few times since Daddy left, but it's pretty dusty."

"I saw Mr. Noble this morning down at the filling station. That's how I found out you were here."

"Yes, he's been a big help for these last three months."

The kitchen was large and old-fashioned, with a sink and cabinets dating from the 1930s. She sat at the large breakfast table in the corner. "I stopped by the state store on the way down from Montgomery and picked up a fifth of bourbon," Rob explained. "You know that Daddy never drank anything much except a little wine."

"Just a little with a lot of water," she said.

He poured bourbon into two glasses. He fished an ice tray out of the refrigerator, broke out the cubes, and put them in the glasses. He then filled the glasses with water at the sink, and sat down at the table, passing the lighter colored drink to Pookie. They sipped and chatted about her family.

He sat listening to her, looking at her. She had always held an attraction for him, but he found her more appealing now than he had in their high school and college years.

Rob switched the subject. "I don't know what I'll do with this house. To let it go would be like losing a member of the family."

The reddish hues of early sunset suffused the kitchen and a faint breeze passed through the open windows. His grandfather Shepperson's design of this house was ideal for the climate of middle Alabama. The tall, wide windows were arranged to provide maximum cross ventilation, allowing even small stirrings of air to be felt.

They were quiet for a few moments. He sipped his drink.

"Well," he sighed, "I suppose I should have married somewhere along the line, but don't rule me out yet."

Dusk in Remberton and talking with one of the old crowd alone in a way that he had not done for a long time brought back one of Rob's most unpleasant memories of those youthful years—Ippy Ratcliff. Daughter of the bank president, vivacious, irreverent, and sexy, she was the one with whom he had truly—so he thought—fallen in love. They had had a fling in junior high school, drifted apart for a few years, then revived the relationship about the time he went off to law school. Much more independent than most Remberton girls, she went to Atlanta and took a job with an interior decorator. She visited him in Charlottesville on several big weekends, but then out of the blue she took up with the son of a real estate developer in Atlanta, and it wasn't long before they were married. As he admitted to himself later, she was really interested only in going to parties and having a good time. Rob looked back on that episode in his life with a measure of disgust at himself, wondering how he could ever have been smitten with someone so shallow. Worse, he had probably made a fool of himself.

He rattled the ice in his glass. "Let's have a touch more," he said. Her glass was still a quarter full.

"Just a tiny bit. I've got to go in a few minutes."

The deepening twilight and the loud rising and falling of locusts wailing filled him with a sense of nostalgia. Here in this house and in this town, he had never been able to think of anything but the past. It crowded out the present, engulfing him with memories of childhood, the growing-up years, and beyond that, decades of history, the upheavals of war and reconstruction, high water, boll weevil, and depression, all of which he had absorbed and breathed in naturally as part of the atmosphere.

She resumed the conversation. "I always had a feeling that Remberton was too small for you; but then I had a feeling that Mr. Ed wanted you to come back and practice law with him. After you went off to Virginia, I figured that you wouldn't be coming back."

"Well I guess that's so," he said. "Several of my classmates were planning to go on to Wall Street law firms. I had all the credentials to do that too—grades, law review, and so on. To the others, coming back to Remberton seemed to be an admission that I was not up to the big league. I resented that, but in the end I gave way and went to New York."

"I remember thinking that you really took to New York."

"I knew that Daddy was disappointed that I had not come back to the state, although he never said so. Knowing that he felt the way he did preyed on my mind. This may sound strange, but every day I compared New York and Remberton. Can you imagine that Remberton was the standard against which I measured things there? Here when I went to the post office or to the grocery store or the drug store or the bank, people knew me when I walked in the door. If someone got sick or died, people came around and helped."

"Then why didn't you come home?" she asked in a quiet voice.

"Well, about that time I was beginning to feel an itch to teach, so I solved my dilemma by coming back to Tuscaloosa to teach in the law school."

The sunset had now faded, and darkness was fast moving in. They had not turned on any lights.

"I think I may be approaching another one of those big decision points in life," he said, leaning back in the chair and stretching his legs out full length.

"What in the world do you have in mind now?"

"I'm not sure. I just sense that I'm in the mood for change. I'm beginning to doubt that I'm doing much good where I am, and I'm beginning to feel a little stale in Tuscaloosa. Now that Daddy is gone perhaps I should try a change of setting."

"Maybe your trip to Germany will give you a new lease on life," she said, smiling sympathetically.

The telephone began to ring. He shoved his chair back and headed toward the hall.

"Robby, this is Richard," boomed the voice in the receiver.

He heard Pookie's voice from the kitchen in a startled exclamation. "Oh my Lord! It's Richard back from Montgomery and probably wondering where his supper is. I've got to run."

Rob exchanged brief pleasantries with Richard and hung up.

"How long will you be here?" she asked, getting up from the table.

"Probably a couple of days. It depends on how long it takes me to sort things out with the house."

They walked up the hall toward the front door. He pushed the screened door open, and they stepped out on to the veranda. Dusk had given way to darkness. The street light was masked by the two large oak trees in the front yard. It was quiet except for the night insects which had struck up their noisy humming and chirping.

"I really do appreciate your coming by," he said, his arm around her shoulders.

"It's grand to see you. You're looking good in spite of your costume. We'll be in touch." Then down the short walk she half ran and plunged into the station wagon, driving away with hurried determination.

Rob stood on the porch for a few minutes, savoring the cool night air, refreshing after the sultry day. From a hundred yards up the street he heard the laughter and shouts of children. The sounds brought back the childhood joys of playing out after dark on summer evenings on this very street.

Here was his point of origin. The house, the trees, the chorus of insect noises, and children's playful yelping were just as they had been. Up these steps, across this porch, and through this door he had come thousands of times from infancy onward. This was home. He had no other. Yet it was not the same. Too many people were gone. He had been too far, seen too much. Had the time come to close it all out, get rid of the house, sever himself from his only fixed point of reference? He did not know what to do.

As the screened door clicked shut behind him, his eyes fell on that puzzling photograph and German letter he had hurriedly tossed on the hall table. He paused, pondering them for a few moments. Where had they come from? Why were they in his father's footlocker? Perhaps, he realized with a mixture of sadness and frustration, the answers lay forever entombed amidst the magnolias and camellias in the cemetery at the edge of town.

Chapter 2

THE MORNING DEW WAS NOT QUITE dry on the grass when Rob left the house. He knew that Uncle Noble arrived at his office early and would be expecting him. The sky was vividly blue. The morning was cool, but the promise of the heat to come could be seen in the unobscured sun, already well up in the heavens. Although he could have walked to the law office in fifteen minutes, Rob took his car. He wanted to get there fast, and he wanted to get back to his housecleaning task without delay.

The clock in the Victorian courthouse tower, which dominated uptown at the head of Center Street, was striking eight as Rob edged his car into a parking space in front of the hardware store on the corner. Passing a plaque reading Kirkman & Shepperson, Attorneys at Law, Upstairs, he mounted the wooden steps running up the side of the two-story building.

The steps looked as if they sloped away from the building, giving the impression that they might suddenly become detached and fall into the street below. Until he had gone off to college and seen the world beyond Remberton, Rob assumed that law offices everywhere were reached by rickety wooden steps going up the outsides of buildings. Law offices were always, in the nature of things, he had thought, upstairs over hardware stores, feed stores, or drug stores.

At the top of the steps he entered a short, drab hallway, with worn linoleum covering the floor. Beyond an unmarked wooden door was a glass-paned door with lettering proclaiming that here could be found Kirkman & Shepperson.

As he entered, a plump, elderly woman leaped from behind a desk, charged around it, and hugged him, exclaiming on the way, "Well, Robby, we've been expecting you. How have you been doing out there with all those old clothes and papers and books? I know Mr. Ed had saved a whole lot of stuff. I surely wouldn't want the job of straightening it all out."

This was Miss Evelyn, the principal secretary in the office for over thirty years. Rob could not remember when she had not been there. He greeted her warmly. "I don't know what I can do with the house and everything in it. You know I have only a few days here before I leave for Germany."

He was standing in a room that had changed little since his childhood. The most notable new features were the overhead fluorescent lights and the window air-conditioning unit now humming away. There were more filing cabinets; and some chairs and a coffee table had been added ten years ago. Off to the side was the small file room in which he had been based for two summers in his law school days. Opposite the entrance door were two closed wooden doors, one leading to his father's office and the other to Uncle Noble's.

The latter abruptly opened, revealing Noble Shepperson, Jr. Little Noble, as he was still called by the old-timers around town, stood six feet two inches tall, weighed two hundred pounds, and looked to be short of his seventy years. His steel-gray hair was thinning only slightly, and his gray-blue eyes were alive. He had the physique of an aging athlete. He was in his shirtsleeves with tie and collar loosened, showing signs of having been hard at work for some time.

"Come on in, Rob," he boomed out. He was the only person in Remberton who called Rob by his adult name. "I've been wondering when you were going to come out of your cocoon over at the house and pay us a visit. I hear you're going to Germany to talk about how German and American judges manage their cases."

"That's right."

"Well, I'll tell you this. The judges in these parts don't manage anything very well. They're politically elected and afraid of offending any of the lawyers." Noble intoned this in his usual authoritative and emphatic voice. The voice still rang with the resonance of the parade ground. Although Noble had twice left the army for civilian pursuits, the military flair had not departed from him.

In the late nineteen-twenties, the glamour of military life had faded fast in the doldrums of the peacetime army. By that time, Ed Kirkman, a young lawyer in Remberton, had married Noble's sister Emily and persuaded Noble to resign the army, go to law school, and come back to Remberton to go into partnership. The two diplomas hanging on the back wall of the room evidenced the shift of careers. The heavily embellished scroll from the United States Military Academy hung alongside the plainer parchment of the University of Alabama law degree.

Rob had vague childhood memories of Noble's return to Remberton with his New York wife. Except for the Jewish couple who ran a dry goods store, his Aunt Nan was the only non-Southern inhabitant of Remberton. She fit in well, however, she did have trouble keeping cooks and maids. Rob's father had always said that she didn't know how to manage them, as Northerners generally did not. The turnip greens and snap beans were never quite right at her house because she wouldn't let the cook leave them on the stove long enough or put in enough of the right kind of seasoning.

Sitting across from his uncle, looking at the West Point diploma, Rob recalled Noble's account of December 7, 1941. That Sunday afternoon, Noble had gone to his office to catch up on some work. Nan telephoned him there to tell him that the Japanese had bombed Pearl Harbor. He sat frozen in his chair for a long time. His thoughts were racing. There would surely be a general war, and it would be a big one and a long one. There was not a tincture of uncertainty in his mind as to his course of action. He would immediately seek to be recommissioned. He had missed the last one because he was too young. He resolved then and there that he would not miss this one. In January of 1942, Major Noble Shepperson reported for active duty at Fort Benning. He was put into a desk job at post headquarters. This was not what he had had in mind, so he spent the next year calling West Point classmates all over the country until he wangled himself into an armored division.

Noble leaned back in his large swivel chair, swung halfway around, and gazed out of the window. From this second-story vantage point at the rear of the building, one looked over a new automobile dealership a block behind Center Street, and beyond that some nondescript houses and open country. Cotton once filled every acre to the horizon, but not a stalk now was to be found between Remberton and the river. It was just as well, Rob thought, that the Shepperson gin and cotton warehouse were lost to the family in the thirties, because there would be no cotton to gin or store today.

"I really miss your father," Noble mused aloud, his eyes on some unidentifiable distant point. "He was a fine man, a fine lawyer, a fine citizen, and my best friend. It's not often that a man is privileged to have a brother-in-law, a law partner, and a friend all in the same person. He drafted all the wills and did all the real estate work. I never did care for that kind of stuff. Litigation is my type of law practice, but your father was fascinated with the deed records and those musty probate files at the courthouse."

Miss Evelyn came in carrying a bulging file and put it on the desk in front of Noble. He cleared additional space, stacking several volumes of the Alabama Code and some yellow note pads on one side of his desk. He opened the file and began turning the papers over, looking at each for a moment.

"This is a relatively simple probate matter, as you know," Noble said, continuing to turn the papers in the file. "You are welcome to look all this over if you want. Everything is left to you. That means the house and the stocks, bonds, and cash in the bank. Outside of the house, all of this adds up to about $50,000. That's not a whole lot of money, but it's a right tidy sum to be handed out of the blue."

"Actually it's a lot more than I thought was there," Rob said.

"Your father was not really interested in money. It was refreshing to know someone like that. He seemed content in these last years if he had an adequate supply of shotgun shells and fishing bait. He always said that he would be happy if he could provide a roof over his family, put food on the table, and put you through college. And he did all those things in good style, I would say."

"I agree," Rob said. "Many a time I have heard him say that a good name is rather to be desired than great riches. Another of his favorites was this: 'What shall it profit a man if he gain the whole world and lose his own soul.'"

The courthouse clock clanged the half hour. Rob stirred to rise. "Well, I have a lot to get done, so I should be running along. If you don't mind, I'll take a look in Daddy's office."

"Check around in there and see if you want to take any of the books. They're yours, but any you want to leave here we'll be glad to keep. Anyway, Nan and I will see you tomorrow for supper."

Rob moved out into the reception room. Miss Evelyn was pounding away on the typewriter. A hard-bitten countryman was sitting in one of the straight-back chairs against the wall. As he opened the door into his father's office he heard Noble saying, "Come on in, Frank."

Rob closed the door. He stood for a long while, looking at the empty desk, the high-back leather swivel chair behind it, and the closed glass fronts of the bookcases lining two walls. Never had he seen the room so bare. There was not a paper anywhere to be seen, not a book casually laid on a table or desk.

Rob remembered coming here as a little boy, holding his mother's hand. The room looked larger and more impressive to a four-year-old, but it had not changed with the passage of forty years. Its walls, like those of all the rooms of Kirkman & Shepperson, were a dirty beige that always looked in need of painting even when they had been freshly painted. The floors were covered with a dark brown linoleum.

Rob saw his father sitting behind the cluttered desk, files and papers sloughing off the sides, and volumes of the Alabama Code and the Alabama Reports piled on top of each other on nearby tables. He felt tears welling up in his eyes, tears for an era gone, a life ended, tears for himself, now alone without a father or mother, without brothers or sisters, and without a wife or children.

Rob sat in his father's chair and looked at the pictures and other framed memorabilia that had been left for him to collect. On one wall was the

University of Alabama Law School diploma and the certificate of admission to the bar. On the table was a picture of his mother taken when she was in her thirties. Hers was a peaceful face with large, thoughtful eyes. Beside it was a photograph of the family—himself, his father, and his mother—sitting on the front steps of their house. He remembered distinctly when it was taken by Noble. It was on a Sunday during his senior year in high school; they had just come home from church, and Noble and Nan had come for dinner, bringing a new camera.

On another wall was a photograph of the house at Trepnitz Hills. It was a massive two-story brick structure in a late antebellum Greek revival style. Four huge white columns across the front supported a portico and second-story veranda. This was the house in which his father, Mr. Ed, and three generations of Trepnitzes before him were born and reared. The house was part of the warp and woof of Rob's makeup, for it was there that he spent every summer until he was eleven years old. There he had a Welsh pony, given to him by his Uncle Charles Kirkman. With that compliant creature, he had the unforgettable experiences of exploring alone vast expanses of cotton fields and woodlands and river banks.

He remembered vividly the night that world came to an end. He and his parents were asleep in the house in Remberton when they were awakened by a loud pounding on the front door. It was a cold February night, and he was bundled deep under the covers. He sensed that it was long into the night, maybe approaching dawn. The pounding repeated, stirring within him the feeling that something very strange and perhaps awful was afoot. He heard his father coming into the hall, moving quickly toward the front door, calling out in a loud voice, "Who is it?"

Then Rob heard from beyond the door a man's voice saying, "It's Charles and Mama."

Rob was by then in the hall in his pajamas. He saw his father open the door. Charles and his grandmother pushed in, looking as he had never seen them before. Both were black all over, with clothes torn and hair bedraggled.

"My God, what's happened?" his father asked in a loud, perturbed voice.

"We've been burned out," Charles said with all the sadness and resignation that one could imagine in a human utterance.

Rob's mother was in the hall now in her bathrobe, rushing forward to take her mother-in-law by the hand. They came back to the kitchen and sat down. Rob was standing in the doorway from the hall.

As his mother got coffee for them, Charles told the story. He and Mama had gone to bed early, about half past nine. They had a fire in the parlor where they had been sitting, but it had died down, they thought. Charles was awakened around midnight by banging sounds. The night was windy, and at first he thought some of the loose shutters were being slammed about by the wind; but he caught the smell of smoke. He got up and went downstairs. When he opened the parlor door, he recoiled from the heat and boiling black smoke. He ran to his mother's room. Yelling to her to start collecting her things from the bedroom, he ran out the back door, down the steps of the rear veranda and across fifty yards of the back courtyard.

There on a twenty-foot wooden tower was the heavy bell that for sixty years had called the field hands to work in the morning and summoned them in at evening. Now he began pulling on the rope with all his body weight, slowly down, then releasing the rope quickly, then down again, activating the slow deep-throated bong . . . bong . . . bong. He had no idea how many would respond. Since the auction and foreclosures, many of their former hands had gone to work for others, and some had left altogether. But a ringing bell in the middle of the night deep in the countryside can mean only a dire emergency, so they came. Within fifteen minutes, over twenty men and women were there, running in and out of the house carrying chairs, tables, and anything they could grab.

The nearest fire truck was ten miles away. Even though Charles thought it fruitless, he dispatched one of the men in his car to summon it.

By then the fire had spread upstairs and was leaping across the hall on the main floor. The dining room was already too hot and smoke-infested to permit an attempt to rescue the silver and china, an accumulation of a hundred and fifty years, some of it having been brought from Germany. A bucket brigade passing water from the artesian well in the rear of the house had been of no value in stemming the raging fire. In the end, all that they managed to save were a couple of dozen pieces of furniture and some of Clarissa's personal effects.

Finally, they all stood back a hundred yards from the house and watched the walls go, one by one. The wall along the parlor and dining room went first, collapsing inward, sending clouds of fiery smoke and debris skyward. Then the front wall buckled outward, taking the four columns down with it. Only small portions of the other outer walls were still standing. The roof and the entire interior had totally disappeared. It was all over by four in the morning.

Charles told this story as he sat in the Remberton kitchen, holding a coffee cup in his blackened hands. Rob looked at the clock on the kitchen wall. It was then six, and he saw through the windows touches of a cold February dawn.

The office door opened suddenly, jolting Rob back to the present. He swung around in the chair and saw Noble Shepperson standing there. "That chair and desk and this room are yours if you are getting tired of haranguing law students. In fact, sitting there, you look a lot like your old man when he was around your age. Anyway, you know you are welcome to join the office."

"It beats the twenty-fifth floor on Wall Street," Rob laughed as he stood up. "But the classroom has probably still got me, at least for a while. I appreciate the offer though. I really should get on back to the house now to keep the papers and other stuff moving."

Noble walked with Rob out into the hallway. "Oh, by the way," Rob said, "did you ever hear Daddy say anything about an old German letter and photograph that he had kept from the First World War?"

"No," Noble said slowly, as though searching his mind. "But we talked about so many things that I could have forgotten it."

"Well, I'll see you tomorrow evening."

As Rob started down the flight of slanting wooden steps still miraculously attached to the outside brick wall, he almost collided with a harried-looking man in overalls, no doubt a client in trouble. The picture of the Trepnitz Hills house had drawn his mind back to things German. He had already been absorbed for weeks on that subject in preparation for the Marburg conference. Then there was this curious letter and photograph from the footlocker. How strange it was, he thought as he had often thought before, that this German name of Trepnitz had been implanted in the heart of the Alabama River country. In this land settled by English and Scots, it was probably the only German name within a hundred miles, except, of course, for the handful of Jewish merchants in Montgomery and Selma. So far as he knew, he was now the only living person in the state—probably in all of America—who still carried the name.

As he reached his car in front of the hardware store, Rob heard a female voice shouting his name from across the street. It was Rosa Craighill, now Rosa Short. She ran up and gave him a quick hug and a kiss on the cheek. She had uncommonly short hair, a nose on the sharp side, and a sunblistered face suggesting a recent stay down at the coast.

"Mama told me that Pookie told her you were here. I guess you've just been playing hermit."

"Pookie told me that she had run into Miss Betsy and that she is still trying to get me married," Rob said with a wry smile.

"Oh, you know that Mama wants to take care of everybody," she said laughing, "and you've always been one of her favorites."

It was well understood around town that she and her husband, an Auburn dropout who had come home to sell insurance, maintained their more-than-comfortable standard of living only with substantial subsidies from Rosa's father, Dr. Lucius Craighill. Known generally as Dr. Loosh, he delivered Rob into this world, took care of his entire family for decades, shepherded his mother out of it, and came to the house in response to Lucy's call that morning last March to pronounce his father's departure via a heart attack in his sleep. He was the only graduate of Johns Hopkins ever seen in the flesh by most people in Remberton. This circumstance, which he was not reluctant to mention, gave him a special aura of distinction.

"I suppose you've got too much to do to come for a swim?" she asked.

Rob reluctantly agreed that he did. They walked to his car, where they hugged and parted.

The courthouse clock, a block away, was booming nine. Several denizens of establishments along this stretch of Center Street were heading toward the drug store for the morning coffee gathering. Rob saw some who had been in business in these spots since his youth, and others, newer and younger, whom he did not recognize.

The men were attired in what had come to be the standard summer dress for Remberton businessmen—a short-sleeved sport shirt and no tie. About the only exceptions to this dress code were the lawyers, the judge, and the doctors. It was curious that in the days before air conditioning, all of the merchants and businessmen wore coats and ties on the job; but now that air conditioning had pervaded every business establishment and home, they had gone to sport shirts and no ties.

Rob drove along the lines of trees separating uptown from downtown, past the Confederate monument, past the Baptist, Methodist, and Presbyterian churches, and past the picture show, which had closed due to competition from the drive-in theatre and television. At the bank, he turned into Jeff Davis Road, passing the older houses. He knew every one of them—who had lived there, who had died there, and who had grown up there, but were now long gone to other places. He was moving along yesterday's streets.

He came to Morgan, a long shady street named for an Alabama senator from the Victorian age. Midway along the street was Rob's house. Set not far back, it was one story with a high-pitched roof, oak trees in front, and pecan trees in the rear, surrounded by a multitude of camellia plants put there by his father through half a lifetime.

For a long while Rob sat in the car in the driveway, debating with himself. What should he do with this house, his home? Indeed, what should he do with his life? He had wanted to make a worthwhile contribution of some kind to the world, but he counted what he had done so far as slight. "If a man is going to make a mark," his father once said, "he will make it by the time he is forty." That was discouraging, but he had always been a late bloomer. Anyway, he couldn't sort all of that out now. He would clean up what he could here in another day or two, then he had to get back to his preparation for the Marburg conference.

Chapter 3

ROB CIRCLED THE HOUSE to look again at his father's many camellias. His favorites were the Professor Sargent, the Pink Perfection, and the Alba Plena—a red, a pink, and a white. In the rear was the fenced area where the hunting dog, an English Setter, used to stay. Next to it the scuppernong vines were growing on two parallel wires strung out for some thirty feet—a much-improved system, according to his father, compared with the old-style overhead arbor.

As he came in the front door, he saw the German letter and picture still on the hall table. He looked again at the bright-eyed face of the young woman. He had to conclude that she was the writer of the letter—Martina, Baroness von Egloffsberg. But who was she? And how did these papers come to be in his father's possession?

He remembered then that he must clean up the First World War mess that he had left on the screened porch the previous evening. Sam Browne belt, puttees, and assorted khaki items were scattered on the floor. He had not yet reached the bottom of the locker, so he resumed digging in the contents. He hit another clump of old newspapers. Most of them must have been saved by folks at home and given to his father when he came back from France. The most dramatic was the Montgomery Advertiser for November 11, 1918. The headline proclaiming the armistice was in bold letters several inches high. After socks, webbing, and underwear—all in khaki—he reached a large brown envelope.

He pulled out several sheets filled with handwriting. After reading the first couple of lines his attention was riveted. The document was headed Trepnitz Hills, April 9, 1919. It read:

> Having recently arrived home from the war, I want to record an unusual incident. There have been many extraordinary events in the last year and a half, and perhaps someday I will undertake to

describe many of them. I take the time now to set down this one because it has especially lingered in my mind. I cannot get out of my thoughts this incident, which lasted only a few minutes. I do have tangible reminders of this moment in the form of a photograph and a letter, to which I will attach these notes.

When the final American offensive began in the Argonne in October of 1918, my division was involved in a series of attacks directly against the German lines. On the day of this incident, my company began an advance shortly after daylight, after an intense bombardment by our supporting artillery. The Germans were entrenched in this wooded, uphill terrain. We also had supporting mortar fire laid down on the enemy trenches. All of this finally weakened the German defense, with its deadly machine gun fire.

My company was able, at about mid-morning, to overrun a German trench. My men and I jumped down into a sickening scene. As always, the air was filled with smoke. Everywhere was the unforgettable acrid smell of cordite and a general stench. In this German trench there were bodies torn and mangled and bleeding beyond anything I had seen. Our artillery and mortar fire had done their work. We jumped down among these dead and dying bodies. Our men fired shots at those still living and attempting to put up a resistance.

We spread out up and down the trench. I was running along it when I rounded a turn and came upon a German officer lying against the back wall in the mud and slime. He was badly wounded. His uniform was torn and bloody, but I could tell that he was still alive. The natural instinct of all of us in this situation was to shoot. It was not the place or time for amenities. But instead, without thinking, I rammed my pistol into the holster and knelt down beside him. There were no other Germans nearby. He was mumbling, but I could not make out what he was saying. I pulled out my canteen and gave him a drink of water. He took a swallow, and then took another. In a moment, he slumped over. I felt his pulse. It was clear that he was dead.

Through his torn blouse I saw some paper. Instinctively I pulled it out. It was a letter. The envelope was bloody. I pulled out of it a photograph of a young woman and two children. The envelope was addressed to Hauptmann Bruno von Egloffsberg. For some impulsive reason, which I do not now understand, I crammed the photograph and letter into my pocket. Because the envelope was bloody, I decided to jam it back into his blouse, thinking also that it could be useful for identification purposes.

At that moment, my sergeant ran up and said that the order had come to resume the advance. So I moved on.

Here I sit now looking at this picture and letter, wondering who this young widow might be and where she is. Did she ever know what happened to her husband? I will, of course, never know. I crave

to tell her, for some strange reason, that I did not kill her husband, that I gave him water, but I will never have the opportunity to do so.

R. E. K.

P. S. I note that today is the fifty-fourth anniversary of the surrender at Appomattox Court House. In view of what I have experienced over the last year, I will never again think of that war in the way that I did earlier. Also, in the last few months, I have wondered whether the Germans now feel the way people in these parts felt after April of 1865.

Visions of the First World War battlefields flooded Rob's mind. Shortly after his law school graduation, he had driven from Ypres to Verdun—along the entire British front as well as much of the French—and then attempted to retrace the positions of the American Expeditionary Force. He had hoped to follow the route of his father's unit, so he had discussed the terrain beforehand with his father and studied maps of the campaign, but he was never certain that he had tracked his exact footsteps. It was a somber and unforgettable journey.

Among the many sights forever imprinted in his memory was the Menin Gate at Ypres. On its walls were inscribed the names of over fifty-three thousand British soldiers missing in that sector of the line. Every evening, rain or shine, summer and winter, all traffic is stopped at the gate; and complete silence falls over this busy thoroughfare. A bugler walks into the middle of the road and sounds "Last Post." Its haunting notes reverberate through the tunnel-like gate. When the last note dies, the thundering traffic resumes. This ceremony has taken place here for over fifty years, except during the years of the German occupation in the second war.

As he sat slumped in the wicker chair rereading his father's account of that poignant moment in the German trench with the dying captain, he could see the shattered trees, smell the acrid smoke, hear the thudding of mortars and the whining of machine gun and rifle bullets. He imagined the German officer in his torn and bloody field-gray tunic. He looked at the photograph of the young woman, becoming a widow at the very instant his father was jamming her picture into his pocket.

This photograph and letter, he mused, must have been at one time in the envelope with his father's typewritten explanation. Somehow they had become separated; the photograph had been lying near the top of the footlocker. Rob contemplated the peculiar notion that the mother and the two boys at the Schloss Bachdorf, the wounded captain in the trench, his father, and he were all linked in a mystical way, in a uniting moment of death and chaos. Given the vicissitudes of time and the later German catastrophe, perhaps he alone was still alive.

The deep rose-colored light of sunset was filtering through the house when a tired and hot Rob concluded that he had done about all that he could do for one day—and even one trip. He had become increasingly ruthless in pitching things into the trash. He may have run roughshod over the claims of history and posterity, but he doubted that he had thrown away much of any real value. His father had discarded little since his mother's death. There were fifteen years of hunting, fishing, and gardening publications stacked in the study and on the back porch. Usable space in the study had been cut in half by this accumulation, all of which was now piled high outside for the trash man.

Rob had stripped and was adjusting the water in the shower when the telephone started ringing. He quickly cut off the water and trotted to the rear hallway to answer. Fortunately the front door was closed, so no one could see him standing there stark naked in the fading sunlight.

"Mr. Robert Kirkman?" inquired a female voice.

"Yes," Rob answered hesitantly.

"Will you hold please for Dean Pembroke at the University of Virginia?" the voice requested.

Alexander Randolph Pembroke was a name to reckon with at the University of Virginia Law School. He was a property man and had taught Rob in his first year. He was a commanding figure in the classroom, part actor, part orator, part ham, part lawyer, and part scholar. Rob waited now, curiosity building, for the rolling cadence of the familiar Virginia accent.

"Rob, Alex Pembroke here."

"Yes sir. How are you?"

"Fine. I've been trying to get hold of you all day," said the dean. "Finally I found that you were hiding away in some obscure spot in the middle of Alabama."

Rob explained what he was doing and why. The dean extended condolences over his father's death and then moved on, a bit impatiently, to explain that one of the faculty members had suddenly decided to go on leave, and that the law school needed a visitor to cover Procedure and Federal Courts.

"The faculty unanimously decided that you are the man we want, so I hope you can make arrangements there and pack your bags and get ready to enjoy the delights of Mr. Jefferson's country for a while."

An invitation to come back to Virginia for a season was something Rob had dreamed of intermittently for years. However, the suddenness of the offer, coming at this unlikely time and place, caught him off guard. In any case, he needed to see what the situation was at the law school in Tuscaloosa. He could not leave them in the lurch.

He and the dean chatted a few minutes about salary and courses. Rob thanked Pembroke for the call and assured him that he was interested and he would be back in touch as soon as possible, perhaps in a couple of days.

For a long while, Rob stood in the quiet of the hall, in the dying daylight, devoid of clothing, hand still on the replaced telephone receiver. Like a lightning bolt, Pembroke's call had instantly illuminated the obscure landscape of his future, revealing wholly new possibilities. The prospect of a new academic setting and a return to the law school from which he had graduated, and for which he had great affection, was irresistible. It came to him, as he stood there reflecting, that Pembroke's call was the answer—at least for next year—to his restless worry about the future course of his career.

He found himself picking up the phone and asking the information operator for the residence of the law school dean at Tuscaloosa. The dean generally got along well with his faculty members by letting them do what they wanted to do. So it was that a few minutes' conversation led to a decision that Rob would take leave and go to Virginia in the fall.

Under the warm, soapy torrent of the shower, he mulled over the unexpectedness of life's events. His spirits had instantaneously lifted. Amidst the droning of the shower he launched into an off-key rendition of "Danny Boy."

PART TWO
Germany

Chapter 4

THE AUTOBAHN RUNNING NORTH from the Frankfurt network curved gradually to the east, toward the border of the German Democratic Republic. Rob had been driving the rented Opel for over two hours. It was now early afternoon. Arranging for the rental of the car in Frankfurt and clearing the traffic-congested city had taken longer than he had anticipated. He was driving a steady sixty-five miles per hour, the maximum speed at which he felt safe on a foreign road, but the German drivers were passing him in an unbroken line.

Gently rolling grass-covered fields stretched away from both sides of the autobahn. Hills and valleys came and went. Occasionally a minuscule patch of woods appeared. He was hardly ever out of sight of at least one village—they were sharply defined villages consisting of several dozen houses tightly clustered around a church. The village edges were clear-cut; fields and grass began there. There was no dribbling away of residences mingled with filling stations, fast food places, and other unsightly and nondescript structures. These compact settlements appeared to be units constructed somewhere else and placed on the green landscape by a giant hand. Often Rob could see two or three of them at once, dotted across a valley only a couple of miles apart, each clearly delineated with no sprawl between them.

The three weeks since he had left Remberton had been hectic. He had gone to Tuscaloosa to wrap up his paper for the Marburg conference and make arrangements for his absence during the coming year. Then he made a stop in Charlottesville for two days. He located an apartment off Rugby Road, just a little north of the university grounds. It was then on to Washington, where he left his car with a friend and took a flight from Dulles to Frankfurt. At Marburg, he sat and talked through three days of the conference on comparative civil procedure, trudging each morning up the steep slope to the castle high above the town and back down at the end of the day. Back in Frankfurt, he rented a car, and he was now on his way to East Germany.

By the reckoning of most people, the trip ahead would seem crazy. He had enough suspicions of its insanity himself that he had told no one about it. He did not mention it to anyone in Alabama, and he said not a word about it to anybody in Charlottesville or Washington. They only knew that after the Marburg conference he planned to rent a car and drive for a day or two around Germany.

The idea had come to him on his last night in Remberton as he was packing to leave the next morning. He had had a pleasant supper at the Sheppersons' house. They discussed a lot of family history and what to do about Rob's just-inherited house. Sitting on the screened porch after supper, Rob brought up the subject that had been growing in his mind ever since his footlocker discovery.

"Did Daddy ever talk to you-all much about his experiences in France during the first war?" he asked.

"No," said Noble, "he wasn't one who liked to talk about that period in his life. I remember when I was heading overseas he joked with me and said he was glad that I was going on this visit to Europe and not him. I recall getting a letter from him when we were beginning to move through France. He said that we had it mighty easy, just riding in tanks and not slogging through mud and lying for days in trenches."

"Did he ever say anything about the last big push through the Argonne? Did he ever mention whether he came face-to-face with any Germans?"

"I don't recall anything in particular. He did used to say that they were mighty good soldiers. I think that he felt a little the way I felt after the second war—that the Germans probably were the best soldiers in the war, and we whipped them in the end by sheer weight of numbers of men and material."

"Let me show you something I found in a footlocker," Rob said, reaching over to a table where he had put the brown envelope. "Have you ever seen or heard of these before?" Rob extracted the photograph, letter, and notes, and handed them to his uncle.

Noble looked quizzically at the picture of the woman and two children and then read the notes. "Well, I'll be damned," he said as he finished. He passed the papers over to Nan. "You'll have to translate the German for me."

Rob told him what it said, and then asked, "Don't you find it unusual that he never mentioned an incident that impressed him enough to write it down months after he got home?"

"As time passes," Nan said, "what seemed important sometimes fades. I suspect that once he settled down in law practice and got married, he pretty much forgot about incidents in the war. I know that Noble hardly says anything about what happened to him."

"Well, I never had a personal encounter of this kind. The Germans I saw were either dead or lined up as prisoners."

"Do you have any notion where Bachdorf might be?" Rob asked.

"Not the foggiest," Noble said. "There are hundreds of villages all over Germany, and lots of them have a schloss. It could be in East Prussia, which is now in the Soviet Union, or it could be in Silesia or some such place, which is now in Poland or East Germany."

When he returned to his house that night to pack, Rob looked again at the pretty young woman and the infants in the yellowed picture. He read again the hand-penned letter from the Baroness von Egloffsberg with its finely engraved crest. The question persisted in his mind: could these people still be alive? The woman would likely be in her late seventies, the boys nearing sixty. Of course, the idea was crazy. After the vicissitudes of the thirties and forties, the Nazis, and the devastation of the Second World War, was there a chance that these people were alive or could be located? They were total strangers. They meant nothing to him. But since reading his father's account of how he came into possession of these items, he had not been able to shake off these images.

He had gone to the university library in Tuscaloosa and found a turn-of-the-century German atlas. No place named Bachdorf was listed in the index, but he persisted and examined every square inch of the maps. On the fourth map he found it. It appeared to be a very small village, north of Meissen and east of Leipzig, on the Elbe River. It was not on any railroad and seemed to be well off any major road. His elation at this discovery was dampened by his realization that this might not be the Bachdorf where the Egloffsberg schloss was located. It was not rare to find the same name used for two entirely different places. Then he realized that this place was now deep in East Germany. After the Nazis and the war came the Red Army, years of Soviet occupation, and the present-day Communist regime. It was most unlikely that these people were still at Bachdorf. All of this uncertainty only made the hunt more exciting. Despite growing doubts as he approached the border, he was now committed to the undertaking, and there was to be no turning back.

Rob's enthusiasm for the venture had been bolstered by an unusual coincidence in Charlottesville. On one of the two days he had paused there to look for an apartment, Dean Alex Pembroke and his wife, Mary, had asked him to accompany them to a cocktail party. They met him at the Colonnade Club, where he was staying, and they walked up the Lawn together to the party in Pavilion I.

Among the numerous guests to whom he was introduced was Peter von Reumann, a thin, almost emaciated man, wearing dark-rimmed glasses and a black German suit. His heavy German accent suggested that he had not been long in the United States. Rob quickly learned from him that he had come to Albemarle County from Germany only two years before; he had bought a house near Ivy; and he was spending his time developing his library, which consisted of several thousand volumes of German genealogy.

"A perfectly marvelous library," broke in an effusive lady who happened by at that moment, but gushed along to join another conversation.

"Have you by any chance ever heard of a German family with the name of von Egloffsberg?" asked Rob.

Von Reumann furrowed his brow. His eyes narrowed behind his heavy glasses. In his slow, German-flavored English, he said, "The name does have a certain familiarity. I think the family may have come out of Silesia or Saxony. Of course I can look it up in my books. Why do you want to know?" he asked in the blunt German style.

Rob was not prepared for the question. A white-coated waiter interrupted with a tray of ham biscuits, giving him time to formulate an answer. "Well," he said, groping for an explanation that was true but did not reveal what he thought might sound ridiculous, "I think the family may be remotely connected to my family." Rob explained that he was on his way to Marburg for a conference. "I will have some extra time, and I might want to see whether any of them are still there."

This seemed to satisfy von Reumann. "When do you leave Charlottesville?" he asked.

When Rob said he would have to leave the next afternoon, von Reumann said that he should come to his house around eleven in the morning, by which time he would have checked his books and would have available for Rob whatever he could find.

The upshot of that chance meeting was that Rob now had in his suitcase three photocopied pages from a volume of German genealogy, showing successive generations of the von Egloffsberg family back to 1530.

Rob could hardly conceal his delight when he looked at these sheets, all in the heavy German Gothic-style print. What he was searching most eagerly for he found. There in the latest generation listed was Bruno Karl Hans von Egloffsberg, born at Bachdorf on March 13, 1895. Because the book had been published in 1905, nothing later was shown. With these pages, though, he knew he was dealing with a real family and a real man and a real place.

Passing another exit sign, Rob checked his map and calculated that he was about ten miles from the East German border. Although he was convinced that there was little danger in this trip, despite what uninformed persons had been telling him, he had taken some precautions with printed material. In the Frankfurt airport, he had checked the bag in which he had put all the papers relating to the Marburg conference and everything not essential to the East German exploration. He had made duplicate copies of the genealogical pages and of the photograph and documents from his father's footlocker. He had one copy in his suitcase and another copy in his coat pocket, figuring that if one should be found and confiscated in a border search, perhaps the other would not.

He was equipped with a road map officially issued by the state travel agency of the German Democratic Republic. As on prior trips, he had with him his 1904 edition of *Baedeker's Travel Guide to Germany.* With the destruction of the Second World War, no contemporary travel guide could provide the essential historical information. He had placed *Baedeker* well down in his suitcase, hoping that the border inspection would not penetrate to it. The other important paper Rob had was a photocopy of the map from the atlas showing Bachdorf, a place not shown on the GDR road map.

Traffic had disappeared from the autobahn. Rob's car was rolling along alone. In the distance to the south he saw another village. Perhaps it was the last before the border, he thought, the people living there having been saved by a hair from Soviet occupation, and hence the GDR, when that line was drawn on the map by the British, American, and Russian planners in London in 1944. The autobahn ended, and barricades forced him onto a two-lane, winding country road. The road ran parallel to the autobahn for a mile, then curved to the north. Before losing sight of the autobahn, he glimpsed its end. The multilane superhighway was ripped up, coming to a jagged termination, as if a giant finger had torn through it, thereby making it impossible for a motorist to continue a journey eastward.

Rob was heading for a spot on the map named Wartha, one of the official crossing points designated by the East German authorities. And that was all that it was—not a town or a village, but simply a point in the countryside where a lonely road crossed this line. Beyond this crossing point, this route would take him through the places of greatest historical interest to him—Weimar, Jena, and Leipzig.

The road leveled out. There were no other cars in sight, and the earth seemed deserted. A gray cloud cover had formed overhead. The day had gone somber, mirroring Rob's mood. He felt bereft of all human contact. He was alone, heading across the East-West divide, and no one knew where he was or where he was going.

Far ahead, he saw several low wooden buildings—the only intrusion on the natural landscape. Now a sign appeared by the side of the road, a shabby, almost homemade-looking sign: German Democratic Republic. Rationally, Rob said to himself, there should be no problem here; there is no danger. He had discounted all those stories about this totalitarian regime and its police-state measures. After all, he was an American citizen carrying a United States passport. Nonetheless, there was an ever-so-slight tightening in his chest and stomach as he approached that sign. His mouth was dry. His pulse rate had quickened. There was still time and opportunity to turn back. All he had to do was simply stop the car, turn around in this narrow road, and head west. By dark he could be comfortably ensconced in a Frankfurt hotel, looking forward to a fine meal amidst the bright lights of a city in the free world. But he dismissed such tempting thoughts. He had decided on a course of action, and he would not turn back.

A hundred yards beyond the sign he saw a wooden arm across the road. A green-uniformed guard wearing a black pistol holster walked toward his car as he brought it to a stop in front of the barricade.

"Pass," the guard said matter-of-factly. His face was impassive. Rob pushed his passport through the open car window, his motor still running. The guard looked at it for a long moment, then handed it back. The arm lifted. The guard waved him forward, telling him to pull over at the building ahead. Rob was now on GDR terrain but not yet really *in* the GDR.

It was another quarter mile to the one-story frame buildings that seemed to be the only man-made structures at this desolate spot. High fences closed in on the road. Rob could no longer see anything to his left or right. Several of the green-uniformed guards were standing in the road ahead in front of the buildings. One motioned him over to a parking lane. He looked closely at the crisply tailored uniforms with high black boots and visored caps, the outfit of the border police, thinking that the Germans certainly knew how to design snappy military apparel. He parked the car, cut off the motor, and got out.

He was directed into an unpainted structure which reminded him of the temporary wooden rooms put up on building sites by construction companies to provide shelter from the weather for the foreman and construction engineer. The afternoon was growing late, but he was still hoping to make Weimar before dark.

Inside, the building was stark. A long wooden counter was on one side of the room. Two heavyset and plainly dressed women were on duty behind it, one at a desk with what appeared to be a teletype machine, the other talking with a man on Rob's side of the counter. Two bare electric light bulbs hung on cords from the ceiling. The man left, and the woman at the counter turned to Rob.

She examined his passport, filling out a form at the same time, then she asked a series of questions: Where did he want to go? How long did he wish to stay in the GDR? Why was he there? Where will he exit?

Rob stated his plans. He was here as a tourist. He wished to spend one night in Weimar and two nights in Leipzig. The woman wrote on a form as Rob talked, then gave the completed form to the teletypist. That woman, who appeared to be older and dowdier than the other, came over to Rob and interrogated him as to the price he wished to pay for room and meals. There were three levels of prices, she explained. He must pay here for all rooms, and that payment would include an amount for meals. Rob elected the middle rate, although he was puzzled as to how the meal arrangement was to work.

The woman returned to her desk and began typing into the machine. She paused at intervals, and the machine clattered away on its own. This went on for ten minutes. There was no sound in the room except the raucous machine noise. When she finished, she tore off a segment of paper that had been ejected by the machine and came over to Rob.

"There is no room with private bath available at the Elephant in Weimar," she reported brusquely. "You can have a room without private bath."

"That is good," Rob said in his simplest German.

"In Leipzig," she announced, "there is a room with private bath for two nights at the Deutchland Interhotel." Rob nodded approval.

She went back to the desk. The machine sprang to life again, and another ten minutes passed.

These women appeared to be in their thirties. The guards outside were younger. Not one was old enough to remember the war. To them, this tightly sealed border probably seemed only a natural feature of the landscape. They had known nothing else. Rob found it difficult, standing in this dingy room, to believe that he was indeed on one of the most heavily fortified frontiers in the world. He had seen no hint of fortifications or military presence as he approached. It was all to the east of where he stood—high fencing, barbed wire, guard towers, and a broad belt of cleared, raw dirt. With all of its powerful physical presence, this border did not exist politically or legally in official West German theory. Although the existence of two German states had been grudgingly recognized, on the west side of this line the view was tenaciously held that there was but one German nation.

The woman at the machine returned with more papers. Now she wanted West German marks. Rob counted out the stated amount. She went to a drawer and then returned with East German marks, explaining that this was his money for meals. He could not re-exchange this money; he must spend it in the GDR. She gave him the papers evidencing his reservations at the hotels.

Rob smiled at this first encounter with Marxism-Leninism. This hotel system struck him as a good example of the centralization he had read about. Here there was no concept of meandering through the countryside and finding a hotel or motel room wherever night found him. No, rooms for each night of the trip had to be firmly booked and paid for at the border before he was allowed to enter, and the rooms had to be in the relatively few state-operated hotels.

As he walked out, a guard directed him to pull the car to the next building fifty yards farther along. At a window there, he produced the car rental papers, the insurance policy, and his driver's license. As these documents were being looked over and more forms filled out, Rob turned and saw that the car was undergoing inspection. All four doors were open, and guards were peering under the seats, front and back. One man was on his stomach on the floor boards. The hood was up. A guard came over and asked Rob for the keys to the trunk. As he extracted them from his pocket, he suddenly realized with considerable unease that he had never opened the trunk. Anything could be there. Fortunately, nothing was there but the spare tire.

Now came the personal baggage inspection. At a guard's direction, Rob hauled his suitcase from the back seat and opened it on the ground. The expressionless guard ran his hands through its contents, pulled out *Baedeker* and leafed through it.

"Tourist?" he asked, looking at Rob.

"Yes."

The guard shrugged his shoulders and put the small book back in the suitcase. Rob held his breath for some seconds as the genealogical pages, photograph, and letter were passed over after a cursory glance. The suitcase was shut. Rob was given the car papers and a visa card.

"That is all," the guard snapped.

The barrier lifted. He drove slowly ahead, but he then saw that he was not yet quite in the clear. Two hundred yards farther on he came to another barrier. Here a guard checked all the papers again—passport, hotel reservations, visa card, and car papers. The barrier rose, and Rob pulled away, at last really inside of East Germany. He had been at this entry point for two hours. The cloud cover had broken, and the sun was now low in the western sky to his rear.

The road ran uphill. On top of a rise just ahead, Rob saw a guard tower—a box set on four twenty-foot legs. The road passed close to its base, and Rob and the guard looked directly at each other. A pair of field glasses slung around the guard's neck rested on the front of his dark green uniform. Under the visor of his cap was that same lean, youthful, and expressionless face Rob had just seen at the entry point. Perhaps his imagination was too vivid, but he felt sure he had seen those same faces in almost the same uniforms in old photographs of the SS. High above the guard tower, three birds darted westward, their wings glinting in the evening sun.

Chapter 5

SHORTLY PAST THE GUARD TOWER, the winding road swung onto an autobahn. According to the map, this was an eastward continuation of the autobahn on which he had been traveling earlier. The East Germans must have cut a gap of at least three or four miles in it to let the fortified border pass through. Before 1945, he could have covered this distance in five minutes; today it had taken him over two hours.

One after another, he passed exit signs announcing historic towns—Eisenach, Erfurt, Gotha. These were not the sturdy steel reflective signs seen on American interstate highways. Rather, the names appeared to be painted on wood. Somewhere out there in these Thuringian Hills was the medieval seat of the von Trepnitz family and the birthplace of the Baron von Trepnitz who had long ago gone to America.

Rob felt a twinge of excitement at the realization that near here in the darkening countryside, Friedrich Karl Hans, Baron von Trepnitz, had been born in 1735. He studied at the University of Jena and then entered into official service at the court of Frederick the Great at Berlin and Potsdam. The baron, as he was always known in family folklore, then became restless. The American Revolution was just coming to a close, and he was excited by the promise of the New World. He, his wife, and their youngest son eventually sailed to the New World, leaving their older son with his grandmother.

They landed in Charleston, and he purchased two thousand acres along the Broad River to the south, where he lived until his death fifteen years later. His son Charles, like his father before him, became restless for new country. The lands along the Alabama and Tombigbee Rivers were being opened for settlement, and this fertile region offered rich possibilities for cotton growing. So in the early 1820s Charles, his wife, and their two sons sold the South Carolina place and set out for the

Black Belt in the new state of Alabama. The westward journey came to its end on the high ridge which Charles named Trepnitz Hills.

It was Charles's grandson, Henry, who built the great house that had stood there. By the time he came home from the University of Virginia and married, the cotton kingdom was nearing its zenith. The Trepnitz holdings had been expanded to eight thousand acres and nearly a hundred slaves. Several hundred bales of cotton were loaded on river boats at Trepnitz Landing every fall to be taken to Mobile and thence to the mills of New England and the English Midlands. When the storm of 1861 struck, Henry Trepnitz raised a company of infantry from the county, and they were assigned to an Alabama regiment that eventually found its way into the Army of Northern Virginia. His daughter Clarissa, Rob's grandmother, grew up in the house at Trepnitz Hills and married Robert Kirkman, who was then working as a newspaper editor in Montgomery. After marrying Clarissa, he renounced the newspaper world for the life of a cotton planter at Trepnitz Hills. It was he who put in the vast pecan orchard and combined the raising of hogs with the raising of cotton.

While growing up, Rob had been fascinated by his great-grandfather, Henry, and his exploits in the campaign of Northern Virginia. He had often stared at the gray-clad man in the daguerreotype on the wall of his father's study. One of his favorite childhood stories was his grandmother's account of a day burned in her memory.

"I was four years old," she would begin. "It was a summer day, and I was playing with my nurse out in front of the steps to the house. Mama was sewing on the veranda. We heard a horse coming at a gallop. I looked up and saw a man mounted on this horse coming up the drive. He was coming fast. The man pulled him up to a stop just a few feet in front of me. The horse was all shiny and black, covered with sweat, breathing hard with nostrils flared. The man was huge and roughly dressed. I was afraid, so I ran to my nurse. The man got down and went straight up the steps."

"He went on to the veranda, took off his large, dusty hat, and said, 'Mrs. Trepnitz?' My mother nodded, and he said, 'I have come straight down from the governor's office in Montgomery, and I have a personal letter from him.' He pulled a letter out of a pouch slung over his shoulder. Then he said, 'I'm sorry to say, ma'am, that it's bad news.' He stopped for a moment. Then he said, 'I regret to inform you that Colonel Trepnitz was killed at Spotsylvania Courthouse a little over a week ago. The governor just received word from the War Department in Richmond yesterday.'"

"Mama took the letter and just said, 'Thank you, thank you very much for coming all this way.' Then she turned and walked in the front door of the house. The man did not say another word," his grandmother continued, "and he never looked at me. He jumped back on the great black horse, turned, and broke into a gallop. To this day, I have an irrational fear of black horses."

This story brought Rob's mind back to the photograph in his father's footlocker. He imagined that young German woman at Schloss Bachdorf living out the months and years of war, her officer husband far from home in the fields of France. Did some hard-breathing and sweating horse and rider rein in at the schloss to bring the long-dreaded word? In some form, the fateful word reached this woman at Schloss Bachdorf in 1918 just as a similar message had reached his great-grandmother at Trepnitz Hills in 1864.

His mind tightened on a curious linkage. The great-grandson of the Baron von Trepnitz died in Confederate gray; the Baron von Egloffsberg died in field gray. Both ended their lives in armed combat against the United States. His father was intimately tied to both, as the son of the little girl left fatherless by one and as the only human present at the death of the other.

Dusk had deepened into darkness, and Weimar was still twenty miles away. It was a darkness that he had not experienced since his childhood at Trepnitz Hills. There were no stars or moon. The blackness was total, except for the channel of light created directly in front of him by his headlights. He had met only two cars in the last quarter hour. He saw no lights of farmhouses or villages, and no city lights reflected against the sky. Where were the people and what were they doing?

At last, a faintly lettered sign reading Weimar appeared in the narrow periphery of his headlights. He almost missed it. For several miles, he then moved through the inky void on a small road until he entered the streets of the city. In his innermost being, he again felt a welling up of excitement concerning the German past. An abiding interest in the grand and tragic history of this land had been instilled in him by his college history teacher, Professor George Marks Wilton, who had studied at the University of Halle before the First World War. Rob sensed a keener than usual edge now because, for the first time, he was in that part of Germany that had been sealed off from the Western world for nearly thirty years. In all that time, few Americans had been in this cultural seat, where one could commune with the spirits of Goethe and Schiller and see the place where hope for a democratic Germany was born in 1919—in vain as it turned out.

There were no pedestrians. Street lights were far apart. In the houses he was passing there were only occasional lights. The trees lining the streets and the large facades of the darkened houses suggested that here was once a rather elegant neighborhood. Turning a corner, Rob entered the central square, and there was the Elephant. It was an old hotel, four stories tall, occupying one side of the square. It had been for decades the town's finest hotel.

Rob pulled the Opel into a designated parking area in the center of the square. Weimar was not afflicted with a parking problem; the square contained only four other cars. Not a single human being was in sight. He took his suitcase from the back seat, locked the car, and walked with considerable curiosity and a little anxiety into the lobby, prepared to check in for his first night behind the iron curtain.

Sounds of a string quartet filled the air. The music was coming from the dining room at the rear of the lobby. It stirred his imagination, and for a moment he could see himself walking into the Elephant in the twenties or perhaps before the Great War.

The clerk at the desk dispelled the fantasy. He was anything but an elegant figure from the old days. He had a sallow complexion and an underfed look; he could have been a ticket seller at a small-town railroad station. He inspected Rob's reservation form, matching it with a paper that he produced from behind the counter. He asked for Rob's passport, saying that it was necessary that he keep it overnight for the police to check. Rob was uneasy about surrendering the only lifeline he had to the outer world, the only evidence of his identity and existence as a human being in this collective regime. However, he quieted himself by remembering that this was a standard custom in Western Europe also.

His room had a grand view of the square. The huge feather-filled pillow, the mattress, and the eiderdown cover were as comfortable as any he had experienced.

Dinner and its setting turned out to be surprisingly elegant, though no match for the best dining rooms in Bonn, Munich, or anywhere else in the West. The head waiter was wearing a dinner jacket. The string quartet continued with waltzes and lilting pieces from the last three centuries. The white tablecloths were spotless. The food was solid German fare. The wine list carried nothing from West Germany. Although the Rhine and Mosel—two of the world's greatest wine-growing regions—were no more than three hours away by car, the leading dining room in Weimar had not a single bottle of their produce. Instead, the list featured a few varieties from Czechoslovakia, Yugoslavia, Hungary, and Austria.

The next morning, Rob arose at six for a walk around Weimar. Everything he wanted to see was within a few blocks of the Elephant. He went to the National Theater, scene of the 1919 convention. Goethe and Schiller stood together on a pedestal in front of the building. He walked to their one-time residences, charming eighteenth-century townhouses, but both were closed for renovations. From there, he walked to the splendid park running through the city. A long, wide stretch of grass was flanked by trees, and a lively stream ran through it. On the far side was Goethe's garden house, a three-story residence with a high-pitched roof. Walking along the edge of the stream among the trees, he came unexpectedly upon a life-sized statue of William Shakespeare. It seemed strangely out of place until he recalled that Shakespeare had been greatly admired in Germany at one time. Weimar struck him as a charming little island of gardens and old houses, seemingly detached from the contemporary political regime.

Driving away from the square in front of the Hotel Elephant, on his way out to Jena, he was unsure about the correct route. He saw an elderly woman—one of the few pedestrians in sight—standing at a corner, waiting to cross the street. He pulled the car over to the curb in front of her.

"Excuse me, please," Rob said. "Can you tell me how to go to Jena?"

"Yes," she said without hesitation, speaking in a businesslike voice. "You go straight ahead for two blocks, then left. After three blocks, you turn right; then you are on the road to Jena." She animatedly demonstrated the turns with her hands.

Rob saw that she was a handsome woman, probably in her sixties, no ordinary member of the working class. He sensed education, culture, and good breeding.

She looked at him as she completed her directions and said questioningly, "Are you Swedish?"

"No, American," Rob said.

He thought he saw at that instant—perhaps he imagined it—a change of expression on her face, a wistful sadness flicker through her eyes. He had a powerful urge to talk with her, to find out about her life and what experiences she must have had, born before the first war, and surviving the decades in an almost elegant style. But there was no way that he and this strange woman could converse. The gulf was too large, the moment too fleeting.

He simply said, "Thank you," and pulled away.

At the last intersection, where he paused to turn eastward out of town, he saw one of the large wooden-looking road signs, one end shaped into a point to indicate the direction. The single word on the sign slammed into his eyes, almost like a flash bulb on a camera that goes off unexpectedly in one's face. That one word—*Buchenwald*—summed up the darkest of all strains in twentieth-century German history.

"It is difficult to understand," Professor Wilton had often said. Although he enthusiastically admired Germany before 1914, he thought that almost everything there since then had gone wrong. "Future historians will have to grapple with these camps in the longer perspective of time. There are theories, of course," Rob remembered his saying, "as to why the Germans turned on the Jews with such ferocity, but they do not explain it very well to me. And it was not only the Jews. These camps had multitudes of others—Christians, Communists, and all kinds of political opponents." He would sigh in the face of an inexplicable mystery of such magnitude.

Rob recalled hearing George Marks Wilton also muse aloud over another dark chapter in history—slavery in North America. Rob himself had last brooded over that subject a few years earlier on a nostalgic visit to Trepnitz Hills. There he had encountered Sam Marshall, one of the last survivors of the Kirkman and Trepnitz employees, an aged black man who had run the blacksmith shop near the mule barn when Rob was a boy. When Rob gave him a ride to the river where he was going to fish, Sam lapsed into talking about the fire.

"It was the worst sight I ever seen. It was like God Almighty hisself come down from heaven to wipe out everything."

Sam grew silent for a moment, then resumed. "Last time I ever seen Mr. Charles, he said I could stay on if I would keep the big weeds out of the cemetery. Then next thing I knowed, they was bringing Mr. Charles over here to be buried. Then it won't too long 'fore they was bringing Miss Clarissa here. I been keeping the weeds out of the cemetery ever since. Mr. Ed done told me the same thing Mr. Charles said."

They rode without talking for a few moments. Pieces of gravel churned up by the car's tires slammed into the undersides of the fenders. "Whatever happened to that boy of yours?" Rob asked.

"He went to Detroit and got a good job."

"That's fine," Rob said. "What does he do?"

"He works in a big plant making automobiles. He makes more cash money in a month than I ever made in a year. Sends us some of it too. Sends some every month. He got a boy of his own."

"So you're a granddaddy?"

"That's right. And that boy say he going on to college. How 'bout that, Mr. Robert, my grandboy in college?"

"I know you're proud of that."

"Yes sir, I am. You know that ain't but one black boy ever been to college from around here. He was the son of your grandma's cook. He went off to Tuskegee."

They had come now to the river landing—Trepnitz Landing it had been called since steamboats began stopping there a century and a half ago. None had stopped there, however, for sixty years. The river at the landing is two-hundred yards wide, a yellow-brown belt of water, somber, powerful, quiet, but moving. It bears the mud of creeks and rivers far above—the Cahaba and the Talapoosa—and the soil of thousands of acres of land. The movement is slow in appearance but mighty in force. Such a tide as moving seems asleep, too full for sound or foam.

Except for the road he had driven down on and the small cleared area here at the landing, the scene was as the Indians knew it long before European man ever laid eyes on it. There was no human being or hint of civilization in sight. The Old South grew and thrived and ultimately died along this river and a dozen or more like it all the way from the Potomac to the Mississippi. Devoid now of steamboats and cotton, this mighty belt still flows everlastingly on to Mobile, the Gulf of Mexico, and the waters of the world.

After Sam Marshall had said goodbye and gone upriver to fish, Rob sat on the bluff, fifteen feet above the water at a point where it eddied around a collection of dead tree limbs. The muddy, swirling movement was mesmerizing, like watching a crackling fire on a cold winter night. The mystery of it all haunted him. In a hundred and twenty years, men and women named Trepnitz and Kirkman, far from their ancestral origins, came here and built a hidden kingdom. They had their place in the sun for a little while, and then vanished, all within a tick of history's clock. Why had it all gone?

Sam Marshall's words had stuck in his mind. "It was like God Almighty hisself come down from heaven to wipe out everything." Could it be that a divine hand had indeed intervened? Was judgment pronounced on this family and all their works? Words floated into his memory from his Presbyterian Sunday school days: "Except the Lord build the house, they labor in vain who build it."

The sins of the fathers shall be visited on the third and fourth generations. But what were the sins? He had no way of knowing everything his ancestors had done, what dark deeds might lie forever buried with them. They were supposedly upright citizens—men and women of honor. But all fall short, he had been taught, all are sinners.

Slavery was one dark suggestion that he was unwilling to accept but which he could not quite suppress. The men who came and lived and died here did not create slavery. They were born into the system. They could be held no more accountable for it—perhaps even less so—than those Yankee shipowners who went to Africa and obtained the slaves and sold them for good profits to the Southern planters. Nor could these folks here be blamed for the system any more than the textile mill operators of New England and the English Midlands who bought and profited immensely from the cotton produced by the slave system. Instinctively, he would not let his ancestors be indicted on the slavery charge while those who furnished the slaves and benefited from the products of their labor went about clothed in moral self-righteousness. And yet . . . and yet . . . he wondered.

The road to Jena passed through country that was hilly and wooded and sprinkled with small apple orchards. This was the route of the American army in April of 1945, in its last dash to overrun the crumbling German resistance. He had often examined the framed map of Europe that hung on the wall of his Uncle Noble's law office. A blue pencil traced the movement of the armored division in which Colonel Shepperson served. The line began at the Normandy coast, went south, then eastward across France until it took an abrupt northward turn, indicating an emergency call to the relief of American forces being pressed in the Battle of the Bulge. From the Ardennes, the blue line went eastward again, crossed the Rhine, and continued through the region south of where Rob was now, and stopped at the Mulde River.

"We really had them on the run," he had heard Uncle Noble say many times. "We could have overrun the whole country and been in Poland in a couple of weeks."

When he first heard this account shortly after the war, Rob had asked, "Why did you stop?"

"Political judgments higher up," Noble had responded in a disgruntled tone. "Of course, we would have met the Red Army somewhere ahead, but at least we would have shown them who really took Germany. But then, worst of all, we had to turn around and hand over all this territory we had taken to the Russians. We left a few million Germans to the tender mercies of the Communist Party and the Soviet Union."

It was hard to grasp that the country through which he was now driving had been crawling with Americans for an interlude of two-and-a-half months nearly thirty years before. Looking at the elderly farmers and villagers along this road, Rob wondered what they remembered of his countrymen, what they thought of them, and what they thought of the switch from American to Russian occupation almost overnight. These questions were getting increasingly academic. A person would now have to be at least forty years old to have any solid recollection of the Americans; those younger had never known anything but the Russians.

Reaching the middle of Jena, Rob parked his car at the central marketplace, next to the large church that dominated one side of the square. It was a magnificent midsummer day. The sky was blue without a cloud. A light breeze blew across the open space, so it was not hot—nothing like a July day in Alabama or Virginia.

He was curious to know what the position of the churches was in this Marxist-Leninist land. He had arrived now in the heart of Protestant Germany—the domain of Martin Luther and the Reformation—yet this Communist regime was officially atheistic. He opened a side door into the church and passed through a vestibule into the main sanctuary. It was incredibly quiet. The light was soft and gray, like the stone of which the building was constructed. The interior was like that of dozens of churches in Western Europe and England. Chairs were arranged in rows on both sides of a central aisle. He sat down in the back row to ponder and look over the interior more closely.

At first he thought he was alone, but then he noticed a woman standing up near the altar, arranging flowers. He sat and watched her for perhaps five minutes, then she walked forward from the altar. He guessed that she was in her early fifties. Acting on impulse, he arose and walked toward her.

"Good day," Rob said.

"Hello," she said in return.

Groping for conversation, he asked, "Are there regular services in this church?"

"Yes, every Sunday and sometimes during the week," she answered crisply. She was an intelligent-looking woman wearing the usual dowdy GDR dress. "The church has been undergoing renovations lately," she added, pointing to scaffolding in the far corner, "and it was closed for a while, but it recently reopened."

Rob was still not at ease talking with East Germans. This was the first chance he had had for a real conversation. He craved to pour out a stream of questions. How was life here? Did the authorities interfere with the church at all? What did she think of this system? Of the Soviet Union? Of the United States? How did she earn her living? They were here in this house of worship all alone—or at least they appeared to be—but he held back. He did not want to court trouble, nor did he care to jeopardize a woman strong enough to remain dedicated to the church in an atheistic environment. She asked him no questions, even though it must have been obvious to her that he was a foreigner.

Crossing the square, past the statue of John the Magnanimous, said to be the father of the university, Rob saw for the first time in his life a live, flesh-and-blood Russian army officer. He was striding across the great open place, dressed in the mustard-brown Soviet uniform. A red band circled his visored cap, and he wore high-top black boots reminiscent of a cavalry officer's. He had a round fleshy face and black eyes which stared straight ahead. Without looking at Rob, he passed within ten feet of him. Where were the rest of the Russians? Western intelligence maintained that there were between three and four hundred thousand Soviet soldiers in this small remnant of the former German Reich. He had expected to see throngs of them on the streets.

For Rob, Jena was a mandatory stop. Schiller, Hegel, and many other luminaries had taught at the university here. Here the notorious custom of fencing among German university students originated. But most important of all to Rob, it was here that his ancestor, the Baron von Trepnitz, had studied.

Two hundred years and five generations had passed away since the young von Trepnitz had walked these streets. A few buildings that Rob saw were probably there then. Others had been built in the early nineteenth century. In a long row in front of these university buildings were busts of the academic greats of the past, left undisturbed by the Marxist-Leninists of today. Against the skyline to the west was a contemporary intrusion, a high-rise building with the name Carl Zeiss emblazoned across the top. The world-famous optical concern had survived to become a state-owned enterprise under the new order.

Soon after leaving Jena, Rob picked up the autobahn heading northwest. It led ultimately to Berlin, that is, to East Berlin, although the prefix was never used in the GDR. All signs proclaimed the city to be the "Capital of the German Democratic Republic." As Rob progressed northward, he spotted the sprawling Leuna chemical works, one of the largest in Europe and an enterprise in which the GDR took great pride. Rob could see the flickering flames at the tops of tall slender chimneys, where gas was being burned off. Chemical-colored smoke drifted in long wispy streaks across the sky.

It was late afternoon when Rob entered the outskirts of Leipzig. Block after block of row houses flicked past his car windows—three- and four-story buildings dating probably from the twenties and earlier. These must have been handsome residences then. Rob imagined the comfortably dressed merchants, bankers, book publishers, and professional men in that era coming home from the day's work at about this hour. The houses were shabby now and needing paint. Traffic here was thicker than it had been in Weimar and Jena, but it was not heavy. Rob was heading for the Ring, the thoroughfare that half-circled the old part of the city, passing the main railroad station and the university. According to the fragmented directions provided by the hotel reservation woman at the border, his hotel was in that vicinity.

The shadows were lengthening as Rob neared the center of Leipzig. Suddenly, without realizing it, he found that he was on the Ring. The railroad station, the Hauptbahnhof, was on his left. For the first time, he saws signs of the war—open spaces covered with rubble and weeds, new and cheap construction, and building materials and equipment parked at various points. Then on his left he saw his destination, the Deutschland Interhotel. He found a parking place directly in front of the hotel with no difficulty. Gathering up his bag and reservation papers, he entered the lobby of this styleless post-war concrete structure, fronting what *Baedeker* told him was Charles Augustus Platz, but a sign stated to be Karl Marx Platz.

His room turned out to be smaller with lower ceilings than his room in the Elephant, but the furniture was the same. All hotel beds, desks, and chests of drawers must have come from the same Peoples-Owned Enterprise. The room was on the third floor. Again his luck had placed him on the front of the hotel. From his window he could see all of Karl Marx Platz. With *Baedeker*'s 1904 Leipzig map in hand, he studied the buildings.

Across the way was the Opera House. What he saw there, however, was not the Opera House that *Baedeker* described, but a striking example of contemporary architecture. To the south, beyond a new splashing fountain surrounded by a cluster of red flags flapping in the breeze, where *Baedeker* showed the university, he saw a group of barely completed buildings, one rising to more than twenty stories. Cranes and other construction equipment still surrounded it. At the site of the renowned concert hall, known as the Gewand Haus, he saw only rubble and construction machinery. An appalling realization came over him: Charles Augustus Platz had been destroyed, wiped out by aerial bombardment. Thirty years had passed, and it had not yet been rebuilt entirely. This destruction had given the East German regime an opportunity to create a wholly new architectural constellation on this renamed space, and thereby project the image of a new order—a new society erected on the ruins of the old.

There was probably another hour of daylight left. Feeling denuded by the surrender of his passport for the overnight police check, Rob walked out of the hotel to investigate the oldest part of the city before dark. *Baedeker*'s map directed him through a small park behind the Opera House into the old marketplace. Here the idiosyncrasies of modern bombing were evident. Here and there a medieval structure remained, but whole blocks of nearby houses and shops were obliterated. The town hall—the Rathaus—had been reconstructed. Signs of rebuilding were everywhere, with numerous gaps still remaining to be filled with buildings. He found Auerbach's Keller, said to have inspired Goethe for some of the scenes in *Faust*.

Walking south from the marketplace, Rob came to the Thomas Church. It seemed intact, but he learned later that extensive repairs had to be made on it after the war. In front stood a statue of Johann Sebastian Bach, who served as choirmaster here for over twenty years.

As Rob entered the church, he was overwhelmed by thundering organ music. Only a scattered handful of people were sitting in the dim sanctuary. He surmised that the organist was practicing and that this was not a church service. The music rolled on, some of the most magnificent organ music he had ever heard. The high, slanting roof and walls seemed to tremble. It was nearly deafening, but it was awe-inspiring.

Rob sought out one other historic building before heading back to the hotel for dinner. The massive structure was erected in the 1890s as the home for the Imperial Supreme Court. This was the highest court in all of the Reich, that territory stretching across 750 miles from Metz in the West to Memel in the East. The building escaped war-time destruction, and there in the twilight Rob saw the great dome, rising to well over two hundred feet. The statue of Truth that once stood atop it according to *Baedeker*, was gone, as were the statues of the two Kaisers Wilhelm that were in the niches on the front. The building now housed a small museum, but it was closed for the day. The Supreme Court of the GDR sat in East Berlin, not here. Its truncated jurisdiction extended over territory only one-fifth the size of the territory over which this court sat. Here before him in the Leipzig twilight was a ghost of the German Empire.

The dining room at the Deutschland Interhotel was crowded and bustling when Rob entered. Unlike the Elephant, there was no string music or pretense toward bygone elegance. The room was garishly lit and noisy with the babble of voices. A female receptionist led him through the maze of animated Germans to a table for four already occupied by a lone woman. In European style, the receptionist directed him to sit there, without asking the permission of the woman, who was already underway with her meal.

The menu was similar to that at the Elephant. He ordered a Wiener schnitzel, on the theory that it was probably the safest option. The wine list was also similar, but it included two East German white wines. Although he had never heard of vineyards in this part of Europe, he ordered one, curious to sample the local products.

The woman across the table from him was, he guessed, somewhere between her upper twenties and early thirties. She had a sad and worn face, reflecting not affluence, but a life of work. However, it was not the face of a peasant. She had a businesslike air about her and was dressed professionally. In fact, compared with the dress of most GDR women he had seen for the past two days, hers bordered on downright fashionable.

The question in Rob's mind was whether to try to strike up a conversation with her. He had said no more than a few words to any human being since leaving Marburg four days before. He yearned to talk with somebody—almost anybody.

"You are a visitor here?" She had looked up from her plate and was staring him straight in the face. She spoke in English, although with a German accent.

Rob was thrown off stride. He had not heard a word of English since entering the GDR. Her voice was soft and slightly husky. Her eyes showed a hint of brightness.

"Yes," Rob said, recovering from his surprise. "I am visiting in Leipzig for just a short while." He spoke in English for the first time since leaving West Germany. After an awkward pause, he added, "You speak English, I see."

"Yes, I speak some English, but I do not have many occasions to practice it."

"How did you know that I speak English?" he asked.

"I thought that you must be American. Is that correct?"

"Yes, I am, but how did you know?"

"I see many Americans on television," she said.

"Television? Where do you see Americans on television?"

"On the stations that broadcast from West Berlin and from the Federal Republic."

"Do you see those programs here in the GDR?"

"Yes," she said with a touch of pride. "I live in Berlin, and we can see all of the Western programs there."

"Do I look like the characters in those television shows?" He smiled cautiously.

She smiled in return. "Your clothes."

Rob wanted to shift the talk away from himself and on to her. "You say that you live in Berlin. Are you also just visiting in Leipzig?"

He sensed a faint hesitation on her part. He had read of the risks that citizens of the East bloc countries ran by talking with foreigners. Maybe she was thinking that she had gone too far. But after only a second's pause she resumed.

"Yes. I am here for a professional meeting."

Rob concluded that although she might be willing to continue talking, at least for a bit more, she would volunteer little and he would have to extract information from her piece by piece.

He decided impulsively now to abandon his reticence to talk with East Germans. After all, she started this conversation, and she could stop it.

"Have you been to Leipzig many times before?" he asked.

"Yes. I am here often in my work," she said.

"What kind of work do you do?"

"I am a medical doctor, and I work on diseases of the eyes—especially problems of blindness."

He said nothing, trying to conceal his surprise. After a moment she went on.

"Blindness has been a big problem in the GDR. About twelve thousand German soldiers in the Fascist army lost their eyesight, and over three thousand of them lived in the East—what is now the GDR. So the subject has received a lot of attention since the war."

The waitress arrived with Rob's Wiener schnitzel, accompanied by a gigantic mound of potato noodles. The East German white wine arrived at the same time; he took a sip, and it was not bad. Talk between the two ceased for a while as Rob began to eat his meal. The waitress set a piece of cake and a cup of coffee in front of the woman.

Rob resumed the conversation. "Do you work in a clinic or hospital?"

"I work mainly in the Charité Hospital. Have you heard of it?"

"Yes. It is a very old and famous hospital in Berlin."

"You are well informed," she said approvingly.

"I did study German history. Exactly what do you do in the hospital?"

"I work on detached retinas, glaucoma, cataracts, and some other problems. In the GDR, we still have a shortage of medical doctors, so I am not so specialized as some American doctors are, at least as I understand it."

At a nearby table there was a sudden scraping of chairs as several men seated there stood up hurriedly. A tall, elderly man had entered the dining room and was approaching that table, where he was obviously well known.

"That is a distinguished psychiatrist," she said. "He is here for this meeting."

As the doctor approached to shake hands with those who had risen to greet him, Rob saw in his lapel the small gold pin that signified membership in the Socialist Unity Party of Germany, the SED, which forms the vanguard of the working class, and they say will lead them to a classless society. So the good doctor, Rob mused, was also a good Communist.

Rob now shifted to personal matters. "Do you have any family in Berlin?"

She responded abruptly. "No, my parents both died in the war." Then she quickly changed the subject. "And what do you think of our country?"

In these words Rob thought he detected the voice of the socialist citizen, the formal question to an outsider by a person reared under this regime, schooled through the Young Pioneers and the Free German Youth, and committed "to the full realization of socialism," as the GDR literature put it.

"It's an interesting country," he said, trying to be complimentary yet not dishonest. "It's full of important historical sites and a lot of impressive scenery."

She had finished her coffee. Rob was cleaning up the last of the potato glue and the sizable slab of meat on his plate. A burst of laughter came from the table where the psychiatrist had seated himself. In his sixties, with gray hair and rimless glasses, he was the center of attention among the half dozen other men at the table. All were in black suits, and at least two were wearing SED pins. The other diners around the room were a mixed lot; many of the men had open collars and no ties, and some had no jacket—all in the spirit of the classless society, Rob assumed.

"I noticed that there is a bar just off the lobby. Would you join me there for an after-dinner drink?" Rob ventured.

She seemed flustered. "No . . . no thank you. I must go. I have papers to read for the meeting tomorrow." She pushed back her chair and stood up. Rob half rose from his chair to say good-bye, but she was gone before he could speak.

He watched her leave the room. Her willowy, well-formed body had escaped his attention while she was seated. Her departure was so abrupt that he wondered whether he had violated some fundamental code by asking her to have a drink. He realized then that he had never asked her name, nor did she know his. A subtle charm radiating from this young doctor, different from any he had encountered, did nothing to lessen his disappointment over this lost opportunity for a real conversation with a GDR citizen. "Oh well," he mumbled to himself as he sat back down to finish his coffee, "What difference does it make?"

Chapter 6

THE LAND EAST OF LEIPZIG was level, a marked contrast to the hilly and wooded terrain around Weimar and Jena. It was under intensive cultivation, with few trees. By eight in the morning, Rob had cleared the city, traveling with little interference along Route 6, a two-lane road heading due east. At intervals, he saw workers in the fields, as many women as men. The tractors they were riding reminded him of the antiquated models he had seen in photographs taken on Soviet collective farms. The wheels were wooden-spoked without the rubber tires that one sees on modern American tractors. Horse-drawn wagons and carts outnumbered trucks.

Rob's planning for the last three weeks had been directed toward this day. Ever since that last night in Remberton, his mind had been absorbed in this mission, almost to the point of distracting his thoughts from the main point of this trip to Germany—the conference at Marburg. He had risen early that morning to study again the photocopy from the 1900 atlas and the current GDR road map.

The village of Bachdorf indicated in the atlas was not shown on the road map. That posed a special challenge because the road map showed no roads at all leading off this main trunk road toward the Elbe River. He had no way of knowing how he was to get over the last few miles to his destination, nor what would be in that vicinity. For all he knew there might be a Soviet army base there; maybe that was why the map showed no roads.

By comparing the 1900 atlas with the current road map, he had narrowed the critical area down to a relatively small piece of territory. At the town of Wurzen, Route 6 began angling to the south, and it was heading almost due south by the time it reached the town of Oschwantz. Both of these towns were on the GDR road map. The Elbe ran roughly parallel to the highway at this point. He estimated that between the highway and the river the distance varied from ten to fifty miles. The village of Bachdorf should be somewhere in the quadrilateral of land formed by these two towns, Route 6, and the Elbe. The problem would be finding a road leading off Route 6 to the east, toward the river.

This morning Rob felt the exhilaration that usually overcame him when he embarked on a venture to historical sites off the beaten track. For him, it was not enough to read about places where great events took place, not enough to look at pictures of them. He needed to set foot on the very ground, to feel the soil and turf underfoot, to breathe the air, and to see the trees and hills and sky of the spot where men lived and acted out their roles and died. It was this zeal that sustained him through days in the cemeteries and trenches of the First World War, and drove him to walk miles through the woodlands of the Virginia battlefields during his three years in law school. Now this quite different exploration was aimed at an obscure place in the German countryside that might not even exist and had only a remote connection with anything. Yet it gave him that same thrill of anticipation.

According to Rob's calculations, the Elbe was not more than forty miles east of Leipzig as the crow flies. Allowing for all the uncertainties and false probes and mistakes, he estimated that he ought to reach Bachdorf within a couple of hours. The flat, cultivated fields were zipping by, and he was encountering only an infrequent vehicle on the highway. Suddenly he was crossing a sizeable stream. It had to be the Mulde River. He could not let it pass without a closer look.

After crossing the bridge, he pulled well off on the shoulder of the road. He looked at the map unfolded on the seat beside him. It was indeed the Mulde. Chills ran through him as he looked back across the water. Just behind him, on the west side of the Mulde, the Americans stopped their eastward advance in April of 1945 to await the Red Army coming from the east. Rob walked back across the bridge. It was quiet here on this summer morning nearly thirty years later. He heard only bird calls and the faint, distant, rasping motor of an old tractor. This was farther east than he had ever been before, and no American soldier had gone any farther. As he had often heard his Uncle Noble say in disgust, the way was clear, resistance had evaporated. Pressing on to the Elbe and beyond would have been easy. Churchill enjoined the Allied armed forces to push on, to take Berlin, and to "shake hands with the Russians as far east as possible;" but Ike decided against it. He ordered the advance to stop at the Elbe in the north and at the Mulde in the south. The Mulde ran into the Elbe to the north of this point, and together they formed an unbroken line from the Baltic to Czechslovakia. So on this Elbe-Mulde line, the Americans stopped and waited while the Soviet forces overran everything to the east. Ike's main reason for halting while so lightly opposed was that the occupation zones for the Americans, British, and Russians had already been set by the London Protocol of 1944. To have penetrated farther eastward would have been pointless because this territory would have to be turned over to the Russians.

But would that necessarily have been the case? Rob had been troubled by this question. It had seemed to him that Churchill, always touching on the grand themes, was then speaking for Western civilization. He was unwilling, Rob had surmised, to allow the war that had been fought to destroy Nazi totalitarianism result in Communist authoritarianism over much of the same territory; but that was exactly what he and the Western world got. But, he countered to himself, he should not judge Ike by hindsight.

Rob thought of Noble Shepperson and the map on the wall of his law office; the blue line stopped at this river. When he had supper with Noble on his last night in Remberton, he had no idea where Bachdorf was and thus no idea that he would shortly be standing near where his uncle had stood in the climactic days of the world's greatest conflict. He would have to talk to him about this country when he got home. He imagined Colonel Shepperson standing on the banks of this river, scanning the country on the far side, looking for the crumbling and disappearing German forces, and perhaps mumbling oaths to himself that his tanks were not being allowed to get at them.

Back in the rented Opel, Rob moved on. He was now in territory where the people had never seen Americans. Those living to the west of the Mulde—at least those over forty years old—had a brief chance for a couple of months to get a glimpse of American soldiers. Here, though, there had been nothing but Nazis and Communists since 1933. A German living here now would have to be well over fifty to have even a vague memory of some other form of government and way of life.

The land was a bit more rolling than it had been. There were more trees, although cultivated fields still dominated. He passed through Wurzen, and the road began to angle toward the south. From now on, he must be attentive to every side road leading off to his left. Bachdorf could be anywhere between this highway and the Elbe, which he figured to be not more than ten miles to the east.

He passed a small side road just beyond Wurzen, and then another in another mile. He decided that both of these were too soon. After three more miles, he came to another narrow road leading eastward. There were no signs to indicate where it went. On the spur of the moment, Rob decided to take it. He had assumed that this would be a trial-and-error search, so he was prepared for several false trails. He knew that he must move eastward at some point, and this seemed to be a good place to start.

The road was barely two cars wide. The surface was old asphalt and needed redoing. The fields were gently rolling. In the distance were a few chunky middle-aged women with hoes and rakes. They were wearing the farm work clothes of both sexes; their heads were covered with scarves. Across a field, he saw the brick roofless walls of what appeared to have been a small church. Several thousand churches were destroyed during the war; he assumed this to have been one of the victims. In another mile, he was in a village straddling the road. It was a cluster of red brick farm houses, nothing else. On the far edge, an old man was standing by the road, apparently engaged in nothing other than standing by the road. On impulse, Rob pulled over, leaned across the front seat, and called out.

"Excuse me." Rob raised his voice above the idling motor. The man was quite old and looked as if he could be hard of hearing. "Is Bachdorf on this road?"

"Bachdorf?" the man repeated in a raspy, hesitant voice.

Countrymen here, Rob thought, must be like countrymen everywhere; they were suspicious and cautious about strangers. Surely this tendency must be heightened here, considering the circumstances and all they had been through.

"Yes, is there a village named Bachdorf ahead on this road?"

This second try seemed to activate the man's mental processes. "No, Bachdorf is not on this road."

This man was a careful witness. He was going to answer precisely the question he was being asked without volunteering any additional information.

"Do you know where Bachdorf is?"

"Yes," came the slow response, accompanied by a nodding of his shaggy gray head.

Rob waited for elaboration, but the man said no more. "Can you tell me how to get there?" Rob continued.

The man's communication facilities were finally triggered. "Go straight ahead four kilometers, then turn to the right. Go about three kilometers. There you will come to a crossroads. Turn to the left. You will get to Bachdorf in about two kilometers."

"Thank you," Rob called out cheerily and with great relief. He gave the man a salute and surged off.

At last, the basic question had been answered: Bachdorf existed. At least *a* Bachdorf existed; there was still the possibility that there was more than one place with that name and that this was not the right one. He should have asked about the schloss, but there would be time enough for that when he got to the village. He concluded that there must be nothing particularly unusual or sensitive about it—no military base or munitions plant was there—otherwise he would not likely have gotten such clear directions.

The old man's instructions were excellent. Rob had made the two turns, and now abruptly, as he rounded a curve, a small sign appeared beside the ever-narrowing road: Bachdorf. Immediately, he was into the main street of the village. It was larger than those he had passed through in the last half hour. A few side lanes turned off the central street. There were brick houses close together with small gardens, and there were some clusters of row houses. Nondescript shops were scattered amongst them. All were likely built well before the First World War, and all had that unkempt look and lack of maintenance characteristic of GDR structures. Rob came to an intersection, apparently the center of the village. To his right, a block away, he saw a church, a weathered and abandoned-looking edifice. He drove on in the direction he had been going, but he saw nothing resembling a schloss, and there was no hint of the river. In less than a mile, he was out of the village and into the countryside again.

Leaving the village, Rob drove for another mile or two. Fields and woods ran along the narrow road; but no schloss or anything that could arguably be called a schloss materialized. He turned around and headed back to the village. He was now mildly sickened by the thought that he had come all this way on a wild goose chase. That is exactly what his friends would have told him if he had confessed his plan before he left.

He considered asking someone in the village whether there was a schloss in the vicinity, but he resisted the impulse. He did not want to arouse curiosity. An American in these parts would be strange enough. Inquiries about this seat of the von Egloffsberg family could invite suspicions because the family was probably remembered—if at all—as wealthy landowners, and in the Marxist-Leninist vocabulary, as "enemies of the people."

In the middle of the village, he came to the principal crossroad. The church was now to his left. He decided to explore the road to the right. It lead eastward toward the Elbe, he surmised. Only a few pedestrians and even fewer cars were on the village streets. It was a bright, sunny July morning, but there was a half-deserted air about the place. He passed a large banner stretched across the top of an unidentifiable two-story building. It read in foot-high letters, "The Program of the Party is the Program of the People."

Within half a mile, he was in open country again. He passed a group of farm workers gathered around one of those antiquated tractors; then, as he came around a long curve to the right, he saw in the distance what he had first imagined as he held that letter and photograph on the porch at Remberton—what he had come over seven thousand miles to find.

There to his left, in the direction of the river, was a long line of trees leading back from the road—a double line, flanking a drive. A hundred yards back from the road was a massive gray—almost black—stone manor house. It was three stories tall and broad across the front, with a wing running to the rear.

Rob slowed the car nearly to a crawl. He drank in the scene, parking at the mouth of the lane leading to the schloss.

Now that the long-hoped-for moment was at hand, he realized that he had given no thought as to what he would say or do at this point. He had become convinced, almost to certainty, that it was unlikely that he would meet any member of the von Egloffsberg family. All the circumstances and forces of history worked against that. In the first place, they might not have survived the Second World War. Bachdorf was directly in the path of the Red Army advance. The two little boys in the picture would have been the right age for military service, and they could have been killed. On top of that, lands such as these were confiscated in the sweeping post-war land reforms in the Soviet zone. There was not much chance, he guessed, that a von Egloffsberg would have been attracted to or welcomed into the Communist party. The immediate question in Rob's mind was not whether a von Egloffsberg would be here, but who *would* be here and what would be said about the fate of the family.

The bright sunlight of the July morning had now gone. Dirty gray clouds had moved in, draining the landscape of color. A fresh wind was stirring the leaves in the trees. Suddenly Rob felt cold. His heart was thumping as he turned off the road. He had been advised in Washington and Marburg not to do anything unusual in the GDR. Abide by their rules, they had said. Everybody who has gotten in trouble there was doing something that was out of the ordinary. And here he was, venturing off the beaten path into he knew not what.

The dirt lane leading to the great house was rutted. Its formerly grassy shoulders were sliced by the tracks of trucks and wagons. The trees flanking the lane did not form unbroken lines. Stumps marked gaps where some had been felled or shattered. Ahead loomed the dark facade of the medieval schloss—somber, ominous, and foreboding. The structure was wide; there must have been ten windows across the front on the upper two floors, but the glass was gone from several. Rob now noticed that a walled courtyard protruded from the front. Some forty or fifty feet beyond the gateway was the front entrance to the schloss.

Rob pulled off the lane and parked near a flatbed truck of the same vintage as the tractors that dotted the fields. Wooden carts and wagons were parked here in no particular order. What appeared to have once been a grassy expanse was now a place for the dumping of miscellaneous farm equipment. Rob turned off his motor and got out. It was quiet; only the chirping of birds broke the silence. The slamming of the car door resounded like a gunshot.

Rob's lingering doubt that this was the place he sought was dispelled in the next few moments. As he approached the main front entrance—massive double wooden doors up three steps from the cobblestone courtyard—his eyes fell on a coat of arms etched in the stonework over the doorway. It was the coat of arms that was embossed on the stationery on which the Baroness von Egloffsberg wrote her final letter to her husband in October of 1918—a letter, he now knew, that was written right here by that young wife, then proceeded westward to the Argonne, where it came to rest in the pocket of the dying German captain. It resumed its journey in the pocket of an American lieutenant, and thus found its way to Alabama and finally to the footlocker in Remberton. Now the photograph and the letter had returned over seven thousand miles and over half a century later to the very house from whence they originated.

Rob's reverie on things past was broken by a rough German voice saying, "*Guten Tag.*" A few feet in front of Rob, a tall burly man stood in the open half of the doorway. He was in brownish-colored work clothes. His collar was open and his sleeves rolled up above the elbows. Dusty boots protruded below his coarse-looking trousers. His hair was thick and dark, capping an oval, weathered face. He appeared to be about Rob's age.

"*Guten Tag,*" Rob said in response. He tried to sound firm and confident. "I'm an American traveling through the GDR for a few days. I have a special interest in old houses and historical places. I saw this schloss from the road. It looked interesting, so I thought I would take a closer look. Can you tell me anything about its history?"

There was an awkward pause. Rob waited tensely, hoping that he had satisfactorily explained his presence at this unlikely spot. The man looked at him intently with no emotion showing; then he plunged into answering the question. He seemed to ignore the fact that Rob was American, behaving as though Americans passed through there every day, when the reality was that Rob was probably the first American who had been there in decades and the first that this man had ever seen.

"This schloss was built in 1590. Before the war, only one family lived here—only one family in this huge house." With these last words his voice took on an emphatic tone, conveying both amazement and disgust. "After the war, twelve families lived here. Now this is headquarters for our agricultural collective."

"Did all of the land here belong to the family who lived here before the war?" Rob asked.

"Everything from the river to the village," he said, sweeping his arms from left to right, "and for several kilometers in that direction." He pointed down the road. "But when the Fascists surrendered, the land was divided among the people."

Rob felt the dilemma that had plagued him ever since entering the GDR: wanting to probe below the surface for information, but hesitating lest he incur trouble. But his reticence was diminishing.

"What happened to the family then?"

The man shrugged his shoulders indifferently. "I do not know. I was not here. I have heard that they left before this place was liberated by the Red Army."

"Do you know the name of that family?"

"I do not know," the man said.

Rob groped for a way to continue the conversation and possibly learn more. "My family was engaged in agriculture for a long time," he blurted out. "I have always been interested in farming, but I have not had the opportunity to do such work. Do you work here on this collective?"

"I am the director," he said with a note of pride in his voice.

"You say that this is the headquarters. What do you do in this house?"

"We keep the records. We must have papers showing production, and we must have records on the workers.

"I am very interested in old houses like this. May I see the main rooms?" Rob watched the man's face closely as he asked this venturesome question. His features were almost Slavic. His eyes seemed to cloud over, but his expression revealed nothing. For an instant, Rob thought he had run up against the usual Marxist-Leninist paranoia over disclosing information, no matter how innocuous; but then came a response.

"*Ja*," the man said slowly and uncertainly. He was obviously weighing an unusual request; but then he turned briskly and reentered the open door, motioning for Rob to follow him.

They entered a wide hallway with high ceilings. Dark gray stone covered the floor. The walls were a dark wooden paneling, whether black or brown was not discernible. On the right side of the spacious hall was a wide stairway leading upward to a landing where it turned to the left and continued out of sight. Its broad wooden steps were worn deeply by generations of feet. Beyond the stairway, some sixty feet to the rear, a door stood open to the outside.

They passed through a double door on the left into an extraordinarily large room. The clattering sound of a manual typewriter struck his ears. Several old wooden tables, like army field tables, were lined up in this room. At one, a stocky woman in her thirties was seated at an old-style typewriter with stacks of papers on both sides of her. Papers and file folders were scattered on the other tables. The room was handsomely paneled. Three tall windows opened onto the courtyard. Opposite the windows, at the far end of the huge room, was a massive stone fireplace.

"Here at that table," the man said, pointing across the room from the typist, "is the place from which I manage the collective." On the table was a sign reading *Direktor.* "But," the man went on, "I must also spend time on the land to see that the work is done and that quotas are being met."

A cool, damp breeze wafted through the open windows, swaying a bare light bulb hanging at the end of an electric cord. The typewriter noise stopped, and the woman shuffled some files from one stack to another. She had closely cropped hair and wore work trousers and a brown shirt identical to that worn by the director. In fact, she might have been mistaken for a man if not for her oversized breasts straining at the shirt buttons. She ignored Rob's presence, barely glancing up at him.

"May I see the rear of the schloss?" Rob asked, pretending to be casual.

Without answering, the director headed through the doorway into the hall and on toward the open doorway at the far end. Rob followed, and they emerged into a large shabby courtyard.

"Four families live upstairs," the man volunteered, pointing to the upper floors as they came outside. Wash was hanging out to dry in two of the upstairs windows.

On the left was a wing extending to the rear. The outer wall was standing, but the interior was gutted. The surprised look on Rob's face evidently moved the director to explain this ruin.

"The Fascist soldiers had a command post and machine gun position here. The Red Army had to clean them out when it liberated this place."

They strolled out of the neglected courtyard and across a dirt drive. At that moment Rob caught sight of the river. There it was, the Elbe at last. It was perhaps a quarter-mile away, down a long slope. It was wide and slow-moving and brown. What a grand site for a grand house, Rob thought. Rivers stirred him spiritually, and he was gripped by this belt of water moving northward through the heart of history, past Dresden, past Meissen, Wittenberg, Magdeburg, and on to the sea.

A herd of cows grazed on the grassy slope between the schloss and the river. Droppings were everywhere, right up to the edge of the former courtyard. The director again volunteered an explanation. "This is one of the pastures for the collective. Before the war, this was a garden with hedges and pathways and flowers; but when it was given to the people, they made it into grazing land."

Rob pointed to a long low brick building a hundred yards off to the right. "What is that?" he asked.

"That is where we keep tractors and wagons. Before the war it was a stable. There were many horses here then."

They turned and walked around one end of the schloss. Far off a dog barked. A tractor engine snorted in the distance. Rob's historical curiosity was intense. He craved to know more about this house and this family, but answers were not likely to be had here in this agricultural collective from this man who knew nothing of the past and cared little about it.

They reached the front of the schloss where Rob's car was parked. Rob stood in the gateway, drinking in the entire facade of this venerable stone structure. Under the thickened clouds, in the absence of sunlight, it had a grim, forbidding appearance. He saw again the outline of the von Egloffsberg crest above the doorway. This sprawling stone edifice held four centuries of stories and secrets.

However, it was not that long sweep of time that captured his imagination at the moment. Rather, he saw in his mind's eye the scene that must have taken place in that time before October of 1918. The young officer, Bruno von Egloffsberg, was saying good-bye to his family. Perhaps they were all gathered on the front steps in the courtyard where he now stood. According to the letter, the father was ill in October, but perhaps he was out here to say farewell on that earlier day. And surely the attractive woman in the photograph and the two infant children were here. Bruno might have been driving away in some kind of motor car or he might have been leaving in a carriage drawn by one of the many horses in the stables. In any case, he was leaving this great house, these vast holdings along the Elbe and a loving family for the hellish trenches of France to fight for—and, as it turned out, to die for—the Fatherland.

The Baron von Egloffsberg was leaving also, Rob reminded himself, for that brief meeting in the last moments of his life with Lieutenant Robert Edward Kirkman of the United States Army and Trepnitz Hills, Alabama—a remote spot in the New World of which the young baron had never heard. But was it really so different? The houses, the lands, and the rivers, though radically different in age and setting, suddenly struck him as having much in common. There came over him again a curious sense of kinship with these vanished people.

Rob and the director shook hands. "Thank you," Rob said, smiling and trying to be affable, but he saw no sign of a smile in the large, impassive face. The director stood motionless, watching Rob get in the car and drive slowly out the rutted lane between the trees. After turning onto the narrow black-topped road, Rob paused and looked back for a long minute to imprint in his memory the schloss and its surrounding fields.

Arriving back in the village, he pulled his car up near the church and parked. The day had darkened further, and rain was now clearly in the offing. He walked through an opening in the church's low stone wall. The church was gray stucco with a small bell tower at one corner, looking the way one would expect a village church to look almost anywhere in Europe. It was set back a few feet behind the wall. The walkway to its main front door was clear, but on either side foot-high weeds had overgrown what had probably been a lawn. The heavy wooden door was closed and locked with a chain. There was no human being in sight, and no sound of life anywhere.

Rob followed a path around the front corner, and there in the rear of the church in a dense growth of trees was what he had been hoping to find—a cemetery.

He had long viewed cemeteries as among the richest sources of historical information. They recorded the myriad names, dates, and places of those who had formed the human drama. They held the remains, the secrets, the joys, the sorrows, the hopes, and the fears of countless men and women who at one time walked the earth. Cemeteries provided tangible evidence that these people did actually exist, each playing out a role in this ongoing pageant. He felt inner excitement as he approached this small cluster of graves in this Saxon village to see what it would reveal about the family long gone from the schloss on the Elbe. In his hand he had a copy of the pages from the German genealogical book.

There were no fresh graves. The most recent dates of death on the gravestones were in the middle nineteen thirties; most were much earlier. Rotting leaves and moss covered many of the marble and granite markers. He surmised that few people came here or invested any effort in keeping it up. A high stone wall ran along the rear and one side of the cemetery. In the corner formed by the wall, he saw several large upright granite memorials. As he walked closer, he could make out the names. His pulse quickened. Deeply chiseled into the first stone was the name *von Egloffsberg.*

There were half a dozen graves in this plot. He unfolded the genealogical pages and took out a pencil. He came first to Hans Gottlieb Baron von Egloffsberg, born March 5, 1852, died October 17, 1919. At this instant, Rob felt a special debt of gratitude to the little bespectacled German and his unusual library back in Albemarle County. The page from that library that Rob now held in his hand showed that this was the father of Bruno. He was the father "not feeling well" in the letter of October 1918. Next to him was his wife, Katharina, who died six years earlier and thus would have known nothing of the Great War and the fate of her son. The largest and most impressive of the stones bore the name of Wolfgang Karl Heinrich von Egloffsberg, born April 3, 1824, died January 29, 1899. Rob's pages revealed him to be the grandfather of Bruno. An inscription revealed that he was in the service of Saxony and Prussia and that he was a general officer in the army. The other graves were those of brothers, wives, and sisters of these earlier generations, all of whom were on his genealogical list. On the far edge of the plot, he found the most recent graves—those of Ludwig Winfrid von Egloffsberg, who died in 1933, and his wife, Ursula, who died in 1936.

With no Egloffsberg grave in this cemetery later than those dates, Rob concluded that the young widow and her two sons did not die in Bachdorf before the close of the Second World War. A faint mist began to fall. He stood for a long while, pondering the mystery. Was this the end of the trail, or was there someone in this remote village who knew what had become of this prominent family? Surely there must be; but he did not feel free to walk up and down the street asking shopkeepers or passersby.

As he stood among the shadowy graves, he heard a door being unlocked and opened. He turned and saw a woman emerging from the church with a broom in her hands. She began sweeping the steps of a side entrance without noticing him. He walked toward her. She looked up with a faint start. She appeared to be in her mid-thirties, a bit more attractive and less rustic than the women he had seen working in the shops and fields.

"*Guten Tag,*" he said, trying to inject a friendly tone into his voice.

"Guten Tag," she responded uncertainly.

"Are there regular religious services in this church?"

"There are services once a month," she said, looking quizzically at Rob as though he had dropped down from Mars.

"Does the pastor live here?"

"No, he does not live here. He comes here once a month. We are preparing for a wedding this evening. He will be here to perform the marriage ceremony."

"I have always been interested in old cemeteries," he said, pausing to let that point get across. "I was just looking at some of these old graves, and I noticed some large grave markers bearing the name of von Egloffsberg. I assume that must have been an important family here. Is that correct?"

"*Ja,*" she said with no hesitation. "They lived many years ago in the schloss between the village and the Elbe."

"Do you know where any of them are now?"

"No, they were gone before I was born."

Having gone this far, Rob decided to press on. "Do you know anyone who might know anything about that family?"

She hesitated; then turning to re-enter the church door, she said, "Wait a moment please."

Rob was in a world of gray—the church walls, the cemetery, the sky, and the light of the misty afternoon now wearing on. Two dogs were barking not far away. A truck ground along the main road a short block from the church. Standing alone in the somber gray quiet, he was struck with the realization that he had encountered no restraints on his mobility in the GDR. Since crossing the border at Wartha, he had sensed no limitations on where he could go. He could drive up and down all city streets, out into the country, and wherever he had wanted to drive or walk. Indeed, he had not seen a policeman all day. He was actually beginning to relax and feel bolder about talking to people. A lot of Americans, he thought, smiling to himself, would probably not quite believe this.

He heard footsteps inside the church. An elderly woman appeared in the doorway. She was short and strongly built. She had a scarf tied on her head and wore a plain work dress. She was very much the type he had seen along the roads in the fields—sturdy German peasant stock. In her hand was a large dust cloth.

"*Guten Tag,*" she said in a heavy but not unfriendly voice. "You are asking about the von Egloffsberg family?"

"*Ja,*" said Rob, "do you know where they went?"

"When I was a young girl, I worked at the schloss before the war. The Baroness von Egloffsberg was living there then. When the war started, I went to Leipzig and worked in a factory." She stopped, as if wondering whether that was what he wanted to know.

"Were there other members of the family living at the schloss when you worked there?"

"The baroness had two sons and a daughter. Her husband had been killed in the first war, and her children were not living at the schloss when I worked there."

"Do you know where they were?"

"No, I only worked in the kitchen and knew nothing about the family's business. The baroness and I never saw each other."

Rob was surprised at the news that there was a daughter in addition to the two sons. "Did the baroness remarry after the death of her husband in the war?"

"I do not know. I was a servant in the kitchen and did not know much about the family."

"What happened to the baroness after the second war?"

"When I came back from Leipzig at the end of the war, she was gone. Fourteen families were living in the schloss. Most of them had come here from Silesia, I believe. The schloss had been damaged, but there were still enough rooms for them to live in."

"Did you ever hear what happened to any members of the family?" persisted Rob.

"People who stayed here during the war said she went to the West. When I worked there, the cook would sometimes say that the baroness would visit some of her own family at Prinzenheim, so maybe she went there. I do not know."

"Prinzenheim? Where is that?"

"They said it was a long way to the west. Maybe it is in Thuringia or Hesse or Bavaria. I do not know."

Rob sensed that this was all he could extract from this woman. Somebody might start asking why he was so interested in this family—a family likely classified as Fascist by the SED. He thanked the woman and turned to leave.

"God be with you," she said, and went back into the church.

Chapter 7

TWO DAYS LATER, in the early afternoon, Robert Kirkman was again driving through the German countryside approaching a remote village. But he was now far to the west of Bachdorf. He slowed as his car flashed past a small sign: Prinzenheim 2 km. The sign lifted his spirits, dispelling for the moment his recurrent doubts about this crazy mission, doubts as to whether he had lost all sense of perspective in taking time to pursue people he did not know who were probably dead. Nonetheless, he was exhilarated at successfully locating an unlikely place and at the prospect of peeling back a piece of a mystery that had him in its grip. It was all the result of the sheerest of happenstances. If he had not chanced to talk with the old woman at the church in Bachdorf, and if she had not happened to utter the word *Prinzenheim,* this venture would be over. It might be over anyway, he reflected, depending on what he found in the village he was now entering.

He had covered a lot of ground over the past two days. Leaving Bachdorf, he had driven back to Leipzig through a heavy rain, with earth and sky and houses all one wet, gray mass. After a hot bath, he had dinner in the Interhotel there, but was mildly disappointed not to see the young female eye doctor again. He had spent an hour studying his maps of East and West Germany, but found no Prinzenheim. Checking out early the following morning, he had managed to clear the border at Wartha and reach Frankfurt by early evening. The Wartha crossing procedures were much less complicated than they had been on his entry to the GDR. Apparently the East Germans were less concerned with the departure of an American than they were with his entry.

After breakfast in Frankfurt that morning, he had walked to a travel bureau to inquire about the existence and whereabouts of Prinzenheim. A crisply dressed woman spread road maps and guide books out on the counter. She was joined by another, and they jabbered away, flipping pages of an index and looking puzzled. One of the women turned to a man who was seated at a nearby desk scribbling on some official-looking forms.

"Villy," she asked in a slightly exasperated tone, "have you ever heard of Prinzenheim?"

"Prinzenheim?" He paused reflectively. "Yes, I believe that is the name of a village near the Taunus Mountains." He rose and came over to the counter. Pulling one of the maps closer to him, he looked intently at it for a few seconds. "Ah, here it is," he exclaimed with the lilt of success.

"Villy always answers our difficult questions," one of the women said to Rob.

She twisted the map around so Rob could see it. With her pencil point on Frankfurt, she said, "Here you are. You go north on this autobahn here." She traced the route with the pencil. "Then you take this road to the east. There is one turn here and then you will be in Prinzenheim." The women agreed with Rob's estimate that the place was probably only a little over an hour's drive.

Now Rob was entering the village. It seemed to be about the same size as Bachdorf—perhaps a bit larger. Certainly, it had a more prosperous appearance. Here the houses and shops were well painted. Nothing had that rundown look so characteristic of the GDR. Automobiles were plentiful, as were motorcycles. Small shops were sprinkled along the main street, with signs announcing their names. People were on the sidewalk, and not all were dressed in farm workers' clothes. He considered stopping to ask someone whether anyone named von Egloffsberg lived here, but he decided first to drive through the entire village.

After nearly a mile, the central street began to curve and ascend a slight hill. At the top of the rise, a high wall ran alongside the road for some distance. An opening appeared in the wall, and through it Rob saw a large house set back about seventy-five feet. A short way beyond this point, Rob pulled over to the side of the road and parked. Here and there were small houses surrounded by gardens, but the village had thinned out.

The walled place he had just passed was obviously the most imposing in Prinzenheim. Rob had to get a closer look, so he walked back to the gateway. Only an occasional car zipped past, and there were no pedestrians. At the gateway, he paused to examine the house more closely. It was three stories high and built of dark red brick. Vines covered most of the front almost to the roof line. Between the front of the house and the wall that ran along the road was a cobblestone courtyard. It was empty as far as Rob could see. At the front door were six curving steps. There were eight or ten windows across the front on the upper two floors; the lower floor had fewer. Beyond the house, to the left, were some low buildings that could have been garages or stables. The entrance to the courtyard, in which he was standing, was wide enough to admit an automobile.

The architecture here was quite different from that of the schloss at Bachdorf. It was more of a country manor house than a castle, but the structure still amply qualified as a schloss.

His eye caught sight of a small stone panel in the wall just to the right of the gateway. He walked over for a closer look. There, cut into the surface of a weather-stained stone, was a single word: Mensinger. Just below that aged stone was a modern-looking metallic plaque. It too had lettering, but in raised metal, forming another single word: *Egloffsberg.*

Rob stood there for a long while, transfixed by the letters. He then walked slowly back to the car and sat behind the steering wheel, oblivious to all else. He suddenly realized that he again did not quite know what to do. Here he was at last at the moment of revelation, the moment when the existence or whereabouts of the woman in the photograph and her two sons might be revealed, and the moment for which he had come several thousand miles. Oddly, he had not thought much about how he would present himself.

How was he to explain to whomever was here, why he, Robert T. Kirkman of Alabama, was knocking at the door on this July afternoon? Somehow it seemed inappropriate and too abrupt to announce at the threshold: "I am Robert Kirkman from America, and I have a photograph of the Baroness von Egloffsberg." No, he must have some other way of introducing himself. He conceived a plan. If it worked, and he could gain access to the house, he could then decide when and how to bring forward the photograph and letter.

With his pulse rate accelerating, Rob walked through the gateway and across the cobblestone courtyard. He stopped at the bottom of the six wide semicircular steps. The place seemed deserted. There was no vehicle in the courtyard, and he had not seen any along the drive to the rear of the house. He hesitated as he had the silly thought that he would be relieved if no one were here, but he composed himself, mounted the steps, and banged the heavy metal doorknocker on the ornately carved wooden door.

A full minute passed. No sound came from within. A car swished past the gateway heading out of the village. He debated whether to knock again. He had come too far and invested too much time in this foolish venture to back off now. He knocked again, this time louder and longer.

All remained quiet for another moment, then he heard a bolt turning. The door swung inward, and there stood a middle-aged woman whose dress and general appearance suggested to Rob that she was probably a maid.

"*Guten Tag*," Rob said.

"*Guten Tag*," she said in a cautious but not unfriendly tone.

"My name is Robert Kirkman. I am an American." Rob spoke slowly in his careful German. "I am a professor of law. I am on vacation, traveling through Germany to see interesting villages, old houses, and historical sites."

She was looking intently at him, but he could not gauge the nature of her reaction. He pulled from his pocket one of his business cards that gave his name and address. "Here is my card," he said, extending it toward her. She took the small rectangle and looked at it for a moment.

"Yes? And what do you want here?" she asked in blunt Germanic style.

"I have been at a conference at Marburg. I have wanted to see some of the country away from the autobahns—especially old places. I was driving through this village and saw this schloss. It looked quite old, so I stopped my car in the road outside the gate to get a better look. Can you or anyone here tell me something of its history? Also would it be possible to see the larger rooms inside?"

Rob realized as he uttered these last words how ridiculous they sounded. It was unlikely that anyone in his right mind would let a total stranger inside a house like this. He could be a fraud or worse, a common criminal bent on robbery or other foul play.

"Wait a minute," she said, much to his surprise, and shut the door. He heard the clanking of a bolt.

He had made his initial move, for better or worse. He convinced himself that he was not being dishonest in this approach. What he had just said was in fact true. It simply did not disclose all the reasons—indeed the real reason—that he wanted to get into this house. He stood there gazing over the venerable facade of brick and vines and musing over what he would do if this overture got him nowhere. He might then be forced to produce the picture and letter right here at the door.

At least ten minutes must have gone by. The July sun was shaded off and on by large white clouds passing in scattered formations against a blue sky. Birds chirped in trees on either side of the courtyard, and cars passed at irregular intervals, breaking the silence. He could see them for only a split second as they flashed past the opening in the wall across the courtyard.

Suddenly the bolt turned and the woman reappeared. "The Baroness von Egloffsberg says that she will be pleased to talk with you. Please come this way."

Rob followed her with a high heart. The baroness, yes, but which baroness? She could be the wife of one of the sons. For her to be the very lady in the picture would be to expect far too much. His luck at this point already seemed to have vastly exceeded reasonable expectations.

Inside the door, which slammed shut behind him, Rob found himself in a high-ceilinged hall. It was neither long nor wide. A wooden stairway began just a few feet inside the door. The walls, stairs, and banister were all made of the same dark, massive wood.

"This way, please," the woman said, starting up the stairs. Deer antlers lined both walls—pairs of antlers of all sizes and configurations. The steps creaked under their feet. Rob felt as if he were ascending into the past—the dark German past—not merely of decades but of centuries.

At the top of the stairs, a long hall ran in both directions, again crowded with antlers—more than two dozen pairs—on both sides of the dim hall. Rob followed as she turned to the right, pushed open a door, and stood aside to let Rob enter alone.

Across the room, through a pair of tall windows, he looked out over the courtyard and the wall that ran along the road. Beyond the tops of the village houses, he saw the rolling grassland of the open countryside leading to distant hills.

He surveyed the room. To his right a sofa stood against the wall; in front of it was a table flanked by several high-backed, upholstered chairs. A pale gray cloth covered the table, on the center of which stood a colorful arrangement of cut flowers. On the wall above the sofa hung a tapestry about ten feet long and eight feet high depicting men on horseback in a medieval setting.

At the far end of the room, at least forty feet away—hung a similar tapestry. The room was about twenty feet wide. A massive wooden cabinet stood along one wall, a heavy desk at the far end. Along the front wall was a table on which several magazines and books were scattered. In the corner of the room, near the door through which he had entered, was a tall stone fireplace. The dark wooden floor was almost covered by a well-worn carpet. The ceiling was some fifteen feet high. Although the walls were a whitish color, the dominant hue was a mixture of gray and green. The tapestries, the draperies at the windows, the coverings on the furniture, and the carpet were all in those shades.

All of this he examined for several minutes. He had not moved from the door he had entered. He was not certain what he should do. The room and the house were quiet. Despite the hot July afternoon outside, it was cool here. For an instant, he imagined he was in the large, quiet rooms of Trepnitz Hills in his childhood—pleasant on even the hottest summer days.

On the table across the room, he spotted a cluster of framed photographs behind books and magazines. He did not want to intrude into the personal affairs of the people living here, but his curiosity was powerfully aroused by these pictures. Hearing no one in the corridors, he walked hesitantly toward the table. A dozen or more photographs of various sizes stood there, some in silver frames and some in wooden.

His eye fell on one. It was a photograph, taken in better days, of the great stone schloss that he had visited only three days before. The trees and grassy fields around the sprawling gray structure were well tended, and there was no sign of unsightly farm equipment.

Peering from several frames were faces of elderly men and women who meant nothing to him, dressed in turn-of-the-century garb. His eyes passed over these, and rested on two pictures. Each showed a man in the uniform of an officer in the German Wehrmacht of the Second World War. He studied them closely. The two men could have been brothers. Each had medium dark hair combed straight back. Their faces were somewhat thin with sharply defined cheekbones and noses. One had a more intense expression than the other. The latter, who appeared to be slightly older, had a devil-may-care look.

Behind those frames was another, half hidden. Rob's muscles locked. His flesh tingled. There, in enlarged size, was the very photograph he was now carrying in his pocket, the photograph from his father's footlocker. There was the young lady with the hairstyle of the First World War and her infant sons. It was incredible that it was exactly the same picture, but there was no doubt in Rob's mind, as he examined it closely, that it was. Next to it in a handsome silver frame was a German army officer of the first war. That could be no one else, he surmised, but Bruno von Egloffsberg. He looked long into that Teutonic face—the face his own father had seen in its death throes.

He had at last found the place which he had sought. But who was here? He suddenly felt like an intruder, as though he were peeping through a keyhole into private lives. What legitimate business did he really have here? What difference did it make to these people now that he had a copy of this picture? Perhaps, though, he could let them know for the first time how Captain Bruno von Egloffsberg died, if anyone who cared were left alive.

The door handle clanked suddenly and sharply to his rear. Startled from his reverie, Rob wheeled around too fast, almost guiltily. He saw, standing in the open door perhaps twenty feet away, a tall, thin woman. She was simply but stylishly dressed in a long-sleeved, high-collared blouse and a casual brown skirt. Her granite-gray hair was ear-length and slightly wavy. Her fair-skinned face, showing only a few wrinkles, was accentuated by prominent cheek bones and a rather large but thin nose. She was smiling with an intensely curious expression. She stood erect, a remarkably attractive woman for her age—which Rob guessed to be in the seventies.

Walking toward Rob, she said, "You are Mr. Robert Kirkman?" She spoke in clear English, though it was unmistakably tinged with a German accent.

"Yes," replied Rob, still working to regain his composure. "Yes, I am Robert Kirkman." His hand went forward to meet hers. They shook hands, her hand clasping his with more warmth and vigor than he expected. She continued to look into his eyes with an intensity that he found a bit disconcerting.

"Would you have a seat over here?" she said, motioning him toward the group of chairs surrounding the table and sofa. Rob sat down in a high-backed wing chair at the end of the table. She sat on the sofa just to his left.

"I understand that you are an American visiting in Germany," she said. "What brings you to Prinzenheim?"

Rob had been examining her face as intently as she had been looking into his. He was searching for the answer to the question foremost in his mind: Was this the woman in the photograph? In this face of seventy-odd years he was searching for evidence of a face in its twenties.

"I am on a vacation after a conference at Marburg. It was a meeting of law professors and judges from several countries to discuss court procedures." Realizing that she had never said her name, he added quickly and casually, "I understood from the maid that you are Baroness von Egloffsberg."

"Yes, please excuse me for not introducing myself. I am Martina von Egloffsberg."

That was what he was waiting to hear—the name *Martina*—the name signed on the letter that at this very moment was inside his breast pocket. The age, the name, and the physical appearance all tallied. He remained uncertain about what to say, but he picked up on her question.

"I have long been interested in German history. I have been in Germany twice before and have visited several cities and regions, but I have not been in this part of the country. I am driving through villages off the main roads to look at the architecture and the land."

"Your card says that you are a professor of law. Is this not a strange trip for a professor in that subject?"

He laughed. "Law professors in America have many interests. Many study history as a matter of personal interest. I enjoy it in the same way that some people enjoy music."

"But German history surely must be an unusual interest," she said.

Her pleasant expression remained, but Rob was beginning to feel slightly uncomfortable. He had an uneasy feeling that she did not quite believe him.

"Germany is a country of major importance in the United States. I read some statistics once saying that about ten thousand Americans attended German universities between the middle of the last century and the First World War. That is more than attended all the universities of Britain and France combined. Those American students brought back influential ideas about education and government." Here Rob heard himself repeating the words of Professor George Marks Wilton. "Also," he added, "German courts have been a growing subject of study in the States."

"So you have an intellectual interest in this country?"

"Yes, that is correct," he said. Still not sure how to reveal his real mission here and wanting to get more facts first, he decided to advance another reason for his German interest by injecting a personal note. "In addition, I do have ancestral connections here. My great, great, great, great-grandfather came from Germany to America right after the American Revolution. I have had a curiosity, because of that, to learn about Germany. I have never had the time to trace either the ancestors or descendants of the one who came over."

"Oh, you are part German then? What is the German family from which you are descended?"

"Von Trepnitz," he said cautiously. He had always been uneasy talking about family backgrounds and personal histories in Germany. He had concluded long ago that it was probably better not to go into the subject—especially with someone born before 1930—but he was relieved at her reaction.

"Von Trepnitz," she repeated slowly and thoughtfully. "I have heard that name, but not in a long time. Do you know whether any members of that family live in Germany today?"

"No, I know nothing about the family in Germany at present. I have always understood that the Baron von Trepnitz who came to America was born in Thuringia. Some day I hope to explore the family seat here to see whether there are any members still living in Germany."

The slight tension he had been feeling seemed to relax. Could it be, he wondered, that the mention of his German ancestral link had established a communal relationship with this woman, some vague connection in the German past that made him more acceptable?

"Would you like some coffee?" she asked suddenly.

"Yes, that would be nice."

"Good," she said, rising from the sofa. "Please excuse me for a few minutes." She closed the door behind her, leaving him alone again.

Rob pulled the photograph from his inside coat pocket and examined the face of the young lady. The eyes, the nose, the mouth, and the shape of the face were, he now decided, a decades-younger version of those he had been looking at for the last several minutes. The dress and the hair-style were, of course, radically different, but he was feeling increasingly confident that this was the woman who had been sitting here on the sofa.

He looked at the handwritten letter on the Bachdorf stationery with the engraved von Egloffsberg coat of arms at the top. He was awed by the realization that this elegant, elderly woman and the woman in this fading picture who wrote this yellowed letter fifty-five years before were one and the same. He was overwhelmed by a sense of time gone.

A host of questions crowded his mind. What had she been doing all these years? The turbulent Weimar Republic, the rise of the Nazis, Hitler, and the destructive war years had come and gone. Where had she been and what was she doing during those traumatic periods in twentieth-century German history? And what of those two babies? Were they the Wehrmacht officers whose pictures were on the table a few steps from where he was sitting? Were they dead or alive? And what were they doing from 1933 to 1945?

Rob was surprised by the cordiality of the reception he had received. He had expected at most a cool, formal greeting, if indeed he had been let in the house at all. Europeans generally tended, in his experience, to be stand-offish, lacking the easy, cheerful informality of Americans. Most Germans he had encountered were blunt, certainly in contrast to genial Southerners among whom he had grown up. But here was a smiling, friendly woman clasping his hand warmly, inviting him to sit down and have coffee. Although he was a total stranger, he had now been twice left alone here in this room full of undoubtedly valuable tapestries, furniture, and silver artifacts.

Apart from this hospitality, this woman seemed different in other ways from German women he had met. There was no hint here of the frumpy *hausfrau.* Instead, here was a slender, tall—she was about five feet ten inches—and delicately refined female. Vaguely, she reminded him of Marlene Dietrich. It was all a bit puzzling, but exciting.

The door handle clanked, and the carved wooden door to the hall swung open. The maid who had met him at the front entrance came in with a large silver tray. She set it on the table in front of him and left the room without acknowledging his presence. The tray held a silver coffee pot, three porcelain coffee cups and saucers, three slices of a creamy chocolate pie, spoons, forks, a sugar bowl, and a pitcher of milk. In another minute, Martina von Egloffsberg entered the room, closing the door behind her. She resumed her seat on the sofa, expressing the hope that he liked chocolate.

"Are your parents living?" she asked casually.

"No," he replied slowly, "My mother died about fifteen years ago. My father just died this past spring."

"Oh," she said in a tone of surprise and sadness. "I am sorry to hear of that."

There was a momentary lapse in the conversation as she began to take the coffee cups off the tray and place them in the saucers. She turned her face back toward him.

"Had he been ill for a long while?"

"No, he had not been ill at all. He died quite suddenly of a heart attack," Rob said, thinking wistfully of his father and of how he might be both bemused and saddened if he knew that his son was sitting here in the heart of Germany with the widow of the man whose death he witnessed and ministered over in the Argonne Forest. Some of his most enjoyable times with his father had been the conversations they had had, usually about some of Rob's recent travels or experiences. He could see the two of them now on the screened porch at Remberton, his father pushing back and forth in his wicker rocking chair. He would surely be fascinated to hear an account of this scene.

The baroness's words broke into the clicking of the ceiling fan on the porch at Remberton. "Was your father also a professor?"

Rob chuckled mildly. "No, but he probably should have been. He had the right kind of personality, and he was very studious. He told me that he thought about it when he was young. He also thought about going into farming on his family's place. They had been there farming for several generations, and he loved the land. In the end he became a lawyer."

"I saw on your card that you are a professor at the University of Alabama. Was your father's home in Alabama?"

"Yes. He was born and reared there. The place was far in the country in one of the main cotton-growing regions. In fact, the place was named Trepnitz Hills because it was settled and the main house was built by members of that family. The *von* was dropped in America. When my father grew up and entered the practice of law, he moved to a small town about thirty miles away. That is where I grew up."

She had placed a cup in front of him and was beginning to pour coffee into it. He glanced at the third cup which she had placed in front of the chair to his right.

Noticing his glance, she said, "Oh, I should have mentioned that my son is here today, and I have invited him to join us. I hope you do not mind. I think that he would be interested in meeting you."

"I would enjoy meeting him," Rob said, feeling his pulse pick up ever so slightly. Here was another surprise. At least one of the sons was alive and was actually on the premises. His luck was holding up beyond his best hopes.

"I think that I should tell you that my son is—"

Her sentence was interrupted by a vigorous clanking of the door handle. Rob looked up as the door swung open and a man entered.

"Wolfi," Martina said, raising her voice in his direction and speaking in German, "Here is our guest. He is Herr Kirkman—or perhaps I should say Doctor or Professor. He is a law professor from America."

The man stood still listening to her, just inside the closed door. He was about the same height as Rob but stockier in build. His thick, dark hair, flecked with gray, was combed straight back from a widow's peak. His long-sleeved blue shirt was open at the collar; he was wearing rumpled dark slacks but no coat. He looked directly at Martina while she was speaking, but he seemed oblivious to Rob's presence. He walked straight toward the chair closest to the door, and placed both hands on its back. There was something odd about his movement.

Martina, turning to Rob, said, "This is my son, Wolfgang."

Rob rose from his chair and extended his hand. As he did so, Martina said, "Wolfi, Professor Kirkman is on your left."

Wolfgang's right hand came forward toward Rob and stopped. After a moment's hesitation Rob grasped it. He said, "Hello, I am glad to meet you."

"It is a pleasure to meet you," responded the heavy German voice. Wolfgang edged around the side of his chair and sat down facing the table.

Rob was perplexed by the man's jerky movements and peculiar stare. There was an almost spooky air about him. Rob examined his features more closely, trying to appear not to do so. Then it hit him. Suddenly he remembered similar movements and facial expressions of a long-ago college professor. Wolfgang, he realized, was blind.

Chapter 8

THE THREESOME SAT for a moment in awkward silence beneath the medieval tapestry. Robert Kirkman was absorbing the sudden insight that he was seated at the table with a blind man—one of the little boys in the faded 1918 photograph now grown to middle age. The baroness's voice mercifully intruded. "Professor Kirkman, do you speak German?"

"Yes, but I do not consider myself completely fluent. I can get along reasonably well in a normal conversation."

"Well, Wolfi and I like to practice our English, so perhaps, if it is agreeable with you, we can all talk mainly in English."

"*Ja*," said Wolfgang, beginning in German but abruptly shifting to English, "I do speak it but some of the complicated words give me trouble. And what you call slang I do not understand."

"I do not understand much of that myself," Rob said, chuckling politely.

"Mama, I would like coffee, please," Wolfgang said.

The man's face was almost handsome, but not quite. On one side, it was slightly misshapen, as though someone had molded it in clay and pushed one cheekbone askew. The skin at that point was of a different hue from the rest of his face. He had the thin lips and nose of his mother; but his most arresting feature was his eyes. They were dark and deep-set and gave the impression that he could see.

Martina came around with the coffee pot and poured a cup for Wolfi. "Here is the sugar," she said, sliding the sugar bowl toward his right arm, which was resting on the table. "I am giving you a little milk," she said as she poured a splash out of the pitcher. His right hand went around the sugar bowl and rose to intersect the protruding spoon. He filled the spoon and moved it over to meet his left hand hovering over the rim of the coffee cup.

In Rob's entire life, he had known only one blind person: an English professor at the University of Alabama from whom he had taken a course in Shakespeare. Rob had seen little of him outside of class. The main thing he remembered about this professor was that he knew Shakespeare's plays by memory, at least those that they studied. Rob saw now in his mind's eye that blind, erudite teacher standing in front of Woods Hall behind the Gorgas Library, waiting in the late afternoon to be picked up by his wife. Many times Rob passed within a few feet of the man, but he did not speak to him. He did not know what to say or do. After all, what can one say to a blind person? Since those days, Rob had read magazine articles explaining that one should deal with blind people the same way that one would deal with anyone else. Yet, he had never felt comfortable in their presence.

As though clairvoyant, Wolfgang turned his head in Rob's direction and said in his accented English, "As my mother may have told you, and as you have perhaps noticed, I do not see."

Rob was caught off guard. He did not expect to be confronted so directly with this uncomfortable fact. He did not know what to say, but silence would not do. He mumbled the only words that seemed acceptable: "Yes, I understand."

They stirred and sipped their coffee. Martina distributed the chocolate pie, and all three began digging into it with forks.

The moment of revelation must come soon, Rob reminded himself. The afternoon was wearing on, but he wanted to put it off at least a bit longer. "This is an extraordinary experience for me," he said. "I have never before been in such an old and impressive residence in Germany. Can you tell me when this house was built?"

The Baroness von Egloffsberg now took on a more serious demeanor. "This house was built in 1686. It has been in my family ever since. Until the last century, there were no village houses nearby. The village was tiny and was a kilometer away; but gradually it grew. Now houses come all the way up the road, as you probably noticed. Originally, my family owned a lot of land here. There was much farming and many pigs and cows. The men liked to go on stag hunts—you saw their horns on the walls when you came in. Gradually the land was sold or divided up among heirs, so today we have only a little around this house."

Rob was listening with fascination. "Could you tell me about this house?" he asked.

"Yes. This is the main floor. I do not know what this room was originally, but we use it as a sitting room. It is cool in summer, and we can heat it in the winter although it is quite large. At the other end of the house," she said, waving her hand, "is a fine hall, a great room that was used, and is still sometimes used, for large dinners. It is the finest room in the house. Across the corridor from us," she continued, pointing toward the door, "is the library where we have many fine books. On the floor above us are apartments and bedrooms. There is a wing to the rear where we have some family apartments."

Wolfgang was eating his pie and intermittently stirring his coffee. His dark, sightless eyes revealed nothing. A hundred questions pressed for answers in Rob's mind; but he must not be too aggressive or overly inquisitive, he thought.

"Have you always lived here?" he asked.

She placed her cup in its saucer and looked at him for a long moment. Her inquiring eyes made him uneasy.

"I was born here," she began slowly as though she was settling in to tell her life's history. "I was sent to a girls' school in Frankfurt for several years and then was married. I then went to live at my husband's home. It then seemed a long way from here. It was beyond Leipzig on the Elbe."

"That is indeed a long way," murmured Rob, "deep into East Germany."

"Yes," she almost snapped back, "It is. We have been cut off from that place for years. Sometimes I think that it is just as well that my husband and my son did not live to see what has happened there."

"Your son?"

"My other son, Kurt. He died in the second war."

She picked up her cup and took a sip of coffee. Rob followed suit with the discomfiting sense that he was guilty of an inexcusable deception. Internally, he was engaged in a running debate with his conscience. There was basically nothing deceitful in what he had done, one voice argued. He had appeared at the door announcing himself to be an American law professor, which was true. He had said that he had been to a conference at Marburg, he was on vacation, and he was interested in seeing historical structures in off-the-beaten-track villages. All of this was likewise true. But, his conscience countered, he knew that he had not told these people why he was really here. He knew who this woman was, who her husband was, and where she lived; he had just been to the schloss on the Elbe that she was telling him about. And she had now accounted for the other son—the other little boy in the picture. Nevertheless, he was sitting there letting her tell him all about these things as if he knew nothing of them. Shifting uncomfortably in his chair, he realized that the longer he delayed imparting the full facts, the more difficult it would become to do so. He would have to leave soon, so he could not long put off the moment of truth.

Just then he heard his own voice as though it were coming from an entirely detached source. "Would it be possible for me to see the great hall and library that you have described?"

"Yes," Martina said. "I can show them to you." She stood up and edged around the table.

"I will stay here," Wolfgang said, reaching for the coffee pot. Rob watched uneasily, thinking of the scalding coffee, but Wolfgang clasped the pot handle firmly, brought the spout deftly into position, and filled the cup almost to the brim.

Martina led Rob down the long corridor lined with horns. At the end they went through double wooden doors, dark and ornately carved, into a room that made Rob catch his breath. What he saw was beyond anything he had imagined. The room ran for at least sixty feet in length and was some thirty feet in width. The wood-panelled walls rose to a height of some twenty feet, then slanted to a peak that must have been nearly thirty feet above the floor. On the outside wall, opposite the door, was a stone fireplace with an opening that was his height. Daylight streamed in from four tall windows. However, what captured Rob's attention were the portraits hanging on the four walls, some full-length and life-sized.

Rob and Martina stood in the middle of the room. Neither spoke. In the silence of this huge hall, he was overwhelmed by a sense of long-gone history. He felt physically linked with three hundred years of time. He had had similar sensations in some of the country places of England, but the feeling here was different. He was gripped now by a peculiar sense of his own past intertwined with that of this family. It was not rational, but it was odd too that he should feel a greater closeness to German history than to that of England. The horrendous schisms of the two world wars surely should have put Germany on the far side of the historical stream from England and America. Despite that circumstance, he was caught in a powerful magnetic force of commonality.

On the far wall was an officer of the Kaiser, arrayed in the finery of the times prior to the First World War. Close by, in an ornate frame, was a full-length painting of an officer standing beside a cannon, bearing all the earmarks of the Franco-Prussian War. Rob's eyes swept along the line of portraits. Back and back they went, through the Napoleonic wars to the time of Frederick the Great and earlier. He was surrounded by an unbroken line of Germans, all—quite appropriately he thought—army officers. Much of the story of Europe for nearly three centuries could be told by retracing the lives of these men.

"Here is my father," Martina said, walking over to the portrait of a tall gray-haired figure in a colorful uniform, wearing a sash and saber. "He served in an artillery regiment but was retired because of an injury he received on maneuvers. He died when I was a young girl, before the first war. My family name was von Mensinger. Every generation of the family is represented here, back to 1650, which was shortly before this schloss was built."

Rob yearned to remain in this room and to ask for the biographies of every man portrayed on its walls. But he was brought back to reality by the slanting rays of the sun coming through the western window, reminding him that his time was running out.

"Over there," Martina continued her explanation, "are three portraits from my husband's family. They are all that I could bring with me from his home at Bachdorf."

Rob walked toward them for a better look. One was of a robust man with a heavy mustache attired in riding clothes.

"That is my husband's father," Martina said. "The other two are of his grandfather and great-grandfather. Each is a von Egloffsberg."

"May I see the library?" he asked.

They left the great hall and walked back along the antler-lined corridor. *Bachdorf.* The word echoed in Rob's brain. She had just said it, actually uttered it for the first time. He must tell her within the next few minutes that he had been there.

As they passed the head of the stairway leading down to the front entrance, Martina asked, "Had you ever heard of Prinzenheim before?"

"No, not until this visit to Germany. It is not mentioned in any of the tourist literature that Americans see."

Beyond the room where they had been sitting, the corridor ended at a door. Martina pushed it open, and they entered a corner room. It was no more than twenty by thirty feet. Book shelves lined two walls from the floor up to a height of at least ten feet. For a library buff and lover of old books, it was a gold mine. There were all shapes and sizes of publications. Many volumes were bound in black, some in white, and some in brown leather. Hard-to-read German Gothic lettering abounded on the spines. There had to be several hundred volumes on these shelves, Rob thought. He yearned to spend hours, days here exploring these treasures. It was obvious that most were very old.

The baroness noticed his mesmerized reaction, and she asked with a fresh smile, "You like old books?"

"Yes," he said, "and this is indeed an impressive collection."

"Most of these belonged to my family and have been here for many years; but some of them came from Bachdorf."

Rob moved closer to read titles. "I see that some are law books," he said, pointing to a shelf where his eye had caught the names of Savigny and von Jehring.

"Yes. They belonged to my husband. He had inherited some of them from his grandfather. Both of them studied law in the university."

The more Rob saw and heard in this house, the more he wanted to know. Whole layers of the German past were lying just below the surface, and his historical curiosity was becoming intense. But he was reconciled to leaving with that curiosity unsatisfied.

They passed through another door back into the tapestried room where they had been sitting. Wolfgang was not there. The coffee cups and service tray were gone.

"Please wait here," she said, "I will be back in a moment."

Rob paused at the table holding the assortment of framed family pictures. He looked again at the two young officers in the Wehrmacht uniforms. Neither clearly resembled Wolfgang; but one of them had to be. With his hand, he covered the mouth and cheeks of one, allowing himself to see only the eyes, forehead, and hair. It could be Wolfgang, but he was not confident. There was something odd about the face he had observed at the table, something unnatural about its shape and texture.

His eye caught a photograph that he had not noticed. A woman stood in the center. Two boys were standing on her right—probably in their early teens—and a much younger girl was pressed against her on her left. He thought he saw Martina in the woman's face. He heard again the voice of the old woman at the church door in Bachdorf: "The baroness had a daughter." The point came back into his mind for the first time since he had been ushered into this room. There had been no mention of a daughter. Where was she? Martina must have remarried, but where was that husband?

He heard faint steps approaching just in time to move to the chairs around the coffee table before the door opened.

The moment never seemed quite right to disclose his real purpose in being here, but he knew now that, without further delay, he must sit down with this woman and lay his information before her.

"Professor Kirkman," Martina said as she entered the room, "I have talked with Wolfgang. He and I invite you to stay here in this house for dinner and for the night. There are only the two of us and Olga, who lives downstairs. There are many rooms. We have a room especially reserved for guests. We are expecting no one else tonight."

This is all incredible, he thought. These members of the German aristocracy had neither seen nor heard of him until a couple of hours ago. They knew almost nothing about him. Now he was being asked to stay overnight under their roof. Although taken completely by surprise, Rob knew instantly that he would accept. He would have a more leisurely opportunity to absorb the atmosphere of the place, to delve more into the past, and perhaps get answers to the questions pressing most insistently on his mind. Better still, he could put off until tomorrow revealing the papers from the Argonne that were almost burning through his pocket.

He felt obliged to protest. "That is extraordinarily kind of you, but I think it would be an imposition. I can drive back to a hotel in Frankfurt."

"No, no, that would not be a good thing to do. If you need to be in Frankfurt tomorrow, you can drive there in the morning. No, we insist that you stay here."

Rob intended no serious resistance, so with a mild show of reluctance he agreed. He went out to the road and retrieved the car, parking it in the courtyard. Olga met him there and took his suitcase. They climbed the wide and creaking wooden stairs to the top floor—the floor above the sitting room, great hall, and library. Martina met them at the top of the stairs and led him along a narrow, poorly illuminated corridor to a corner room. The room was spacious, but it was crowded with dark, carved furniture. A massive post rose at each corner of the high bed. A wardrobe, a chest of drawers, and two chairs almost filled the remaining space.

"Here you are," Martina said. "The bathroom is next door."

"Thank you. I am sure that I will be very comfortable."

"We will meet in the sitting room below at seven for dinner. Wolfgang is walking to the center of the village in a few minutes. He has asked me to invite you to walk with him. You have time. It is only five o'clock."

"Yes, I would enjoy going with him.

"Good. He will meet you on the front steps in about ten minutes," she said. "I will see you at seven."

The road curved away from the wall and gateway of the schloss and sloped gently down toward the center of the village. Rob and Wolfgang were striding along briskly. Rob let Wolfgang set the pace. He held a long white cane which he flicked deftly from side to side as he walked. On close examination, Rob determined that it was fiberglass with a flat, round, metallic tip about the size of a quarter. Wolfgang held the cane at his waist. When his right foot went forward, the cane tip went to his left, touching the ground briefly. When his left foot went forward, the cane tip went to the right. There was a rhythmic synchronization between feet and cane as the silvery tip flashed in an arc from right to left and back.

Since they had set out from the house, they had said little. Rob had concluded that Wolfgang was reticent and maybe unfriendly. He had said almost nothing while they were seated at the table having coffee. Yet the invitation to walk into the village suggested that he might eventually warm up. Rob decided that he had to take the initiative in conversation.

"You certainly move along well with that cane," Rob said.

"I have had a lot of practice. Also, I had good training."

Rob had surmised from the photographs that he had seen that Wolfgang had not been born blind. When had his blindness come on?

They passed two middle-aged men walking along the road. Both were in working clothes and showed signs of having spent a long, hot day outside. "*Guten Tag, Freiherr*," said one. "*Guten Abend*," replied Wolfgang. Rob nodded and smiled at the men.

"Where did you take your training?" asked Rob, deciding to press the subject now that Wolfgang had opened it up.

"In a school for the blind in Berlin. Several such schools were operating in Germany. About twelve thousand German soldiers were blinded during the war. Later, I went to Marburg, where there is a school for the blind."

"I was just in Marburg for a conference at the university. We met in the castle at the very top of the high hill."

"I walked up there many times while I was there; but I had not been there before the war, so I have never seen Marburg with my eyes. But I feel that I know it very well.

There was silence for a few seconds. The tapping of the cane tip on the asphalt surface of the road maintained a steady beat accompanying their footsteps. Though quite warm, it was a beautiful late afternoon. The sky was deep blue with only a few white clouds high above. Just as Rob was about to make some small talk, Wolfgang resumed.

"The library for the blind—where they made braille books and recorded books—had been in Leipzig for many years. I visited there when I came out of the rehabilitation school in Berlin; then the war ended, and we had this East-West division."

His voice hardened on these last words, and Rob thought he detected a hint of bitterness. They walked on in silence, passing a few more villagers who nodded and spoke.

"From what you say, I assume that you lost your sight during the war," Rob said tentatively. Wolfgang seemed to be loosening up, growing more willing to talk. "Yes, that is right. I was not a natural soldier. For generations, most of the men in my family had been officers—at least for a part of their lives—and my older brother was attracted to the army as a career. But I was not. I had gone to the University at Breslau and then to the University at Berlin. I was interested in theology and was considering going on to the University at Leipzig, which had a strong Protestant theology faculty; but the war was then coming on, and there was a great patriotic spirit in the land. Like almost all of the men of my generation, I felt a duty to the Fatherland. I must add, because Americans are suspicious on this point, that I was not attracted to the Nazi party. I was not a member, and I thought that most of them were—how do you say in English—scoundrels? Anyhow, I became a staff officer in the Wehrmacht."

Wolfgang abruptly rounded a corner, turning into a street leading away from the main road. He stopped at a mail box, pulled a letter from his rear pocket, and posted it.

Church bells not far away began to ring, the double German church bells, one deep and slow, the other, intermingling with it, higher pitched and more rapid. The air was suffused with this rolling, booming, and clanging emitting from the church tower a couple of hundred yards ahead.

"Evening services are conducted here one afternoon each week. My mother and I sometimes go, but we go to church mainly on Sunday mornings."

Birds dipped and darted overhead. The bells rolled on, getting louder as they approached the church—bong . . . bong . . . dong . . . bong . . . dong . . . dong. . . bong. Pedestrians scurried along, some heading toward the church, some in the opposite direction.

Several roads intersected just as they reached the church. In the center of the intersection was a small grassy plot with a large stone monument. They stopped directly in front of the church. The duet of bells rolled overhead, the booming bass and tenor filling the whole square. The sound of these multiple German church bells always stirred Robert Kirkman deeply, touching all the recesses of his mind and soul. In this slow pounding music, he heard and felt the history of the church across the ages. Bells like these had been ringing through centuries of German history, from the earliest settlements of the Middle Ages through the Reformation, through the time of Frederick the Great, through the nineteenth century and the golden age of a united Germany, through the First World War and its humiliating end, through the tumult of the postwar years, the rise of Nazism, the catastrophe of the second war, and into the divided Germany. The bells ringing through all those decades were ringing here on this July evening in a quiet village. Standing beside his war-blinded host, beneath the heavy tolling of the bells, Robert Kirkman was painfully aware that he carried next to his bosom the secret of their fathers' battlefield meeting.

Raising his voice to be heard above the bells, Rob said into Wolfgang's ear, "I would like to go over to see the monument."

They crossed the narrow street to the grassy plot on which the massive granite slab stood. On the long rectangular side which they approached, Rob saw a short German inscription which said simply: The

Fallen and the Missing, 1914-1918. Then there were the names, column after column, row after row.

"I am looking at the names under 1914-1918," Rob said, again lifting his voice over the bells, "There are so many from such a small village."

"Yes," Wolfgang said thoughtfully, "but the list on the other side is longer."

Grasping Wolfgang's elbow, Rob moved him around the granite stone to the opposite side. Wolfgang was right. Here the names ran on and on to more than half again the length of the other list. The inscription at the top read: We died for you, what do you do for us? 1939-1945.

"There are over a hundred names here," Wolfgang said in measured tones, "from this village of no more than eight hundred inhabitants." He seemed to be lost in thought. Then he added, "Herr Kirkman, this was a very high price to pay for a divided country; and every village in Germany paid this price. And for what purpose? Was it to bring Marxism-Leninism into the middle of Europe?" His voice was low and harsh, barely audible above the bells, as if he were talking to himself.

The bells suddenly subsided. The quietness was startling. Cars and people had disappeared. The sun was lowering in the western sky. The two stood in front of the monument. Wolfgang stared ahead, inscrutable, detached, not distracted by the world around him, a faint evening breeze ruffling his graying hair.

Rob looked again at both sides of the monument. Putting together the names from both of these lists added up to a staggering biological loss in this small cluster of humanity. No American community had suffered such losses, he thought, unless it were some counties or towns in the South. Yes, the South would come nearest in the United States to something like this. Images flickered in his mind of the many Confederate monuments he had seen, bearing a similar simple inscription: 1861-1865. His ancestors had experienced one disastrous defeat over a hundred years ago, but these people had been through two far more cataclysmic defeats right here in the twentieth century within a generation of each other.

Wolfgang broke the long silence. "My brother and my father are not here," he said quietly. "We were not originally from Prinzenheim. Only my mother's family had its home here. My father's family—Egloffsberg—had its seat far to the east. But there are no monuments there to preserve their memory."

"From what your mother said, I assume that you lost your brother in the second war."

"My older brother, Kurt, died at Stalingrad. We do not know the circumstances, and we will never know. He was a batallion commander in a panzer division. I do not know how much you may have read of the

Sixth Army at Stalingrad. The army had been ordered not to retreat. One week before it was surrounded by the Soviet army, we received a message from Berlin that he had been killed. We were not able to learn about his death because nothing more was ever heard from any of the German forces in the Sixth Army, except fragments from a few prisoners of war who finally came back. I have talked with some of the officers and men who came back from the Soviet prison camps years later, but no one knew my brother's battalion. Thousands of German families have had that same experience."

Gradually the pieces were falling into place. Rob resisted the temptation to ask Wolfgang about his father out of his reluctance to be guilty of further deception. But what about Wolfgang himself? And what about the daughter the old woman at the Bachdorf church had mentioned? She would be Wolfgang's sister. The evening lay ahead, so perhaps he would draw out the whole story, bit by bit.

"It will soon be dinner time," Wolfgang said. "We should walk back toward the schloss."

As they turned to leave the grassy plot, Rob's eye caught a short inscription across the end of the great stone, appearing to link the two lists of the village's sons: All in God's Hand.

Chapter 9

THEY WERE SEATED FOR DINNER in a dining room just off the corridor near the great hall. Although the room was larger than the typical American dining room, it seemed small compared to the other rooms in the schloss. Martina sat at one end of the table. Wolfgang was at the other end, and Rob was on the side between the two. In the center was an ornate silver candelabra. Its six candles provided the only light. Their places were set with silver forks, knives, and spoons, but as yet no plates.

Rob felt refreshed after the walk to the village, a good bath, and a change of clothes. Wolfgang had changed into another open-collared shirt and was wearing what Rob had always thought of as a smoking jacket. Its brass buttons glinted in the candlelight. Martina had gotten out of her casual blouse and skirt and was now attired in a simple rose-colored dinner dress. Despite the softening effect of the candlelight, she looked older to Rob than she had in the more casual afternoon attire. Nevertheless, she was well-preserved and fashionable for a woman of her age.

Olga entered with a tray laden with plates. Placing the tray on a sideboard, she served them plates bearing huge quantities of roast pork, potato dumplings, and green beans. Despite her short, fat figure, Olga moved easily and quickly around the table. Her build was more in line with Rob's image of most German women than the tall, slim frame of Martina.

"We eat simple food here," Martina said. "You are being served what we would have if you were not here."

Olga had left the room and now returned with an opened bottle of wine. "We do not keep a large variety of wines," Martina commented, "so I hope you like Johannesberger Riesling."

"Oh yes, I like almost all of the Rhine and Mosel wines." Olga filled their glasses then put the bottle on the sideboard.

Silence ensued for some seconds as the three of them cut away at the slices of pork. "Professor Kirkman," Martina abruptly said, "tell us about yourself and your work."

Rob launched into an account of his life, telling briefly of his college and law school background, his short time with a firm in New York, and his years of teaching.

"As for my family," he went on, "I am the last one. I do still have one uncle, my mother's brother, but I have no brothers or sisters. The name Trepnitz has disappeared as a family name. It is my middle name. My great-grandfather was the last man to bear the Trepnitz name; and if I do not marry and have children," he added with a laugh, "there will be no more Kirkmans either."

"That is like our family," she said. "I do have cousins with the Mensinger name. They live in the north of Germany, but they are in another branch of the family. The von Egloffsberg name will disappear when Wolfgang and I are gone."

"I do not know about that, Mother," interrupted Wolfgang, speaking facetiously in his labored English. "I may marry some beautiful young lady and have many children." There was a twinkle in his sightless eyes and a joking smile on his face.

"Well, I have always said that the women of this country were missing a great opportunity with you," his mother replied.

Olga refilled their wine glasses, and conversation turned to the contemporary German scene. They talked of Frankfurt and Berlin and their hotels, restaurants, art galleries, and theaters.

"I have a granddaughter in West Berlin," Martina said.

Rob was startled at this news, but tried not to show any change in his expression. "Oh," he said, "Whose daughter is she?"

"She is the child of my daughter. After the first war, I remarried and had one child, a girl named Helga. My husband died suddenly when she was only two years old."

"She is seven years younger than me," interjected Wolfgang. "But we grew up in the same house. Since our fathers were both dead, we were quite close. I was happy to have a little sister."

"Where is Helga now?" asked Rob, excited by the confirmation of a daughter and becoming increasingly less reluctant to ask questions.

There was a pause; then Martina spoke. "It is unusual. She and her husband live in the East Zone."

The words *East Zone* had an odd ring, but Rob had noticed on his previous travels in Germany that many of the older people referred to the GDR by that name. It was a carry-over from the occupation days, but it also reflected an unwillingness to recognize that part of Germany as a separate country.

Martina continued, "She married a pastor during the war. He had come from a small town in Brandenburg, and of course, Helga had grown up at the Bachdorf schloss. They felt that their home was in the East, so they stayed there after the war. At that time, we all thought that the occupation would end and Germany would be one country again. Even when it became clear that a Communist state was being created there, they believed that their place was with the people in the church, and they did not leave."

Olga appeared with a fresh bottle of Johannesberger Riesling and refilled the glasses. Their plates were almost empty. Olga inquired about their desire for another helping of pork. When they all declined, she removed their plates and disappeared again.

Rob leaned back in his chair, twirling his wine glass absently. He could tell that mention of her daughter had stirred emotions in Martina; but he was not sure why. He wondered whether there was an estrangement between the two or whether she was upset by the East-West separation. He resisted the temptation to ask more about Helga and her family. Wolfgang took a sip of wine, seemingly lost in thought. Martina resumed talking.

"After the wall went up in Berlin, we went ten years without seeing her. Two years ago, we had a visit with her and her husband when they were permitted by the East German authorities to attend a church conference in the West. I am happy to say, though, that we have often had visits from her daughter, my granddaughter, who lives in West Berlin."

Martina rose from her chair, saying, "We will have coffee and dessert back in the other room."

They walked along the antlered corridor to the room where they had sat in the afternoon. Olga followed them within a few minutes with coffee and apple strudel. Martina resumed the conversation by telling of her experiences on a trip to New York and Washington several years earlier. Rob noticed that Wolfgang said little when his mother was present. She was not at a loss for words, and he apparently let her do the talking. Whereas she had a bright and lively air, he had a somber demeanor, smiling little.

Martina went to the large cupboard and came back to the table with a square, short bottle. "Here is a bottle of the von Mensinger family schnapps," she said. "It was made here for about two hundred years. It was made for only a few years after the war, but no longer. This is one of the last bottles. We save it for special occasions. And," she added graciously, "this is one of those."

Rob could read the word *Mensinger* on the label, but he could not make out the other writing from where he sat. Martina placed short-stemmed glasses in front of Rob and Wolfgang, and filled each with the clear liqueur.

"I will excuse myself and leave you two to talk," she announced. "Professor Kirkman, you and I will eat breakfast together tomorrow morning. Wolfgang must leave very early for a business trip to Frankfurt."

Rob rose. She extended her hand and took his in it, saying, "It is an honor for us to have you with us. I hope you find your room comfortable."

"Thank you very much for this unexpected hospitality. The dinner was delicious."

"Wolfi, I will be up to see you off at six. Professor Kirkman, we will have breakfast in the dining room at eight. Good night." In her voice now was the authority Rob had detected in many German voices, male and female. She closed the door and was gone.

The quiet of the night filled the room. Rob took a sip of the Mensinger schnapps. A trickle of fire ran down his throat and lined his stomach. He momentarily shut his eyes and swallowed hard, relieved he had taken only a small sip. Opening his eyes, he saw Wolfgang lift his glass to his lips, tilt it abruptly, and return it to the table. It was half empty. Wolfgang sat perfectly still, eyes closed, as though he were waiting for his body to absorb the fiery effect.

"Your mother is an attractive and charming woman," Rob said, looking for a good way to open a conversation.

"I remember her that way. She was a very attractive woman when I last saw her, but that was thirty years ago. Of course, I still know the warmth of her love and know her as a person even though I do not know how she looks."

"Do you mind telling me how you lost your sight?" Rob would not have dared ask this five hours ago; but the conversations of the afternoon and evening, along with the wine and schnapps, had removed his reticence.

"No, I do not mind," Wolfgang said. His right hand slid lightly across the table to the schnapps glass, firmly clasping the stem. "It was in the war. I was in the army, as I told you this afternoon."

The schnapps glass rose to his lips. There was a quick upward motion, and the glass returned to the table empty. Rob sipped again from his glass. The fire tingled again down his throat, and he wondered how anyone could take the entire glass in two swallows. In a moment, Wolfgang resumed.

"In 1935, I entered the University at Breslau. I was eighteen years old. At first, I was interested in history. Military conscription had then been introduced, so after a year at Breslau I spent a year in the army. I then went to the University at Berlin and enrolled in the faculty of theology. I had a vague feeling that I might want to go into the church and become a pastor or perhaps a professor of theology. Berlin was different from Breslau. There it was not possible in those days to avoid government and the international situation. The university was on Unter den Linden in the midst of it all. The chancery was on Wilhelmstrasse, just three blocks away, and we were surrounded by government ministries of all sorts. Military parades took place often. Student groups and the Hitler Youth were very active, but I was not interested in all that. I was a serious student, wanting mainly to read in the library. I know that Americans have said that every German since the war has claimed—and they think falsely—that he had nothing to do with the Nazis. For many Germans it is, of course, ridiculous to claim that; there were millions who admired Hitler, although many of them did not join the Party. I will tell you the facts about myself. I was not a Nazi party member. My feelings about Hitler at that time were mixed."

He paused and leaned forward across the table, his hand moving back and forth until it intersected the schnapps bottle. "Have some more of the schnapps," he said, pushing the bottle toward Rob.

Rob's glass was three quarters empty, so he topped it up. "I will fill your glass also," he said to Wolfgang, who simply nodded.

"I was sure of only three things. I was sure of them then, and I am sure of them now. First, I loved Germany, my country—all of it, from Metz and Strasbourg in the West to Koenigsberg and Memel in the East. I should say that one of those areas is now in France, and the other is in the Soviet Union. My second belief was—and still is—that the most deadly threat to civilization on this earth is communism, or I should say Marxism-Leninism. My third point is this. Almighty God is ultimately in charge, and our fates in the end will be decided by Him—our fates in this journey as well as on the day when we stand in judgment."

Wolfgang's voice had taken on the tone and volume of one making a speech. He was holding forth with more force and verve than Rob had imagined he possessed. Although his English was good, it did not come easily. He hesitated frequently to search for the right word; but he spoke impressively, and Rob was awed by the power with which he presented his three beliefs. At the same time, he was wondering what this had to do with the blindness.

"One day in the spring of 1939," Wolfgang continued in a quieter, less emphatic tone, "I was walking along the street in front of the Adlon Hotel in Berlin. It was not far from the main university building on Unter den Linden. A taxi stopped at the hotel door, and an army officer stepped out. I saw that he was a general. As he turned to go into the hotel, we recognized each other. He had been one of my father's friends, and our families had known each other for many years before the first war. He and his wife had visited us several times at Bachdorf, but I had not seen him for a few years. He asked me to have a drink with him while he waited for a friend with whom he had an appointment. I remember that afternoon very well. I can see the two of us sitting together in the bar at the Adlon. He was the picture of the proper Wehrmacht general, and I was a rumpled young university student.

"'The Wehrmacht has need of bright young men to serve as officers,' the general said. 'There is a strong likelihood of a war in Europe, and the officer corps must be increased. I can get you into staff training school, and you would be in a good position to move up if war does come.'

"I explained that I was deeply involved in my university studies and did not want to interrupt them unless it became necessary. He knew that my older brother was already an officer in a panzer unit, but I think that he also thought that I would be better suited for staff duty than for a combat assignment. He was correct on that."

Wolfgang paused to sip from his glass. "By that time, I was developing a strange feeling about events in Germany. Let me ask you a question, Herr Kirkman. Have you ever heard of Dietrich Bonhoeffer?"

"Yes, I have read about him, but I don't know the details of his life. I know that he was a Protestant pastor and that he became involved in the German resistance after the war started."

"That is correct. Then you also know of the Confessing Church and the Barmen Declaration?"

"Yes," answered Rob, "but only in a general way."

"Among those Protestant pastors, there was a growing worry about Christianity and the actions of the German authorities under the Nazi regime. Dietrich Bonhoeffer, who was one of them, talked at private gatherings in Berlin in those days. By the time I came there, he was officially prohibited from public preaching; but I heard him talk several times. He became something of a hero to me. He had a fine mind and a wonderful way of explaining the scriptures. I have never heard anyone like him. I was thinking more of entering the service of the church than of the army."

As if he realized that he was rambling, Wolfgang said apologetically, "I know I have not yet told you how I lost my sight, but this background is necessary to understand how it came about."

"No, I do not mind at all. You have a fascinating story."

In the after-dinner quiet of this high-ceilinged room, Wolfgang von Egloffsberg began to appear to Robert Kirkman in a different light. In the afternoon and through dinner, he had seemed inarticulate, reclusive, and weak. Now Rob saw a man of force and of deep inner conviction.

Despite his eyes' lack of linkage with his brain, they were now alive. He seemed to relish this opportunity to retell these long-ago events.

Rob now had a better chance to examine Wolfgang's physical features. His dark, gray-speckled hair swept straight back from a faint widow's peak, with no noticeable thinning and only the suggestion of a receding hairline. His face below the eyes was markedly misshapen on the left side. The peculiar texture Rob had noted earlier now appeared to be skin grafts. He had a strong urge to go over to the table, get the photograph of the young Wehrmacht officer, and compare it with this living countenance.

Wolfgang was warming increasingly to his story, having replenished his glass and again pushed the squat, dark bottle toward Rob. "I was becoming what you call in English . . ." He paused, mentally searching for the word. "I was what you call, I believe, ambivalent."

"That is a good word," Rob said, reassuring him. "It suggests an uncertainty, a doubt about which of two things one should accept."

"Yes," Wolfgang said, "that is what I mean. I believed deeply in my country, just as you probably believe in the United States of America. For many generations, my family has served Germany and its people. You saw those portraits here in the great hall. Those are some of my mother's ancestors, the von Mensinger family. There was an equally distinguished line in my father's family, von Egloffsberg; but fate in the twentieth century has cut us off from the schloss and most of everything that they had. . . ." He drifted off, detached, the sightless eyes closed.

To bring him back, Rob said, "I understand your dedication to Germany. You say that was one feeling that you had. What was the other part of the ambivalence?"

"It was growing dislike for Hitler and the Nazi party and doubt about what they were doing. When Hitler became chancellor in 1933, I did not think much about it. I was young and not interested in politics. I do remember that my Uncle Ludwig at Bachdorf never had any respect for Hitler. It was when I arrived at the University in Berlin that I began to think on these matters. I remember now what was a small point in the whole picture, but it stands out in my mind. I asked myself: 'Why is this strictly party symbol of the swastika now the official flag of the German nation?' It was as though the symbol of your Democratic party, which I believe is a donkey, had become the flag of the United States when Franklin Roosevelt was elected president. That one small point started me thinking about the entire regime."

Wolfgang was given to lapsing into a dreamy silence after each of his dramatic assertions. Rob had to think of questions to pull him back and keep the conversation going. So he asked, "How well did you know Dietrich Bonhoeffer?"

"Not well personally. An older student in the theology faculty introduced me to him one Sunday afternoon. That student later married my sister Helga. I had introduced them to each other when she was in Berlin for a visit. But back to Bonhoeffer: He was a large, impressive man. He must have been absolutely fearless, with complete faith that no earthly harm would matter since he was with God. I did not see him after the summer of 1939. Four years later, when I was in the hospital, one of my old theology professors told me that Bonhoeffer had been arrested. I was upset by the news. It was not until the war was over that I learned that he had been killed at the Flossenberg concentration camp."

The mention of Flossenberg surprised Rob. It was the first time he had ever heard a West German voluntarily refer to any of the concentration camps—the cancer that scarred German culture, perhaps forever. In Munich, he had once asked a local resident to tell him something of Dachau, which was not far away. After an awkward hesitation, the middle-aged German said, "Dachau? Ah yes, Dachau, famous for its nineteenth-century school of painting. It has always been a center for artists." And so the conversation had gone.

For an instant, Rob thought that with Wolfgang he now had a long-awaited opportunity to pursue the forbidden subject with a German old enough to remember. Questions almost burst from his mouth. Did you know about the camps in the thirties? Did people talk about them? What do Germans think about them now? The scene at Dachau, the one camp he had actually visited, was clearly etched in his mind. Other names floated by—Buchenwald, Bergen-Belsen, Sachsenhausen, Ravensbrueck—but he caught himself and, as usual, refrained. He wanted to be diplomatic and courteous in this house where he was a guest. He decided to keep Wolfgang going with his own story.

"You were talking about your ambivalence. I take it, though, that you did join the army."

"There was no choice after war broke out in September of 1939, but I was not totally reluctant. My friends were all going, and—you must not forget this—it was my country. I contacted the general and told him that I would accept his proposal. He was delighted. Within six weeks, I was in uniform and enrolled in staff school. The general was stationed at army headquarters at Zossen, and he had me assigned there when I completed the school. Later, I went to a field army headquarters on the Russian front."

Rob noticed that Wolfgang's glass had been empty for several minutes. "May I pour you more schnapps?"

"*Ja, bitte,*" Wolfgang replied, nodding his head slowly.

Rob filled the glass, Wolfgang's fingers steadying the stem. His own was still half full.

Wolfgang took on renewed vigor. "Now, Herr Kirkman, you asked how I lost my eyesight. I am coming to that, but your question has brought to mind all of these events leading up to that event. I have relived all of them many times, wondering how I could have acted differently; but we cannot change the past, and I have often told myself that there is a purpose in all of this. I believe that, but I am not sure exactly what the purpose is. It is not usually revealed to us." He closed his eyes and took a sizeable swallow of schnapps.

"Where was your brother at that time?" Rob asked.

"He was a commander of a panzer unit stationed near Aachen. He had aspired to a military career and had been in the army for several years. He and I were different. He was much more of an athlete and sportsman. I was the student. The last time that he and I were together was at Christmas of 1941. We were at Bachdorf on leave with my mother and sister. He had just recently been married to a woman from a prominent family in Pomerania, and she was there too. Also, he had just been promoted to major and had been assigned to a panzer division in the Sixth Army in the Soviet Union. I remember his enthusiastic talk about the big offensive that would end the war in the East by summer. That Christmas was the last time I saw—actually saw with my eyes—Bachdorf and my mother, brother, and sister."

Thoughts of that last Christmas with vision stopped him. Seconds ticked past. The night air drifting in through the large open window brought a sound Rob had not heard since his arrival. It was the distant striking of the clock in the church tower in the village. It struck ten times.

When it fell silent, Rob spoke up. "What happened to you after that?"

"I was transferred from Zossen to a field army headquarters in the Ukraine. Is it not strange, Herr Kirkman, that my last sights on this earth were not of my native Germany or of my family and old friends? My last sights were of the steppes, days and days of dusty roads in summer heat and miserable-looking Ukranian villages, mostly burned. I remember perhaps more clearly than anything else the thousands of bright sunflowers along the roads—kilometer after kilometer of them. Those large yellow sunflowers stretching along the endless, flat road are forever in my memory as among the things I saw on that last hot dusty day that I saw anything."

"What happened on that day?"

"Our convoy of vehicles had just come through a burned out village. There were about ten armored cars and staff cars. We had slowed to go through the main village street. At that moment, firing broke out on both sides of the road. It was sudden and violent. The lead vehicle was hit immediately. A second later, a tremendous explosion ripped my staff car apart. A sheet of flame shot up out of the engine. I felt myself being thrown upward and burned. Then everything went black. When I woke up, I was in a German field hospital far to the rear. I was told later that some partisan guerilla units had attacked our convoy. An hour after the attack, another German unit had come along and found us. All of our vehicles had been destroyed. The only men alive were a corporal and me."

Another silence ensued, but then Wolfgang continued.

"When I woke up in the hospital, I was in great pain around my head and arm. It took me a few minutes to realize that I could not see. This was immediately after I had reached the hospital, no doctor had seen me, and no bandages had been applied. I thought that perhaps I simply could not open my eyes. There was so much pain that I could not be sure. Someone gave me a shot, and I became unconscious again. But, Herr Kirkman, to make a long story short, as I have heard Americans say, my sight was gone."

They sat for a while in silence. Rob swallowed the last of his schnapps. Wolfgang's glass was empty. The faint sound of a car passing along the road on the other side of the courtyard wall penetrated the late night quiet. Rob was tired, but he could not bring himself to leave at this point.

Wolfgang roused himself from his thoughts. "So, Herr Kirkman, that was the end of the war for me. And I thought for a long while that it was also the end of my life. They shipped me to a hospital in Berlin. They did plastic surgery on my face, then I was put in a school for the rehabilitation of the blind. I found my life later, but my family lost our home and land along the Elbe. I have come to despise the Nazi party, but Hitler did have one valid point—that communism was the great threat to the West and Germany was the buffer between the Soviet Union and Europe. So you can think of the German attack to the East as a move on behalf of Western civilization. Now I doubt that you Americans see it that way; but that was what I thought when I went east in 1942. Many Germans believed later in the war that America and Britain were naive, that they did not realize that they were fighting the wrong enemy. It was only after the war that the Western powers came to see that. As a result, we have communism all the way into the middle of Germany and Europe."

Wolfgang's voice was taking on a heightened intensity.

"I believe," he continued, lowering his voice and speaking as though he were uttering a solemn declaration, "that a divine judgment was rendered on Germany. As I have read about the actions of the Third Reich, I have become even clearer in my belief that Almighty God decreed her doom. I say this even though Germany's destruction brought communism—the antichrist—into power over much of our land and people. But this division cannot last. Just as the rejection of Christianity brought disaster to Germany, Christianity will bring reunion."

"Do you think that a majority of the German people really want to reunite?" Rob asked.

"That is a difficult question to answer. Some people do not care. Others may be happy with things as they are. But millions of others with divided families and lost homelands do want to be one country. For myself, I detest this artificial division. I do not recognize it. I have dedicated my life to two objectives: trying to help blind people in all of Germany—West and East, I make no distinction—and reuniting the two parts through the church."

Wolfgang leaned back in his chair with a sigh, as though the speech had exhausted him. Despite his portrayal of himself in his youth as a nonathletic bookworm, he now appeared as a man of great physical force, an aggressive leader with strong convictions.

"I must leave early in the morning, so now I will say goodnight to you, Herr Kirkman." Wolfgang rose, extending his hand toward Rob. "It has been a pleasure having you as a guest. Perhaps we shall meet again some day."

Rob held onto the hand a moment longer than necessary, staring into the face that could not look back at him. He sensed an extraordinary magnetism and determination. He was suddenly hoping that they would meet again; he could go on for hours, he imagined, listening to these accounts of not-so-ancient history. He regretted that Wolfgang did not yet know of the improbable circumstances that had brought them together, but he would have to learn of them from his mother.

Alone in his bedroom on the top floor of the schloss, Robert Kirkman stood looking out of the tall casement window. It was open, letting in a faint breeze carrying a not unpleasant odor of manure and freshly cut hay, a characteristic odor of the German countryside. Rob imagined that this scent of mingled hay and manure must be one of the truly unchanging elements of a radically changed world.

Under the sliver of a moon, he could see the dark form of the courtyard. Traffic sounds had disappeared. Over the wall, he saw the small houses lining the road that curved down to the center of Prinzenheim. A few street lights marked the intersection near the church.

Although it was July, Rob found himself snuggling under the eiderdown to ward off the chill of the breeze circulating in the room. The massive corner posts of the bed loomed above him in the darkness. It had been a long and extraordinary day. He was tired, worn out by the high-pitched emotional setting, but he did not go to sleep. His mind was recanvassing the sweep of German history to which he had been exposed for the past few days.

The dark and tragic convolutions of the twentieth-century German drama were replayed in his mind amidst the ghostly shadows of this three-hundred-year-old room. The dynamic industrial, scientific, and educational golden age into which the nation seemingly had entered at the dawn of the century had turned into one of the world's greatest catastrophes. Some undetected cancer had struck at its heart and soul. He saw again that endless network of ghastly trenches that he had trooped along for days, from Ypres to Vimy Ridge to the Somme, and on to the Marne and Verdun. There began the biological hemorrhage that gushed forth anew only a short generation later.

In only thirty-one years, from 1914 to 1945, Germany had come from the heights to the depths, suffering a level of destruction new to human history. The von Egloffsberg family reflected the dimensions of the disaster—the father killed in the First World War, one son killed and one son blinded in the second, the family home and holdings gone, and the survivors cut off from their homeland by a new order bent upon what Wolfgang saw as a godless remaking of Western civilization. The lengthy list of names on the stone marker for this one small village, as in a multitude of villages all over Germany, haunted him. The might-have-beens were overwhelming. If the European powers had taken another path in 1914, the world might be an altogether different place.

Questions crowded his mind about this family into whose midst he had been unexpectedly cast. What about Wolfgang? What was this business in Frankfurt and what did he mean when he said he had dedicated his life to the reunion of the country? What did he mean when he said that he worked with East and West? What was the significance of this fascination with Dietrich Bonhoeffer? And what of his sister, or half-sister, Helga, who lived in East Germany?

The bizarre nature of the situation almost amused him. Here he was in this comfortable bed in this great house in the heart of Germany as the result of his chance discovery of a 55-year-old letter and photograph in his dead father's footlocker. That happenstance in turn flowed from the chance encounter at death's edge between that Alabama lieutenant and the German captain from the Bachdorf estate. This last thought brought back the disquiet he felt whenever he contemplated the inevitable moment at which he must tell the Baroness von Egloffsberg what really brought him to her. That moment had to come in the morning. With that realization, he rolled over, determined to get some sleep.

Chapter 10

ROBERT KIRKMAN WAS AWAKENED by the sound of an automobile engine and the rumbling of tires over cobblestones in the courtyard below. It was daylight, and he saw blue sky through the window. His watch showed five minutes to six. The car stopped; a door opened and shut. Rob rolled out of bed and went to the window. Below, just to his right, was a black Mercedes-Benz. Standing beside it was a man dressed in a dark business suit. He was about Rob's age. Rob could hear the heavy wooden door being opened at the entrance to the schloss.

"*Guten Morgen*," said the man standing by the car.

"*Guten Morgen*," Wolfgang's voice said in response. A second later, Wolfgang came into sight from below the window. He too was dressed in a dark business suit. The two looked like London bankers. Wolfgang was carrying his long white cane and a medium-sized suitcase. The younger man moved forward quickly from the car, took the bag, and put it into the back seat.

Now Martina came into sight. From this angle, she seemed taller and thinner than she had on the previous day. Although dressed casually, she still had a touch of elegance about her. She gave Wolfgang a light kiss on the cheek. They exchanged words which Rob could not quite hear, although he caught the words "a week." The two men got in the car, and it pulled away, disappearing through the gateway to the road. Martina stood there watching it go, and then slipped from his sight back into the house.

At eight o'clock, Rob walked into the dining room. He was wearing a light gray summer sport coat and an open-collared shirt. In his right inside pocket, he had three items: the photograph of young Martina and her two baby boys, her handwritten letter to her husband dated October 1918, and his father's account of finding these two items on the dying German officer. He was now going to deliver the photograph and letter to the hand from whence they had come. He would also be informing her of the circumstances of her husband's death in that long-ago autumn.

Martina was standing at the sideboard putting the finishing touches on an arrangement of fresh flowers. Although she belonged to his parents' generation, she reminded him of his grandmother at Trepnitz Hills. Indeed, this whole place was reminiscent of the great columned house in the Alabama Black Belt with its heavy air of things past, of days and men of greater glory, of profound loss and defeat.

"Good morning," she said cheerfully. "Have you had a good sleep?"

"Yes," replied Rob. Despite his turbulent tossing before getting to sleep, he felt remarkably refreshed. "The bed is unusually comfortable."

"That room has been the main guest room in this house all my life. Many distinguished visitors have slept there—generals, ministers, and even some professors and lawyers." She smiled broadly with a twinkle in her eye.

"I am honored to follow in such company. It is certainly quiet and pleasant. I imagine that I am the first American ever to sleep there."

"Please sit here," Martina said, touching a chair along the side of the table and ignoring his last comment. "I will be back in a moment." She went through the door that apparently led toward the kitchen.

Only two places were set at the table. Rob was sitting on the side. The other place was to his right at the end. Martina returned and took her seat there. Olga followed her and commenced serving coffee, orange juice, and large chunks of white bread with butter and marmalade.

Since the day before, Rob had been preparing his little speech. The moment for its delivery was at hand. He would tell her that his arrival here at her residence in Prinzenheim was in fact not a coincidence. He would tell her the whole story of the photograph and the trip to Bachdorf. He would apologize for not having related all of this the previous evening, and he would say that the conversation and company were so pleasant that he could not bring himself to mention this subject. At some point in this speech, he would produce the documents from his pocket and lay them before her.

His nervous apprehension over her reaction to this dramatic revelation kept him from enjoying his breakfast. In fact, he could hardly eat at all. He had no idea whether she would be angry, insulted, sorrowful, or grateful. She was pouring him a second cup of coffee, and he had finished a small piece of bread smeared with butter and marmalade. The time had come for him to plunge into his story.

He was clearing his throat to begin when she looked at him and spoke in a tone of voice that was different: "Professor Kirkman, yesterday I asked you whether you had ever heard of Prinzenheim before this trip to Germany, and you said that you had not."

"That is correct. I had not."

"Let me ask you this." Her hazel eyes were boring in on him. "Had you ever heard of a place called Bachdorf before this trip?"

The question caught Rob off-guard. He could think of no good way to answer it except to jump into his more-or-less prepared speech. "Well, yes. I had heard of it," he said slowly. Her look gave him an uneasy feeling, and he hesitated with his explanation. "Why do you ask?"

"This may not come as a surprise to you. I have reason to think that you may not have come here merely by chance."

When her voice stopped, the silence in the room was total. They were looking directly into each other's eyes. There was a wistfulness in hers. How could she possibly know anything about him or the extraordinary and remote twist of circumstance that brought Bachdorf to his attention?

"I see that you are puzzled," she continued. "When and how did you first hear of Bachdorf?"

"Why, uh, only about a month ago."

She took a sip of coffee, not taking her eyes off him. Rob sat motionless, watching her. She touched her mouth with her napkin. When he did not speak she resumed.

"Yesterday, when Olga brought me your card, I immediately recognized the name," she paused for a long moment, "You see, Professor Kirkman, I knew your father."

The words fell on his ears with a mesmerizing effect. When . . . where . . . how . . . could the two have met? After a long moment, he was able only to repeat the words slowly and incredulously: "You knew my father?"

"Yes," she said solemnly with a slight sigh, "but only for a short time, and it was very long ago. Did he ever mention to you the name of von Egloffsberg or that he had visited me?"

"No, he didn't," Rob said hesitantly, still stunned. He was embarrassed to say this. He was also perplexed. What surely must have been an unusual occasion in the life of Edward Kirkman—one that she still remembered—he never once mentioned in all these years.

"Let us go to the other room where we can be more comfortable." They arose from the table and walked along the dark corridor, passing under the countless pairs of antlers. They came from the gloom of the corridor into the welcome light of the high-ceilinged sitting room. She took a position on the sofa, and he sat in the upholstered wing chair where he had spent much of the previous afternoon and evening. The windows were open, letting in the warm morning air.

"You know nothing of this story?" she asked as they settled back.

"No, nothing at all," Rob responded weakly.

"Then I will tell you," she began. "It was the early spring of 1923. I was living in the von Egloffsberg schloss at Bachdorf, as I had been since my marriage. One of my husband's uncles was living there with his wife. Their two children were grown and living in Dresden. Uncle Ludwig managed the place. After my husband's death, I considered coming back here to Prinzenheim to live, but I knew that my husband wanted his two sons to be reared at the family seat at Bachdorf. So out of my love for him and respect for his memory, I stayed there. Uncle Ludwig and his wife, Aunt Ursula, were like parents to me, and they treated Wolfgang and his older brother Kurt as though they were their grandchildren. It was rather lonely for me as a young widow. Bachdorf is just a tiny village, far from a city; but life there was pleasant, and it was a good place to bring up two little boys.

"But I am getting away from the story," she said. "It was the early spring of 1923, near the end of March, I believe. It was still cool, but there was a touch of green on the grass, and buds were beginning to appear on a few of the trees. I was in my upstairs sitting room when one of the house servants came in. She said that there were two young men downstairs in the front hall asking whether a Baroness von Egloffsberg lived here. One had said that he was an American, and the other had said that he was English. She said that they spoke a little German but not very well."

At this, Martina smiled for the first time since the subject of Rob's father had been mentioned. Then she continued.

"I could not imagine who they were. I did not know any American or English men. 'Is Uncle Ludwig here?' I asked. 'No, he is out on his horse,' she said. 'How do they look?' I then asked. 'Oh, they are well-dressed young gentlemen,' she said. I felt uneasy, but I said, 'Well, you come with me, and we will go see what they want.'"

"So the two of us went down the stairs to the front hall. There I saw the young men. I could tell immediately that they were not German. There was—more so then than now—a certain look about German men that those two did not have."

Olga pushed open the door and came in with a tray holding a pot of coffee and two cups. She set the cups in front of Martina and Rob, filled them with coffee, and left.

After pouring milk into both cups, Martina went on. "I approached the men and said, 'Good day, may I help you?' I spoke in English. I had learned English well in school, and I thought that this was my chance to use it. One of the men stepped forward and said, 'Good day. Are you the Baroness von Egloffsberg, Martina von Egloffsberg?' I said that I was that person, and he then introduced himself and his friend. I can hear him now, speaking in a soft, slow accent, not like any I had ever heard before. He said, 'I am Edward Kirkman from the United States. This is Harold Titheringham from England.' He went on to explain that they were studying at Oxford and that they were on spring vacation traveling through Europe."

Rob recognized the name Harold Titheringham. He had heard his father mention him a few times as being his best English friend during the year he had spent at Oxford. He had come across a few pieces of correspondence between the two in his father's files. The letters were all dated in the late nineteen-twenties. From them he knew that Titheringham had become a barrister, but contact between him and Edward Kirkman apparently had ceased around 1930.

Martina continued: "They seemed to be nice and polite and well-dressed young men, so I invited them into the parlor. That was a large room at the front of the schloss. It was a grand room, larger than this room." She gestured with a circular motion, indicating the expanse of the room. "On the wall opposite the windows there was a magnificent stone fireplace. Even though it was spring, a low fire was burning there to keep the chill off. We sat on large sofas on either side of the fireplace. They sat together, and I sat facing them. I can see that scene now as though it were only last year."

Rob too saw the scene in his mind's eye. He was entranced by the thought that only three days ago he himself had stood in that hall, the hall where his father and this woman had stood fifty years earlier—the spacious hall with the gray stone floor and the broad dark wooden stairway. He saw again the massive wooden balustrade flowing upward, curving at the landing and moving out of sight, his father and Harold Titheringham standing there in their twenties-style English blazers. He had come across some photographs of them in his father's file boxes only a month ago, standing together in the gardens of Wadham College. Judging from the way they were dressed, the picture must have been taken on a Sunday or just before some special function. He imagined that they were dressed in similar fashion when they appeared at Schloss Bachdorf. He could see them moving into the huge parlor, the room where he himself had just seen the shoddy tables stacked with dog-eared files and the mannish big-breasted typist pounding away on the clattering, old machine beneath the bare electric light bulb.

"I was naturally curious as to why they were in that remote spot. They said that they had been at Leipzig and were on the way to Meissen and Dresden. They had taken a train at Leipzig and had gotten off at a station about ten kilometers from Bachdorf. That was the closest station to us."

She took a swallow of coffee and put the cup back in its saucer before continuing. "Then your father looked at me with a very solemn but kind expression and asked, 'Baroness von Egloffsberg, may I ask whether your husband was an officer in the German army during the late war?'"

"The question took me by surprise, but I said, 'Yes, he was an infantry captain. He was killed in France in 1918.' Then your father said, 'Do you know the circumstances of his death?'"

"I thought these questions were strange coming from a person I did not know, but I said that we never knew exactly how he died. He then asked, 'Was your husband named Bruno von Egloffsberg?' When I said that he was, he went on to say that he had some information about his death that he wanted to make known to me."

"You may imagine how I felt on hearing that statement. The war had been over nearly five years. The first year or two after I received word of Bruno's death had been quite sad for me; but I had gradually come to accept the situation and put all my thoughts on raising my sons. I had even had thoughts of possibly remarrying, although there were few prospects. Now here was a voice out of nowhere—a complete stranger—bringing the whole dreadful event back up again. When I said nothing, but sat there looking at him blankly, he went on.

" 'I realize that this may be painful for you,' he said, 'and I am sorry to be the one to bring you this information; but I decided that I could never rest easy with myself if I did not see you or some member of the family and tell what little I know about the matter.' He paused for a moment. Since he seemed a little nervous and embarrassed, I told him that I appreciated his concern and would be grateful for any information that he had.

"He then told me that he had been an American infantry officer on the western front. He started telling the story of the advance of his unit through the Argonne Forest. There was heavy fighting, and the German opposition was stiff. He said that American artillery and mortar fire was pouring on the German positions and lifted just before his unit made a rush to take some German trenches. It must have been a horrible scene. I had bad dreams about it after that day. He said that he and his men jumped down into a German trench. He came upon a German officer who had been badly wounded by a shell burst, but he was still alive. Your father said that he gave him a drink of water from his canteen, and a few moments later he died. An envelope was sticking out of his pocket, and your father said that he impulsively grabbed it and looked inside."

Martina was telling this in a matter-of-fact way, slowly and with no emotion. Rob was tracking the account mentally from his father's handwritten record of the event which was at that moment in his inside coat pocket. Her version matched with it exactly—a remarkable feat of memory, he thought, after half a century. He had sat motionless since she had begun talking, transfixed with incredulity that such a conversation as this ever took place. But she had the facts; her story had to be true.

"In his slow, soft voice, your father went on to say that the envelope contained a letter signed Martina and a photograph of a young woman and two small children. The return address, Schloss Bachdorf, had brought him to my door. He said that he intended to return the letter and picture to me, but he had left them in America. He said that he would send them to me."

Rob stirred uneasily, feeling vicarious embarrassment for his father's failure to keep such a solemn promise. He also felt increasing guilt for himself for sitting there in possession of these documents. "Is that all my father had to say about the event?" he asked.

"That was about all. He did say that Bruno did not suffer long. He had just been hit only a few minutes before the Americans overran the trench, and he died only moments after your father discovered him. He did not say anything before he died. I thanked God that he did not suffer long."

"Did my father and the Englishman then leave?"

"At that moment I felt myself on the edge of crying. I did not want to break down in front of those men, so I quickly excused myself and said I would be back. I ran up the stairs to my room and was overcome by emotion. I fell into a chair and sobbed for several minutes. When I was drained of tears, I got up, washed my face, and tried to look normal again. I then went to Aunt Ursula's apartment and asked her permission to invite the men to stay for dinner and spend the night. She thought this a strange request, but she agreed after I told her what your father had said and that they were well-mannered Oxford students."

"Your hospitality was as generous then as it is now," Rob said. "Did they accept your invitation?"

"At first they protested. They said that they had left their bags at the station and had planned to take a late afternoon train to Meissen. When I urged them to stay and said that I would send a man for their bags, they agreed. I must say that I was excited over their presence. It was quiet and lonesome there in the country."

Martina stood up from the sofa and walked around Rob's chair to the table near the window. She pulled open a drawer and took out a lacquered box. She rummaged through layers of papers and extracted a small picture. Walking over to Rob holding it in her outstretched hand, she said, "Here is my only memento of the occasion."

Rob took it, still having trouble comprehending what he was hearing. There were the three of them standing outside in front of the entrance to the schloss. He recognized the doorway behind them. Overhead was the von Egloffsberg crest etched in the stone, the crest that he had seen himself three days earlier. Martina was standing in the middle, flanked by the two men. She was much more striking in appearance in this picture than she was in the 1918 picture that he was carrying. Her face had filled out a bit, her hair was cut in a more becoming style, and she was putting on a broad smile for the camera. Edward Kirkman was on her right and Harold Titheringham was on her left. They too were smiling. They looked almost foppish, dressed in the male high fashion of the day. Both men were lean six-footers; Martina was not short, possibly five-nine or ten. He figured his father to be about the same age as Martina, maybe a year older.

Rob placed the picture on the table in front of him. Martina had resumed her seat on the sofa. A cacophony of bird calls drifted through the open window. Two cars passed by in quick succession on the road beyond the wall.

"Baroness von Egloffsberg," Rob said in a tone of solemnity appropriate to the announcement he was about to make: "I am now going to keep my father's promise to you. It is fifty years late, but as we say, better late than never."

As he uttered these words, Rob drew from his coat pocket the two pieces of paper. He unfolded the letter and laid it and the photograph face up on the table in front of Martina.

Now it was her turn to be startled. Her eyes narrowed and her lips parted. She stared at them for a long moment. Then her hand went forward hesitantly, her fingers lightly touching first the letter and then the photograph. It was as though she needed to assure herself that they really existed, that she was not hallucinating.

Picking up the letter gingerly, as though it might disintegrate from age, she said softly, "Yes, this is the last letter I wrote Bruno. I had not known whether he ever received it until your father told me of having found it."

She placed the letter back on the table and focused on him with a penetrating gaze. "You said a little while ago that you had heard of Bachdorf before you arrived but that you had heard nothing of your father's visit there. Is that correct?"

"That's right. He never mentioned it. I only learned of Bachdorf when I found these papers in his trunk a month ago. It does seem strange, doesn't it?"

"Yes, it does; but it was long ago. I suppose that in a busy life across the ocean it was easy to forget." She had shifted her gaze from him and was staring wistfully out of the window.

The silence lingered. Finally Rob spoke. "Along with those two items, I found in my father's trunk his handwritten description of the scene in the Argonne. I have brought a copy for you." He pulled the photocopy from his coat pocket and handed it to her. "As you can see, it was written several months after the war was over. He was back home in Alabama at that time."

Martina sat very still on the sofa, reading the account slowly and with careful attention to every word. When she had finished, she rose, the pages in her hand, and said, "Please excuse me. I will ask Olga to bring us some more coffee." She quickly left the room.

A quarter hour passed. Olga arrived with fresh coffee. She asked in German whether he would like some. He had decided that she spoke no English. When he nodded affirmatively, she filled his cup and then left.

Rob sat sipping the coffee and wondering what he should do now. His mission had been accomplished; but he had stumbled into more than he had ever imagined. He had thought it odd that he had been asked to spend the night here. Europeans were not usually that friendly to total strangers. The warmth of Martina's initial greeting had also surprised him. Now it had all come clear. But why had his father never mentioned his visit to Bachdorf? Why had his father never returned the photograph and letter as he had promised? This all seemed out of character for Edward Kirkman, the kind and scholarly lawyer from Remberton.

Rob tried to remember what his father had said about traveling through Germany. He could not recall many details. He had heard him mention that he and Harold Titheringham had taken their spring vacation together, traveling to Cologne, Berlin, Leipzig, Dresden, and Munich. But he would be prepared to swear under oath that his father had never mentioned Bachdorf or any place like it. The trunk containing most of his father's letters and other papers from the early and mid-twenties had burned in the fire at Trepnitz Hills. And now his father himself, like those papers, was gone forever.

The church clock was striking ten. He should make some gesture to go soon. He did not want to wear out his welcome. Now, though, he sensed an affinity for this woman and her family, a relationship that he did not want to terminate.

The heavy door to the corridor swung open, and Martina entered. Her face was pale but composed; she had been gone for nearly half an hour. Resuming her place on the sofa, she poured herself a cup of coffee. He pushed his cup forward, requesting a refill.

"I must be leaving shortly," he said, "but before I go, I wonder whether you could tell me about the remainder of my father's visit at Bachdorf. How long did he and Harold Titheringham remain? What did they do while they were there?"

As he finished the question, he saw that Martina was leaning back on the sofa, gazing into the distance. The smile and the brightness that had wreathed her face most of the time since his arrival were gone. There was a sadness to her countenance that he had not seen before. Without the smile and twinkling eyes, she really looked her seventy-plus years. Anyone who had lived through the first seven decades of the twentieth century in Germany, Rob thought, had experienced history that few human beings in the western world are condemned or privileged to experience. They had seen it all—glory and degradation, triumph and defeat.

Martina stirred, as if refocusing her memory in preparation to speak. Rob regretted that he had asked her to dredge up more details of his father's visit. She was having to cope with a double remembrance—her husband's death and the painful occasion five years later when she learned of the last moments of his life. Rob's appearance had rubbed salt in those old wounds. He decided that he must not ask any more questions and that he should now leave as quickly as he could.

"Their visit was one of the brightest spots in my life during the five years following the war," Martina said, remembering. "We had tea later that afternoon on the terrace to the rear of the schloss. There was a beautiful view there across a garden and down a slope to the Elbe."

Rob saw the scene in his mind, almost as though he had been there. But he also saw a later scene—the ruined wing of the schloss shattered by mortar fire, the rubble-strewn terrace, rutted ground, and dilapidated farm machinery of the agricultural collective. He resolved that he must tell her about his visit there, and how it was that he found her at Prinzenheim.

"We took a walk along a path through the woods to the edge of the river. At that point, you can see far to the south along the Elbe, but to the north it turns westward. Some fishing boats were on the far side where the land slopes upward. The day had grown warmer. I remember it was a beautiful late afternoon of early spring. We sat beside the river for a while, and I told them about the history of the von Egloffsberg family, of how it could be traced back to about the year 1100 in Saxony.

"The three of us gathered for dinner that evening with Uncle Ludwig and Aunt Ursula. I later learned that Uncle Ludwig had been quite irritated when he first heard that we were having two strangers to dinner, especially an American and an Englishman. I would never have guessed that from the way he behaved at dinner. He was lively and almost jovial at times. He spoke almost no English, and your father and Harold Titheringham spoke only some basic German, so I acted as an interpreter. Uncle Ludwig did get serious and almost angry when he began to talk about the political situation in Germany. He said that it had been a mistake to abolish the monarchy. In his view, that deprived the country of a stabilizing force—a rallying point. He thought the chaos and inflation would lead to some dark disaster that he could not predict. He did live to see Hitler come to power, but did not live to see the disaster. It is just as well."

Rob spoke up. "Did Titheringham or my father comment on this or ask any questions?"

"One of them—I forget which—asked Uncle Ludwig what he thought of the Weimar Republic. He said that he thought it was a failure, that it could not govern. Then he took up one of his favorite themes: the threat of international communism. He said that a Communist party had been founded in Germany in 1919 and that it was growing in strength and was tied closely to the Soviet Union. I remember well one statement he made. He looked sternly at them and said, 'I will probably not see this, but in your lifetime the Soviet Union and international communism will present the most serious challenge to Western civilization that it has seen in a thousand years.' He went on to say that Germany is on the frontier and would have to bear the brunt of the struggle. He said that England and the United States do not understand this now, but in time they will. 'We fought each other in this war,' he said with great emphasis, 'but who knows, someday we may stand together to block this menace.'"

"He was at least half of a prophet," Rob said.

"Uncle Ludwig was a rather serious thinker. At that time, he had finished serving a term in the Reichstag and had become disillusioned by what he had seen there. He lived until 1936, and I talked with him many times about politics. One of his theories was that the greatest threat to a decent and civilized society was disorder. That is why he was disturbed by the disorder of the twenties. He said that people crave order and safety; if they do not get it, they will eventually turn to extreme means."

She paused, her eyes drifting into the distance again. Rob spoke up. "As the only man in the house, he must have had an influence on your sons."

"Yes, I think he did, more so perhaps on Wolfgang than on Kurt. Kurt was a natural outdoorsman and athlete. He grew up with an ambition to go into the army, and that is what he did. But Wolfgang did not have that inclination. He spent more time reading and talking with Uncle Ludwig. He became an officer, reluctantly, when war broke out; but his attitude changed when Germany went to war with the Soviet Union. He felt then that he had a cause to which he could give his full energy. I always thought that this attitude was a result of Uncle Ludwig's views."

"Going back to Titheringham and my father," Rob said, "I assume that they departed the next morning."

"Yes. After breakfast they said that they must go. It was just before they left for the railroad station that Aunt Ursula took this picture," she said as she picked up the photograph and looked at it again.

"I was very sorry for them to go. As I said, life was quiet and rather uninteresting at Bachdorf. I had known English people before the war. My English teacher at Frankfurt was an English woman. She is the one who taught me to enjoy afternoon tea. But I had never seen an American before. Both of them were different from German men, but your father was the most different. He was so relaxed and friendly, talking and laughing with ease. You have the same expression and manner. When I walked into this room yesterday and saw you standing there, I was a bit startled. It was almost as though I were seeing a ghost. The image of your father had come clearly back to my mind when Olga gave me the card with the name Kirkman on it. So when I saw you, I almost gasped. Something told me that you must be his son."

"And I had no idea that you had any notion as to my identity. I assumed that I was intruding here as a total stranger."

"There is something that puzzles me, Professor Kirkman," Martina said, becoming a bit more serious. "But first, may I call you Robert? You are younger than my son, and I feel as though I have known you for a long time."

"Yes, by all means. As you know, Americans are quite informal."

"My question is this: How did you find me here at Prinzenheim?"

He was glad to hear the question. He no longer felt any awkwardness about this woman, although he was a little sheepish because he had not told her of his venture at Bachdorf. At last he would give her a full account.

At this moment, the two heard a car pulling rapidly into the courtyard beneath the open window. It stopped abruptly; the door opened and slammed. A few seconds later, there was a loud and vigorous knocking on the heavy wooden door at the main entrance to the house.

"I do not know who that is, but Olga will find out," Martina said. "So perhaps you could explain how you found me here."

"Yes, I will be glad to do so. I have intended to tell you about it all morning, but there has not seemed to be the right moment. I apologize."

They heard rapid footsteps in the corridor. The door to the room opened, and a young woman burst in breathlessly.

"Grossmutti!" she exclaimed to Martina, who leaped up off the sofa and went forward to embrace this new arrival.

"Christa!" she said. "What a surprise. What are you doing here?" They were both speaking in German.

"I have been at a meeting at Bonn and decided to rent a car and drive here to see you."

They hugged again. Martina turned and said in English, "We have a guest, Professor Kirkman from America. Professor Kirkman," she was now looking at Rob, "this is my granddaughter, Christa Schreibholz."

Chapter 11

A NOTE OF EXCITING FRESHNESS had been introduced into the room. This bright-eyed and vivacious young woman seemed strangely out of place in this centuries-old house. He stood to greet her under the great tapestry depicting medieval German knights advancing on horseback across a rolling plain. He guessed that she must be in her late twenties or early thirties. Her wavy blond hair came almost to her shoulders, framing a face that resembled Martina's. Her large blue eyes had a friendly but intense look. Her face had a natural, well-scrubbed appearance, and he suspected that she used no make-up. She was wearing a closely-tailored dark suit, much like those he had seen on the increasing number of female lawyers in Washington and New York; it was the professional uniform of the breed. Her attractive head and face were matched by the figure that was evident beneath the jacket and skirt of the suit.

"Hello," Rob said, extending his right hand.

"Hello," she said, taking it warmly. "You are a professor?"

"Yes, a professor of law." Turning to Martina, Rob added with a half laugh, "I thought you said you would call me Robert."

"I did," Martina agreed. "So, Christa, we should call him Robert. He has a very old connection with our family that I will explain to you sometime."

"Christa herself is a lawyer," Martina said to Rob, "so I think she would enjoy talking to you."

"Oh, that's interesting," Rob said with a slight note of surprise. He should have guessed it from the uniform.

Christa spoke up. "I have known some American lawyers in Berlin, but I have never before met an American law professor. But Grossmutti," she said to Martina, reverting to German, "before I sit down to talk, I would like to go up to my room and make some notes on the meeting in Bonn and also make two or three telephone calls. May I do that and come back here a little later?"

Rob intervened. "Excuse me, but I really must be going. I have already imposed on your hospitality too long, and I should be getting back to Frankfurt."

"No, I tell you what," responded Martina, exuding the authority she had been exercising as head of the house for several decades, "You must at least stay for lunch with us. We will eat in another hour. That will give us an opportunity to talk after Christa finishes her work. Surely, Robert, you can remain a little longer. You can drive to Frankfurt in an hour."

Rob hesitated. He felt in danger of abusing her hospitality; but the invitation did seem genuine, and he did still have questions—even more now. But most of all, he had to admit to himself, here was this quite appealing female who had just burst on to the scene.

"Yes," Christa said before Rob could speak, "you should stay for lunch. That will be a good time for us to talk. I would like very much to hear what you do and why you are in Germany." She spoke English well, flavored with only a moderate degree of German accent.

"All right," Rob said, "You've persuaded me, but then I must leave when lunch is over."

"Good," Christa said with a broad smile. It occurred to Rob that she had inherited her grandmother's gracious smile and personality. "I will join you again within an hour," she said as she went out the door.

As the door to the corridor closed behind Christa, Rob turned to Martina and said, "So that's your granddaughter, and a lawyer too!"

"Yes, she is a fine person," Martina said. "Let us sit down," she added, motioning toward the cluster of chairs around the table and sofa.

Rob saw through the tall open window that this was another glorious July day. The sky was deep blue with only a few white clouds scattered high above. Over the wall separating the courtyard from the road, he saw the tops of houses in the village sloping down along the curve in the road. From this vantage point, he could see almost the entire village. Nothing was higher than two stories except the church tower. He could see the sharp line of the village edge in the distance. Beyond the far line of houses, green fields began. Low hills marked the horizon. It was a peaceful, quiet scene. He could stay here a long time, he thought, especially with the immensely rich resources of the library that was just down the corridor.

As they sat down, Rob asked, "Could you tell me more about Christa?"

"Christa is the daughter of my daughter Helga. I think I mentioned Helga to you yesterday. Helga is Wolfgang's half-sister. I remarried in 1923, not long after your father and his friend came to Bachdorf. Several months before their visit, a man from Berlin had taken an interest in me.

His name was Hans Kremser. I first met him when I went with Uncle Ludwig and Aunt Ursula on a visit to Berlin. We went to a reception at the home of some of their friends in the Tiergarten. He was there and was introduced to me. He was an official in a large Berlin bank. During the war, he had served in the Ministry of Finance. He had weak eyesight and had been ineligible for military service. He visited me twice more while we were in Berlin, and from then on he showed increasing interest. He was several years older than I was, but he had never been married. He was a nice-looking man, polite and considerate, but I had no serious interest in marrying him, at least at first. But it was important to me that my two sons should have a father.

"Hans came from Breslau originally. Uncle Ludwig knew people all over the country, so he found out that Hans came from a reputable family of merchants there. They were not of the German nobility, but they were respected citizens of Breslau. Hans visited us several times at Bachdorf, and he came once here to Prinzenheim while I was here with the boys visiting my mother. I came to like and respect him, and I finally decided to accept him. We were married in September of 1923."

"From what you said yesterday, I gather that he did not live many years after you were married."

"That is right. Helga was born in the spring of 1924. Hans died two years later, suddenly, with a heart attack."

"I assume that Helga is the little girl in the picture with you and the two boys over there on the table."

"Yes. After Hans's death, I moved back to Bachdorf. In case you are wondering, I have never again married. I took back the name of von Egloffsberg."

Almost every hour that Rob spent in this house brought forth some new revelation about the lives of these people and threw illumination into still another dark corner. He suspected that there was much more that he would likely never know.

Martina's voice broke into Rob's mental wanderings. "Helga grew up and married, but all of that is another story. Christa is her only child. But now, Robert, I want to hear how you found me here at Prinzenheim."

Rob told her the whole story, beginning with his research into maps to locate Bachdorf, the chance meeting with the German genealogist in Charlottesville, his trip into East Germany, his stops in Weimar and Leipzig, and the successful search for the schloss on the Elbe.

"I have not seen Bachdorf or that schloss in nearly thirty years," Martina sighed. "I cannot believe that you have just been there." Her attention had been riveted on him as he was telling of his trip. Now she said, barely above a whisper, "Tell me exactly how the schloss is. Did you go inside? What is there now?"

He heard the heartbreak in her voice and could see it in her face. It was one thing to have nostalgic memories of a place that neither she nor anyone around her had seen or even heard of for three decades; it was another to be sitting in the presence of one who had been there this very week. It was as though a long-dead loved one was being exhumed from the grave.

Despite this, Rob felt compelled to describe the scene as he had seen it. He told her that the schloss was now the headquarters of a large agricultural collective. He described its director and the hard-bitten typist sitting in the great front parlor. He tried to give her details of that room and of the main front hall with its stone floor and massive wooden stairway. He told her of going onto the rear terrace to see the Elbe, where the shattered wing of the schloss loomed broodingly over the scene. He could sense that all of this was painful, but he continued telling her of the dilapidated appearance of the grounds and the run-down farm machinery parked helter-skelter around the schloss.

"Yes," she murmured with a sigh, "a refugee who came through a year or two after the war told us that the place had survived the Red Army, but that the rear wing had been badly damaged. And, of course, we knew that all the land and the schloss had been confiscated by the Communist authorities."

Without thinking, Rob asked, "Was there any compensation given to you or the family?"

"Ah," she exclaimed scoffingly, "of course not. A place that had been in the family for nearly four hundred years and probably worth several million marks is gone just like that," she said bitterly, snapping her fingers. "You must know that those people have no respect for life or property or God."

He felt naive and embarrassed for having asked such a question. He did indeed already know the answer. He had forgotten where he was.

"We were not alone in what happened to us. All land holdings that were much larger than a very small farm were taken by the state. There were no payments to anybody. But," she said after pausing a moment, "I still do not know how you found us here in Prinzenheim. Surely the director of the collective farm did not tell you," she added with mild sarcasm.

"I have an interest in old cemeteries. They are rich sources of information. Many times they are located near churches, so I went to the church in Bachdorf, and there indeed was a cemetery. You may imagine my excitement when I found some von Egloffsberg graves. You were talking earlier about Uncle Ludwig. I saw his grave there, and that of his wife too. They are the most recent. I looked for the grave of Bruno von Egloffsberg, but I didn't find it."

"It was a matter of great sadness to me that Bruno was not buried there with his parents and other ancestors. We were informed after the war that his body had never been recovered. That often happened. So he lies today in a nameless grave in France."

Her eyes were again glazed and distant. Rob waited for a second or two and then resumed. He told her of the old woman at the church door who had said that the baroness had gone to the west. The name Prinzenheim, he said, was mentioned by the old woman almost as an afterthought; and that was the sole piece of information that brought him here.

"Did that old woman tell you who she was?"

"No, but she said that she had worked in the kitchen at the schloss when she was young. I think she said that she never talked to you."

"I dealt mainly with the cook and head housekeeper. You may be interested to know that Olga's mother was the cook there. I brought her here with me, along with Olga and Olga's little brother; they were both children then. Olga was married here in Prinzenheim and had three children. Her husband is now dead, and her children all are grown and work in Frankfurt. Olga has been with me here in the house for several years."

"I assume that you left Bachdorf at the end of the war and came here," Rob said.

"No," she said, "I left before the war was over. In January of 1945, we knew that the Red Army was massing along the Oder and Neisse Rivers. Those of us who were realistic, and I counted myself among them, knew that it was only a question of time, and probably not much time, before the Russians would be at our doorstep. We had heard many stories coming out of the East about the Russians' behavior. It was not pleasant to think about. Wolfi was then about to be released from a rehabilitation school for the blind, and of course, Kurt was gone. Helga had married and was working in a hospital in Berlin, so I was at Bachdorf alone with a handful of servants. I decided that the time had come to leave. I was very fortunate to have this place to come to. My mother's brother was still living here, and he had been urging me to come. So in January of 1945, I made the move. Wolfi joined us here shortly after that."

"That must have been an upsetting decision. Did you consider that you might have been moving away from the Russians but into the path of the Americans?"

"Yes, certainly, but, my dear Robert, thousands of my fellow countrymen—hundreds of thousands—made that same decision in the closing months of the war. If they did not make it then, many more made it over the following two or three years. Have you never realized that this westward movement of people was a tribute to the United States perhaps greater than that which has ever been paid to any other nation in history? There are few indeed who moved eastward to get out of the way of the Americans and put themselves in the hands of the Russians. Members of the Communist party were probably the only ones."

Rob nodded, contemplating how a German facing defeat on two fronts would view the Stars and Stripes as compared with the Hammer and Sickle.

"For a time right after the war, we had eight families living in this house. There were about thirty people here. They had all come from the East. We had not known most of them, but everybody was taking in refugees. It is hard now for the young people to believe that such times ever existed. Most of those moving westward had no place to go. We were extraordinarily blessed, and we felt that we should take in as many as we could accommodate."

"Did American army units eventually come to Prinzenheim?" Rob asked.

"Yes, and I remember that day vividly. For days, German soldiers and vehicles of all sorts had been passing through here, moving eastward. They were the saddest and most beaten-looking elements of the German army I had ever seen. I stood out there at the gate and occasionally talked to some of the soldiers. They were moving back to regroup. We were then caught in between the two armies. We had discussed leaving, but there was no place to go. So we had decided to stay here and hope and pray. In my heart, I had long thought that the war was lost for Germany. So in those days, I wanted it to end as quickly as possible."

"Did you have any sense as to how far the Americans were when the German troops were passing through?"

"We could hear artillery in the distance. A German officer told me that the main American thrust would probably go north and south of here. I think the Americans must have been perhaps thirty kilometers away then."

"When did you first see any Americans?"

"The stream of German soldiers finally stopped. For a day or so it became very quiet. The artillery had stopped. Not one human being passed through this village. It was late March, and I remember thinking of spring and how lovely the coming weeks would be if it would just remain as quiet as it was then. The next morning very early—it was barely daylight—Wolfi opened the door to my bedroom and came in. He had come home from the rehabilitation center just shortly before. He said, 'Mama, I hear tanks coming.' "

"I jumped out of bed and put on a robe. We then went together to the room where you slept last night. That room affords the best view to the west of any in the house. We stood there together with the window open, listening. Very faintly at a great distance to the west, I could hear what seemed to be the roar of massed engines. It reminded me of the distant coming of a storm. 'There is no doubt that they are tanks,' Wolfi said. 'I have heard the same distant sound on the eastern front. The sound will gradually grow louder. What we don't know is whether they are headed our way or will go past us. My guess is that we are in their path; but with no armed German units here we should be safe.' "

"Did he have any idea how far away they were?" Rob asked when Martina paused.

"We stood at the window for several minutes in absolute silence. In the early gray of dawn there was a mist lying over the village, obscuring the fields and hills beyond. Then I asked Wolfi how far he thought they were and, if they were heading our way, how long it would take them to get here. He guessed that they would be in Prinzenheim within two hours."

"It is hard to imagine what one would do or could do in that situation," Rob said.

"Wolfi and I dressed quickly and walked down to the center of the village. The only people left in the village were old people, children, and their mothers. People were in the road in front of the church wondering what to do. The noise of the tank engines was now clearly audible. Some people had already hung white towels or sheets out of the windows of their houses. We all agreed that everyone should do so, and that people should stay in their houses and show no hostility to American soldiers. Some were crying, but I could not tell whether this was for a lost Germany or out of fear for themselves. Wolfi said almost nothing on our walk down to the village and back. I did not know what he was thinking."

Martina had again reached one of those points at which she lapsed into a detached dreaminess. Rob let a few moments pass and then asked, "Do you remember what you were thinking?"

"Yes," she said slowly. "I said to myself, here we are again, coming to the close of another horrible war. I had just seen again that long list of names from the first war on the stone monument in front of the church. How long would the list be this time? The first one had taken my husband. Now this one had taken one of my sons and blinded the other. We were only twenty-six and a half years from the end of the other. I, like all Germans, had paid an enormous price. And for what?"

They sat in silence for a while. Outside, a truck coming into the village from the country was throttling down and applying brakes as it passed the gate. The church clock began to strike the noon hour.

The striking of the clock seemed to reactivate her memory. "We hung a white sheet out of an upstairs window and put one out at the gate. Then I sat at the window in your room to watch and wait. The noise was growing closer. At about mid-morning, I saw the first tank come around a curve in the road about three kilometers beyond the village. When the road curved again, I saw a single white star on its side. Behind it came an endless line of tanks. They spread out on both sides of the road into the fields to encircle the village. Then vehicles of all sorts began to pour through the streets."

"That must have been quite a sight for this peaceful place," Rob said.

"Of course, I had never seen anything like it. Wolfi was familiar with such things from his army experience, but he was only hearing the sounds. The roar of motors was everywhere. Something I later learned you call a half-track stopped at the front gate. Several soldiers wearing steel helmets and carrying rifles ran into our front courtyard and circled the house. I decided I would go down to the front door and speak to them."

"That must have taken a lot of courage," Rob commented.

"Well, I had to meet them at some time. Wolfi went with me. I opened that large wooden door and walked out on the steps with Wolfi. At that moment, another group of soldiers was running through the gate. They spread out in front of the house, and an officer walked out of their midst toward me. I knew enough of American insignia to know that he was a major. Wolfi at that time was wearing dark glasses and had a walking stick; he must have looked blind to the American, and perhaps that softened him a bit. There I was, a middle-aged woman surrounded by armed American soldiers."

"If I had been either you or the major, I am not sure that I would have known what to say," Rob said.

"I spoke first. I said in English, 'Major, this house is undefended. The only persons here are me, my blind son here, and two servants. You and your men are free to search the entire place if you wish.' He seemed to be taken somewhat by surprise. Then he spoke. He said that he was commanding officer of the second battalion of some regiment and division I do not now recall. He spoke in a kind of American accent that I had not heard before. He did not sound like you or your father. In later years, I came to know that as a midwestern accent. He said that his soldiers would be occupying the village for a while, that they meant no harm to any civilians here, and they would do no harm to persons or property as long as the people went about their business peacefully and caused no trouble for his soldiers."

She was half smiling at this last statement. Rob smiled back. "So that," he said, "is how you met the invading American army and brought the Second World War to a close for yourself."

The door from the corridor swung open, and Olga entered. "Lunch is served," she said.

"Good," Martina said, rising from the sofa. "Please tell Christa to join us in the dining room."

Chapter 12

MARTINA SAT AT THE HEAD of the dining room table, flanked by her two guests. Rob's position directly across from Christa afforded him an opportunity to examine her more closely. Her soft, wavy blond hair and blue eyes, combined with her smile and lively manner, confronted Rob with what he considered to be a rather beautiful woman.

As they sipped the leek soup, they chatted about the summer weather and German food. As at dinner the evening before, Johannesberger Riesling was poured. The main course was a delicious white fish which Rob could not identify. It was accompanied by roasted potatoes and a salad consisting of tomatoes and lettuce.

Through the previous afternoon, evening, and morning, Rob had been reliving with Wolfgang and Martina the vicissitudes of Germany in the two world wars. The luncheon conversation brought him joltingly into the present. Here he was across the table from a member of the new generation—a woman reared since the cataclysm of the nineteen-forties—who knew nothing firsthand of that story.

"I understand that you are a lawyer. What kind of work do you do?" Rob asked as they began cutting into the fish.

"I live in Berlin—West Berlin, I should say—and work in the offices of the Senator for Justice. That is what is called the Minister of Justice in the rest of Germany. West Berlin, as you probably know, is different in many ways.

"What are your duties there?" Rob asked.

"For a while, I worked in a section responsible for legal matters relating to the American forces in West Berlin. That is where I became acquainted with several American lawyers. Now I am in a section responsible for legal problems in relation to the East Berlin and GDR authorities."

"Which do you find more interesting," asked Rob with a wry smile, "the Americans or the East Germans?"

"Well," she said with a slight laugh, "that is hardly a fair comparison. I like Americans very much. In fact, I must say that in many respects I find American men more interesting and attractive than German men." Rob thought that he caught a faint, devilish twinkle in her eyes. "But," she continued, "the Germans are, after all, my fellow countrymen."

"So you consider the East Germans to be your fellow countrymen?"

Martina shifted in her chair and made a slight clearing noise in her throat, bringing her napkin to her mouth for a second. Olga appeared and topped up the glasses with Johannesberger Riesling.

"I do," Christa said, her face becoming serious, "because in fact they are. I was born in what is now East Berlin, and I grew up in the GDR. Both of my parents live there and have lived there all of their lives." She looked at Martina with an impish smile and said, "I know that you do not like to admit it, Grossmutti, but our entire family, except you, are all from the East—both of your husbands, my grandparents on my father's side, my parents, and me. And you lived there for many years."

Martina listened with a resigned air to this recitation of the family roster of the eastern-born. "Yes, that is all certainly true," she said matter-of-factly.

Christa addressed Rob. "You must find it strange that one who grew up in the GDR now works for the West Berlin government. And you are probably wondering what my parents are doing there."

"Yes, you are a good mind reader. I would like to know."

"My grandmother here can tell you much more about the beginning of it all than I can. As I have been told, my mother and father met in Berlin during the war and were married there. He was a theology student in the university. He had been exempted from military service because he had been born with one leg slightly shorter than the other. This has never been a serious handicap for him, but, thank God, it was enough to keep him out of the army. He and my mother both worked in the Charité Hospital after the Berlin bombings started. I was born during that time. My father became an ordained Protestant pastor. They made a decision that many others did not make. They decided to remain in the Russian occupation zone after it became the GDR. They often explained to me that they had both been born and reared in that part of Germany and they felt an obligation to remain among those people to help them as much as they could. They said that those in the West would need them far less than those in the East. Who can argue with that?"

"What did your parents do after the GDR was formed in 1949?" Rob asked.

"After the war, my father served as pastor of a church in Rostock, which, as you probably know, is up on the Baltic coast. I was a little girl then. Later, we moved to Halle, and they have lived there ever since. He is pastor at the main church on the marketplace in the center of Halle. It is an old and famous church. Martin Luther preached there several times."

Her mention of Halle instantly brought to Rob's mind the image of the formidable George Marks Wilton, his college history professor, who had studied at the university there before the First World War. He was the person who had stirred Rob's abiding interest in the German scene. Halle was a place Rob had always wanted to visit, but he had written it off because it was behind the iron curtain—a barrier he had now discovered to be quite penetrable by an American tourist. Perhaps he would reconsider, but that was for another day. At the moment, he wanted to hear more from this bright and charming product of East Germany.

"Do you mind telling me how you happened to end up in West Berlin?" he asked.

"When I was growing up, my parents were always concerned about my education and my future in the GDR. They often told me that I should not feel bound to stay in the GDR merely because they had done so. It was difficult to grow up there and be actively involved in the church. The entire government and political apparatus is hostile to religion. As you know, Marxism-Leninism is atheistic. They reject the concept of any divine authority. I guess the miracle is that they allow churches to exist at all. When I was fourteen, I became eligible to join the Free German Youth, which is the official youth organization—really an arm of the SED, the Communist party. There was no way I could join, we thought, and remain faithful to Christian doctrine. But without joining, my future was bleak, so they eventually decided to send me to live with my father's brother and go to school in West Berlin. You must remember that in those days there was no wall. People could move freely in and out of all parts of Berlin. I came home to Halle to see my parents nearly every weekend."

"It is hard now to recall the time when West Berlin was not sealed off," Rob said.

"I was about to enter my last year in the gymnasium when the wall went up. I will never forget that day. I have read in American books and magazines that all Americans who were alive on the day that the Japanese attacked Pearl Harbor remember exactly where they were and what they were doing when they heard that news. It is that way for most Germans in connection with the wall. Sunday, August 13, 1961, is forever fixed in their minds. I was right here in this house. I had come to visit my grandmother. You remember that, don't you, Grossmutti?"

Martina stirred from her somber detachment. "Of course. That is one of those dates that cannot be washed out of the mind. It is like September 1939 and August 1914. Or perhaps a better comparison would be those two days at Bachdorf when death's messenger arrived—first for Bruno and then for Kurt. Yes, that is most like the news of the wall on that Sunday. That was word of the death of a city and the death of a dream."

No one spoke. Then Rob asked, "How would you describe that dream?"

"Oh," she sighed, "It was a dream of a reunited Germany, the idea that there was only one Germany."

"But isn't that idea still the official policy of the West German government?"

"It certainly is," Christa said in an emphatic tone.

"Do many Germans today really believe in that policy?" Rob asked.

"I will tell you one who does," Martina said. "He lives right here in this house: Wolfgang."

"Yes, I am afraid that Uncle Wolfi is romantic about that notion," Christa said. "He believes that although God has inflicted just punishment on us, the German people are destined to be united again. He believes that the Communist regime in the East is part of the forces of darkness—part of Satan's forces, you might say—or the antichrist, and that such cannot prevail. Now I should say that Uncle Wolfi is not alone in that view. Many other Germans believe that too; however, others are ready to come to terms with the situation as it is."

Rob wanted badly to ask her what she herself thought about the matter, but he did not pursue it. Instead he said, "Your parents must be truly extraordinary people."

"Indeed they are," Martina said, speaking before Christa had a chance to respond. This was the most positive and energetic statement she had made since Christa had first mentioned her mother. Rob had begun to imagine that there was some kind of estrangement between Helga and her mother, the mistress of Prinzenheim, comfortably situated here in the West. But that theory evaporated in light of what Martina went on to say.

"Helga was a darling girl when she was growing up, always especially concerned over other people's difficulties. Her husband, Ernst, is the same kind of person. Their decision to stay in the East entitles them, in my opinion, to elevation to sainthood. Since the border was closed and the wall was built, we have seen each other only rarely. I miss them very much. But fortunately Christa does visit me." Martina smiled warmly at

Christa, adding, "And through her, I stay in touch with Helga and Ernst."

"It is fortunate that the work of my office usually brings me to the Federal Republic two or three times a year. I try to use those times to visit here," Christa said to Rob. "Because my parents cannot get here and I can, I play the part of a living link between them and my grandmother. However, when and how often I see my parents depends on the whims of the East German authorities. They change travel restrictions for West Berliners into the GDR as they think the political situation requires." She paused and suddenly shifted the subject. "Tell me something about your work."

Rob outlined his career, describing his short time in New York in law practice, his years of teaching, and his subjects. He wound up by telling her of his forthcoming year at the University of Virginia and of his own days as a law student there.

"One of the American lawyers I knew studied law at the University of Michigan. Another studied at the University of Georgia, I believe. Are American law schools all alike?"

Rob proceeded to give her a description of the realm of American law schools. "American higher education owes a lot to the German universities," he said. "The seminar is a German invention, as is the concept of the university professor as a combination teacher-researcher."

"I studied law at the Free University of Berlin. When I was there, we still had a few of the old professors who had been educated before the war. They were part of the group that had come over from the old university on Unter den Linden, which was in the Russian sector, to found the Free University in the American sector."

Christa had a marvelous command of English. Her grammar and pronunciation were excellent, but the German accent was unmistakable. Martina's English was equally good, but the two spoke in different accents. Here was a clear generational gap, the difference between those Germans who learned English before the Second World War and those who learned it afterward. Martina spoke with the pronunciations of England, having learned the language from an English woman long before there was any American influence in Germany. Christa, on the other hand, used the language and accents of America, predominantly of midwestern America. Martina's speech was more elegant, but to Rob they both spoke with that entrancing quality of English infused with a female German accent.

"I still must make another telephone call and record some material on the meeting in Bonn," Christa said. "So I must excuse myself in a moment. I do wish that you could stay longer so that we could talk some more."

To Rob's mild surprise, Martina spoke up: "Robert has said that he must be going back to Frankfurt. We do not want to delay him any more."

"Yes, I really do need to move along," Rob said, picking up her cue.

"How long will you be in Germany? Are you coming to Berlin?" Christa asked.

Rob smiled and hesitated. "I don't know exactly. There are some people I may want to see in Munich, but I don't have exact plans."

"Then you should plan to come to Berlin," Christa said with an emphatic enthusiasm in her voice. "Have you ever been to Berlin?"

"I am embarrassed to say that I have not."

"I would be glad to show you around. Here is my card," she said as she rooted in a small purse she had extracted from a pocket in her jacket. "Here, I will write my home telephone on it." She jotted a number below her office number. "I will be back there on the day after tomorrow."

Rob slid his chair back from the table. "I will now excuse myself and go to my room for my bag."

"Robert, I will meet you on the front steps," Martina said.

"Then I will say good-bye to Christa here," he said, coming around the table and extending his hand to take hers. "Perhaps we will meet again in Berlin some day."

"Yes, I look forward to that," she replied, grasping his hand.

In the upstairs guest room, Rob closed his suitcase, which was lying on the bed. The four corner posts, each larger than a man's leg, rose above his head. Through the window he looked out over the village westward to the fields and hills beyond. He was enraptured by the scene and found himself not wanting to leave. Three hundred years had passed through and around here. The clattering of horses' hooves on the cobblestones of the courtyard had signaled the arrivals and departures of men bound for the court of Frederick the Great, for the Napoleonic Wars, for the Franco-Prussian War, and for the opening of the twentieth-century tragedy in August of 1914. Then came the intrusions of the internal combustion engine, with the roar of motorcars and trucks. Swastikas had fluttered on the village streets, and doubtless there had been men from Prinzenheim wearing the black of the SS. It was from this vantage point that Martina had seen the armored might of the United States approaching from the west in March 1945—American tanks heading eastward to meet those of the Soviet Union—changing fundamentally and perhaps forever the face of Germany and the Western world. He had been in this house only parts of two days, but he felt intimately identified with it, almost as though he had always been there.

He walked down the two flights of wide, creaking wooden stairs with their heavy, dark balustrade, descending beneath the horns of countless stags that had roamed the dark forests in the nearby hills in bygone decades. He reached the bottom of the stairs in the small entry hall and pulled open the massive door to the outside. As he walked across the courtyard toward his car, he saw Martina plucking flowers along the side of the drive that led to the rear. She approached him as he was placing his bag in the trunk of the car.

"Baroness von Egloffsberg," Rob said, "I cannot recall ever having had a more interesting two days, nor have I ever experienced warmer hospitality."

"You should call me Martina," she replied with a smile warmer than any he had seen from her since Christa's arrival.

"I will be glad to, if that is what you prefer."

"It has been nice having you here," she said with a return of the detached quality that had been puzzling him. "I thank you for your thoughtfulness in seeking me out to bring the letter and picture. It was a gracious thing to do. Your father must have been very proud of you."

"I am glad that I was able to find you and to learn of my father's visit to Bachdorf. I hope that we may have an opportunity to see each other again."

Martina hesitated, a flicker of shadow crossing her eyes. "You know at my age life becomes more and more uncertain. Your visit here has been enjoyable, but we cannot plan on another with certainty."

There was an aloofness and sadness about her now that contrasted with the warmth of her greeting just twenty-four hours earlier. "Of course, that is so," Rob said, "but if you should ever come to the States, please let me know. Also, if Wolfgang ever goes there, I would like to have him visit me. There is a good chance that I will go to Berlin. It would be nice to see Christa again."

Martina made no response. Behind her he saw the red brick facade of the schloss with leafy vines climbing to its roofline. Above and beyond the curving bank of stone steps leading up to the main front entrance, he saw the windows of the room where they had talked at such length, and above them, recessed in the brick wall, the window of the room where he had slept. He looked longingly at the scene, thinking of the treasures it contained in the library and the portraits of generations in the great hall. His eyes soaked in all the details because her last statement left him with the melancholy feeling that he would never again see this place. He and the baroness and the von Egloffsberg family had briefly touched each other, just as they and his father had done over a half century ago, and he, like his father, would never return.

"Your granddaughter," he said to break the awkward pause, "is really a bright and attractive woman."

"I expect that she will be getting married sometime soon," Martina said quickly.

"Oh," Rob said with slight surprise, "Is she engaged?"

"No, I do not think so at the moment, but I think she may be serious about someone in Berlin."

"In that event, I doubt she would have much time to show me around."

"That is probably true," Martina said in a blunt German tone.

"Now I must go," Rob said, taking her hand. "Thank you again, and please thank Wolfgang for me."

She held his hand with a curiously intent look in her eyes. "I thank you again." She moved forward and embraced him lightly.

He turned and opened the door of the car and got in. As the motor sprang to life, she backed up a few steps and stood to watch him pull off. He looked once more at the tall slim figure, the short and grayed hair, and the aging but elegant face of this survivor who had known his father before he had known him, the living flesh behind the photograph in the footlocker of the late Lieutenant Robert Edward Kirkman, AEF.

"*Auf wiedersehen*," she said, waving her hand slightly as the car moved toward the gateway. In another instant, the car slipped into the road, and the schloss and Martina, Baroness von Egloffsberg were gone.

Chapter 13

Robert Kirkman peered out of the airplane window at the East German landscape below. One advantage of the restrictions requiring planes to fly below ten thousand feet from West Germany to Berlin was that the passengers were treated to a much closer view of the terrain. So it was that Rob, on this cloudless day, could see plainly the level countryside of the German Democratic Republic. From the air, West Germany was a patchwork quilt formed by innumerable small farms. But here, over the East, the patchwork had been erased. In its place were only long, unbroken stretches of cultivated fields and pastures of collectivized farms.

After returning to Frankfurt from Prinzenheim, he had intended to go on to Munich. But an evening's reading in *Baedeker* about the capital of the German Empire, coupled with his meeting with Christa, had convinced him that he should proceed to Berlin instead. Overnight this trip had become imperative.

The plane was beginning its descent. Rob still saw only open countryside below, with occasional tight clusters of red houses forming the villages. Time seemed hardly to have touched them. He surmised that he was over what had been the province of Brandenburg. It was no more. The GDR authorities had abolished all the historical territorial configurations and names and had divided the country into fourteen administrative districts, each named after its principal city. Suddenly houses began to appear in a quickly thickening pattern as the plane was coming in over Berlin. In a moment, Rob realized that he was about to be provided with a spectacular treat. The plane flew eastward past most of the city and then began a slow banking turn back toward the west to make an approach to Tempelhof Airport.

Eagerly and almost frantically, his eyes moved back and forth over the scene. He wanted to take it all in but realized that in the fleeting moments before landing he would catch only a few of the key landmarks.

There was Alexanderplatz. He knew from his study of city maps and photographs where to look. He felt genuine exhilaration when his eye spotted the Brandenburg Gate, with the broad expanse of the Unter den Linden stretching eastward. Immediately to the west was the Tiergarten. The heart of Berlin was now in view. And then he saw it—the raw dirt strip and the Wall slashing through its middle from north to south. One could hardly imagine a more disruptive structure. The Wall plowed remorselessly across streets and through squares at no natural intersections. It was as though some blindfolded giant had raked his finger across the city without regard for buildings, streets, or human arrangements. As the Wall reached the outskirts of the city, it changed to wire fencing, watch towers, and a wide dirt strip that bent off to the west, engirdling all of West Berlin and sealing it off from the surrounding GDR countryside.

What a dramatic way to be introduced to the Wall. He had been afforded a perspective of the city and its central scar that no amount of moving around on the ground could have provided. He now tingled at the prospect of exploring every block of front-line East-West confrontation. It was one of the few places in the world which presented simultaneously the old and the contemporary—physical evidence of the challenge of Marxism-Leninism to Western civilization.

The travel office in Frankfurt had made a reservation for Rob at the Hotel Am Zoo, "an excellent location with relatively moderate rates," an agent there had said. Although the rates were hardly in the economy class, in all other respects the hotel was just right. It was on Kurfurstendamm, the principal thoroughfare of West Berlin, only a block from the Kaiser Wilhelm Memorial Church, or rather, the ruins of that church. Rob's room faced an inner courtyard and was so quiet that no one would have suspected that the hotel was in the center of a city.

Rob took off his coat and tie, washed his hands and face, unpacked a few things, and sat down in one of the two overstuffed chairs to think about a plan of action. According to her announced intention, Christa would be remaining with her grandmother in Prinzenheim through that night, presumably returning to Berlin the following day. That gave him the next twenty-four hours on his own.

After an hour with Berlin maps spread out on the bed, *Baedeker* at hand, followed by a discussion in the travel agency next door to the hotel, he had his plan formulated. In the morning, he would take a bus tour of West Berlin. In the afternoon, he would take a bus tour of East Berlin. Together, these tours would give him an overview of the entire city, East and West. He would then decide on the places to revisit on his own and explore in greater detail.

Rob felt tired. The emotional experiences at Prinzenheim and the exhilaration of arriving in Berlin had drained him. He ate an early dinner in a restaurant near the hotel and went to bed. But he spent a restless night. He slept a while, woke up, tossed and turned, slept some more, and woke again. Each falling asleep brought a new dream. After daylight, he did not go back to sleep but lay in bed reflecting over the kaleidoscope of the dream world through which he had passed. The strange mixtures of times and places and people bothered him.

In one of the dreams, it was Christmas at Trepnitz Hills. He must have been about nine or ten years old. The great Christmas tree—over twelve feet tall—stood in the main parlor, suffusing the room with its fresh cedar aroma. The multicolored balls, tinsel, and icicles all glistened in the reflected light of the crackling fire with its oak logs piled up behind the brass andirons. It was approaching dusk on Christmas Eve. Uncle Charles was growing impatient for darkness to come so that he could unleash his fireworks—mainly roman candles and sky rockets. Uncle Noble and Aunt Nan were there with their two small children, Rob's first cousins. Rob's mother and father were there. All was as he remembered the magical Christmases of his childhood except for a glaring incongruity.

There in the group mingling in the parlor and hallway were Wolfgang von Egloffsberg, his brother Kurt, and their younger half-sister Helga. Wolfgang and Kurt were in their Wehrmacht uniforms, looking handsome and young. Kurt's willowy Pomeranian wife was also on hand, her flaxen hair pulled back, accentuating her lean face. They were all chatting amiably together, and Rob's grandmother, Clarissa, was telling the Germans about her father's grand adventures in the Army of Northern Virginia and of how he died gloriously for the Lost Cause. Making the scene even more out of joint, Noble Shepperson was attired in his freshly fitted new army uniform—pinks and dark green blouse—with the gold major's leaves glinting in the candlelight. Martina did not seem to be present, and Rob kept looking for her. No one knew where she was. Helga was at the piano playing "Silent Night." He was standing behind her, marveling at her musical ability. He heard Wolfgang asking Mr. Ed, "Did you know my father? He also served on the Western Front."

At another point in the night, after thrashing around in the commodious Am Zoo bed with fantasy and reality blending, Rob drifted off again and saw his father and himself at the schloss at Bachdorf. They were walking in the garden between the rear terrace and the Elbe. As they walked around the side of the somber gray structure toward the front, his father was talking about the wonderful fruit trees. An apple orchard a short distance away particularly attracted his attention.

Then he was standing alone in the courtyard at the front entrance of the schloss. Along the lane from the main road came a horse, moving rapidly, his hooves scattering the drifts of autumn leaves. Clattering across the cobblestones, the black, panting horse stopped just short of the steps to the schloss. The rider dismounted and strode to the double entrance door beneath the von Egloffsberg crest. He was clothed in olive drab with a stiff, high-necked collar, Sam Browne belt, and riding boots that came almost to his knees. He rapped the heavy iron door knocker, removed his cap, and stood waiting. Rob saw then that it was his father, the young First Lieutenant Robert Edward Kirkman, AEF.

A maid opened the door, and they exchanged a few words. The maid disappeared and returned in a minute with Martina. She was young, looking just as she did in the photograph with her two baby boys. The lieutenant bowed slightly from the waist and handed her an envelope that he had been holding in his hand. She opened it, took out a single sheet of paper, and fixed her eyes on it. Then she sagged against the doorway and slowly slumped to the stone floor emitting an agonized moan. The maid, rushing up from her rear, knelt beside her. Running her arms under Martina's shoulders, she asked in a half crying voice, "Is it the baron?"

Rob looked at his father, now standing beside him, and asked, "Is it?"

Mr. Ed slowly nodded his head. "Yes, it was the Argonne. I was there."

In still another confused episode, Rob was in Remberton. He was at a party at the house of Scott Clevmore, one of his boyhood friends and part of the Remberton crowd with which he had grown up. The house was twelve miles out of town on land where the Clevmores had established themselves after the Civil War. Rob had always been unclear about their origins and earlier history. However murky the past, they had put together a substantial acreage and become big cotton farmers, but in recent years they had been turning to soy beans and beef cattle. When Scott married, he built his house in the edge of a pecan orchard about a mile from his parents' weathered Victorian house. His bride came from Birmingham, and having grown up in Mountain Brook, had some difficulty at first in adjusting to Remberton—not to mention living twelve miles out in the country—but she gradually fit in. Scott's house was of the 1950s ranch style—one-story and air-conditioned, with a large screened porch with two ceiling fans. The party in progress must have been in spring or fall because people were drifting back and forth between the porch and the den through the wide-open double doors. If it had been summer, the house would have been sealed and the air conditioning going full blast, with no one on the porch.

The party must have been under way for a while because several there were showing signs of having had too much to drink. The Remberton pattern was to gather at about seven and eat at about ten. The bizarre feature about this party was that Christa was there. Although she was a dozen years younger, she looked the same age as everyone else. He had introduced her all around, and she had entered into the animated conversation as though she had known the group for years. This Remberton crowd was always hospitable, at least to anyone sponsored by one of them.

Suddenly he found himself locked in an embrace with Christa in the hallway of the house. His father appeared abruptly and said to Christa, "You shouldn't be here. It's getting late. It's time to go home."

The vividness of these dreams left him confused about reality. The agonized, pained look on Martina's face as she read the message handed to her at Bachdorf was burned into Rob's mind. He thought of his grandmother's story of the messenger on horseback bringing word of her father's death to the front steps at Trepnitz Hills. In such quiet settings, deep in the countryside, came these two fateful communications, one in 1918 and the other over half a century earlier in the summer of 1864. He felt as though he had been present at both moments in time. The causes and the places were different; but, he wondered, how different were they? In both, the causes were lost. Could it be said that both men died in vain?

Then there were the descendants of the dead men in that strange Christmas Eve gathering at Trepnitz Hills. The incongruity of two officers in the uniform of the German Wehrmacht as guests in the Alabama Black Belt shocked him into an uneasy wakefulness. The thought had crossed his mind more than once in the past week that the feel and ambience at Bachdorf and Prinzenheim and Trepnitz Hills were not all that different. His great-grandfather, Henry Trepnitz, wearing the Confederate gray, could have ridden up on his horse to either of the great German houses, dismounted, entered, and found congenial surroundings.

Dominating all else out of this restless night was the strongly lingering sensation of his embrace with Christa. He reflected on that heated moment as if it were indeed reality. He even embellished it a bit. He saw the two of them drifting into the hall of the house, deliberately getting away from the others at the party. He mentally reconstructed a holding of hands and then a rush to grab each other. Best of all was the long, warm kiss, their bodies clamped against each other. His father's interruption of this blissful moment angered him. It made no sense. He, Rob, was a grown man, and Christa was a grown woman over whom his father had no authority whatsoever. He found himself, ridiculous as it was, becoming angry with his dead father over this incident that never happened and never could have happened.

The low buzzing of his travel alarm clock penetrated his post-dawn slump back into sleep. He barely had enough time to dress, have a cup of coffee and a croissant in the hotel breakfast room, and board the tour bus parked across the Kurfurstendamm. The bus took him on a wide sweep of West Berlin, passing all the major sights—the Tiergarten, Charlottenburg, the 1936 Olympic Stadium, the Free University, and the city hall.

Like most visitors, he found himself fixated on the Wall. Photographs and verbal descriptions simply did not convey the emotional feel of being there, seeing it, touching it, and looking over it. He climbed up the wooden steps to a platform the West Berliners had erected. From there he looked across the bare dirt strip to a guard tower on the other side. Two East German guards in green uniforms looked blankly back at their curious observers. People on this platform stood in silence or spoke in low voices. Everyone's thoughts seemed to be throbbing with an overwhelming but unanswerable question: how could a civilized society in the late twentieth century do this to a city, and especially to its own people?

Rob stood equally absorbed before the Brandenburg Gate. Through this great ceremonial portal, nearly two hundred feet wide and as high, formerly thundered five lanes of traffic, passing in and out of Unter den Linden. Now it was a dead end, the broad thoroughfare blocked by a concrete wall nine feet thick. Beyond it was the heart of old Berlin, the center for decades of the German Imperial Government, of the city's commercial life, the libraries, theatres, and museums, the seat of the university. Atop the Brandenburg Gate, mounted in the Quadriga, fluttered the black, red, and gold flag of the German Democratic Republic, seemingly flaunting the brute fact that what lay beyond now belonged to another world. All of what he saw beyond the Wall Rob would see at closer range during his afternoon tour of East Berlin.

Back in his room at the Am Zoo that evening, Rob luxuriated in a long, hot shower, washing away the heat and fatigue of the hours on sightseeing buses. As the hot water pummeled him, he wondered where the monuments were to the men and events that had shaken Western civilization—and Germany in particular—to its foundations in the twentieth century. In all of Berlin, East and West, he had seen no monuments to the leaders of the momentous happenings of either of the two world wars, at least none erected by Germans to Germans. The tree-lined length of Monument Avenue in Richmond popped into his mental vision, with its heroic equestrian statues of Lee, Jackson, and Stuart. There was nothing to compare with it in Germany for the two great wars of this century. There had to be something at work here in Germany other than defeat. Something had gone so profoundly wrong that the survivors did not want to remember or to be remembered.

The only sign of remembrance he had seen in West Berlin was the ruined Kaiser Wilhelm Memorial Church, a block from where he was now showering. The partly destroyed tower was itself a somber monument. Inside the starkly modern and newly built church adjacent to the tower was the sole inscription: To the Protestant Martyrs, 1933-1945. On the other side of the Wall on Unter den Linden was the East's single memorial, established in a restored classical structure. It too bore but a brief inscription: To the Victims of Fascism and Militarism. Thus, the memory was recorded, East and West, only of those who had suffered. No great statesmen, no generals or admirals, and no tumultuous or glorious historic events did this society, on either side of the divide, want to preserve for posterity. The defeated Germany had no Robert E. Lee or Jefferson Davis.

As he dried himself with an oversized hotel towel, Rob's mind returned to his most immediate interest. The time had come to call Christa. She should have returned from Prinzenheim by this hour. He had deliberately waited to give her ample time to reach her apartment, on the chance that she had been at her office. It was now past six. Although it was unlikely that she would be available for dinner tonight, he reasoned, at least he could try to make arrangements for the next night.

He picked up the telephone nervously. She had told him to call her if he came to Berlin, but had she really meant it? Brushing doubts aside, he dialed her apartment number.

After the fifth ring, his spirits sagged. Irrational as it seemed, he had expected her to be there and answer the phone promptly. The sixth ring passed. He would give it one more ring and then hang up. The seventh ring was interrupted.

"*Hallo,*" said a male voice speaking in German.

Taken off guard, Rob momentarily did not know what to do. What should he say? Perhaps he had a wrong number. Hanging up might be the best course. But he rallied.

"May I speak to Christa Schreibholz?" he said in German.

"She is not here," the voice said in that authoritative tone to which the German language lends itself so well.

Rob hesitated. His impulse was to hang up, but that would be too frustrating. "When will she be in?"

"I do not know," intoned the German. "Who is calling?"

The question was said in a way that seemed to command an answer, but Rob decided to abandon the inquiry.

"Thank you," he said, "I will call again." He quickly replaced the receiver.

His hand still on the receiver, Rob sat stunned in the chair beside the phone. What was a German male doing in Christa's apartment? The voice seemed older, more mature than he would have expected from a man of Christa's age. He sensed a mixture of perplexity and concern. Was something awry? Could she be living with this man? Such a possibility, he realized, had never occurred to him, and he now found himself mildly shocked by the thought. But why should he be concerned one way or the other? He had no reason to think of himself as her protector. There was something about her that had taken hold of his mind in an odd way.

Oh well, he mused, he should forget the whole thing. Christa had her own, busy life in Berlin, and there was no reason to think that she would give him the time of day, as they used to say in Alabama. He might still try to telephone the next day, but contacting her had receded to low priority. He would concentrate on his projected exploration of Berlin, especially on the east side of the Wall.

Half an hour later, Rob was pushing his way through the throngs of pedestrians along the wide sidewalks on the Kurfurstendamm. It was the height of the summer tourist season. Americans were here in abundance. Many were college students, usually walking, laughing, and shouting in clumps of three or four. Most were in blue jeans and T-shirts bearing their college names or inane phrases. Then there were the middle-aged Americans on group tours. Their voices sounding in the accents of New York, Chicago, and Texas could be heard all along the street. These were not settings in which he was proudest to identify himself as an American. Germans too were here in all ages, shapes, and varieties of dress, from the peaks of elegance to the depths of hippiedom.

The street was as crowded with vehicles as the sidewalks were with people. He was beginning to wonder whether anyone in West Berlin owned any kind of automobile other than a Mercedes-Benz, BMW, or Audi. He did see an occasional VW. He had not yet seen a taxi that was not a Mercedes-Benz. The whole scene for blocks was like a carnival with bright lights, trees, kiosks, outdoor cafes, animated people, and expensive cars.

Rob walked for more than an hour along the Kurfurstendamm and into some of its side streets before plopping down at a table in the open air in front of one of the restaurants near the Kempenski Hotel. He had become voraciously hungry and thirsty—a condition intensified by the long wait he had to endure before being served. He ordered and devoured a Wiener schnitzel. He accompanied it with a sizeable quantity of Berliner Pilsner. He sat at a table only ten feet from the passing parade on the sidewalk, a never-ending show of humanity in all of its international richness, sprinkled with a special Berlin flavor.

He had risen and was standing beside his table counting out some marks for a tip when he heard a female voice at his side exclaiming, "Robert Kirkman!" He jerked around in surprise. There, coming through the opening from the sidewalk, was Christa Schreibholz.

"Robert, I did not know you were coming to Berlin so soon," she said in her Americanized English.

"I hadn't planned on it," he replied as they shook hands. She was out of the professional uniform. Instead of a two-piece dark suit, she was wearing a form-fitting pink silk dress that almost matched the color of her cheeks. The blue eyes and wavy blond hair seemed more lustrous in the soft light of the cafe than they had in the schloss at Prinzenheim.

Behind Christa loomed a tall brown-haired man vaguely resembling Jimmy Stewart. He was wearing a light blue sport coat and a striped tie. Turning, Christa said to Rob, "This is Major Douglas Catron of your American army." To the major she said, "This is Robert Kirkman. He is the law professor I told you about from the States."

The two men shook hands. "How do you do," said the major in a solid voice that exuded confidence. Rob had heard the voice from regular army officers numerous times.

"I'm glad to meet you," responded Rob.

"We were walking to a little bar just around the corner when I saw you here," Christa said. "Won't you join us for an after-dinner drink?"

"Well . . . ah . . . I don't want to intrude on your evening," Rob said uncertainly. Actually, he could think of nothing more enjoyable at the moment than sitting down with her in a quiet place, even in the presence of this American stranger.

"Oh, come on," she urged, "we will not be long. We must go to work in the morning."

"Yes, come on and have a drink," commanded the major.

Ten minutes later, they were seated in a rear corner of a quiet and semidark cocktail lounge just off the Kurfurstendamm. Rob and the major each ordered a brandy; Christa ordered a rum drink. As they were being served, she explained that she had just returned that day from West Germany and that she and the major had eaten dinner in a nearby restaurant. Rob, in turn, described his change of plans in not going to Munich and how he had been playing tourist all day.

Through all of this the major sat quietly, the brandy cupped in his hands. He had an honest, open face.

"Are you stationed here in West Berlin, Major?" Rob asked.

"Well, yes and no," he said.

"He has an unusual assignment," Christa added.

"I am quartered in West Berlin," he continued, "but I am officially assigned to the U. S. Military Mission in the GDR."

"Do you mean to say that the United States has a military mission inside East Germany?" asked Rob with surprised disbelief.

"That's right," the regular army voice replied. "Not many Americans realize that. It is one of the last vestiges of the occupation of Germany by the Allies. The Soviets, of course, have a similiar mission in West Germany."

"The GDR puts so much emphasis on its being a sovereign state that I'm surprised it would tolerate an American military entity on its soil."

"Well, I can tell you that the GDR authorities don't like it; but there is nothing they can do about it because the Soviet Union is firmly in control. The Soviets get a lot out of being able to have their mission in the West. They know that if we were put out of the GDR, they would be put out of the Federal Republic."

"Where is the U.S. mission actually based?" asked Rob.

"At Babelsberg, which is almost in Potsdam. We are just a short way beyond the western border of West Berlin. If it weren't for the border, Babelsberg would be considered a suburb of Berlin."

"So that's why you're able to be quartered in West Berlin and still be stationed at the mission in the GDR?"

"Yes," said the major, "it's only a fifteen-minute drive from my quarters through the checkpoint to our mission. You may have heard of the Glienecke Bridge. That's the place where people are sometimes exchanged between East and West. Francis Gary Powers, the U-2 pilot, was swapped there. It's right on the line. I cross that bridge every day going to and from work."

"Doug has some very interesting experiences," Christa interjected. "He deals mainly with the Russians."

"In this work do you have to speak both Russian and German?" Rob asked with concealed admiration for anyone with such language skills.

"That's right," the major said, his voice more relaxed and less military. A momentary silence ensued as if all were reflecting on this fact.

Then in a quick change of direction, the major said, "Did I understand Christa to say that you are a law professor back home?"

Anticipating a series of questions, Rob briefly explained his work in the law school, described the Marburg conference that had brought him on this trip in the first place, and outlined what he would be doing at Charlottesville in the coming fall.

"Have you been to East Berlin or the GDR?" the major asked.

Rob said that he had taken the standard bus tour that afternoon and that he had previously driven through Weimar, Jena, and Leipzig. He did not mention Bachdorf. Christa said nothing, although she must surely have been told by her grandmother of his unusual exploration there.

The major said, "I would invite you to visit the mission in Babelsberg, but the Soviets and the East Germans don't want visiting Americans trooping around that neck of the woods. We keep the place strictly limited to the U.S. military personnel assigned to the mission. There are only about a couple of dozen of us."

"Oh, I certainly understand," Rob said.

"But perhaps I could at least show you the justice offices here," Christa said.

Rob went for the opportunity without hesitation. "Yes, that would be interesting."

"Perhaps you could call me tomorrow and we could discuss it then," she said.

Their glasses were empty. Rob wondered about the man in her apartment, but he saw no way to work that subject into the conversation decently. He agreed that he would telephone in the morning. They left the lounge. On the sidewalk in front Rob said goodnight, he and the major stating that each hoped to see the other again. They parted in opposite directions.

Chapter 14

At the intersection of Unter den Linden and Friedrichstrasse, traffic was moderately heavy at mid-morning of this sunny July day. There was a scattering of Wartburgs and Trabants—the two East German-made cars—and an occasional Lada from Poland, Skoda from Czechoslovakia, and Swedish Volvo—the preferred vehicle of GDR officials and high-ranking Party leaders. Buses passed in trainlike configurations, two or three joined together and packed with standing people.

Rob had been standing at this famous intersection for several minutes absorbing the scene. He had boarded the S-Bahn at the Zoo station, only a short walk from his hotel, and arrived at Friedrichstrasse Station in East Berlin twenty minutes later. After crossing the River Spree, the train had slowed as guard towers and barbed wire fences closed in abruptly on both sides. It had taken Rob nearly an hour to clear the tightly controlled passport and currency processing points after making the mandatory exchange of West marks for nonexchangeable East marks at absurdly unrealistic rates. His final inward-bound clearance gave him a great sense of relief as he walked out of the station into Friedrichstrasse and thence to this intersection.

He launched this venture into East Berlin on his own only after telephoning Christa and being told by her, with agonized apologies, that she had an unexpected array of matters requiring urgent attention and she could not see him during the day. Much to his surprise, however, she agreed to meet him for dinner that evening.

To his right, Rob looked westward down Unter den Linden toward the Brandenburg Gate. Parallel lines of Linden trees, freshly replaced since the war, stretched for several blocks along the median, dividing the lanes of traffic on the two-hundred-foot-wide boulevard. The Embassy of the Soviet Union loomed on the far side, filling an entire block.

To his left, Rob looked eastward past the State Library, the university, and the restored Opera House. If he had been standing there before 1943, he would have seen the Imperial Palace at the head of the street, over half a mile away, a sprawling seven-hundred-room edifice housing the Hohenzollerns and their retinues through those bygone years of German glory. Now in its place stood the starkly modern Palast der Republik, the seat of the Peoples' Chamber and symbolic manifestation of this new German state. Its contemporary architecture reminded him of the Kennedy Center in Washington.

With his *Baedeker* map of Berlin in hand—a detailed street map from the first decade of the century—Rob set out to see the historical points at closer range. Heading toward the Brandenberg Gate, he was looking for Wilhelmstrasse, the chief government street of the German Reich for decades. It was not where it should have been according to *Baedeker.* After some perplexed searching, Rob discovered that the Wilhelmstrasse was now Otto Gronewald Strasse. As he discovered later, numerous streets had been renamed to reflect the revolutionary replacement of the imperialist, capitalist, and bourgeois heroes with Marxist-Leninist heroes. Turning down this street, Rob saw that the site of Bismarck's house and the Reich Chancery was now open fields of rubble and nondescript new structures. From the street, he could see across this depressing desolation to the mound of dirt and weeds marking the site of the bunker where Hitler met his end. Beyond that was the Wall. The street was almost deserted, obviously an area which the ruling party did not wish to commemorate.

Back on Unter den Linden, Rob stood in the middle of the street not more than a hundred feet from the massive and soaring columns of the Brandenburg Gate, a truly immense ceremonial construction put up under the direction of Frederick the Great. Where Rob stood now, it would have been impossible to stand forty years earlier. Lines of traffic would have been pouring between the gate's five columns. Now, though, he was in a quiet parklike setting. Flowers had been planted in beds to mark the end of the street. A handful of armed green-uniformed guards stood just beyond the metal rail which marked the point beyond which pedestrians could not go. Tourists milled around. A middle-aged German man asked Rob to take a picture of him and his wife. In response to Rob's inquiry, he explained that he was a worker from a town outside Berlin, in the city for a one-day holiday. Rob accommodated him, taking a shot of the smiling couple with the gate in the background. He noted that the Wall would not likely show up in the photograph. It was low at this point, enabling tourists on two-story West Berlin busses to peer over it and through the gate's columns into Unter den Linden.

Rob walked eastward a few blocks, crossing Friedrichstrasse and coming to the front of the main university building. The central structure, originally erected as a royal residence before 1800, was three stories tall and made of dark stone. It was set back from the street and was flanked by two wings of the same height coming forward almost to the sidewalk. This U-shaped arrangement formed a courtyard which was separated from the sidewalk by a tall iron railing. The complex had been badly damaged in the war. Rob had seen photographs of it taken in May 1945, when the buildings were pocked with shell marks, windows were out, and much of the interior was gutted. The restoration had been remarkably well done. This was true of most of the other buildings along the length of Unter den Linden.

Where he was standing now had been the focal point of the final drive by the Red Army to take Berlin. To the damage already inflicted by Allied air bombardment the Russians added the immensely destructive effects of artillery, tank fire, and street fighting. Yet, as he looked around, much was as *Baedeker* had described it seventy years earlier.

Rob went into the university courtyard to look for the statues of the academic greats of the past that *Baedeker* reported to be there, but they were gone. He circled the block to the rear of the buildings and discovered that the statues had been relocated to various points to the rear and sides. Hegel had been taken to the entrance of a new seminar building to the rear.

The statues of the two Humboldts had been moved to the sidewalk bordering Unter den Linden. Rob was examining these two seated figures whose name the university bore. Alexander was on one side of the entrance to the front courtyard, and Wilhelm was on the other. As he stood there musing over the scene, he heard the approach of a rhythmic, metallic tapping. For a moment his view in that direction was obscured by a group of students emerging from the courtyard. They moved past him, crossing the street to the bus stop on the other side. He then saw a blind man coming along the sidewalk in his direction. The man was tall with dark hair and was wearing a gray suit better tailored than the usual attire seen east of the Wall. The man was moving at a steady clip, swinging a long white cane back and forth in front of him, its metal tip giving a sharp click each time it struck the pavement. Rob moved to the side to give him more room.

Suddenly, his eyes became riveted on the face passing him, its sightless stare fixed straight ahead. It was Wolfgang von Egloffsberg.

Rob was startled into immobility. His first impulse was to run after Wolfgang, greet him, and announce his identity. But he held back, overcome by the strangeness of the encounter. How extraordinary it was that a blind man, who apparently felt so strongly about the fundamental evil of this society, should be walking confidently through the middle of East Berlin—and alone at that. What could he possibly be doing here? Without thinking, Rob fell in behind him.

Wolfgang continued westward along Unter den Linden to Friedrichstrasse. There he turned right. Rob was staying some twenty or thirty paces to his rear. After a block, they came to the intersection with Clara-Zetkin-Strasse. There Wolfgang paused, turning to his left. After waiting for the traffic to clear, he crossed Friedrichstrasse and continued westward. Rob marveled at the blind man's adeptness in avoiding obstacles and sensing the traffic flow. In his hands, the long white cane was an almost magical instrument.

In the distance, Rob could see the Wall. Clara-Zetkin appeared to run directly into it and end there unceremoniously. The Wall was now no more than a block and a half away. The street was devoid of cars, and Rob saw only a handful of pedestrians. They crossed the last street before the Wall, which was now no more than a couple of hundred yards ahead. Rob was still keeping about twenty paces behind Wolfgang.

Suddenly the blind man turned around and stood looking directly at Rob. "What do you want?" Wolfgang's powerful voice sounded as if it were coming through a megaphone on this quiet street.

Rob had stopped instantly. Could this man really be blind? He was looking straight at Rob. He must have the hearing of a hound dog or some batlike antennae, Rob thought. He had heard of extraordinary senses possessed by the blind. Now he felt trapped, but he could not bring himself to reveal his identity. He suddenly felt shabby, deceitful, unworthy.

The German voice boomed again, "You have been following me. Who are you and what do you want?"

Rob looked to his rear. There was no other person within a block. He took what he considered a coward's way out, but the wisest course under the peculiar circumstances. He tiptoed backward for several yards. After retreating, he crossed the street, putting more distance between himself and Wolfgang. He went into the next block, but he kept his eyes on the solitary blind figure who had not moved, but remained alertly poised with his white cane as if to fend off an attack.

After a long minute or two, Wolfgang turned around and resumed walking. He began tapping the side of the building with his cane until he reached a doorway, which he entered. It was the entrance to a four-story office building of no particular character. It was less than a hundred yards from the Wall. On the other side of the Wall to the West the dome of the Reichstag—the building constructed to house the national parliament when Imperial Germany was at its zenith—loomed with impressive clarity.

Rob waited several minutes and then walked slowly toward the entrance of the building that Wolfgang had entered. The street was still deserted. He saw a plaque beside the doorway listing the offices of four organizations or government agencies. One name caught his attention: The Association of the Blind and Visually Handicapped in the GDR.

Rob stood in front of the sign, puzzled. So here was Wolfgang pursuing his interest in helping the blind—East and West—just as he had mentioned during their late night conversation at Prinzenheim. In light of what he had said then, it should hardly be surprising to find him calling on the East German organization for the blind. However, he had announced that he was going to Frankfurt. Also, he had obviously not just come in from West Berlin. He had been striding along the street from the opposite direction, from Marx-Engels Platz and Alexanderplatz, the center of the Party and government offices. There were no entry points from the West in that direction. Then, too, how did Wolfgang get around the limited access to the East allowed by the GDR for West Germans?

Rob did not feel comfortable loitering here. Yet he had a consuming curiosity to find out more about Wolfgang's presence in East Berlin. He could not simply walk away from this scene, so he drifted across the street and strolled slowly back toward Friedrichstrasse. He intended to keep within sight of this building entrance and to wait at least for a while to see whether Wolfgang emerged and where he then went.

He had not gone far when he saw a woman walking hurriedly along the sidewalk on the side of the street he had just left. She was headed toward the building Wolfgang had entered. She was a slim, youngish woman wearing a gray, unstylish dress like a hundred he had seen on women in the GDR. Her fast pace and intense look suggested that she must have an urgent mission or be late for an appointment. He backed into the doorway of an apartment building to observe what she did.

As he watched her from his vantage point directly across the street, Rob had a faint sensation that this woman looked familiar—that he had seen her somewhere before. But this could not be. He knew no one in East Germany. Then the flash of recognition broke through. This was the woman with whom he had sat at dinner at the Interhotel in Leipzig a week earlier, the woman who had described herself as a medical doctor from Berlin who specialized in problems of the eyes.

Rob remained for several minutes in his recessed position, his gaze fixed on the building diagonally across the street into which the woman had disappeared. It was the same building that Wolfgang had entered. A high cloud cover had slid across the blue sky, cutting off the sun and cooling the Berlin streets. There was hint of a late afternoon shower. A jet floated westward, slowly descending toward Tempelhof, allowing its passengers to witness the spectacular panorama of the Wall cutting the city at its heart.

The only person in all of East Germany with whom he had had any conversation was now in the building with Wolfgang von Egloffsberg, the man from West Germany at whose house he had just been a guest. Her visit to the blind association was actually not odd, Rob reasoned, as he remembered their dinner talk in Leipzig. But did these two know each other? Was their arrival here within a quarter hour of each other a pure coincidence? He was hooked now. He had to see this little drama through.

He had received plenty of advice before going into the East. Mind your own business, everyone had told him. Obey all the rules, don't do anything suspicious, and you will be all right. Now here he was, tailing someone, keeping a building under surveillance, and generally acting suspicious. He must do something. He could not stand indefinitely in this doorway.

Occasionally glancing at the building containing his quarry, he sauntered a block toward Friedrichstrasse and back three times before he saw them emerge. He stepped quickly into a doorway.

Wolfgang and the woman walked side-by-side. They were chatting, but even though the neighborhood was quiet, Rob could not catch what they were saying. Their words were interlaced with the tapping of the cane tip. After they passed his position, Rob followed from the opposite side. When they reached Friedrichstrasse, they turned left, heading toward the railroad station. Rob surmised that Wolfgang intended to take a train to West Berlin; but when the pair arrived at the station entrance, they did not enter. They walked instead to a taxi stop. The woman signaled a taxi, then she and Wolfgang shook hands, and he got in, closing the door behind him. The taxi pulled off, heading northward, away from the city center.

The woman began walking rapidly back in Rob's direction. He stepped into a shop entrance and began looking at its modest stock. In a moment she passed, striding purposefully toward Unter den Linden. Rob resumed his tailing procedure, staying well behind her. Keeping up with her was now more difficult. People were beginning to get off from work. The street was more crowded with cars, buses, and pedestrians than any street he had seen in the East. He would lose sight of her for a few seconds, then after charging ahead through throngs of workers he would catch sight of her again. At the corner of Unter den Linden, she turned left. He now almost ran to the corner, hoping not to lose her altogether.

Then he saw her standing at the next corner, waiting to cross the wide boulevard. A green-uniformed policeman was in the middle of the intersection directing traffic. With a whistle and machinelike motions, the policeman instantly stopped all vehicles in one direction and commanded movement from the other. She started across the street. Rob followed, now not more than twenty paces behind her.

On reaching the other side, she went into a cafe next to the corner. Now the moment of decision was at hand. She was in a confined space, a public place. Here he could go in and speak to her, possibly even join her at a table. He hesitated, pondering whether to forget this foolishness and head on back to West Berlin. It was only three hours before the time he and Christa had agreed to meet. There was no way to know how long it would take him to clear through the railroad station and get out of this place. Also, it suddenly occurred to him that he did not know what he would say to this East German female doctor if he had another chance to talk with her. He realized that he was too caught up in the mystery of Wolfgang's presence here and the meeting of these two to abandon matters now. Taking a deep breath, he opened the door to the cafe and walked in.

He came first into a foyer with the usual coat-check room. He had yet to see a GDR restaurant without a mandatory coat-checking procedure. Having nothing to check, he passed into the large dining room. The front windows faced directly on the sidewalk along Unter den Linden. Through the rear windows he could see trees and flowers. He stopped and looked around. There was no receptionist on duty. At a far table, he saw a waitress serving a beer to a lone man. Although it was still early for an evening meal, several people were eating, but most were drinking beer or coffee.

At first he did not see her, but after scanning the room for a minute, he spotted her sitting alone at a table next to the rear windows. She was gazing out toward the leafy courtyard, chin in hand as though lost in thought. He circled to the other side of the room so as to approach from her side and rear.

"Excuse me," he said in German, as he reached the table, "I believe that we have met before."

Startled, she dropped her hand and swung her head abruptly toward him. She looked directly at him with a severe, slightly befuddled expression.

Continuing in German and making an all-out effort to sound surprised, he said: "I believe that you and I sat at the same table in the dining room at the Interhotel in Leipzig just a week ago."

He waited for a response, almost holding his breath for what seemed to be an interminable moment. A hint of a smile flickered at the corners of her lips, and her eyes lost their blankness.

"Yes, I believe that is correct," she said in an official, expressionless voice.

"I decided after seeing Leipzig to visit Berlin. I have just come to have a cup of coffee. You can imagine my surprise when I recognized you sitting here."

"It is a surprise to see you again and here in Berlin," she said, her voice warming slightly.

Rob was standing awkwardly by the table. She showed no inclination to invite him to sit down. He had the choice of leaving or groping forward.

"May I sit here and have a cup of coffee?" he asked, motioning toward the chair opposite her. He felt somewhat less ill at ease in making this inquiry because of the custom in Europe of sharing restaurant tables with strangers—a custom he had noticed generally observed in the GDR.

"Yes, of course," she replied in a manner that revealed neither pleasure nor displeasure at the thought.

A waitress appeared just as he took his seat. "Let me buy you something to drink," he said, studying her face.

"That is good of you," she said. "I would like a cup of coffee," she said to the waitress. Rob ordered the same, and the waitress left.

"I believe that we were speaking English when we were at dinner in Leipzig," she said. "Do you often speak German?"

"My German is not excellent, but I do try to speak it to get practice. If you would like to practice your English, I would be happy to help," he said with a broad smile.

Her professional features relaxed a bit, but there was no real smile.

"Yes, perhaps we should speak in English," she responded, switching to it.

"Well, that makes it easier for me," Rob said. "If my memory is correct, you are a medical doctor, and you were in Leipzig to attend a medical meeting."

"Your memory is very good. And if my memory is correct, you are an American, and you are visiting the GDR as a tourist."

"You are right," Rob said, beginning to feel more comfortable. "I also recall that you are an eye doctor and you work at the Charité Hospital here in Berlin."

A flicker of surprise showed in her face. "You do indeed have a good memory. What else do you remember?"

"Not much else, except that," he added after a pause, "you were a very attractive woman."

"That is the kind of statement I hear American men making on television."

"It was intended to be a compliment." Something told him that she was not seriously offended. He even wondered whether she was half joking.

The waitress arrived with two cups of coffee. As she placed them on the table, Rob studied the woman across from him. There was a somber beauty about her. Her light brown hair was ear length and almost straight. Her large green eyes had a sad and haunting quality.

When the waitress left, they each sipped coffee. Rob broke the silence. "Incidentally, my name is Robert Kirkman. I am a professor of law in an American university. I don't think I told you that in Leipzig."

"No, I do not remember that," she said.

Rob had hoped that the announcement of his name would prompt the announcement of hers, but she said nothing more.

"If I have a problem with my eyes while I am here, should I come to see you?" he asked, hoping to get to her identity indirectly.

"No, I would not be the person to see. I am engaged mainly in research. I do see patients, but only with a senior doctor."

"Well, I don't expect to have any problems. I have good eyes. But, in any case, could you tell me your name?"

"Why do you want to know my name?" she asked in the typically blunt German style. She was deadly serious.

"Oh, no special reason," he said with a soft laugh, trying to lighten the mood. "It's customary in the States for people to introduce themselves to each other when they meet, so I gave you my name. I thought as a matter of courtesy you might also introduce yourself."

She sipped more coffee. She appeared to be deep in thought. She put the cup down, gazing out the window toward the trees and flowers that filled the small patio. Then she looked at Rob and said, "I think that Americans must be more casual about that than Germans. But I will tell you my name. It is Maria Egloffsberg."

Rob had just lifted his cup to take a sip of coffee. As the name struck his ears his muscles locked. He bent every ounce of his concentration on remaining expressionless. Slowly, he lowered the cup to its saucer and dabbed his lips with his napkin.

He repeated matter-of-factly, "Maria Egloffsberg." Then he added in a low voice, "Let me see. Is that spelled—*auf Deutsch*—E-g-l-o-f-f-s-b-e-r-g?" He said each letter with its German pronunciation.

"Yes." She appeared to be about to say something else but then stopped and took a swallow from her cup.

Rob's mind was whirring. An East German female doctor named Egloffsberg is seen walking along an East Berlin street with Wolfgang von Egloffsberg. That sight, puzzling enough in itself, now assumed the aura of profound mystery. Although the woman announced no "von" with her name, that did not seem strange. The use of that prefix had been dropped in this workers' state, probably because almost everyone entitled to such had either gone west, died, or been killed.

He searched her face, looking for a family resemblance. The shape of the head and face were not markedly different from Martina's, but he could not find a close resemblance to anyone he had seen at Prinzenheim. Moreover, in all of the discussion there about the family, he had heard no mention of any such person as this.

"I now remember something else you said in Leipzig," Rob said, wanting to burrow into this mystery but not knowing quite how to proceed.

"What is that?" she asked with a mild touch of interest.

"I think that you said you work with blind people."

"I may have said that," she said, her flat, detached voice returning. "I do work with the blind, and I was visiting the library in Leipzig that makes tapes and Braille material for the blind.

"Does your work give you any opportunity to meet people from other countries who are involved with the blind?" he asked cautiously.

"Occasionally it does. There is a European organization that includes every country in Europe. We meet with their representatives sometimes."

She glanced at her watch. "I must be going," she said, pushing her cup forward and putting her crumpled paper napkin on the table.

Desperate not to let her disappear into the void of East Berlin, Rob asked uncertainly, "Would it be possible for me to come by the Charité Hospital sometime and see it on the inside? It is a famous place."

"I do not think that is possible," she said in a straight East German business tone. "Only authorized persons are allowed in the hospital. You would need to have authorization from the hospital director or the Ministry of Health, and they give authorizations only to persons who need to go there on business."

"Well, I am sorry to hear that," he said with a disappointed air. "Would there be any possibility that I could visit the offices of the blind organization?" he added, groping for some way to keep a hold on her.

"I really do not know. You would have to make inquiry there. You must realize," she said in a lowered voice, "that it is not normal for Americans to come into the East and simply walk into various places, and I cannot help you."

She was standing up. He rose with her. "Thank you for the coffee," she said, extending her hand, a gesture that he had not expected. He grasped its warm firmness and held it for some seconds.

"Perhaps we shall meet still another time," Rob said with a smile.

Her face was unreadable. She said nothing. Their eyes met for an instant, but hers communicated nothing that Rob could interpret. She turned and walked rapidly through the tables of the dining room, out through the foyer, and into Unter den Linden.

For the second time he was watching her leave a restaurant with no reason to think that they would ever meet again, but there was a difference this time. She was no longer a totally anonymous East German woman. He now knew that she actually knew Wolfgang von Egloffsberg and had the same last name. He could not rest with that unexplained.

Chapter 15

THE KEMPINSKI HOTEL AND its dining room had to be counted among the best in West Berlin. That reputation had moved Rob to select it as the site for his dinner with Christa Schreibholz. His sense of history also attracted him to it because it bore the name of an old, well-known prewar Berlin hotel. For West Berlin, the Kempinski could hardly have been more centrally positioned. It was on Kurfurstendamm, only two blocks from the Am Zoo where Rob was staying.

The dining room was of moderate size, and it exuded a quiet elegance. Spotlessly clean glassware, china, and silver glistened in candlelight. An ample supply of waiters in dinner jackets moved efficiently about the room. Rob and Christa sat at a table for two positioned against the wall. They had placed their orders, including a bottle of Mosel wine that she had suggested.

She asked about his day's experiences in East Berlin. He described with more hilarity than he had felt at the time, his protracted clearance process in the Friedrichstrasse station and his explorations of Unter den Linden, the side streets, and the university.

"Did you get to Alexanderplatz?" she asked.

"No, I was so absorbed with the other sights that I never reached it." He had decided, at least for the moment, not to mention his spotting of Wolfgang and the diversion which it caused. "I want to go over again, and I'll cover that then."

"I go over almost every month on business. The ministries I deal with are around and near Alexanderplatz."

"Exactly what do you do?"

"A lot of it is sensitive, as you can understand. My office has charge of all legal matters concerning the relations between the two Berlins. You would be surprised at how many questions arise—many of them small and not spectacular at all—things like sewage and water service, the

S-Bahn, electricity, mail, and so on. A lot of the problems are considered confidential, so I really can't talk a lot about what I do."

This East-West division, Rob thought, has created a land of secrecy. On the East side he could not get into a world-famous hospital. Now on the West side he could not hear what a public law office was doing. Shifting direction, Rob asked, "Do you work some with Major Catron?"

"Oh, not much. Sometimes we have a problem that requires discussion with the American military authorities, but he and I are mainly social friends." After a momentary hesitation and a nervous laugh, she added, "It is nothing serious."

"Your grandmother told me that you had some American admirers here, so when I met him last night I assumed that he was one of them."

"I consider us good friends, and that is all," she said, giving Rob a look that he took to convey special sincerity. "But," she went on, "he may have more serious interest than I do."

Their wine had been poured, and the lobster bisque had been served. They had both ordered the same meal. The main course was to be turbot, a North Sea fish highly recommended by the waiter.

"I believe that my grandmother told me that you're not married. Is that correct?" she asked.

"That is correct. I am what we call a bachelor."

"Well, I do not understand that," she said with an impish smile. "How can such a handsome and intelligent man go as long as you have without having married?"

Rob felt a slight blush rise to his cheeks. Comments like that from women made him nervous, but he kept his footing. "I could ask the same question of you: How can such a good-looking woman have escaped all men?"

"Well, for one thing," she said, "men—or at least what could be called eligible men—are not that plentiful in West Berlin. For another, many German men do not appeal to me."

"That leaves the rest of the world," Rob shot back with a laugh. "American men don't seem to be in short supply here."

"I think I told you at Prinzenheim that I find American men more appealing than German men."

Again, Rob felt uncomfortable. He could not interpret her look. Her blue eyes, sparkling in the candlelight, seemed to bore into his. He could not rid his mind of his dream of the Remberton party. The sensation was intensified by what he now saw across the table. Christa was wearing a long-sleeved blue dress with a sharp V neckline. It made a perfect frame for her blue eyes and blond hair. His discomfort was growing, however, because he felt himself being captivated by this German woman to a far greater extent than he thought sensible.

They were now digging into the turbot, which was delicious with a wine and butter sauce. In the exhilaration of the moment, Rob pronounced it to surpass anything he had previously tasted. The waiter had refilled their glasses with the Mosel. It was now time, Rob thought, to move to more serious subjects.

"I had a long conversation with your Uncle Wolfgang at Prinzenheim," he said. "But I didn't quite understand what he does these days. He left while I was there, saying that he was going on a business trip, but I did not hear what his business is." Here Rob stopped and took a bite of fish, hoping Christa would pick up the point.

She took a swallow of wine and said nothing for a long moment. He could not tell whether she was deliberately stalling. Then she spoke.

"I myself do not know exactly what he does. He has no regular employment, but he is active in many things. I would say that he has three consuming interests—blind persons and their problems, the church, and Germany."

Rob sensed a change in her mood. The light, flirtatious air was gone. "What does he do in connection with the blind?" he asked.

"I do not know many details. He works with the Association of Blind Intellectuals based at Marburg. That group and others try to help the blind who have professional jobs, those who are not manual workers. They also work with international blind groups. Uncle Wolfi once went to the States."

"Yes, he said that he had been to a training center for the blind—in Illinois, I believe. In his work with the blind organization, does Wolfgang have occasion now to visit any other countries?"

"I think that he does sometimes make other trips, but I really do not know much about where he goes." Her manner suggested that she preferred not to pursue the subject.

"What of the church?" Rob asked. "Do you know much about his interest there?"

"Only that he believes that the severing of the Protestant church between East and West in 1968 was a disaster. This is closely tied to his ideas about Germany. He is deeply disturbed over the division. He thinks that there is some God-given right for the German people to belong to one nation. After the creation of the two states in 1949, the only uniting force that remained was the Protestant church. He clung to that as the force that would hold Germany together and one day reunite it. When the East Germans forced a church split, he was even more upset. By the way, have you ever heard of Dietrich Bonhoeffer?"

"Yes," Rob replied as he speared the last piece of fish with his fork. "I have read about him. Your Uncle Wolfgang just mentioned him the other day. Why do you ask?"

"Uncle Wolfi actually met Bonhoeffer, had conversations with him, and heard him speak. Bonhoeffer is one of his heroes. He has elevated him to a kind of sainthood. I have a feeling that Bonhoeffer has a strange and almost abnormal influence on his life. I get the impression that he thinks that Bonhoeffer showed uncommon courage as a Christian in the face of overwhelming evil, even to the point of death, and that he—Uncle Wolfi—should follow his example. However, because he is blind, he is frustrated in doing this. I think that he sees the East German regime to be the same as the Nazi regime and believes that he should do now what Bonhoeffer did then."

"How does Wolfgang put these ideas into action? I had the impression that he lived a quiet and retiring life at Prinzenheim with his mother."

"Then you have the wrong impression. He has anything but a quiet life, and he is not at Prinzenheim for much of the time. You just happened to be there when he was home for a few days."

"Where does he spend his time, and how does he pursue these ideas?" Rob persisted.

"I am not really sure," she said as the waiter emptied the last drops from the wine bottle into their glasses and stuck it upside down in the ice bucket. "He has an apartment in Frankfurt where he stays at times, but he moves around a lot."

"Does he ever go into the GDR or East Berlin?"

"I think that he does, but I really do not know."

The brevity—almost abruptness—of her answers told Rob that she did not wish to continue this line of conversation. Although believing that she knew more of her uncle's activities than she was revealing, he thought it prudent to shift the discussion. "I found it fascinating to learn when I was at lunch with you and your grandmother that you were reared in the GDR and that your parents still live there. Do you see them much?"

"Not as much as I would like. As you know, there are restrictions on West Berliners entering the GDR. I have been able to visit them only about once or twice a year, but we have reason to hope that this will improve. Of course, they have not been able to leave at all. My father has just turned sixty-five, so he should be able to visit us in the future. They will allow pensioners more freedom. This is a crazy, sick situation. Here I am in this island in the middle of the GDR. They are physically much closer to West Germany than I am, but I can go there at any time. They cannot come into this island or go west."

They decided against dessert and simply ordered coffee. A group of American businessmen was getting up from a table across the room, laughing and talking loudly with their guest who appeared to be a German.

Rob said, "I've always been curious as to how churches could function in a Marxist-Leninist state. Churches seem to have enough difficulties without the whole power of the government arrayed against them."

"My father would tell you that the church began in a pagan society, and has existed in such societies at various times in history, and has always survived and sometimes even thrived. He likes to quote that line from the Bible saying that the gates of hell cannot prevail against it."

She was interrupted by the arrival of the waiter with the coffee. When he was gone, she continued.

"I mentioned that Uncle Wolfi was a dedicated admirer—I should say worshipper—of Dietrich Bonhoeffer. My father also knew Bonhoeffer, at least casually, and was also profoundly influenced by his life. I think that it was because of Bonhoeffer and his death that Father decided to remain in the East. He could easily have gone to the West before they closed the Berlin sector borders."

For a moment they were quiet, each stirring milk into their coffee. A low hum of conversation mingled with muffled clinking of cutlery and plates, filling the dining room with a pleasant sound of warmth and well-being.

"Say," Rob said suddenly, his face brightening, "I have an idea. Didn't you say that your parents live at Halle?"

"Yes, they do. Father is the head pastor in the main church there."

"Halle is one of the cities I most want to see. My favorite college professor, a history professor, studied at the university there before the First World War. I also want to do some more sightseeing in the GDR. I could rent a car here and drive to Halle. If you think that it would cause no problem, I would like to call on your parents in Halle. And, of course, I would love for you to accompany me, if you could arrange it."

"Well," she said with a smile, "there is nothing I would enjoy more than a drive with you to Halle and the opportunity to see my mother and father. It has been eight months since we have been with each other; but I am afraid that it is not possible for me to go at this time. It would take quite a while to get a visa, if I could get one at all just now. Also, there are some pressing matters that require me to be here."

"That's too bad," Rob said, disappointment showing in his voice. "It would be interesting and fun to have you along to show me the places I should see—as well as for the company. What do you think, though, of my going alone and calling on your parents, at least for a brief chat?"

"Probably," she said hesitatingly, holding her coffee cup just above the saucer, "it would be all right. Do not misunderstand. I would like very much for you to meet them and for them to meet you. I just want to think about it for a minute."

"Well, if there is doubt about it in your mind, I wouldn't want to do it. I certainly don't want to cause them any problems."

"At times," she said, putting down her cup, "there are some difficulties connected with westerners and pastors in the GDR. The authorities are, as you know, suspicious of all things western. And they always have suspected the clergy of somehow being in a conspiracy with the West Germans. However, that hostile attitude has diminished somewhat since the churches in the GDR broke off and formed a separate organization. No," she murmured as though thinking out loud, "I am inclined to think that there would be no harm in your stopping by to see them for a short visit. In fact, the more I now think about it, the more I like the idea. They would really enjoy a visit from an American, especially one who has met my grandmother, Wolfgang, and me."

"If you feel comfortable about it, I think I would like to do it. Tomorrow is Saturday. I could rent a car in the morning and also make a reservation at the Interhotel at Halle. I suppose there would be no difficulty with my dropping into your father's church for the Sunday morning service, would there?"

"Oh, I do not think so. Services are open, and anyone can simply walk in and take a seat. It would probably be better to try to call on my father at his church office. He could then get mother from their apartment. It is not far away." After a reflective pause, she said with fresh enthusiasm, "Here, let me write you a note of introduction."

Christa rooted around in her purse and pulled out a small notebook and pen. Putting the notebook on the table, she wrote rapidly for a couple of minutes. "Here is what I have said," she announced, proceeding to read from the paper she had torn from the notebook.

> Dear Parents,
>
> This note will introduce you to Professor Robert Kirkman. He has recently visited Grandmother and Uncle Wolfi. I have met him there and again in Berlin. He is interested in meeting you and seeing Halle. He is a very nice gentleman, and I think that you will enjoy talking with him. I am fine. I hope that all is well with both of you.
>
> Love,
> Christa

She read the note as she had written it, in German. The melodious Germanic rhythm of her voice shot tingles along the back of his neck. Certain types of female German voices moved him in a strange way. He could not decide which was more sensual—her English flavored with a German accent or the pure German.

When she next spoke, after reading her note, he realized that he had been staring at her. "You notice," she said, "that I have revealed nothing about you except your name and title and have said nothing to reveal the identities of anyone else. I would have liked to have said more, but I wrote it this way in case the note gets lost or by chance the GDR guards come across it in a search at the checkpoint. I think this is unlikely, but we must be careful. At the checkpoints they normally do not search the pockets of Americans, so put this in your wallet or inside coat pocket."

Rob carefully folded the note and placed it in his wallet. The bill had arrived on the table. He counted out the marks to cover it and the tip. Standing, he said, "Let's take a walk and have an after-dinner drink somewhere else."

They walked through the long, rather narrow lobby of the Kempinski and out into the Kurfurstendamm. They turned left and headed toward its culmination amidst a welter of shops, automobile dealerships, restaurants, and night spots. The street was filled with Mercedes. They were again in the midst of the nightime carnival atmosphere. The crowd of pedestrians thickened, and Rob took Christa's elbow to steer her through the mass of old and young Germans, Americans, and unidentifiable others. They reached open space where the crowd thinned. Rob slid his hand down Christa's arm to her hand, clasping it firmly in his. They walked on, not saying anything for a while.

"There is a nice little place just off the Europa Center where we could have something to drink," she said, breaking the silence. "I must be going soon. Even though tomorrow is Saturday, I have to be in the office."

Passing the ruined tower of the Kaiser Wilhelm Memorial Church, they came to the plaza bordering the starkly contemporary structure housing the Europa Center. She led him around a corner and into a small cocktail lounge. Only two tables were occupied. They took seats at the rear. Rob suggested Cointreau, and Christa agreed. The waiter almost immediately produced two small glasses filled with the thick orange-flavored liqueur.

"After you left Prinzenheim, my grandmother told me about you and what you had been doing in Germany."

"What did she say?"

"It was a strange story. She said that your father had found her husband in the trenches on the western front in 1918 just at the moment he was dying, and your father had taken a photograph from him which showed her and her two sons, my Uncle Wolfi and his older brother Kurt."

"So far you have it right. What else did she say?"

"She said that you found the photograph after your father's death a few months ago, then set out to find her. That sounds really odd. Did you really do that?"

"Yes. Incidentally, there was also the handwritten letter from your grandmother to her husband. That is how I knew of Bachdorf. It does all sound strange, but I have always been interested in exploring the unusual—especially the historical. That is partly why I want to go to Halle tomorrow."

"My grandmother said that you went all the way to Bachdorf on the Elbe. That is a long way inside the GDR. My mother grew up there, as Grandmother probably told you, although her father was not of the von Egloffsberg family. My mother never knew her father; he died when she was an infant."

"Have you ever been to Bachdorf?"

"No, I have not. For one reason, it is a long way from any place I have ever lived. It is not directly on a railroad, and we never had a car. Few people in the GDR have cars. A very important reason is that my mother does not want to make known her connection with that family. This is a hard point to explain to outsiders, but I will try."

"Yes, why is that?" asked Rob.

I believe the von Egloffsberg family to be an honorable family. Its members have played prominent parts in German history. My grandmother, whom I love, married one. And I love Uncle Wolfi, who is one. They have suffered all the heartbreaks that millions of Germans have suffered in the twentieth century. Of course, the sensitive time is from 1933 to 1945. As far as I have ever been able to determine, they were not what I would call Fascists. To my knowledge, no member of that family was a member of the Nazi party. It is true that Wolfgang and Kurt served in the Wehrmacht as officers, and it is true that the family owned a huge amount of land on which many worked. For those reasons, the East German authorities and the occupying forces of the Soviet Union deemed them Fascists or, as they often say, enemies of the people. That is a lengthy way of explaining why my mother, who decided to live in the GDR as the wife of a pastor, thought it wise not to disclose her connection to the family, even though there is no blood relationship."

"Is it possible to keep connections like that secret in a state like the GDR?"

"Well," she said, "you must remember that my parents were married before the war was over. By the time the Russsians arrived, she was identified only as Pastor Schreibholz's wife. She has never been in any trouble with the authorities, and they have paid no attention to her. If they ever did begin some kind of investigation, they would probably uncover the fact that before her marriage she had used the name of von Egloffsberg. Then there might be trouble. The irony of that would be that she is not really a von Egloffsberg. Her father was named Kremser, and that is the name she was born with. My grandmother gave her the von Egloffsberg name after Herr Kremser died."

Rob thought now of the sad-eyed and obviously intelligent young woman who had identified herself as Maria Egloffsberg, sitting with him just a few hours earlier in the restaurant on Unter den Linden. She was as pretty as Christa, but in a different way. Given the clothes, the cosmetics, and more attention to hairstyle, she could easily equal, and perhaps surpass Christa in attractiveness, he mused to himself.

"Is the name Egloffsberg common in Germany? Are there any members of the family with that name living in the GDR?"

Christa was holding her Cointreau glass and looking vacantly across the room. "The family is very old," she said hesitantly, "and there have been several branches. It is possible that there are some in the GDR, but I doubt that there are many. Families like that all moved west in 1945 or shortly after the war. As you know, land held by those families was confiscated. There is no doubt that a lot of those people would have been put to death or imprisoned by the Russians or East German Communists if they had stayed."

Once again, Rob sensed a curtain falling around her. He was not getting all the facts. He felt certain of that. He had had enough conversations in Germany to realize that the curtain would rise and fall, at times allowing straightforward information to be imparted, at others shutting off the facts. Perhaps it was her mother's sensitive position as a GDR resident that made Christa reticent. Whatever the reason, he could not shake off the suspicion that she was not telling him all there was to know about the Egloffsberg family in the GDR today.

"This is enjoyable," she said, "but I must go because I have a long work day tomorrow."

"Will I have an opportunity to see you after I come back from Halle so that I can give a report on my trip?"

"I would love to hear about it," she exclaimed with a revived enthusiasm. "That reminds me. I do not think that you have my father's address." she pulled the small notebook from her purse, tore a page out, and scribbled on it: Pastor Ernst Schreibholz, Marienstrasse 21.

"Here," she said, handing him the paper, "put this in some pocket away from my note to my parents. Actually, it would be better if you would memorize the address and then discard this paper before you cross into the GDR. I am probably being too cautious. Americans usually have no trouble, and they are not searched as thoroughly as some others. But you can never be too careful."

"I understand. I can remember the address. I assume this is in the center of the city of Halle."

"Yes. It is only a few blocks from the church, which is on the marketplace right next to the tall twin towers—the Red Tower—the major landmark of Halle. As we were saying a little while ago, it would probably be better if you called first at the church office. My father is usually there on Saturday afternoons and Sundays."

As they emerged from the bar, they were struck with the coolness of the night. A breeze was blowing, rustling the leaves of the trees bordering the street. It was almost chilly.

Their route back toward the Am Zoo Hotel took them through the sunken plaza along Kurfurstendamm next to the remains of the Kaiser Wilhelm Memorial Church. The crowds had gone, and the scene was almost deserted. The splashing water of the fountain in the center of the plaza drowned out all other sounds.

They had joined hands and were standing before the large circular pool of water into which the myriad streams were cascading. In the center of the pool stood a huge sphere, ruptured through its middle. It was a globe, a representation of the whole earth, but an earth badly ajar. In the illumination of street lights, through the plumes of wind-blown water, they saw the brief inscription: The Fractured World.

Rob and Christa stood there for a long time, holding hands and saying nothing under the hypnotic spell of the wavering, splashing streams of water. They stood there as though they were before the altar of a church. There the Berliners had expressed in a simple broken sphere and three words all the heartache, torment, and reality of the late twentieth century. Standing there, with the Wall a mile away, Rob felt himself at the center of the rupture. Tomorrow he would again plunge across that divide and enter the other half of this fractured world. At a deeper level, he sensed too that Germany was only a symbol—maybe even the epicenter—of the whole world divided against itself, as this water-drenched globe in front of him so eloquently stated.

Christa spoke at last quietly and slowly. "I really must go."

"I'll get a taxi and take you to your apartment," Rob said.

"Thank you," she said, "but that will not be necessary. I use taxis alone all the time. Just help me find one."

Rob hailed a gray Mercedes cab. It pulled over to the curb, and he opened the rear door.

"I'll be returning here on Sunday night, but it may be late. May I call you on Monday to tell you about my adventures?"

"Yes," she said, nodding her head. "Be careful, and give my love to my parents."

Rob took her right hand in his, his left hand grasping her arm. Impulsively, she leaned forward, kissed him lightly on the cheek, and stepped quickly into the taxi. As he bent down to close the door, she smiled at him and said in a lilting voice, "Good night."

Rob stood at that spot until the taxi was out of sight. Christa's perfume suffused his nostrils for only a few moments, but the memory of her soft, warm face against his remained. He turned and walked slowly toward the Am Zoo.

Chapter 16

THE NIGHT WIND BROUGHT rain. Saturday dawned wet and overcast. Rob had rented a car—another Opel—around the corner from the hotel and had threaded his way through the rainy streets of West Berlin to Checkpoint Bravo in the southwestern corner of the city. This was an entry point directly into the GDR and not into East Berlin. The inspection, checking of papers, and booking of a room at the Interhotel at Halle had taken only an hour—a quick clearance, Rob reckoned, judged by the usual East German standards with which he was coming to feel familiar.

Beyond the checkpoint, he had passed into countryside for a short distance and then skirted the southern edge of Potsdam. For more than an hour, he then drove through level, open country on a hard-top road that resembled the two-lane roads he had known as a child. The route was punctuated by an occasional village, a cluster of dark red-brick cottages and shops, looking grim and lifeless in the drizzling rain and sunless sky.

Now Rob was in Wittenberg. The 1904 *Baedeker* map of the town did not help him make his way through the outskirts. He went on instinct toward the center and shortly found himself pulling into the marketplace where there were more than enough parking places for the half-dozen cars. He stopped in a spot directly in front of the Rathaus—the fifteenth-century town hall. There, just to his left, was a pedestalled statue of the man who had put Wittenberg on the map for all time—Martin Luther. To Rob's right was an equally heroic statue of Luther's disciple, Phillip Melanchton.

Rob sat for a while in the car, hearing no motors, no traffic, but only the rain drumming on the car roof. He reread *Baedeker*'s text and studied the map some more, feeling again the quickening of his pulse and the slowly rising sense of excitement. He was now on the very ground where Martin Luther had lived, studied, taught, preached, and thundered forth the message of the Reformation, shaking Christendom to its foundations, with ramifications still felt over the entire world.

The rain slackened into a light mist. He got out of the car, buttoned up his raincoat, crammed a crushed, all-purpose hat on his head, and struck off on foot. He had identified three objectives in Wittenberg, and he saw the first just to the east of the marketplace. It was the City Church, the Stadt Kirche, its steeple piercing the low clouds.

He made his way into the sanctuary and sat down in a pew. It was devoid of human life and all sounds of the world outside. Postings on a bulletin board, however, gave evidence that this was a living, functioning church. He sat there for a quarter-hour, letting his imagination play over the scene where Luther had preached many times. That was 450 years ago. Americans had difficulty comprehending such time spans. Jamestown had not even been settled, he mused, and along the Tombigbee and the Alabama there were only Indians and forests, silently awaiting the onslaught of European civilization. All the genes in his body had come from ancestors who were then still on this side of the Atlantic—some right here in Germany, perhaps not far from where he now sat. Did any of them ever hear Luther preach? What did his forebears, the von Trepnitz family, think of the Reformation? It reached them somehow because the Baron von Trepnitz, who reached South Carolina over two hundred years after Luther's time, was Protestant.

Coming out of the church, Rob walked along Colligienstrasse to his second objective, a cluster of buildings standing close by the monastery and the residence of Martin Luther that had at one time housed the University of Wittenberg. The university, however, was long gone, consolidated with the University at Halle and moved there in the early nineteenth century. Its old buildings were now occupied by a variety of state bureaus and district offices of the sort used to keep this Marxist-Leninist society functioning. Luther's house and the monastery were closed, but Rob stood on the sidewalk for a while to record the scene in his mind and to impress on himself that this was the very house of the great man.

He heard across the years the memorable voice of Professor George Marks Wilton saying that Luther was the greatest of all Germans. Wilton had believed that Luther's translation of the Bible, which established a literary standard for all written German, made Luther the most influential German in history. With those words playing in his mind, Rob sensed an almost physical presence of the redoubtable Wilton, who had himself walked the streets of Wittenberg six decades earlier.

He now struck off toward his final objective, the one that excited him most of all. Walking along Colligienstrasse past the marketplace, he came in sight of it a half mile to the west: the Castle Church, where

Luther had posted his ninety-five theses on All Hallows Eve 1519, thereby kicking off the Reformation.

The church was not at all what Rob had expected. Although he had never seen a picture of it, in his youth he had read and heard of that dramatic posting of Luther's theses on the door. He had a clear image in his mind of the scene. In it he saw a village church with a tall steeple, situated in a busy market square. What he now saw ahead of him, however, was a combination palace and castle with round, rather squat towers. There was no church steeple. Indeed, it was difficult to know that there was a church there. It turned out to be a corner segment of the sprawling structure that for centuries housed the Electors of Saxony. The vast and somber complex was set on grounds just off the street, surrounded by grass and trees.

Looking past the palace and into the distance, Rob saw it—saw it for the second time in East Germany—beyond several hundred yards of trees and grass. There, low and wide and brown, flowed the Elbe. He had stood on its banks at Bachdorf, far to the southeast, where it flowed up from Dresden and Meissen. Now here it was again, with its flat, unrippled surface, pushing relentlessly ever northward through the heart of Germany toward the Baltic as it had for ages, not knowing East from West, Protestant from Catholic. Luther had seen it from here, walked along it, and crossed it many times, as had prehistoric tribes and later the armies of many nations. The follies of mankind and the vicissitudes of fortune affected it not. It kept moving inexorably to the sea, as all rivers do.

This ever-flowing band of water came to history's center stage in 1945 when it was made the line beyond which the Americans and British would not go. That meant, Rob reflected, that no American soldiers set foot in Wittenberg, even though from the far side of the river they could see the steeple of the City Church and the squat towers of the castle. There they sat, waiting for the Red Army to pile into this heart of Luther land. Thus the citizens of Wittenberg experienced commisars, the Russian language, and banners bearing the hammer and sickle, while the Americans looked on from across the river.

Now he was standing before the great double doors to the church. The original wooden doors had burned long ago, *Baedeker* informed him, and they had been replaced with bronze doors on which the ninety-five theses had been embossed. All of this he now saw. Standing precisely where Luther had stood, he felt the metal lettering with his fingers, making an effort to translate some of the Latin. The chilly mist of the somber day cut through to him.

Inside, he found the long-ago Electors of Saxony memorialized in statuary. In the floor, in front of the altar, he came to the simple slabs marking the graves of Martin Luther and Phillip Melanchton. The church was deserted. Rob was becoming accustomed to finding churches in East Germany bereft of people, at least on weekdays. Still, he had the sense of a functioning church, but of what magnitude he did not know.

He stood at the graves for long minutes, ruminating again over the tumultuous career of Luther and the wrenching events of German history since his time. What would Luther think and say today, here in this church in the midst of an officially godless society—a regime that rejected, root and branch, all that Luther believed? Somebody has got to be radically mistaken, Rob thought. Either there is a God or there is not. Whatever view one took on that, one proposition seemed indisputable: If God does exist, there can be no question as to who will prevail, and Marxism-Leninism is ultimately doomed.

Rob returned to his car in the marketplace, and in the gray mist of midday he crossed the long bridge over the Elbe and headed southwest toward Halle.

Two hours later, after three stops for directions and one false turn, Robert Kirkman parked the Opel in front of the Interhotel in Halle. The highway had fed into a long street of buildings, residences, and shops, most of the structures dating from the twenties and thirties. Across the front of one ran a hundred-foot banner proclaiming: "Marx Lives in Us and in Our Deeds." He had passed the SED district party headquarters and had come shortly to what appeared to be the newest and perhaps main commercial district of the city. There he had spotted the hotel, a blocklike multistoried construction of no architectural distinction. Strongly resembling other GDR interhotels, it had probably been built within the last ten years.

His room was furnished almost identically to his rooms in Weimar and Leipzig. The single bed consisted of a sturdy wooden frame holding a comfortable mattress, a folded eiderdown, and a soft, mushy pillow. A dresser, desk, lamp, and chair completed the set. Rob again imagined that single "peoples-owned" enterprise—designated, as all the state factories were, by the letters VEB—produced all the room furnishings for the GDR hotels. Life was certainly simpler in this economy. The director of the state-owned hotel enterprise—running all the hotels in the country—would need to waste no time shopping around for furnishings. He could skip all the trouble involved in getting estimates and comparative designs from competitive suppliers and manufacturers. He had merely to place an order with the state-owned enterprise making these beds, desks, dressers, and so on.

It was now four o'clock in the afternoon. The rain had stopped, but the day had grown no lighter. Indeed, with the lateness of the afternoon, it was fading to a duller gray. Rob quickly refreshed himself on the old center of the city with *Baedeker*, and then struck out on foot toward the marketplace to find the church where Pastor Ernst Schreibholz preached.

On leaving the hotel, he came to a large open plaza into which several streets fed from different directions. All was new and of post-war construction. Traffic, by GDR standards, was moderately heavy. He walked on, passing a forbidding-looking monument to the workers' movements. It consisted of a cluster of clenched fists raised skyward. His eye caught a portion of an inscription: 1848.

The monument struck a disquieting chord in Rob. It reminded him that he had turned his passport over to the hotel clerk, as he had been asked to do—"for his convenience"—so that the police could register him. He felt the same sense of being denuded that he had felt after having given up his passport at the hotels at Weimar and Leipzig, with an added uneasiness now. Perhaps it was the depressing somberness of the day, the militancy of the monument, and the strangeness of Halle. Compared to Weimar and Leipzig, Halle seemed more remote, more off the beaten track, a place where one might be more easily swallowed up and forgotten.

It was extraordinary, he thought, and one of the retrogressive features of the twentieth century, that a piece of paper such as a passport could mean the difference between freedom and imprisonment, between being a person and being nobody. Without a passport, a man simply did not exist for official purposes. And yet, here he was, walking through the streets of this town deep inside this Marxist-Leninist country on a Saturday afternoon with no passport. At any moment, the police could stop him. He would have no papers. They could lock him up, and who would know the difference?

This last thought lingered disturbingly in his mind. The only human being who had any idea where he was at this moment was Christa Schreibholz in West Berlin. Perhaps if he did not call her in a couple of days she might wonder where he had gone. But would it occur to her that he had been imprisoned by the GDR authorities? She might assume that he had decided to depart for America and would dismiss him from her mind. He soothed himself slightly by imagining that after a period of weeks he would be missed back in the States, and somebody would initiate an inquiry. Investigation would, he reassured himself, at some point uncover his confinement in the East. But then what? The influence of the United States over the East Germans was not notably strong. As quickly as these thoughts flickered through his mind, he dismissed them as grim fantasy. After all, he had traveled several hundred miles across the GDR, driving and walking where he wanted and had encountered no trouble. No, he concluded, it was perfectly safe. He had been exposed to too many spy novels and too much cold-war propaganda.

Leaving the clenched fists and the busy new plaza behind him, he entered a long, narrow street closed to vehicular traffic. He passed shops and a church that was now a lecture hall and theatre. Turning a corner, he was surprised to find himself at the edge of the old marketplace.

His heart quickened, and he felt the historical impulses flowing again. What he saw before him, around a vast open space, was a scene from the Germany of old. Dominating the square was the venerable 270-foot-high Red Tower immediately next to the Market Church, the main object of this venture. On other sides were solid buildings, those heavy Germanic structures erected just before or after the turn of the century, when the German Reich was at its zenith. And there, just as *Baedeker* had reported seventy years and two world wars ago, was George Frederick Handel, garbed in the English court dress of his day, preserved in statuary form a few blocks from where his life had begun.

Rob had decided to try to make contact with Christa's father now. If he should miss him this afternoon, he would still have another chance to find him the following day. He headed toward the fifteenth-century church, walking diagonally across the square and crossing an intersecting network of trolley tracks before arriving at its steps.

In the narthex, he found assorted notices like those he had seen posted in other East German churches. One gave dates for upcoming weekday services. Another announced the Sunday schedule, showing a service at half past ten in the morning. There he would be, Rob said to himself. Though now quiet and empty, the church was obviously functioning.

Rob walked out to the street, around the corner, and alongside the church building. At the rear, he found an inconspicuous wooden door. A small plaque affixed to it at eye level bore the single word, *Büro.* He pressed the leverlike door handle, and the door opened inward. He stepped into a dim, short hallway. He was startled by the sudden appearance of a woman from a doorway to his left.

"*Ja*," she asked, "May I help you?"

"Is Pastor Schreibholz here?" Rob asked, remembering to speak in German. Christa had told him that few people in Halle spoke English and her father was not one of them.

"Yes, he is here," she said with a look that told Rob that he was not the usual visitor with whom she was accustomed to dealing.

"May I talk to him?"

"Please wait here," she said. "I will see." She went across the hall, opened a door, went in, and closed it behind her.

Almost immediately, she returned and said in a more friendly tone, "Pastor Schreibholz will talk to you."

Rob's apprehensions over this meeting had been growing. He was curious to meet this man. He was Christa's father, the man who had married the daughter of the Baroness von Egloffsberg amidst the disintegration of wartime Berlin. Most impressive of all to Rob was the fact that he was a living and breathing and actively working Protestant minister in the middle of East Germany—a man who had survived Nazis, war, and Communists and was still preaching. Schreibholz had become a daunting figure in Rob's mind, and he felt his pulse thumping as he approached the door being held open by the middle-aged woman.

As Rob walked through the door, the woman closed it behind him. The room was small. It had only one window over which curtains were pulled almost shut, leaving a narrow slot through which the gray light of the overcast late afternoon afforded some weak illumination. A table in the far corner was covered with books and papers. On another table nearer him stood a lamp holding a single light bulb surrounded by a brown paper shade. Beside the lamp, Rob saw facing him a stocky man with iron-gray hair. He was wearing metal-rimmed eyeglasses whose lenses were almost round. His clothes were not what Rob had expected on a clergyman. Instead, the open shirt collar and jacket—something of a cross between a windbreaker and a smoking jacket—were like the attire of many men Rob had seen on the streets all over the GDR.

"*Guten Tag*," the pastor said. "May I help you?" He spoke in a rich, full-timbered voice—a voice whose volume seemed to be turned down to adjust to the small size of the room. It was easy to imagine the volume raised to fill the far corners of a great church. The whole appearance of the man, as Rob could now perceive more clearly, was one of enormous power and strength. In the weathered and slightly lined face, Rob saw character, compassion, and wisdom. It was the face of a man who had seen much of the world's sorrows, but also a face of one who had not given up. His eyes were bright and alert behind the metal rims, and a smile spread into his cheeks as he spoke.

Speaking German deliberately and slowly, as he had to, Rob made his case as straightforward as he could. "My name is Robert Kirkman. I am an American, and I am visiting the GDR as a tourist. I have met your daughter Christa and also met her grandmother, the Baroness von Egloffsberg. Here is a letter that Christa asked me to give you."

Pastor Schreibholz took the paper which Rob handed to him. He unfolded it, tilted it toward the lamp, and read it slowly. "So," he said hesitantly, as though borrowing time to formulate his next words, "you have met my Christa?"

"Yes, sir, I have," Rob said in a firm voice, his apprehensions diminishing.

"Have a seat," Schreibholz said, pointing to a chair alongside the table.

Rob sat down, facing the pastor at the head of the table. This appeared to be his work place. A pencil was lying on a pad of paper, and two books were opened, one on top of the other, beside the pad. The large, sturdy hands rested on the table.

"Tell me now why you are in Halle?"

Rob explained that he was interested in seeing various parts of the GDR, that he had come to West Germany for a conference, that he had heard a lot about Halle years ago from one of his college professors, and that he had then met Christa and learned that her parents lived here. He went on to say that he thought it would be a special privilege to meet a pastor in the GDR and that Christa agreed that it would be all right for him to have at least a short visit with her parents. He concluded his explanation by apologizing for his German.

"You speak German very well. I should apologize because I do not speak English. I studied English many years ago, and I listen to it on the West German radio and television; but I have no way to practice it."

"I would like to talk with you, but I know that tomorrow is Sunday and that you are probably busy now."

"Ah," he exclaimed with a broadened smile, "I can talk for a little while. I am working on my sermon for tomorrow, but I still have time to finish it. Here you see me violating one of the basic points about preaching that I learned as a young man."

"What is that?"

"It is a rule that one should never wait until Saturday to prepare a sermon," he said almost laughing, his volume moving up a decibel or so. "It is a rule that I learned from the most impressive man I have ever known."

"Who was that?" Rob asked after having waited for a few seconds to hear more.

"His name was Dietrich Bonhoeffer. I do not know whether you have heard of him. He has been dead for almost thirty years."

"Yes, I have heard of him. He is well known in America. I must say that I have not read any of his writings. Christa mentioned that he had been an influential person in your life. He must have been an unusual man."

As though he could not contain the nervous energy within his powerful frame, Schreibholz rose from his chair and walked to the window. Rob noticed a slight limp, one leg appearing to be shorter than the other. He remembered that this defect had kept him out of the German army. It may well have saved his life. The pastor turned from the window and stood facing Rob with hands in his jacket pockets.

"I do not know anyone who spent any time in Dietrich Bonhoeffer's presence who was not profoundly affected. He had a spiritual force that could be felt almost physically. He was a large, strong man, and that added to the impression of Godlike presence."

This description of Bonhoeffer, Rob thought, could well be applied to this man himself. His voice had risen, and his face had taken on a glow.

"Bonhoeffer is responsible indirectly for my being here today. I came to know him in Berlin several years before the war started. I heard him talk several times, and I was one of a small group of men training for the ministry who attended some training sessions with him. He had been prohibited from public preaching. We all knew that he had been in America in the spring and summer of 1939 and had been urged to stay there by people at Union Theological Seminary. Instead, he chose to return to Germany to serve his people. In 1942, the Gestapo arrested him. I never saw him again after that. It was many months after the war ended that I learned that he had been hanged. The saddest part of it all was that he was killed only one month before the war ended. Only four weeks more and he would have survived."

"How is he responsible for your being here?"

"Knowing that he returned from safety and comfort in America to serve the German people in a time of great stress and trouble and that he paid for that decision with his life convinced me that I should stay with the people here in the East. I could easily have gone to the West. Many people urged me to do so before the borders were closed, but the memory of Bonhoeffer was burned into my mind, and I could not leave."

The pastor strode back to his chair and sat down. "Yes," he half sighed, "Bonhoeffer was one of the great men of our time. I have here all of his published writings." He waved his hand toward a bookcase behind his chair.

The bookcase was a five-foot-tall set of wooden shelves like countless Rob had seen in second-hand furniture stores. It needed painting, as did the entire room. The bare walls were dingy and devoid of pictures.

"Here is *The Cost of Discipleship* and *Ethics*," he continued, touching the spines of two of the books. "And here is a truly magnificent book that Christa gave me. It was published only two years ago. The title is *Letters and Papers from Prison*. It is a collection of letters that Bonhoeffer wrote to his parents and a close friend after he was arrested and put in prison in Tegel."

"Do you mean the Tegel that is a district in West Berlin?" Rob asked.

"Yes, a Gestapo prison was located there. That is where they held many political prisoners for investigation. Bonhoeffer was kept there for nearly two years. They then moved him to a tougher prison on the Prinz Albrecht Strasse and then finally to Flossenberg."

"It is surprising that so many letters survived," Rob commented.

"It is. His family and good friends tried to save most of those they received. He was limited in what he could write from prison, but they are rich in theological insights. He even wrote some poems and sent them out. Just listen to these lines," Schreibholz said, opening the book to a place where a dog-eared bookmark was stuck. Rob saw that several other bookmarks were sticking out at other points.

"If you are going to read a poem, please read slowly."

"Yes," Schreibholz said, his deep voice full of muted intensity. "Listen to Bonhoeffer speaking to us, speaking to us sitting here thirty years later. This poem is called 'Night Voices at Tegel' " Then he began to read slowly, intoning Bonhoeffer's lines reciting the torments of all sorts and conditions of mankind.

They sat in silence for some moments. "I hear in those words," the pastor said softly, "a call from the depths of human travail—a cry on behalf of all of the suffering. But Bonhoeffer did not despair. Not at all. Listen to these lines." He turned a page as he spoke. "I have had these passages marked here since I first read them." He read again, very slowly, lines in which Bonhoeffer spoke of a midnight brilliance in which the evil perish and the good overcome.

Turning more pages, he said, "And here—I will read only one more—here I think I hear Dietrich Bonhoeffer foretelling his own coming death. He must have had a premonition of it many months before the end. Listen to his words." Bonhoeffer's words depicted the irony of a beautiful summer day punctuated by muffled steps coming for him and his brother prisoners; he enjoined his brothers to think no longer of the present but of the future.

Rob heard in the rolling German cadences of Schreibholz's voice the signs of a powerful preacher. If he had any doubts about his plans in Halle, they were resolved now. He would not miss this man's sermon the following morning.

"This is an excellent collection of writings by one who experienced the torment of his times. He was not just a theorist. Like the writers of the Bible, he wrote from direct personal encounter. I have heard that this book has been translated into English. You may want to read it when you go back to America."

"Yes, I think I will," Rob said.

"But that is enough of my reading," Schreibholz said, replacing the book on the shelf. "Tell me something about yourself. Where do you live? What is your work?"

Rob gave a brief biographical sketch while the pastor listened intently, never taking his penetrating eyes off of Rob's face.

"Ah, yes," he said when Rob finished, "but there is one point I do not understand, and that is how you met Christa. Also, you did not say how you met Martina von Egloffsberg and why you were visiting her." He paused for a moment, and then added, "I hope that you do not mind my asking these questions. It is not common for us to see an American in Halle. Other than two or three singing groups from your country, you are the only American I have seen in Halle since I have been here—and that has been many years."

"I went through Weimar, Jena, and Leipzig, and did not see even one American; so I am not surprised to hear you say that not one has come here. It is very different from West Germany where there seem to be Americans on almost every street corner. No, I do not mind your asking me any questions. My only problem is that I think that you will have trouble believing my story. It is strange."

"The world is full of strange stories. Whatever you say will probably not greatly surprise me."

Rob found something uncommonly appealing about this man. He had felt drawn to him almost from the moment he entered the room. Human warmth and deep conviction radiated from him with near-physical intensity.

So, relaxing and feeling a closeness with this preacher, Rob proceeded to recount the events that led him eventually to Prinzenheim: his father's death, the photograph in the footlocker, and his trip to Bachdorf. He talked without stopping for a quarter hour. As always, when he had to speak German for a lengthy, uninterrupted stretch, he spoke deliberately and haltingly, searching for the right words.

"That is indeed an interesting story; but I must say that in Germany there are millions of experiences just as strange and stranger, stories of the lost and reunited and, sadly, of the lost and never found. The human wreckage of the Second World War is so huge that it cannot be easily comprehended."

"Yes, I know that. Still I am impressed with the extraordinary coincidences that brought me to Prinzenheim and here today."

Schreibholz arose abruptly from his chair and moved to the window with his slightly limping stride, looking like an odd cross between a bookworm and an outdoorsman. He peered into the dusk and then drew the curtains completely together. He turned and began pacing back and forth by the window.

"No," he said after a few moments. "I must tell you that I generally do not believe in coincidences."

"Are you saying," Rob asked with a note of incredulity in his voice, "that my finding that picture in my father's trunk and my hearing of Prinzenheim from the old woman at the church at Bachdorf were not coincidences? And are you saying that the fact that Christa came unexpectedly to Prinzenheim when I happened to be there for one night was not a coincidence?"

"That is what I am saying. But I must also say that I do not really know."

"They all seem to me to be just happenstances, accidents," Rob said.

"No, life is full of such happenings. The Bible is full of them. It is clear to me that many of them, perhaps all of them, are part of a divine plan. We humans, of course, are unable to understand the plan. Sometimes we get glimpses that we think we can understand, but our comprehension is incomplete and uncertain. Perhaps you know that line from Second Corinthians, 'Now I see through a glass darkly.' It is not given to us on this earth to know the full scheme of things or the reason for all the joys and sorrows and the disasters and triumphs that befall us."

This line of conversation had made Rob slightly uncomfortable, and he felt an urge to get out of it. "I am enjoying talking with you, but I know that you have work to do, so I must depart."

"I am sorry that I must return to my preparation for tomorrow. I would like to talk with you some more. Can we meet tomorrow afternoon?"

"Yes," Rob answered after a momentary hesitation, "if you have the time, I would like to see you again. Is there a chance that I could meet your wife? When I was at Prinzenheim, I saw a picture of her when she was a young girl, and I have heard Christa speak of her."

"I am sorry. She is not here. This weekend she is at a church meeting at Naumberg. She will return on Monday. Will you be here then?"

"No," Rob said, genuinely disappointed, "I must return to West Berlin by tomorrow night."

"That is too bad. Helga would be very interested in talking to someone who has seen her mother recently. Could you come back here at two o'clock tomorrow afternoon?"

"Yes, I can. Would it be all right for me to attend the service in the church in the morning?"

"Of course. Services are open to anyone. It is at half past ten."

They shook hands. The pastor opened the door into the hall, and Rob made his way through the short and dark hallway into the twilight of the still overcast day. The atmosphere was now thickened with chemical odors drifting up from the vast Leuna Works south of the city.

Rob emerged from the side street beside the church into the marketplace. High in the tower, the bell tolled six o'clock. A light mist was in the air. Though it was still early for a summer day, a peculiar, premature darkness was setting in, intensified by the chemical smog.

He stood at a corner for a while, watching the arrival and departure of two trolley cars disgorging and taking on clumps of nondescript men and women. When they had bumped and screeched their way across the intersecting tracks and disappeared into side streets, the large square was almost empty. A handful of automobiles came and went. He walked around the sides of the square to see it from different perspectives. At the building with the 1890s look, he found a menu posted beside the heavy double doors. He would not have thought that a restaurant was located there. The absence of commercial advertising or even any prominent identifying signs often made it difficult to spot business establishments; but here was obviously a restaurant with a substantial list of offerings. Not having eaten since breakfast, Rob did not hesitate long before deciding to enter.

He found himself in a foyer from which broad wooden steps led upward. Strains of an accordion, a babble of voices, and the clatter of dishes floated downward. At the top of two flights of stairs, he came upon the obligatory check room with an attendant on duty. It continued to surprise him that in this workers' and peasants' state he had never seen a restaurant without a check room at its entrance coupled with an absolute requirement that all coats be checked for a fee. He had seen waiters refuse to admit patrons who were wearing or carrying coats.

The instant he pushed through the pair of double swinging doors into the restaurant, his ears were hit with a tripling in volume of music and laughter and talk. The room was huge, filled with dozens of tables. Despite what seemed to be an early hour to eat, most of the tables were filled. There must have been close to two hundred people drinking beer, eating, shouting, and talking animatedly. It was a high-ceilinged room with columns separated by arches running along one side. It could have been 1920 or 1935. He had seen beer halls in Munich that looked like the Germany of bygone decades; but this was the first such place he had come across in East Germany. His spirits lifted. Here at last he could escape the sterile and bland cafes and hotel dining rooms of the post-war Marxist-Leninist architecture. A violin and accordion rose above the noise with an old-style lilting German tune. Rob went forward into the crowd in response to the motion of a waiter.

The waiter seated Rob at a table for six, with three chairs on each side. A pair of men were at one end, facing each other. Rob took an end chair, opposite a man who was working vigorously on a massive pile of dumplings.

Rob examined the menu. He tended to go for the familiar rather than the unknown on these East German lists. He glanced at the dumpling eater across the table, and their eyes met for an instant. Perhaps here is a chance, he thought, to talk to an ordinary GDR citizen.

"What kind of meat do you have there?" Rob asked, attempting a friendly note in his voice.

"Bratwurst," came the answer as the man almost simultaneously took a long swallow from his glass of beer, signaling that he did not want to elaborate on his response.

"Is it good?" Rob asked.

"*Ja.*"

"Then I think that I will have that also."

After giving his order to the waiter, Rob focused attention on his table companion. The man was eating with gusto, his eyes fixed on the copious amounts of dumplings, red cabbage, and bratwurst. Rob took him to be in his late thirties—a child when the war ended. He was wearing one of those rough-textured almost black suits—virtually the uniform of GDR officials and managerial types. Most significant of all to Rob was the SED pin in his lapel, the membership insignia of the Communist party. Here was Rob's first and perhaps only chance to talk face-to-face with a Party member. He could not let the opportunity pass.

"Is this an old restaurant in Halle?" Rob asked, searching for an appropriate opening remark.

"I think so," the man said after pausing a moment to swallow. "But I am not sure. I have not lived here very long."

"Where did you come from?"

"I was born in a small village that is seventy kilometers from here."

Rob looked around at other tables and saw a group of men and women arriving and taking seats. He noticed for the first time that few of the other patrons were dressed in suits and ties. Nearly all of the men had open collars and no jacket. Most were perspiring profusely amidst their raucous banter. While Rob was considering what to say next, the man spoke.

"Are you an American?" The question caught Rob off guard. He had not expected to be asked anything.

"Yes, I am an American." Then, not wanting to be a reluctant conversationalist, a style he had mentally criticized in the East Germans, he continued, "I am on vacation and traveling through the GDR as a tourist."

"And what do you think of our country?"

It was the identical question, Rob recalled, that he had been asked in the dining room in Leipzig by the woman who turned out to be Maria

Egloffsberg. The impression these people make on Americans must be an important concern to them.

"I have been interested in many of the historical sites. You have some famous places and some good museums. I am enjoying my trip."

"History is important to us for what it can teach about the future; but we are building a new society. We have moved to a new stage in human history in which the social order is based on equality and peace."

The waiter arrived with a huge platter for Rob, mounded with all of the heavy food he had observed on the plate opposite. Rob welcomed the interruption, as he was unsure what he should say in response to these comments. He began eating. The musicians had taken a break, so the room was quieter.

After a few mouthfuls of the tasty and fattening fare, Rob asked, "Do you think that the GDR today gives you more opportunity and a better life than your father had?" As the words flowed from his mouth, he realized that the answer was easily predictable.

"Certainly. There is no doubt about it. My father worked all his life for a large landowner. He worked from sunrise to sunset for barely enough to feed his family. He had no opportunity for an education. My mother worked the same. My father was drafted into the Fascist army and was almost killed." There was a hard quality to his voice—an almost bitter tone. In Rob's mind there flickered an image of the vast expanse of fields and livestock at Bachdorf and the many men from the village toiling away to sustain that establishment and to provide themselves and their families with food and shelter. For an instant, he thought also of Trepnitz Hills. "Now look at me," the man continued. "I have attended a technical school and studied chemical engineering. I am an assistant manager of a chemical enterprise. I have a house with electricity, good heat, and running water. My wife has a good job as a school teacher. We have two children, and they go to good schools."

"Is your good fortune just a matter of different times? Would you not have the same opportunity and same living conditions if you were living in the Federal Republic, or do you think that it is the GDR that has made all this possible?"

"No, I could not have done this in the West," he answered emphatically. "There I would have needed a lot of money to go to a higher technical school or university. A poor man like me would have spent his whole life working for capitalists. I would have done no better than my father."

Rob had decided long ago that if he had chances to talk with East Germans he would not attempt to debate them but would simply try to get their views. So he made no comment.

At that moment, a loud voice to Rob's rear startled him. "Hallo, Otto," said an overweight man as he almost pounced on the man with whom Rob was talking. Otto rose, smiling, and the two shook hands. The fat man was probably in his forties and, like Otto, was wearing a black suit with an SED pin in the lapel.

"Klaus, how are you?" Otto asked with exaggerated enthusiasm.

"Good. Very good. I am here in Halle for a district Party meeting tomorrow. How is everything at the enterprise?"

"All is running well. We expect to meet all our production quotas this month."

"Excellent," boomed Klaus. "And how is your wife?"

"She is healthy and working hard. This weekend she and the children are visiting her parents in Magdeburg."

"Well, I am certainly happy to see you again and to know that all is well. I must leave now for a meeting we are having this evening at Party headquarters."

"Thank you for coming over," Otto said with a hint of subservience.

"Good-bye. I hope that we will have a good visit sometime soon." Klaus turned and rolled hurriedly toward the door.

Otto sat down, took a swallow of beer, and resumed eating. Rob continued to eat without looking up.

As if feeling the necessity of offering some explanation for this interruption, Otto said, "That was an old friend of mine. He is now a Party official in Berlin. He travels a lot on Party business. He is an important official. I do not see him very often now."

"I could not avoid hearing you say that your wife is visiting in Magdeburg," Rob said. "Was Magdeburg originally her home?"

"Yes, she was born there, and her parents still live there."

"Is that a pretty city? I know that it is an old and historical city."

The question was a mistake. Otto reverted to his solemn, almost sour look. "It was a beautiful city before the war; but then many buildings were destroyed. It was the American army." Hardness had crept into his voice, making Rob uncomfortable. The statement had revealed the mindset of the Eastern bloc about wartime damage. Americans were held responsible as though Germans had nothing to do with the fighting that brought the destruction on the city.

"Do you read or hear much about America in the GDR?"

"Of course we get news from all over the world, and I see some American programs on television."

"What impression of America do you have from those television programs?" Rob asked.

"The people are unhappy. They fight each other. There is much crime, and most people use drugs. Also, there are many poor people, and some very rich people who exploit them."

Rob was strongly tempted for a moment to respond to this standard Marxist-Leninist litany about conditions in the United States; but he quickly gave up the idea. There was no way that he would change this man's mind, and there was considerable likelihood of getting into an unpleasant exchange. After all, he reminded himself, he was not on his home ground, not in the land of free speech. He had avoided trouble in the GDR so far, so he had better hew to that course.

"I saw an old church on the marketplace. It has notices posted about religious services. Are the churches active and well attended in the GDR?"

Otto was taking the last swallow of beer from his glass. "No," he said, shaking his head from side to side with a look of mild contempt. "They are not important. The Party tolerates them. Some old people get comfort there, and they do some good works; but in our new and progressive society, they have no part. They belong to the past, to the bourgeois and Fascist times."

The accordion and the violin had now resumed playing. The crowd noise had risen. It was getting more difficult to hear above the din.

Otto shoved his chair back from the table. "I must go," he almost shouted.

Rob stood and shook hands. "I enjoyed having dinner with you."

"Yes," Otto said. "*Auf wiedersehen.*" And then he was gone.

Rob resumed his attack on the red cabbage. The waiter had just delivered another glass of beer. Although ample, the glasses here were not nearly as large as those to be found in Munich establishments and elsewhere in West Germany. Not having anywhere to go except to the hotel and to bed, Rob went about eating and sipping at a leisurely pace. The going and coming of the customers around him provided sufficient entertainment for a while.

The grimness of the city scenes and the drabness of life in the GDR, as he had observed and read, were belied by what he saw in this huge, boisterous dining hall. The place was filled almost to capacity. No one, other than Otto, seemed to be in an unhappy mood. Nearly everyone was talking and laughing animatedly. An observer might even have described the scene as a joyous gathering of happy, contented people—people for whom life was good and reasonably comfortable. Was this forced hilarity, a mere Saturday night facade, or did it realistically reflect life in the GDR, a state of affairs that Western news media refused to recognize?

Rob examined some of the individuals more closely. There was no doubt that he was in the midst of the working classes. Out of the dozens of men there, he had seen no more than a handful wearing a coat and tie, and that included himself, his table companion Otto, and his friend Klaus. While many may have been office workers, their faces and hands showed that life had not been easy. Perhaps this was a transitional generation, Rob pondered. Born and reared in the families of uneducated laborers in factories and farms, they were now moving up the ladder in education and economic means. For a guarantee of betterment in material status over their parents, they were paying the price of limited mobility, limited speech and assembly, and limited political freedom. In scientific materialism, man had unlocked the secret of history and was moving here in step with it. This crowded mass of fat, sweating, open-collared, and shirtsleeved men with food-mounded plates and copious quantities of beer seemed to testify that it was working.

God was irrelevant to this new age of mankind; He belonged to the past, to the time before the true scientific theory of history was discovered. But what about that church just across the square, and the others he had seen in Weimar, Jena, and Wittenberg? He saw the rugged, gray-topped countenance of Pastor Schreibholz—a man who committed his life in these unappealing surroundings to the opposite proposition. Once again the nagging question pressed on Rob's mind: somebody has got to be wrong. Either these people are correct and there is no God, or else God does exist. He could not figure out any middle ground.

After another beer, he left the nostalgic music, the raucous crowd, and the overheated air, and descended the stairs into a totally deserted marketplace. He looked forward to breaking into the cool, refreshing night air; but he emerged instead into smog laden with chemical odors. Although it was only a little past nine, not a human figure was to be seen. The silence was empty, lifeless, and complete. It was as though the city had been evacuated. He stood still for a long while. The chemically infused fog almost blotted out the far side of the square. Street lights appeared as murky blobs. He strained his ears for footsteps, traffic sounds, voices, anything. But there was nothing. The silence was total, absolute, and unlike anything he had known before. It was spooky, weird, unearthly. He searched for the right word to describe the scene. It was like what he imagined it would be on the last day, when the earth is shutting down, with all human life gone except himself—the last living witness to the close of the human drama.

Now there was a sound in the far distance. It was faint, and he could not discern what it was. It was gradually rising, however, and he suddenly recognized it as an approaching trolley car. What he heard was the sound of its steel wheels screeching on steel tracks as it rounded curves. It grew louder, and now he could hear the sound of the motor mixed with the screaming of metal on metal. Then, from a street to his right, the car came into view, proceeded to the center of the square, and stopped. Its loud electric motor continued to run as its doors jerked open. Two people got off—he could not tell whether they were men or women—and walked up a side street. No one got on; no one had been waiting for it. After another minute with its motor idling, the trolley doors slammed shut, and it moved off, turned a corner with agonized metallic screeching, and disappeared. For several minutes, Rob could hear the diminishing sound of its wheels taking curves in the track, and then there was silence.

Again he was alone in the world, alone in the middle of the centuries-old city of Halle, alone in East Germany. He pondered whether reality lay here in this somber setting or in the brightly lighted, music-filled dining hall amidst all those Germans laughing, drinking, and eating. Through the emptiness, he walked to the Interhotel and to bed.

Chapter 17

BY MORNING, THE SMOG had gone, the sun was shining, and the sky was the kind of deep blue that one expected on a July morning. The world seemed to have emerged from a sinister darkness bereft of human beings into renewed and cheerful life. In the hotel dining room, where Rob had rolls, jam, and coffee, there was a moderate bustle—even an upbeat note among the patrons and the waitress.

Robert Kirkman's spirits were rising again. Ahead he had the prospect of attending a regular church service in the GDR. Thus far, he had seen only notices about services. He would see for himself whether there were only a few old women scattered lonesomely in a nearly empty church.

Before church, though, he had one important mission: to visit the university. Because of the university, Halle had been on the list of places he especially wanted to see in the GDR long before he had ever met the von Egloffsberg family. More precisely, it was because of Professor George Marks Wilton.

Rob had taken Wilton's course titled Europe Since 1815. It covered that magnificent pageant of events from Waterloo to Potsdam. In his senior year, he had taken the course on Germany in the twentieth century. These courses aroused Rob's latent interest in Germany, an interest that had not flagged. Indeed, he reflected as he spread jam on his roll, there was a likelihood that he would not be eating breakfast this morning in Halle and would probably not be in Germany at all had it not been for Professor Wilton.

Similarity of geographical origin and family backgrounds had brought together the student and teacher. This Edwardian-looking academician had been born on the banks of the Tombigbee River, seventy-five miles south of Tuscaloosa. His home county bordered that of the Trepnitz and Kirkman families, and he knew Rob's father and grandfather. Like most

Black Belt families, they had a legion of interconnecting relatives and acquaintances. Wilton had done his undergraduate work at the University of Virginia and was influential in Rob's going to law school there. He had gone on to the University of Chicago for his Ph.D. before going on to Halle. After staff service with the army in France during the war, he returned home and took a position on the history faculty at the University of Alabama. There he remained, with an occasional leave of absence and visitation elsewhere, until he retired soon after Rob graduated.

During spring recess of his last year in law school, Rob called on the old man at his home in Tuscaloosa. He could see now the stooped figure, the still thick but gray hair, and the soft, reflective face of the scholar. They sat and talked for an hour.

"So you're thinking about going to New York to practice law," he had said, after Rob had told him of his thoughts about the future. "I know how you feel about seeing the great world out there. I had the same feeling myself at your age. I wanted to get out of the South and to have new experiences. That was the appeal of Chicago and Germany. I went to those places and a lot of others; but in the end I found that the pull of the home ground was irresistible. It may have been a sense of duty, a felt obligation to the people of my state, or it may have been a touch of homesickness. I'm not sure. But the gravitational pull was there, and I came back. And I might say that I have never regretted it. I predict that you will ultimately follow the same course. For southerners, there is a powerful, almost unbreakable linkage to the land of their origin. This, among other things, is what separates southerners from other Americans. It is a sense of place—an awareness of being rooted somewhere—that other folks don't seem to have."

Those words had replayed a thousand times in Rob's mind. They had turned out to be an accurate predictor of his own course of action. By the time he returned to Alabama, however, George Marks Wilton was dead. It was one of Rob's most profound regrets that his favorite professor had not lived to see that he too had taken the same road home. He had not, in the end, "deserted the house of the fathers," to use a Wiltonian phrase.

Wilton was particularly fond of lecturing on the German universities and their influence on American higher education. With facts and anecdotes, he propounded the thesis that German influence on America was far greater than that of England, the mother country. He was fond of reciting the long list of distinguished American educators and high-ranking government officials who had studied in Germany. Rob could not leave this place without seeing the very buildings and walking the same ground where his mentor had spent those early years.

After two world wars, the Weimar Republic, the Nazis, and a Marxist-Leninist regime, *Baedeker* was still accurate. The text and the map told it as it was and as it continued to be in the vicinity of the university. A thirty-minute walk from the hotel had brought Rob along University Ring to the cluster of nineteenth-century buildings forming the center of the old university. Walking in from the street, he came to the middle of a grassy courtyard around which these buildings were grouped.

Although the university had been founded in 1695, the physical center of it, where Rob now stood, consisted of these buildings erected in the 1830s. Not long before that, the University of Wittenberg had been consolidated with this institution. In later years, the combined entity had been named the Martin Luther University, and the Communists had not altered that designation.

The largest building ran parallel with University Ring, and had been designed by Schenkel, the architect of the German Museum in Berlin. Its entrance steps were flanked by a pair of stone lions, life-size or larger, thus giving the edifice its informal name, the Lion Building. The doors were open, even though it was Sunday morning. Students were walking up by ones and twos and entering the door between the lions.

Rob followed the last of the students and found himself in a large foyer. Ahead was a wide stairway leading to a landing. There, stairs went up to the left and right. Walking toward the stairway, he suddenly saw that it was in a three-story atrium. There, at the second floor level, he saw what he most wanted to see—the murals. He mounted the steps to the landing. From that vantage point, he could see all four walls and the four murals. The voice of George Marks Wilton came through just as clearly as though he had been standing there.

"In the main building at Halle," Rob had heard him say more than a few times, "you will see murals depicting the four faculties. You know, of course," he would add in a footnoting tone of voice, "that from the Middle Ages on, every German university had four faculties—Philosophy, Theology, Law, and Medicine. There is a mural for each flanking the grand stairway."

At the center of each mural was a robed woman holding a symbol for each faculty—a cross for theology, the scales of justice for law, a caduceus for medicine, and an opened book for philosophy. Standing in the stairway, Rob thought of that long line of professors and students who had climbed these stairs over many decades, among them the young Wilton. He would have enjoyed telling Wilton that he had at last seen the murals and climbed the very stairs that the aged scholar had climbed sixty years before and several thousand miles from the Tombigbee. He thought that his father would have gotten a kick out of hearing about this experience as well.

Rob moved on to the top floor. There he entered the Aula—the auditorium, a high-ceilinged ceremonial room, which was the centerpiece of all the old German universities. The room held about four hundred seats. Overhead, in the center of the ceiling, were four circular murals, again representing the four faculties. On one wall hung a line of oil portraits of professors from bygone days. Reading the identifying plaques, Rob noted that Thomasius was the only law professor among them.

In the corridor, just outside the entrance to the Aula, were busts of former rectors of the university. Immediately on either side of the doorway, he saw busts of Martin Luther and Phillip Melanchton. All appeared to be as it must have been a hundred years before until Rob's eye caught a sign over a set of double doors down the corridor: Library of Marxism-Leninism. The words brought him jarringly back to the late twentieth century. He pondered this discordant juxtaposition of the old and the new. What did free intellectual inquiry mean today in this system? What was the meaning of a university? How different was it now from what it was from 1933 to 1945? Each question pushed him back to an earlier question. What had gone so profoundly wrong in Germany after the first decade of this century? It made no sense. He was convinced that there was simply no answer to this riddle. Some weird, cancerous disaster had beset this extraordinary intellectual dynamo, and no one had been able to explain it to his satisfaction. Even Professor Wilton seemed to have given up on this question.

A student was standing at the bottom of the stairway as Rob reached the main floor. Others were going into a room down the corridor. "Is there a lecture or meeting here this morning?" Rob asked.

"*Ja*," the young man said. "It is the weekly lecture and discussion of marriage and the family."

"Is the meeting for university students?"

"Yes. It is held every Sunday morning."

"Do you have many students who are married?"

"By the time they graduate perhaps half are married," the student replied, now looking at Rob with an expression of curiosity. "Are you Swedish?"

Rob smiled and said, "No, I am American."

Surprise flashed over the student's face. "An American," he almost whispered. "We do not see Americans here, except on television. My grandfather told me that he saw American soldiers here in Halle in 1945."

"Well," Rob said, half laughing, "now you see one in the flesh. I am visiting here as a tourist."

"Here comes my girlfriend," the student said as he raised his hand toward a young woman coming through the front door. "We must go to the lecture. *Auf wiedersehen.*" He put his arm warmly around the girl's shoulders as she came up, and the two walked off together down the corridor toward the lecture room.

Rob stood for some minutes in front of the Lion Building. There was little in his line of vision that had not been there in 1913. He felt a sense of spiritual release, a sense of paying a final tribute to George Marks Wilton. He had put his foot on the very ground, climbed the same grand stairway, and walked the same corridors filled with the same pedestaled busts of bygone academics.

A brisk, fifteen-minute walk through the narrow streets of the old town brought Rob from the university buildings to the church on the marketplace. He arrived there ten minutes before the service was scheduled to begin. In the twin towers overhead, the bells were clanging—multiple bells tolling bass and tenor, an intermingling of slow bonging of the deep-throated bells with more rapidly clanging higher pitched notes.

People were streaming in the front door. They were of all ages, ranging from children of ten or twelve years to the very old. This was no tiny aggregation. People were coming from the side streets onto the square and into the church by the dozens, walking rapidly and purposefully in good German style. He fell in behind one group and entered the church, taking a seat in a pew near the rear.

The bells kept up their magnificent tolling interplay, though from within the sanctuary the thick walls gave them a distant and muffled sound. At half past ten they stopped. Almost immediately the organ broke forth in a mighty, thundering swell of music that filled the church and drowned the congregation with seemingly divine force. From a side door, Pastor Ernst Schreibholz and a much younger man appeared, both wearing black clerical robes. They mounted the platform at the front of the church. Schreibholz took his seat in a heavily carved, high-backed wooden chair near a massive pulpit. The other man sat at the opposite end of the platform near a smaller pulpit. The organ continued its performance for some minutes. The pews were almost filled. There had to be at least three hundred people, Rob calculated, gathered on Sunday morning in a land where the government was officially atheistic, where any religious affiliation could do them no good and was likely to be a serious detriment to their schooling, jobs, and future.

The music tapered off and stopped. Pastor Schreibholz rose and stepped to the pulpit. His powerful voice boomed out in prayer. He invoked the blessings of Almighty God on those assembled and gave thanks for all of the blessings that had been bestowed on them. The prayer went on and on for longer than Rob thought necessary. The organ then erupted again, and the entire congregation rose, hymn books in hand. Rob recognized the hymn—it was one that he had heard as long as he could remember—"Now Thank We All Our God." The congregation sang it lustily, filling the great space with their enthusiastic voices. The scene was like that in a thousand churches in America at this hour on any Sunday morning.

The young minister now mounted his pulpit and commenced reading from the first book of Samuel. It was not a passage with which Rob was familiar. It was the story of Saul's search for some lost donkeys that belonged to his father. Saul and a servant wandered through the countryside for several days without finding them. They came to a village where they were told that there was a prophet—Samuel—who might tell them where to find the donkeys. Seemingly by happenstance, they met Samuel on the street. In fact, Samuel had been divinely informed that the new king of Israel would appear before him in the village and that he, Samuel, should anoint him king. That person was, of course, Saul. Thus the two came together on the village street pursuant to a divine plan of which Saul knew nothing.

The congregation rose and sang another hymn, and Pastor Schreibholz mounted the pulpit. He began the sermon with a reminder that he was preaching a series of sermons on incidents from the Old Testament which in themselves seemed trivial, but contained important lessons about the ways in which God plays an unsuspected role in people's lives.

This man had an awesome presence. His resonant voice carried his conviction and commitment to every corner of the church. It would be hard for anyone sitting in these pews not to believe that this man, standing where Martin Luther had stood, was delivering a divinely inspired message. This man had stayed here, where his talents were not likely to be widely appreciated, and where his work might even endanger himself and his family. There was commitment and courage here that Rob had never before witnessed.

"The story in this scripture reading began," the pastor said, "with a commonplace happening. Some donkeys had strayed off. Wanting to recover them, Saul's father dispatched his son to find them. Neither the father nor the son had any notion that there was any significance to this situation. In our lives every day, there are ordinary occurrences like this, and we do not consider that they have anything to do with God's plan.

"Now do not ask me," Schreibholz thundered, "how God spoke to Samuel. He spoke to Samuel in the way that He speaks to you and me today. A feeling comes over us, a thought comes to our minds that we cannot dismiss. Many times something has come to my mind that has caused me to do something. I think of a person, for example, a person I have not seen for a long time, and something—I cannot identify it—says to me that I should visit that person. Often when I have then done so, I find that person to have a serious problem or to be sick or to have lost a loved one. God can speak to us in many ways; so He spoke to Samuel and at the same time led Saul to this village through the seemingly meaningless hunt for lost animals.

"Many would say," Schreibholz continued, "that Saul's wandering into this village was a mere coincidence. I recall numerous times when someone had met on the street a friend or relative thought to have died in the war. They would speak of such events as coincidences. But," he went on, warming to his subject, "much of what we think of as coincidences may not be that at all. Just as God used strayed donkeys as a device to bring Saul to Samuel, so He often uses unsuspecting and ordinary events to guide our lives. Believers can see God's hand in many things where nonbelievers see only coincidences."

The pastor sat down. After the offering, another hymn, and a prayer by the young minister, the service was over. The people flowed out into the sunshine of a warming July day. How like and yet unlike it was, Rob mused, to a Sunday morning at the Remberton Presbyterian Church. Pastor Schreibholz read from the same scripture, said the same prayers, and called on the same God as thousands of preachers were doing around the globe that very day. Though united in this God, these people were divided here on earth; and that was nowhere more painfully evident than in this new German state.

As the clock in the tower was striking two, Rob approached the small wooden door at the rear of the church leading to the office, anticipating a short chat with the pastor before setting out on the drive back to West Berlin.

Rob pressed down on the door handle, but it was locked. He knocked softly. In a moment, he heard a key turning. The door opened a few inches, and he saw Pastor Schreibholz in the crack.

"Come in," he said.

Rob entered, and the pastor locked the door. Rob followed him back into the small study where the two had talked the previous evening. The curtains were drawn, shutting out the brilliant sunshine. The shaded lamp provided dim illumination. The pastor waved Rob into the straight wooden chair. Papers and books were strewn here in greater disarray than they had been on his visit the day before. The pastor took his seat in what was obviously his working chair at the head of the table. There was nothing clerical now about his dress. He was wearing an open-collar work shirt.

"I am glad that you have come back," he said warmly. "I hope you had a restful night."

"Yes, I slept well. This morning I visited the university to see the old buildings. I had a professor who studied there before the First World War."

"Ah, yes," exclaimed Schreibholz, "many Americans did come here and to other German universities in those days. It is sad that they no longer do."

"I saw students coming into the main building and going to a lecture. One of them told me that lectures were held on Sunday mornings on marriage and family."

"Having meetings of that sort to appeal to the young people has been a tactic of the SED for many years. They have them on Sunday mornings to compete with the churches. The Free German Youth leadership makes it clear that a loyal member has an obligation to attend. I am glad that you came to the service here instead of staying there."

Noticing a smile on Schreibholz's face, Rob laughed slightly and said, "I am glad too. Was it a coincidence that you preached today about coincidences?"

"Not at all. I must confess that I wrote this sermon after your visit last evening. I had thought of preaching on another Old Testament episode, but decided to take this story from Samuel after our conversation."

"I am impressed that my short visit with you would change your sermon topic," Rob said.

"You may find it strange for me to say this; but you may understand it shortly." Schreibholz paused as though assembling his thoughts. "I believe that God sent you here to Halle this weekend. This is no mere coincidence. You are, of course, not aware of this, just as Saul was not aware that his search for the donkeys had any significance. I preached that sermon hoping that you would be there, and that it would help you to understand."

The awesome thought made Rob uncomfortable, and he shifted nervously in his chair.

"You know, of course, that this is officially an atheistic government. Church and state coexist, but in tension. This situation is not unusual in history. When Christ himself walked the earth, he lived in a Roman colony, a pagan regime. The state puts severe restrictions on us, although things have gotten a little better since the church in the East divided from the church in the West. However, the authorities are still suspicious of us; they resent anything that they cannot totally control. Many of the officials believe that we are agents of the Western powers. That is untrue. What is true is that Christians do not acknowledge the Party and the state to be supreme in human life. The SED does not like the competition of God. They think of God as being a creature of the West, an ally of their enemies. Since 1949, many of our members and pastors have been arrested on political charges that we consider not well founded. We try to help our people as best we can. Sometimes this help takes the form of getting them out of the GDR, which is in itself a crime under GDR law. We are not able to help them all, but when there is opportunity we try to do what seems possible, knowing that in the end God is in charge of our destinies, not the SED."

The pastor stopped and took off his glasses to wipe them. Without the glasses, his eyes showed a faint resemblance to those of his daughter Christa. The pastor rose, paced a few steps, resumed his seat, and cleared his throat.

"Herr Kirkman, you have visited in the home of Martina von Egloffsberg, and you have met my daughter."

Rob nodded without speaking.

"You have seen that they are decent, upright people. You know something, I believe, of the sorrows and disasters that have befallen this family—a family into which I married, but with which I have had little intimate association because of the division of Germany. Your father, you have told me, was with Martina's husband at his death on the western front."

"Yes," Rob said, "that extraordinary coincidence . . .uh . . . excuse me . . . event is the reason why I am sitting here at this moment."

"Well, however you want to describe the matter, you have arrived here at a moment when we are confronted with an urgent and dangerous situation. The problem is one in which you may be of great help, even essential help. Who can say what God's plan is? So if you want to think of it as an unusual coincidence, that is your privilege. I myself think that the hand of God is involved."

"Can you explain what you mean?"

Schreibholz shifted in his chair and looked even more intently at Rob. "You know, I believe, that when Martina lost her husband in the First World War, she was left with two small sons. One of them, Wolfgang, you have met at Prinzenheim, the other, Kurt, died at Stalingrad."

Rob nodded, his curiosity mounting.

"The year before he died," continued Schreibholz, "Kurt had married. Shortly after his death a daughter was born to his wife."

Rob's ears pricked up. He had heard no mention of a child.

"The fate of Kurt's widow is not clear. Her family's estate was far to the east and was overrun by the Red Army. Her father died during the war, and her elderly mother was living alone with servants at the estate. We do not know what happened to her; the assumption is that she died or was killed during the Soviet advance or occupation. The last word from Kurt's widow was from Berlin, where she was living with friends. Martina had invited her to come to Prinzenheim with the baby, where they would have been much safer, but she did not go.

"We assumed that mother and baby had both died in Berlin. Then one day, about three years ago, I went to the Charité Hospital in Berlin to visit a sick friend, who was having a serious problem with his eyes. While I was at his bedside, a young woman came to examine him. She was a medical school graduate and was in advanced training. As we stood there talking, she introduced herself. She said, 'I am the eye doctor on duty today. My name is Maria Egloffsberg.'"

Rob stiffened. "Maria Egloffsberg," he whispered in unconcealed amazement.

"You can imagine my thoughts at that moment. There was, of course, the possibility that there was little or no family connection. The Egloffsberg name is centuries old, and she could have come from some other branch; but the name Maria and the age of the woman made it impossible for me to accept that theory. Later when I left my friend, I sought her out and found her down the corridor writing up reports in a small office. She was alone.

"Now you must understand, Herr Kirkman, that questions about a person's origin and background are sensitive matters in Germany since the second war—especially in the GDR. So I had to be cautious."

"Yes, I can understand," Rob said, largely to fill the momentary silence.

"I first told her that I was a pastor at Halle who had come to the hospital to see an old friend. Then I said, 'Your name brought back old memories. Before the war I knew a man named Egloffsberg who was a theology student at the university here in Berlin. He was a member of the von Egloffsberg family of Bachdorf.' I was, of course, speaking of Wolfgang. She had put down her pen and was looking at me with a frozen face. I went on. 'He had an older brother named Kurt,' I said, 'and he was killed in the war. Are you related to that family?' With that, she jumped up from her chair and quickly closed the door to the corridor."

Schreibholz sighed. "We were standing face-to-face, only a meter apart, looking directly at each other. 'You say that you are a pastor?' she asked. When I nodded, she said, 'Do you know any pastors in Berlin?' When I said that I knew several, she asked me to name some. I mentioned the names of several. Then she asked to see my identity papers, and I showed them to her. She was being very careful. Then she asked, 'Do you know any members of that family who are still alive?' I told her that I knew two and that they both lived in the West. 'What are their names?' she asked. I said, 'Martina von Egloffsberg and Wolfgang von Egloffsberg. He is the one I knew before the war.' She then asked, 'Did you say that he had an older brother named Kurt?' I said, 'Yes, he is the one who died in the war.' She stared at me for what seemed an eternity, as though searching my mind for any sign of deception. She finally said in a low voice, 'He was my father.' "

The pastor and Rob sat in silence for some seconds. High up in the Red Tower, the clock boomed the half hour; they heard the distant screeching of trolley car wheels on the tracks. Rob was perplexed. Why hadn't Martina told him at Prinzenheim of this miraculously discovered granddaughter?

Pastor Schreibholz sprang abruptly from his chair and began pacing back and forth. Finally he sat down, rearranged the papers on the table, folded his hands together, and looked at Rob.

"When the news of my discovery went out to Martina, she did not greet it with complete joy, as one might have expected. I should say that Helga and Christa were very excited and anxious to meet her. Wolfgang was in between. He was interested, but he was not at first convinced. You see, the problem with something like this in Germany is that there have been cases of fraud—instances where persons appear years after the war claiming to be related to somebody when in fact it is all false. Martina had known several families where that had happened. So she was cautious, and still is, about believing that Maria is really Kurt's daughter. I should add that people who are wealthy tend to be the most skeptical; they are the most likely targets for fraudulent impersonations. So I can understand Martina's attitude."

"Isn't there some way to determine whether Maria is who she says she is?"

"I will tell you all there is on that. Before I left this young woman in the Charité Hospital, we agreed to meet again in Berlin on my next trip there. That came three weeks later. We met in a cafe not far from the hospital. She had with her a photograph of a man and a woman. She said that they were her parents. Although I had met Kurt only once, I had seen pictures of him and his wife. There was no doubt in my mind that they were the two persons in that picture."

The pastor paused and shifted his position in his chair. Rob spoke up. "Couldn't you have others look at the picture or investigate further? Also, since she was a baby when her mother died, how did she know anything about her?"

"She said that she grew up with a married couple who lived near Sachsenhausen. This couple adopted her. They are dead now. She was told that a family friend had rescued her from the collapsed buildings and had brought her there from Berlin. This friend told these people that this baby was the daughter of Kurt von Egloffsberg and his wife, whom she knew; she had this photograph with her. The picture was the only tangible link to her parents."

"Did that picture convince the family?" Rob asked.

"Martina has not seen it, but Helga and Christa are satisfied. There is more to tell, however. At that meeting in the cafe, Maria told me that she had recently been attending some church meetings in Berlin and that she was thinking seriously of joining the church. I invited her to come to Halle and spend the weekend with Helga and me. She accepted and came two weeks later."

"Perhaps this is not appropriate to say, but being in the GDR has made me suspicious. Is there any possibility that somebody like this could be planted by the police to find out what is happening inside the churches?"

"Of course, that is always a possibility. We take chances. In this case, I relied, as I must, on my judgment. Something told me that she was genuine. At least, I was willing to risk it, and nothing has proved me wrong yet. Maria has visited us several times. Indeed she has come to seem like a member of the family, which I believe her in fact to be. She joined a church in Berlin about two years ago. As you can imagine, that has not helped her standing at the hospital."

"What is Martina's view now?"

"She remains in doubt. She wants more specific proof before she is willing to accept Maria as Kurt's daughter."

It dawned on Rob that he had said nothing to indicate that he had ever heard of or met Maria Egloffsberg. Thus far in the conversation he had been too overwhelmed by these revelations to think of announcing this extraordinary happenstance, or whatever it was.

"I must say, the story you are telling is interesting, but I still do not understand what it has to do with me."

"It has taken all of this explanation to get us to the point." The pastor was again on his feet. "We must move on to the immediate problem, but first excuse me for a moment." He opened the door to the corridor, went out, and closed it behind him.

Rob sat in his chair, mulling over what he had heard. Now another question came to his mind. Why hadn't Christa acknowledged the existence of Maria when he had asked her about relatives in East Germany? This must surely be a matter of considerable interest. He heard voices and footsteps in the corridor. The door handle clicked, and the door swung open.

Rob turned and saw Pastor Schreibholz entering the room. Following him was Maria Egloffsberg.

Chapter 18

"I BELIEVE THAT YOU have met each other," Pastor Schreibholz said.

"Uh . . . yes," stammered Rob, unable to gather his wits quickly enough to utter anything other than platitudes. "This is too much. I cannot believe it."

"It is strange," she said, as she took his hand.

There was something different about her. Although she was quite clearly the woman with whom he had taken coffee on Unter den Linden and with whom he had sat at dinner in Leipzig, her face now had an altogether different expression. Gone was the detached, somber, almost unfriendly appearance. Her eyes were alive, and there was a warmth in her look that had not been there before.

The pastor steered Maria around to a chair on the side of the table. "Have a seat. We have much to talk about." He resumed his chair at the head of the table, sitting between Rob and Maria.

"How did you know that we had met before?" Rob asked, looking at the pastor.

"Maria and I talked earlier today. When I told her your name and described you, she told me of your meeting, or rather, two meetings. I was convinced that my sermon was well chosen."

"Did you know that I was here?" Rob asked, turning toward Maria. "This is all very strange."

"Let me explain everything," the pastor interrupted. "First, let me say that I understand that you must be back in West Berlin by midnight."

"That is correct," Rob replied, "My visa expires then."

"Then we must not waste time. I will get straight to the reason for this unusual meeting. Among the many problems the churches have in the GDR is that of obtaining enough Bibles. The authorities permit the publication of a limited number; but after years of little or none, there are not nearly enough. About two years ago, we developed an arrangement under which Bibles printed in West Germany were shipped into the GDR. These Bibles were printed through generous gifts of money from persons in the West. They are printed without any designation of their source. Until recently, we have been successful in getting them into the East."

"Legally or illegally?" Rob asked.

"Most of these shipments have been illegal under GDR law. God and Caesar have coexisted in many places for two thousand years, not always comfortably. I regret that we do not have time now to discuss this interesting question. I have made my decision in this case. I have decided for the Bibles."

Shifting himself in his chair, the pastor continued. "The state police have been suspicious for a long time. Several weeks ago, they arrested one of our key men, which blocked the major means of entry for the Bibles. I am not giving you more detail than you need to know, but I come now to a very sensitive point, Herr Kirkman. To say what I want to say to you, we must have trust in you. I must ask whether you can keep this information in absolute confidence. Based on my observation of you and from what I have been told of you, I believe that you can be trusted. Am I right?"

"I have always considered myself able to keep a secret."

"I must ask you this," Schreibholz said, "as God is your witness, do you swear that you will not reveal to anyone except my daughter what I am about to tell you?"

"I do," said Rob.

"I believe you," the pastor said. "In any case, we are in God's hands. Now I go on with the story. Shortly after our man was arrested, the police took Maria into custody for interrogation. They questioned her about this whole operation. It seemed clear that they have information that involves her in it. Whether the man they arrested earlier talked or whether they have other sources, we do not know."

Maria was sitting impassively. Rob was struck by how much more attractive she was now than she had appeared on the two previous occasions. Her hair, the color of pale sherry, was arranged in a softer style, and her stiff, professional demeanor was gone.

"Maria has now received a notice to report to police headquarters next Thursday. We have learned from a reliable source that she will probably be arrested and charged with importing illegal items. That carries a substantial prison sentence. Maria," the pastor put his hand on her arm, "would you tell us what you want to do?"

"I have decided to leave the GDR," Maria said quietly. "The road to this decision has been long; but now I must act without delay. There is a box of five hundred Bibles in West Germany that we have arranged to transport by truck to West Berlin over the transit route. This gives me an opportunity to leave."

Schreibholz stood and crossed the room. He parted the curtains, glanced out, closed the curtains and returned to his chair, limping slightly.

"How will the shipment of Bibles along the transit route to Berlin give you a way to leave the GDR?" Rob asked.

"We have a plan," she replied. "Any plan to leave the GDR without official authority is dangerous. Attempting to leave is a serious criminal offense, but I face a prison sentence if I remain, so I am willing to take the risk. I have little to lose. The plan is really quite simple. The Bibles will never reach Berlin. The truck will leave the autobahn at a designated point. There the Bibles will be unpacked from the box, and I will take their place in the box. The truck will then proceed to West Berlin. This plan has two features. It gets the Bibles into the GDR, and it gets me out."

"Why are you telling me this?" Rob asked uneasily. "What does it have to do with me?"

Schreibholz took over the conversation again. "Herr Kirkman, for this plan to be carried out, your assistance will be required. In short, we need your help."

Rob looked blankly at Schreibholz. He remembered those warnings before this trip: "Americans have no problems in the GDR if they mind their own business and follow the rules. Every American who has gotten in trouble there has been doing something he ought not to have been doing." He could not tell whether Schreibholz was waiting for him to speak. But he said nothing.

"We have no other way," the pastor resumed, "to get Maria to the point of rendezvous with the truck or of getting the Bibles from that point to their destination in Magdeburg."

They all sat in silence until Rob spoke. "Do I understand that you are asking me, an American, to violate GDR law, to commit two serious criminal offenses?"

Maria's expression was a mixture of sorrow and anxiety. Schreibholz leaned forward, placing his arms on the table.

"That is correct," he said. "We cannot deny it. I know that you are a man of the law, but all of your assumptions about law come from a society where people govern themselves—a government of laws, I believe you say. This is a Marxist-Leninist state where the official policy is that there is no God, and there are no free elections. We are asking your help in bringing five hundred Bibles to families who have no access to the Scriptures and in helping Maria to avoid an unjustified prison term.

"I understand, but I must think carefully about this. How soon do you need an answer?"

Maria spoke up. "By tomorrow. The truck and the driver in Hanover are set to make the trip on Tuesday evening. My summons to police headquarters is for Thursday morning. It must be done on Tuesday night when the truck makes this trip, or it will be too late."

Rob took a deep breath and let out a long sigh. He rubbed his hands together, staring at the table. "Could you tell me more about how all of this is to be done?"

"Here, let me get a map," Schreibholz said, going to a cabinet across the room. He returned and spread the folded sheets on the table. "This is a road map of the GDR. You see here the border with the Federal Republic." His finger traced the meandering line from north to south. "One of the major transit routes to West Berlin is along this autobahn here, beginning at the entry point at Helmstedt." Maria had come around the table and was standing behind Rob. All three were now focused on the map spread under the lamplight on the table.

"Here you see Magdeburg," the pastor continued. "It is not far south of the autobahn, probably under a half-hour's drive. You see here the main road from the autobahn down to Magdeburg." He pointed out each feature as he spoke.

Maria leaned forward, her hair brushing Rob's cheek. "Not far south of the point where the road to Magdeburg leaves the autobahn, there is the site of a former village. It was destroyed by fighting in the last days of the war. The site is about three or four kilometers below the autobahn. A small road turns off the main road to Magdeburg. One kilometer from that point, there is the ruins of the village church, where we plan to exchange the Bibles for me."

"I thought that trucks admitted to the transit route for Berlin were forbidden to leave the autobahn," Rob said.

"They are," Schreibholz said. "But the route is not always tightly patrolled. The situation is actually looser than many people think. If police cars are patrolling near this exit, the driver will pass it and attempt to exit at another place. If the autobahn is not patrolled, he will get off there. We estimate that the process of getting to the church, unloading the Bibles, loading Maria, and getting back to the autobahn should not take more than a half hour."

"What is my role in this?" Rob asked.

"Your role," answered the pastor, "would be to have an automobile and take Maria to this spot and then to bring the Bibles back."

"Bring them back where?" Rob asked.

"To the cathedral at Magdeburg," Schreibholz replied. "People there will take them from you immediately. Then your function will be at an end."

"Just an ordinary night out in the GDR," Rob said, half sarcastically. But he sensed that this was no occasion for smart remarks. Their faces told him that this was deadly serious business. "What is your idea about where I would get a car?"

"You could rent a car in West Berlin, just as you have done this weekend," the pastor said. "Then you could drive on Tuesday to Magdeburg. Of course you would need to make a reservation at the Interhotel there. It is called the International. Maria would come to Magdeburg by train from East Berlin on Tuesday afternoon. The two of you would meet at the hotel that evening and drive after dark to the church near the autobahn. The truck driver plans to reach that spot at ten o'clock."

"Then," Rob added, "I drive back to Magdeburg, take the Bibles to the cathedral, and go back to the hotel and get a good night's sleep."

"That is correct," the pastor said, ignoring the sarcasm. "The next day, you drive back to West Berlin where I hope you find Maria at Christa's apartment."

"Yes," Maria said, "if I make it through the checkpoint into West Berlin, I will go to Christa's. That will be a joyous moment, but it will also be sad. It will mean that I will probably not again see Pastor Schreibholz and Helga and many other friends in the GDR."

Lost in thought, Rob stared at the greenish map, his eyes shifting from Magdeburg to the autobahn to Helmstedt to Berlin. He was mildly irritated at being put on the spot this way. He was an American tourist, interested only in history and seeing Germany and meeting people with fascinating experiences. He wanted no trouble. Yet he was now confronted with a request that all of his humanitarian and religious instincts told him he could not easily decline.

Suddenly he wished that he had never come to Germany, but most of all that he had never found that photograph in his father's footlocker. It was a bizarre idea to delve into such remote events more than half a century gone. If he had only let the past alone, he would not now be trapped by the present.

Pastor Schreibholz spoke at last. "Herr Kirkman, I know that we ask much of you. We ask you only out of necessity. There are few automobiles in the GDR. The person on whom we were relying, who has a car, has himself been detained by the police and is unavailable. We have no other car. I hope that you will consider the matter carefully, and I should add, prayerfully. Of course, there are dangers for you in what we ask. If the police caught you, you would face a prison term. We believe that the chance of that happening is small, but it is certainly a possibility. We should remember that men have always taken risks for good causes. Yesterday we talked about Dietrich Bonhoeffer. He took great risks, and he paid with his life. You may consider that this is not your problem; but that is what many people said about German events in the 1930s."

Maria broke in, as if embarrassed by the pastor's statements. "Herr Kirkman, I do not want you to feel compelled to undertake this task. You have your life to think about. I have been reluctant to ask you to do this. I have agreed to do so only because this seems to be the last way out. I am sorry," she said, struggling to retain her composure. "We should not have told you of this."

Rob felt desperately the need to think the whole thing through. "I would like to help," he said cautiously, "but I would like time to consider it."

"You should let Christa know by noon tomorrow whether you will go or not. I should add that the expenses involved in renting a car and in paying for a hotel room in Magdeburg will be paid by our friends in West Berlin."

"Oh, I am not worried about the expenses," Rob said quickly, embarrassed that they think that this was the cause of his hesitation. Then he wondered what was the cause of his hesitation. "May I ask how my decision will get from Christa to Maria to the truck driver in Hanover?"

"There are means for getting that message to the right people," the pastor replied. "You can be certain that your word to Christa will be sufficient."

"Yes," Maria said. "I will have all the information you need when we meet in Magdeburg. There are two dining rooms in the International Hotel. I will enter the Moscow Room at seven o'clock, and sit down and order dinner. You should enter a few minutes later and sit at a different table. When you have finished eating, get up and leave. I will follow you. Wait at the elevator until you see me coming. We will get on the elevator together, but do not show any recognition of me. I will follow you to your room. There we can talk briefly. From there, we will leave in your car."

Rob had never felt so low in his life. He wanted out. He wanted to be back in Tuscaloosa or Remberton or Charlottesville or anywhere in the Western World. What a fool he had been to think that he could enjoy a vacation in East Germany. This was life-or-death business, not something which one could casually sample. He thought of countless martyrs of centuries gone—the figure of Dietrich Bonhoeffer looming largest of all in the forefront of his thoughts because of his conversation with Pastor Schreibholz.

His distracted reverie was interrupted by Schreibholz. "Herr

Kirkman, perhaps you should begin your trip back to Berlin and think more about this overnight."

"Uh . . . oh . . . yes, I should do that," Rob said, rousing himself from his brooding. "I really must go. The roads are not familiar. It will be dark before I reach Berlin, and I do not want to miss the midnight deadline."

Rob pushed his chair back from the table and began to rise. "Wait," Schreibholz said, laying his hand on Rob's arm. "If you do not mind, I would like to say a short prayer before you leave."

"Yes, of course," Rob said, sitting down.

Pastor Schreibholz then said, "Let us hold hands." He extended his right hand and clasped Rob's; with his left hand he took Maria's. Maria reached across the table for Rob's free hand.

After a long moment, the pastor began quietly but impressively. "Almighty God, we thank you for all your boundless grace and mercy. We thank you for our families and loved ones, those who are with us now and those who have gone before. . . ."

With his head bowed and eyes closed, Rob saw nothing. He lost comprehension of the words. He was transported by the preacher's deep and soothing voice. He was outside himself in some unreal state of suspension—a dream world.

Cutting through this detachment was the feel of Maria's hand gripping his. It was a slender, feminine hand, but it was not the soft silky hand that was characteristic of most American women he had known. It had a roughness about it, a coarseness of texture, although it was not the hand of a farmer or manual worker. He suddenly became aware that his heart was beating more rapidly than normal. He was not hearing what the preacher was saying. All of his thoughts were focused on that warm, female hand that he held in his own—a hand that seemed to be holding on to his as if it were its lifeline in the world. And it occurred to him that it might well be just that.

The preacher's words began to penetrate again. ". . . protect us from the pestilence that walketh at noonday, deliver us from the snare of the fowler, and bring us at last to your eternal peace."

They released hands and stood up. "I hope that I can help you," Rob said. "I will do what I think I can. I will talk to Christa before noon tomorrow."

The pastor and Maria followed Rob as he walked into the hall and toward the door to the street. When he reached the door, the pastor moved ahead of him to turn the lock.

As the door swung open, Rob shook the pastor's hand and said, "*Auf wiedersehen.*"

The pastor took Rob's hand in both of his. "My friend, I hope that we will meet again. Whatever you decide to do, and whatever happens to you or me, remember that God is with you."

Never before in his life had Robert Kirkman felt as he did now, that he was talking directly to an agent of the Almighty. The weathered but kindly face, the intensity of the eyes, and the firmness of the handshake all conveyed to him that he was in the presence of an extraordinary person. At that instant, the rightness of this man's beliefs seemed beyond question. The SED was a pale and feeble shadow by comparison.

Rob turned to Maria and looked into her now drawn and wistful face, her eyes reddened from earlier tears. He took her right hand in his. Their eyes met. "Perhaps we will see each other in Magdeburg," he said in a low voice. Then he was out of the door and into the soft light of the late July afternoon.

Chapter 19

IT WAS DARK BEFORE Robert Kirkman reached Checkpoint Bravo and was cleared by the GDR border police to pass into West Berlin. After reaching the Hotel Am Zoo, he ate a bowl of soup and went to bed. He was tired and emotionally drained, but he could not sleep. Compassion for Maria's plight and interest in his own safety competed within him. One way or the other, within the next twelve hours, he had to resolve this anguished turmoil.

He had no family to be concerned about; therefore, he reasoned, he need not act out of consideration for persons dependent on him or looking to him for guidance. It came to him that the only thing standing between him and this mission in the GDR was his own well-being. It was, after all, his life.

What right did these people have to draw him into such a risky task, to put him on the road toward a GDR prison? They had no claim on him; he owed them nothing. It would be so easy to get on a plane for the States and put all of this behind him. After all, he need never see any of these people again. He had satisfied his curiosity. He had found the woman in the photograph.

During the three-hour drive back from Halle, it had occurred to him that he did not know what led to his involvement in this escape scheme; Pastor Schreibholz had not explained whose idea this was, and Rob had been so overwhelmed by the proposal that he had not thought to ask. As he tried to analyze it, he concluded that Christa had to be behind the whole thing. Now that he looked back on the dinner with Christa, he recalled that she seemed surprisingly agreeable to his calling on her parents. He had let his guard down, mesmerized by the smiling, charming Christa. In this divided world with its sinister past, dark intrigue should be no surprise. But how could she have communicated so expeditiously through the nearly impenetrable Wall? He was angry at both Schreibholtz and Christa for snaring him in this plot, but he found himself also admiring their ingenuity.

He got out of bed several times during the night and stood at the window looking out over the dark and empty courtyard. At one of those moments, as dawn was approaching, he remembered Saul and the lost donkeys. He heard again the deep voice of Pastor Schreibholz saying, "It is no coincidence that you have come here." Standing at the window in the still darkness, Rob's flesh turned cold. Was it possible in this age of science and technology that some divine force had actually brought him to this benighted land? He stood at the window, transfixed by the implications. After a long while—he knew not how long—it became clear that he had no choice.

Rob and Christa met at eleven in the morning at a small restaurant on Kant Strasse. He arrived first and waited on the sidewalk. She appeared five minutes later. She was smiling, but her manner was decidedly businesslike, almost curt. They exchanged greetings, and she led the way in. The restaurant was nearly empty; Christa led him to a table at the rear and they ordered coffee.

"Did you meet my parents?" Christa asked as soon as the waiter left.

"Only your father," Rob answered, relieved to be able to speak English again. "Your mother was away for the weekend at a church meeting at Naumberg."

"Oh, I am sorry. Mother is a bright and interesting woman. I wanted the two of you to meet each other."

"I'm sorry too. I have a feeling that you are aware that Maria Egloffsberg was there. Am I right?"

"Yes," Christa said after a moment's hesitation. "I want to apologize to you for this unexpected and difficult position in which you have been put."

Rob leaned back to let the waiter place the coffee cups in front of them. When the waiter left, he resumed. "I must say that I am somewhat confused by several things. I take it that it was no happenstance that Maria came to Halle when I was there; but how did she know that I was there? What is going on here? When I asked you whether there were any members of the von Egloffsberg family in East Germany, you said nothing about her."

Christa looked hurt and embarrassed. "I realize that this must be perplexing for you. I want you to know that I did not lure you into this. Going to Halle was your idea, wasn't it?"

"Yes, it was; but there is a lot going on here that I have not been told." Rob was showing a bit of irritation.

"I intend to tell you all about it, at least to the extent that I can without disclosing sensitive information. But I am concerned now about time. I must leave in a few minutes in order to get a message through before noon. I need to know right now whether you are willing to help. I know that this is not an easy decision, especially on such short notice, and I will accept your decision not to undertake it. But I do hope that you will."

"Am I to assume that you know the details of the plan?" Rob asked.

"Yes. All I need to know at the moment is whether your answer is yes or no."

Rob was mildly surprised at how calm and confident he was now about his answer. The tormented night had worked all the anxiety out of him. By the time he had arisen and taken a shower, he was quite clear as to what he would do.

"I may be a fool," he said slowly, "but my answer is yes."

"Good," she exclaimed, a broad smile breaking across her face. She breathed a sigh and reached out and covered Rob's hand with hers. "Thank you so much. I will have to tell you later how grateful we all are to you." She pulled her hand back and rummaged in her pocketbook. "I must leave now to make the telephone call relaying this information. There are two things you should do this afternoon: make a reservation for yourself in the International Hotel at Magdeburg for tomorrow night, and rent a car with the largest trunk available. Then there is one more thing," she continued after a pause. "You must come to my apartment for dinner tonight. We will go over all the details then."

Rob was captivated again. He found himself looking at her flashing eyes, her thin, wide mouth, and her shapely torso. All sense of irritation at her for involving him in this dangerous venture had evaporated.

Pulling a pencil and notepad from her pocketbook, she wrote out her apartment address. "It's in Charlottenberg," she said as she handed it to him. "Try to be there at six-thirty." She rose and took his hand, then turned and walked quickly out of the restaurant.

After a light lunch, Rob wandered aimlessly along the Berlin streets, his thoughts preoccupied with the next forty-eight hours. The uplift he had experienced in Christa's presence was gone, and he was filled with foreboding. He circled the Victory Monument, strolled along the Tiergarten, and eventually reached the Brandenberg Gate. He stopped in front of the massive Soviet War Memorial. Guarded by soldiers of the Red Army, it was a discordant fluke of the timing of the arrival in Berlin of the Western allies. The Russians erected it in what was the American zone, but no Americans were yet there. It was an audacious publicity coup, as though the Americans had built a great monument to themselves in the middle of East Berlin. He wondered why the USSR always erected monuments to itself while the United States did not.

The black, red, and gold GDR flag was flapping in the wind alongside the Quadriga atop the gate. The Wall obscured his view of Unter den

Linden, but he could see the needlelike television tower rising in the distance from Alexanderplatz, the East's bold assertion of its technological advances—the symbol that socialism was the way to the future. Sightseeing buses were arriving, parking, and departing, their engines snorting and emitting offensive fumes as they disgorged and reboarded their loads of tourists, all there to gawk at the Wall.

After two hours of wandering, Rob found himself back in his room at the Am Zoo. He could not see beyond the next day. He reviewed the worst possibilities—capture, imprisonment, or death. It was unnerving to realize that at this moment no one in the States knew where he was, and no one would know what had happened to him if one of these dark scenarios unfolded.

He pulled an Am Zoo Hotel envelope from the desk drawer and addressed it rapidly in his large, angular hand: Col. Noble Shepperson, Attorney at Law, Remberton, Alabama, USA. On a piece of hotel stationary, he began to write an abbreviated account of his trip thus far. He mentioned only Marburg, Frankfurt, and Berlin, saying that he would have a lot more to relate when he got home. He concluded:

"Tomorrow I am going into the GDR to spend the night and look around. This will be outside of East Berlin, at a place where American tourists are almost never seen. There is no reason to be apprehensive, but strange things do happen. When I get back to West Berlin, I will cable you. If you have not received a cable from me by the time you get this letter, please make inquiry through the State Department with the American Embassy in Bonn."

At half past six, he alighted from a taxi at the Charlottenberg address that Christa had given him. It was an attractive tree-lined street filled with multistory post-war apartment buildings. Gripping the German visitor's obligatory bunch of flowers, he took the elevator to the third floor.

He stood in the hall collecting his thoughts. Classical music filtered faintly through her door. He knocked lightly. In a matter of seconds, the door opened, and there stood Christa.

She was more physically striking and alluring than he had yet seen her, in tailored black slacks and a long-sleeved white silk blouse. A light gold chain lay at her throat, and gold bangles glittered at her wrists. Her hair looked freshly washed and wind-blown.

"Come in," she said, standing aside to let him enter. "So you know the old German custom. What beautiful flowers." He extended the bouquet toward her, thinking that they looked rather bedraggled.

"Charlottenburg is a pretty district," he said, following her into the seating area. "Your address is easy for a taxi driver."

"Yes, it is convenient here. Sit down while I put these in something."

He sank into a low, soft cushioned sofa. The room was starkly contemporary. The furnishings looked Scandanavian, the colors mainly orange and rust. An abstract painting hung over the sofa. On a glass-topped coffee table was a copy of *Der Spiegel* and some other German magazines that he did not recognize.

Christa returned from the kitchen with the flowers in a vase. "Now," she said, placing the vase on a table facing the sofa, "what would you like to drink?" Before he could answer, she continued. "You told me the other night that you liked schnapps. I have several kinds; would you like to try any special variety?"

"Schnapps sounds good. That is something I do not get at home. But I do not have any special preference."

She disappeared again into the kitchen; he heard the clinking of bottles and glasses. The late afternoon sunlight illuminated the room through mesh curtains. Sounds of a string quartet came softly from a radio at one end of the sofa. The noise of traffic was barely discernible. The scene took on a dreamlike quality for Rob, slouched as he was in the deep cushions, legs stretched out in this quiet retreat in this Western island in the heart of the GDR. The drab office of her pastor father in Halle and the bleakness of life beyond the Wall, hardly two miles away, belonged to another time and place.

She was coming toward him with a pair of slender glasses filled to the top. She placed them on the coffee table and eased down beside him on the sofa. She handed one glass to him and took the other.

"I believe Americans say *cheers,* or is it the English? Anyway, Germans say *prost.*"

They both laughed, touched glasses, and sipped. The liquid fire trickled down Rob's throat, reminding him of his evening with Wolfgang at Prinzenheim.

Christa leaned forward and placed her glass on the coffee table. She pulled a magazine from the stack. "Here you can see some of your countrymen," she said, flipping the pages. "This was an American military parade in honor of the mayor and other officials of West Berlin. You know that there are about six thousand American soldiers in the city."

Rob looked at the picture. There, lined up in perfect order, boots and helmets shining, pants creased and scarves neatly tucked under their chins, were row upon row of his compatriots. A group of rather ordinary-looking Germans in civilian suits was passing down the line in review.

"What good do you think that six thousand men would be if the East Germans or Russians decided to make a move against us? Of course the British and French also have small garrisons here. Suppose there are ten thousand men. The GDR army has over one hundred thousand men, and the Red Army nearly four hundred thousand."

"Those six thousand," Rob said, slightly amused at her seriousness, "are a symbol, I guess, a sign, a kind of pledge by the United States that the freedom of West Berlin is something we take to be important. In my view, those men are not what protects this city—it's a combination of world opinion and the fear of a another world war, especially nuclear war. Maybe those six thousand are necessary as evidence that the threat of war is real if a move is made against West Berlin."

"I suppose that is what it comes down to," she sighed. "Doug Catron says the same thing, but it is a bit frightening to think about the odds against us in this small space."

She leaned forward again and put the magazine back on the stack. She leaned back on the sofa and took a sip of schnapps, looking into space as though lost in thought. Rob could not decide how he should view this woman. He felt drawn to her, but the attraction was not quite sexual. Never an easy conversationalist with women, he groped mentally for something to say.

Suddenly she sat straight up. "Listen," she said, placing her hand on his knee, "I have almost forgotten to tell you that we are having another guest for dinner."

"Another guest?" Rob exclaimed, with surprise and irritation.

"Yes, and you have met him before. He is Uncle Wolfi. I hope you do not object."

"Oh, no," Rob said, trying not too successfully to conceal his disappointment.

"I really had to invite him tonight. He is in West Berlin for a few days and is staying here. He actually pays part of the rent on this apartment. I could not afford a two-bedroom place like this on the salary I get. He comes here on business often, so we share the rent and he stays for a few days once or twice a month. He has always been good to me, and I could hardly refuse his request. Besides, tonight it may be useful for you to talk with him about your trip tomorrow."

Tomorrow. Yes, everything must now focus on tomorrow. The glow of the evening had passed. The unreal moment had gone. "What time is he coming?" Rob asked resignedly.

"It should be almost time. He said that he would return by seven."

Sitting in the fading sunlight, Rob changed the subject to Maria Egloffsberg.

"Her existence in the GDR and our family connection with her are sensitive," said Christa, "and it serves no one's interest to make this known. When you questioned me about our family, I was not sure enough about what you were doing to feel comfortable telling you. I am sorry. You should not feel offended." She put her hand on his arm, and a slight tingle passed through him. "In this strange and divided world, both friends and enemies are all around us, and it is not easy to tell the difference."

"I can understand that. I have come to the point where nothing in Germany surprises me. I suppose you know that she and I first saw each other in Leipzig."

"I learned that after you left for Halle. What do you think of Maria?"

"She seems to be quite intelligent and serious-minded."

"Do you think that she and I look alike? After all, we are first cousins—or at least half first cousins."

"There is something about the hair and eyes that suggests a resemblance. But," he paused with a smile, "I would add that she is not as pretty as you."

As he spoke, he leaned toward her. Just as their lips touched, they heard a key turn in the lock. Rob pulled back, both startled and irritated. The door swung open as Wolfgang von Egloffsberg entered, preceded by his white cane, its metal tip gliding across the floor ahead of him. Rob stood up abruptly, flustered and embarrassed for a moment until he realized that it made no difference how he looked or what he was doing.

"Uncle Wolfi," exclaimed Christa, "come in." She moved across the room and grasped him by the arm, closing the door behind him. "I was beginning to wonder whether anything had happened to you."

"No, no," Wolfgang responded in his deep voice. "I knew that today would be busy."

"We have here as a guest for dinner tonight Robert Kirkman. You remember him, the American who visited recently at Prinzenheim?"

"Yes, of course," Wolfgang said. "Herr Kirkman, I am glad to see you again."

Wolfgang took a step forward, shooting his right hand ahead of him. Rob advanced and grasped it. He had almost forgotten how tall and imposing Wolfgang was, especially so as he stood in a dark business suit, with his nearly full head of hair swept back and his scarred face softened in the waning light.

"This is a nice surprise to see you in Berlin," Rob said.

"I believe that we have important business to discuss this evening. Is that correct, Christa?"

"Yes. But first, would you like to go to your room and rest?"

"I would, for a few minutes. Perhaps Herr Kirkman would like a schnapps."

"He already has one, but I will get you one. And let me say that we need not be so formal. Perhaps I have been with the Americans too much, but I think, Uncle Wolfi, that you could address Herr Kirkman as Robert. Grandmother did."

"Of course. Then he should address me as Wolfgang. Also, Herr Kirk—Robert—I believe that you prefer to talk in English."

"I can talk in German, but it might be easier for you to understand me in English."

"Then we will speak in English," Christa decreed.

In a few minutes, Wolfgang returned, wearing an open-collared, long-sleeved gray shirt. He sat in a chair across the coffee table from Rob, who slid a glass of schnapps into his hand. The music on the radio prompted a discourse from Wolfgang on West Berlin radio stations and the programs they broadcast to the East. Christa was moving back and forth between the kitchen and the dining table, putting plates and glasses in position.

Wolfgang shifted his comments from West Berlin radio to the subject of the blind in Germany. He was full of talk, and Rob said nothing. He described the library that had been founded in Leipzig in 1894 to produce Braille material for the blind all over the German Empire. That library was still there, he said, but it now confined its services to East Germany. It had been necessary after the war to create a similar service in the West. In fact, it had been necessary to create duplicates of many things in the West. The historic German structure had to be rebuilt in the reduced territory—a parliament, the courts, and the ministries. The continued Germany-wide union of the Protestant churches had given him hope for the reunification of the country, but that hope disappeared in the late sixties, when the churches divided because of intense pressure from the GDR. Wolfgang lectured on for a quarter of an hour until Christa summoned them to the dinner table.

When they were seated, Wolfgang bowed his head; Christa and Rob followed. Wolfgang then spoke in a powerful German cadence: "Our Father in heaven, we thank you for the many blessings you have given us—for food, for shelter, for friends, for family, those who are with us and those who have gone. We thank you for bringing Robert Kirkman to us. Be with him, guard him against all harm, and deliver him safely home. Be with all people in this fractured land who call upon you for strength and help. We ask all these things in the name of our Lord Jesus Christ."

Rob had shifted uncomfortably in his chair at the mention of his name. He was not accustomed to being prayed for so personally and explicitly. As the three of them lifted their heads and opened their eyes, he tried not to look flustered. They took forks and began eating the green salads set at each place.

"Today I found an interesting-looking bottle of Austrian wine," Christa said as she filled their glasses.

After several bites, Wolfgang abruptly said, "Now we must talk about the business of tomorrow. My good friend, we are grateful to you for your willingness to undertake this mission. You could have said that this is none of your concern, but you did not. There are dangers, but I do not think they are great; still, who could say what could happen. You really know none of the people involved. The words come to mind: 'Greater love hath no man than he who lays down his life for his friends.' I would add that the love must be even greater in one who lays down his life for a stranger."

Rob stirred. The thought of laying down his life had not occurred to him. "Before we talk further, I must ask a question or two. I am puzzled. I left Berlin on Saturday morning for Halle. Christa was the only person who knew that I was going, and she learned that only the night before. Yet Maria arrived in Halle on Sunday, knowing that I was there. Also, Christa's father seemed to know all about this plan. With East and West sealed off from each other, how could these communications take place in such a short time?"

Dabbing his lips with the napkin, Wolfgang spoke in a low voice as if there were someone across the room from whom he wanted to keep the information. "Robert, we do have means of communicating when it is important and necessary. I don't think that it is wise to go into the details. In a sense, the less you know, the better off you will be. I can say this. We are putting extraordinary trust in you. You are a stranger among us. We know nothing about you. Yet you have been told of a secret plan that is in violation of GDR law and could cost several people their liberty and perhaps more."

"I had thought of that," Rob said, "and wondered why anyone would do that."

"Well, I will explain that," Christa joined in. "You will find out eventually. This, too, is confidential. I asked Doug Catron if he could have you checked out in the States. He has helped us on other occasions. He was good enough, on an emergency basis, to contact the right people in Washington, over a secure telephone line, and request that they run a quick inquiry on you. They found out enough in the States within twenty-four hours to satisfy us that you are reliable enough. There is, of course, still a risk. This was not an in-depth investigation." A twinkle came into her eyes, and a hint of a smile crossed her face.

Both startled and irritated, Rob sat back in his chair. "Do you mean that you got the United States Army to launch an investigation of me back on my home ground?"

"That's right," Christa said. "Some of your friends and colleagues may tell you when you get home that they were called by a government agent, but they do not know why they were called. We have been desperate for some means to get Maria out. When you said that you were going to Halle, that seemed to us to be the best chance we are likely to have. We had to know something more about you. I hope you do not mind."

Her plaintive voice softened Rob. "Well, I suppose it does no harm to arouse the curiosity of folks back there. Most of them have thought that I was a little odd for a long time."

While Christa was removing the salad plates and bringing quiche, Rob resumed his questions. "Pastor Schreibholz told me the story of his discovery of Maria in the Charité Hospital. When you and your mother first heard that news, what did you think?"

"We could not believe it. My mother almost fainted. My brother Kurt had been dead for nearly thirty years. His wife disappeared during the final days in Berlin, presumed dead, so we had always thought that their small daughter had also died. We were doubtful that this young woman was really my brother's child. After Ernst and Helga had both talked with her and looked at the photograph she had saved, they were convinced. Of course, I could not examine the photograph myself, but I was willing to accept their judgment."

"How did you meet her?" Rob asked, still curious about Wolfgang's forays into East Berlin.

"I went to the Charité Hospital and found her on duty," Wolfgang replied.

"Can you simply go into East Berlin at any time?" Rob persisted.

"Not quite, but I do have what might be described as special arrangements. I can go and come more readily than most West Germans."

Rob waited for further explanation, but none was forthcoming. Christa refilled their wine glasses, and they tackled the quiche.

Wolfgang continued. "Maria had been reared in a straight Marxist-Leninist environment. The system had not been too bad to her. She had gone to medical school on a full scholarship and was into a fairly promising career as an eye doctor. That career interest and my blindness drew us together, I believe. It was also clear to me that she was starved for family relationships. Her foster parents had both died, and she was alone. Although I already had one wonderful niece," he reached out and patted Christa on the arm, "I was very happy to find that I had another. It is not bad, is it, to have one niece who is a lawyer and one who is a doctor? It was sad, of course, that one was in the East and one was in the West; but that is the German story of the late twentieth century."

Christa spoke up. "Because I had no brothers or sisters, it was nice for me to learn that I had a cousin. I first met Maria several months after my father and mother had met her. Because of my position in the Justice Ministry here, I too have access to East Berlin that West Berliners generally do not have. So Maria and I have seen each other many times. Of course, she has never been to West Berlin or out of the GDR."

"Wasn't this an awkward relationship for both of you," Rob asked, "because of her Marxist-Leninist rearing?"

"At first I was concerned about that," Wolfgang said. "She was a little cool. She seemed almost afraid to meet and talk. But that is typical of all East Germans when they meet a Westerner. After my second visit with her, I began to think that she was not a true believer in that system. This feeling grew in my mind as time passed."

"I began to see that also after Maria had visited my parents in Halle," Christa said. "I think she began to look on my parents almost as if they were her parents. They were very good to her, and she began to visit them rather often."

"She was progressing well in her training," Wolfgang said, "and she had to be careful about her contacts with the church and with West Germans. Although she had been a member of the Free German Youth—she would have hardly been admitted to the University otherwise—she had never joined the SED."

"Then the most amazing thing happened," Christa said. "About a year ago, she asked my father to baptize her. That was one of his most unforgettable moments. It took place in Halle, and I was able to be there. It was a strictly private baptism. She has kept her church affiliation a secret. In fact, she does not openly associate with any congregation, but she is quite active behind the scene."

"And that is what has now gotten her into trouble with the GDR police," Wolfgang said.

"Do you mean her involvement in importing Bibles?" Rob asked.

"Yes, that as well as other activities. She has helped some people get out of the GDR. You know that leaving the GDR without official authorization, or helping others to do so, is considered a serious offense there."

"Yes," Rob said, "an offense I am now about to commit." He smiled nervously. "What is the penalty?"

"Usually from two to seven years in prison," Christa answered. "But there are exchanges from time to time. You have probably read of some of the dramatic ones involving spies, but many exchanges take place quietly between the East and West Germans. Also, the West German government sometimes pays the GDR to get political prisoners released into the West."

"So if I get caught in this business tomorrow night, there is at least some chance that I will not spend the next several years of my life as a guest of the GDR prison authorities?"

"A very good chance. If you were picked up over there, we would immediately activate all diplomatic channels," Christa said.

"You are thinking too much of the dark side," Wolfgang interrupted. "It is highly unlikely that the police will stumble onto this operation. But you must remember this: God is with you. Whatever happens, you are in God's hands."

They fell into silence. The last light of the summer day was fading. In the deepening dusk, Rob saw the two Germans lost in thought—one of the prewar generation, seared and scarred and rendered sightless; the other a child of the divided residue, a post-war product, living with a split family and shuttling across the barrier.

At home at this very hour, Rob reflected, Americans were likely to be at the beach or on the tennis courts, or simply going about routine business on this July day. They would have difficulty comprehending the scene which he now confronted.

Pushing her chair back, Christa broke the silence. "I will turn on the lights. If the two of you will move over to the sofa and chairs, I will bring coffee and a map."

After she had served them coffee, Christa sat down on the sofa beside Rob and spread out a GDR road map identical to the one Rob had in his hotel room. Wolfgang sat in a chair across from them, cup and saucer in hand.

"You know, of course, how to get from West Berlin onto the autobahn for Helmstedt," Christa said, pointing to Checkpoint Bravo.

Rob nodded, and she continued. "Here you proceed westward along the autobahn until you reach this road." She indicated an intersection about halfway between Berlin and the West German border. "You will have just crossed the Elbe a short distance back. I suggest that you drive by this route to Magdeburg tomorrow, so you can see the area in the daylight."

"Is this the intersection at which the van driver with the Bibles will leave the autobahn for the ruined church?" Rob asked.

"Yes. As you can see, this is the main road from the autobahn down to Magdeburg," she said. "Now, about three kilometers south of this intersection, as you come from the autobahn, there is a small road turning off to the west. It is not on these GDR road maps, but you will have no difficulty finding it; it is the only road turning off to the west for several kilometers. About one kilometer along that road, you will find the ruined church on the site of a former village."

"Will it be on the left or the right?"

"On your left. The church in former times was in the middle of a small village that was almost totally destroyed during the war. It was directly in the path of the American army as it advanced toward the Elbe. In fact, the point where you will cross the Elbe on the autobahn is approximately the place where the Americans first reached that river line in April of 1945. This village was so badly damaged that the Russians and the East Germans did not try to rebuild it. They cleared the site and incorporated it into a large collective farm. They left the church ruins, probably because of the cemetery there. It is about a hundred meters back from the road on which you will be driving."

"How far are any inhabited houses from the church?"

"The nearest village is about five kilometers farther on. Perhaps you know that with the collective farm system there are almost no isolated houses in the countryside. All the workers and farmers live in villages. So you will find no houses along this road."

Christa sounded like an army officer briefing the commander. Perhaps she had picked up the jargon and style from her associations with Major Catron. He studied the map closely, trying to think of other questions he should ask.

Christa reviewed the plan as it had been described to him by Pastor Schreibholz, from the meeting with Maria in the hotel to the rendezvous with the van at the church and the delivery of the Bibles to the cathedral in Magdeburg.

Rob pulled *Baedeker* from his coat pocket. "I have studied this map of Magdeburg," he said as he thumbed through the pages to the city map. "I see here the cathedral near the river. But, of course, this 1904 map does not show the International Hotel, and the street arrangement could be quite different today. Can you update the situation and show me where the hotel is?"

Christa glanced at him with a smile that was both sad and amused. She stared at the little street map. "Well, the streets are still there, the river is still there, and fortunately, the two key buildings are still there. One is the cathedral, which you already know; the other is the railroad station." She pointed to a spot west of the cathedral. "In front of the station is a great open space, a parking lot. Your hotel is directly opposite the station. The station and the cathedral will look as they did in 1904, but not much else will. I went to Magdeburg once with my parents on the train when I was about thirteen. Most of the central part was destroyed in the war."

Rob was back in the noisy and hot restaurant in Halle for an instant, sitting across the table from Otto, the new Marxist-Leninist managerial breed, in his black suit and SED pin. Rob heard again those bitter remarks about the once beautiful city of Magdeburg.

"What could go wrong?" Rob asked, taking his coffee off the table and leaning back on the sofa.

"I will tell you," Wolfgang said. "I should say that I do not consider any of these possibilities to be likely. First, there may be difficulties of some sort at the border, and the van could not get through the crossing. Then, the autobahn could be so heavily patrolled that the van driver could not make an exit to get to the church. It is also possible, but very remote, that someone could discover you at the church. Once you have

Maria in the van and the Bibles in your car, all you have to worry about is delivering the Bibles to the cathedral. It will be dark and late, so there should be no problem there. The most serious threat to the mission will be at the GDR exit point at West Berlin. We can only hope that the GDR border police do not decide to unpack the boxes in the van. On the transit route they do not normally do so."

"How will Maria be concealed in the van?"

"She will get in the box from which the Bibles are removed. In the top eighteen or twenty centimeters of this box there are Braille pamphlets. So even if someone opens the box he will see only Braille material. The box will have shipping labels on it showing that it is being sent to an institute for the blind in West Berlin."

"I imagine," Rob mused aloud, "that among persons coming out of the GDR into the West there are at least a few spies, persons planted by the GDR authorities."

"Yes, of course," Christa said, "that does happen. Our government has procedures for screening new arrivals, but the procedures are not foolproof."

"This may sound unkind or cynical," Rob said, "But has it ever occurred to you that Maria could be such a person?"

"Yes it has," Wolfgang said. "Here one has to be suspicious of almost everything. There is always some risk, but in this case I believe that we do not have a GDR plant, as you put it."

Christa spoke up. "I agree. I believe that Maria is a genuine Christian who has come to see the GDR system as essentially evil. Also, the police investigation that is underway against her seems inconsistent with a theory that she is a GDR spy. We are willing to take our chances."

Rob hesitated. "There is something here that keeps puzzling me," he said slowly. "Why did the Baroness von Egloffsberg not mention Maria to me during all of my talk with her about the family?"

"Her attitude about this is strange," Wolfgang said, placing his empty cup on the table. "She is simply not yet convinced that Maria is really Kurt's daughter. She wants some proof. It is, of course, unlikely that we will ever have that kind of evidence. Ernst and Helga and Christa and I are all willing to accept Maria as what she claims to be. I wish that Mother would also. Perhaps she will later. When we get Maria out of the GDR, she can talk to Mother and show her the picture, so maybe she will put her doubts behind her."

"Yes," Christa intervened, "so much has been lost, so many families have been destroyed, that I am willing to resolve the doubts in Maria's favor. I am convinced that she is a good person, one that we should help all that we can."

Wolfgang stood up. "I have had a long day. I think that I will retire to my room, if you will excuse me." He extended his right hand. "My friend, Robert, you are a man of great courage and good heart. You are undertaking a humanitarian mission for which the von Egloffsberg family is grateful." The two men shook hands. "Christa, my dear," he said, turning to her, "good night. I will see you in the morning."

"Good night, Uncle Wolfi," she said, clasping his arm.

Halfway to his bedroom door, Wolfgang turned to face Rob and Christa again. "*Auf wiedersehen*, Robert," he said, raising his hand in a half salute. "May we meet again." Then he added, "God be with you."

When Wolfgang's door had closed behind him, Rob said, "I must be going too. I want to get a good night's sleep. No telling what time I will get to bed tomorrow night, if at all." His earlier amorousness had faded in the light of the reality lying just ahead.

"Oh, Robert," Christa said, putting her arms around his neck, "we do thank you. You are, as the Americans say, going beyond the call of duty. You must telephone me the minute you get back in West Berlin. By that time, I hope that Maria will be right here, safely in this apartment. We will all get together and have a little celebration."

She moved forward and kissed him squarely on the mouth. He ran his arms around her back, and they remained locked in embrace. The long kiss ended, and for a few seconds they looked into each other's eyes. After an unreckonable amount of time—it may have been a matter of seconds or of minutes—Rob pulled back and whispered, "I really must go."

They walked to the door of the apartment holding hands. "Incidentally," she said, "the weather reports for tomorrow night are uncertain. It may rain; but that would be good. It would mean that fewer people will be out wandering around."

In the opened door, he kissed her again lightly. "I hope to see you on Wednesday. If I don't show up, call out the U.S. Army or somebody." He half laughed, but he was not really amused.

"Good luck," she said, squeezing his hand. Rob thought he saw tears in her eyes as the door closed.

Chapter 20

THE SKY WAS OVERCAST, and the morning was gray and cool. The Mercedes-Benz with Robert Kirkman behind the wheel slipped smoothly along the autobahn. Traffic was running from sparse to moderate. A Mercedes was probably the most conspicuous Western-made car he could have chosen, but it had the largest trunk. Although he was enjoying the feel of the car, he was far from relaxed.

Since clearing the checkpoint and entering the GDR, he had asked himself over and again why he was here. Was it compassion, outrage at the GDR, or part of some divine plan? Or could it have something to do with Christa?

He was unable to assess the divine element, if any. Instead, he found himself feeling that a more tangible explanation was Christa. There was something oddly appealing about her, yet different from that which he had experienced with any other woman. It was not exactly a romantic attraction. He couldn't say what it was.

He had not had a genuinely romantic sensation in years, not since he had been in love—or thought he had been in love—with Ippy Ratcliff. Her defection to the Atlanta real estate developer's son had jolted him and changed his whole attitude about women for years. He had been depressed for months. Fortunately, it came just after his law school graduation, otherwise he might not have made it through his third year.

That summer was etched deeply in his mind. He was packing for New York when he received a telephone call from Archibald Ratcliff's secretary, requesting that he come by the bank. Reluctantly he agreed.

He entered the bank a few minutes before closing time. Mr. Archie and two other bank officers sat chatting in the marble lobby. When Rob arrived, Mr. Archie waved him into his private office.

Mr. Archie closed the door as they shook hands and then sat down behind his desk. He was a heavyset man, his puffy face the color of a dove's foot surmounted by an unruly shock of gray hair. On the wall behind him hung a 1930 survey of the county. Rob sat across from him in the chair usually occupied by supplicants for loans.

"Robby," Mr. Archie began, modulating his normally booming voice, "Ippy has done a lot of damn fool things in her life, but this is the most damn fool thing of all. This fellow she says she wants to marry is no good. I've met him, and I think I'm a pretty good judge of character. What she sees in him I'll never know."

Rob sat expressionless as Mr. Archie described his efforts to talk Ippy out of the whole thing. He had about given up, he said, until a couple of days before.

"I had made discrete inquiries about this fellow through a banker friend of mine in Atlanta. You can understand a legitimate fatherly interest, Robby, I'm sure."

Rob stirred. "What did he find?"

"It seems that about three years ago this boy was chased out of Miami for defrauding a bunch of old folks on real estate deals."

"My Lord," Rob said. "Does Ippy know anything about this?"

"I doubt it. But she's damn well going to find out. Now listen, Robby, I know that you've been pretty keen on Ippy, and I might as well put it right on the table. If you're really interested in marrying her, I'll do all I can. She's coming home this weekend."

Rob sat quietly unresponsive. He could hear the tellers' machines tallying up and balancing the day's transactions.

"Well, what do you say?" Mr. Archie asked.

Something inside told Rob that he was at a crossroad. One instinct pulled him toward a chance to be with Ippy again; but another and more sober instinct was putting on the brakes.

"Mr. Archie," he began deliberately, "you know that I admire you and all of your family. I've known you all of my life. However, this latest move on your daughter's part has forced me to realize that she and I are not really suited for each other."

He had forced himself to utter those words, only half believing them; but he had never regretted it. Still, Ippy had taken a toll on him, and he did not want to risk a similar experience with Christa.

Whatever the reason for this East German venture, Rob kept telling himself that it made no sense; it was crazy. As Mr. Archie would say, it was a damn fool thing to do. What had begun over two weeks before as a lark, a long-shot foray back into history, had taken a grim turn. There was a queasy feeling in his stomach, which he had to recognize as a symptom of fear.

Almost before he realized it, he was crossing the Elbe at the point where the American army had first reached its banks in 1945. Berlin was fifty miles behind him, with only a thin and disintegrating German army in the way; the Red Army was east of the Oder. He dismissed the might-have-beens, but it warmed him to know that he was now on ground once occupied, albeit briefly, by his countrymen.

Much to his regret, Rob had not had a restful night. It had been another one of those nights punctuated by sleeplessness and bursts of dreams. In one dream, he saw his father and Dr. Loosh standing on the front porch of the house in Remberton during his mother's last illness. Mr. Ed's face was a study in sorrow and fatigue. The two men talked in hushed voices in the twilight, but he could not hear what they were saying.

Then he and his father were standing in the courtyard at the schloss in Prinzenheim, and there with them were Martina von Egloffsberg and Maria, flickering and gone. Then there was a disturbing glimpse of himself running through a thick forest in the dark of a rainy night in loneliness and desperation.

On both sides of the autobahn, the land was flat—table-top flat all the way to the horizon—like parts of Illinois he had once driven through. Grain was growing as far as he could see. He imagined long lines of Prussian cavalry sweeping across the flat expanses of North Central Europe one hundred and two hundred years ago. This must have been great cavalry country—and ideal tank country too.

Ahead, the sign indicating the exit for Magdeburg came into view and Rob slowed. A flock of trucks and BMWs and Mercedes swished past him, fast-driving West Berliners and West Germans bound for the border at Helmstedt. He reflected with mild pleasure that this lifeline connecting Berlin to the West was preserved by the solemn commitments of the United States, Britain, and France, as well as that of the Soviet Union. However, he now was leaving this internationally protected corridor and entering unprotected East German terrain.

He headed south toward Magdeburg and passed a lone truck heading north. Otherwise the road was deserted. He had slowed considerably to avoid overshooting the side road, but he almost did. It was exactly three kilometers from the autobahn, as Christa had said. Although it was a black-topped road, it was narrow, hardly wide enough for two cars, if two cars ever happened to meet on it. He had gone less than a mile when he saw the church ruin in the fields ahead to his left.

Traces of the former village were evident. The road was level and suddenly became wider with remains of curbs visible along its sides. Lanes and narrow streets led off at intervals to the left and right but then faded into grassy pastures or brushy growth. The rubble had been imperfectly cleared. Here and there the outlines of foundations could be seen. Most of the site had been put into pasture. A small herd of dairy cows was grazing about a hundred yards from the road on the right side. Rob did not see a single human being.

The church was set back from the main road at the head of what had formerly been a short side street. Despite the damage, Rob could discern that architecturally it was typical of many German village churches. It was made of dark red brick. The single tower at its front had been sheared off at the top, and the structure was roofless. The front wall connected to the tower was largely intact. One side wall appeared to be completely gone; the other side wall and the rear wall were standing to about half their original height. Trees were growing in the middle of the ruin, in what had been the sanctuary; a half-dozen others surrounded the church, all obviously post-war growth.

Looking carefully and seeing no one, Rob turned into the lane leading to the church. If anyone came along, he would say that he was a tourist. He pulled around behind a couple of trees to make his car slightly less conspicuous from the road, then he got out and walked to the rear. There he saw for the first time the churned remnants of a cemetery. Broken headstones remained here and there, and a few were still undamaged; but there were voids and depressions, places, he surmised, where artillery or mortar shells had exploded. His penchant for old cemeteries tugged at him to linger and read the surviving inscriptions, but his cool head told him to move along and not run unnecessary risks.

The clouds had grayed and lowered, and the temperature had dropped. A shiver ran over Rob. He looked across the open expanses up and down the main road, thinking of the people who had been born here, had lived here, and had died here over the decades. They were no doubt sons and daughters of the soil, gathered around a fire in winter or outside on a warm summer evening. The church where he stood was almost certainly the center of their social and religious lives. What difference did it make to these people whether the Kaiser reigned from the Imperial Palace in Berlin or Hitler from the Reich Chancery? The survivors, along with their descendants, were now probably scattered to collective farms or urban factories, reassigned into a communal life that they already had here. It was strange indeed, Rob thought, that in this unknown and forsaken place of ghosts he would have his own rendezvous that very night.

He thought it wise to check out the road for a bit farther to be sure what lay beyond the church. Just as he emerged from the lane, he saw a wagon enter the road from behind a clump of bushes. It was not more than fifty yards ahead of him. It had rubber automobile tires on its wheels, like many other wagons he had seen in the GDR countryside. The single horse was driven by a husky, middle-aged man sitting on a high front seat. The man looked straight at Rob, but made neither a move to wave nor speak.

Having someone spot him here in this car was bad luck, but there was nothing he could do about it. He drove on for another mile and saw no structure or sign of life. He turned the car around and headed back toward Magdeburg.

Twenty minutes later, Rob was entering the outskirts of Magdeburg. He passed high-rise, styleless, post-war apartment houses, then he was in the older streets. Trolley tracks ran down a median strip. At one stop, a weathered trolley car was being boarded by a couple of dozen people, mostly fat women carrying shopping bags. He passed the SED headquarters with the inevitable banner with foot-high letters proclaiming the victory of socialism. In the 1930s the street was probably attractive, even elegant in spots, but maintenance had obviously been neglected for years. The fronts of the buildings, the dress of the people, and the darkening sky combined to give Rob that sense of drabness and blandness that he had felt so strongly on his drive through Leipzig and eastward.

It took two pauses for inquiries for Rob to find the International Hotel. Virtually identical to the other multistoried, white concrete box structures in the Interhotel chain, it stood opposite the redone version of the prewar railroad station. As Christa had explained, an extensive open space separated the hotel from the station. It was the kind of space that Rob had learned to recognize as the site of substantial wartime destruction so extensive that it took the area beyond the reach of reconstruction. Bulldozing the rubble was the only feasible recourse.

Rob was traveling lightly and informally. Instead of his usual coat and tie, he was wearing a short-sleeved, open-collared sport shirt. Because he had noticed few coats and ties in this workers' and peasants' state, he reasoned that he would be less noticeable. He had only a small canvas bag and a trench coat.

With his reservation form, he had no difficulty checking in and getting to his room on the third floor. The one window faced the front, giving him a good view of the railroad station and his car. The room was more spartan than those he had had in Weimar and Leipzig, but it was clean and adequate. He doubted that in any event he would be spending much time in it.

He took out the bread, cheese, and beer that he had bought that morning at a West Berlin delicatessen as he read again the description of Magdeburg from his 1904 *Baedeker*. His normal zeal for probing every corner of a historic city was blunted by his mission. Also, he was feeling more uneasy than usual over having given up his passport at the hotel desk. At this moment, that little booklet with the words United States of America on its cover took on uncommon value.

Half an hour later, as he pulled the Mercedes out of the parking area, he felt like an elephant among donkeys. On the autobahn, the car had blended in comfortably with the transit traffic; but here there was no other Mercedes in sight, and no other car approaching it in size—only a few Trabants and Wartburgs.

He headed toward the middle of the old city. The station was right where *Baedeker* had it in 1904, so from that point he could easily plot the short way to the cathedral, his key midnight objective. The 1904 map worked well here, as it had elsewhere, because the street lay-out had not changed despite radical destruction.

After driving eastward toward the river for a few blocks, he consulted the map. The center should be only a block or two ahead. Abruptly he stopped aghast. He had reached the oldest and most historic part of the city; but there was nothing there. He was accustomed to the large open spaces left by the bulldozing of wartime rubble, but what he saw now appalled him: city blocks of nothing. The streets were there; one could see intersections and blocks, but they marked only a great emptiness.

Rob pulled the car over to the side of the street and simply stared, feeling nauseous. The Magdeburg that he had been reading about in *Baedeker* no longer existed. He now understood what Christa had meant when she had said that it is something that you do not want to see. Otto surged back into his mind, sitting across from him in the noisy Halle restaurant only three nights before. Seeing what lay before him, Rob could understand how a German could harbor bitter thoughts about the invading army. But in God's name, Rob wanted to shout back, what brought the Americans here? There is no way that war can sort out the just from the unjust; all will suffer. What looks so right at one moment in time may look entirely different thirty years later.

Rob edged the car along until he came within sight of the Elbe and the island which had been the site of the so-called Citadel. It was gone. The entry to a handsome bridge ended in space.

He went along the river, climbing to higher ground, until he came upon the cathedral. It and the area around it had somehow escaped serious damage. He had to investigate the place to which he was to deliver the Bibles in the middle of the night. He parked at a distance and began walking toward the cathedral. In a green and well-treed park along the road, he saw an impressive ornate monument to the Prussian soldiers and victors of the Franco-Prussian War. Imperialism had its peculiar uses in the GDR.

Following the instructions that he would have to follow that night, he entered the cloisters. The buildings were all of that distinctively dark red German brick, darkened and made even more somber by the weathering of four centuries. He passed along an arcade which formed one side of a courtyard and burial ground. Interments apparently had also been made in the inside wall of the arcade, as there were numerous plaques with dates running from the late 1600s to the late 1700s. These people were living and dying here at the very time his ancestor, the Baron Heinrich von Trepnitz, was setting off for America.

The place was deserted, and the silence was near total. He stopped and listened. The thought of returning here in the dark of midnight was chilling. A mist was in the air, and though it was only midafternoon, the light was that of early dusk. All in all, this was a forbidding place. His impulse was to get out of it as fast as possible.

At the end of the arcade, he saw in the gloom the large wooden door where he was supposed to knock twice. Then, he was told, a man would appear and take possession of the Bibles. Rob turned and walked rapidly back along the arcade and out into the street.

A few minutes after seven that evening, he entered the Moscow Room, one of the two restaurants in the hotel. It was a large, brightly lighted room, where little effort had been made to add any warmth or attractive decor except an artificial plant at each end. About a third of the tables were occupied, but Maria was not there. He took a table off to one side, sitting so that he had a clear view of the entrance. He ordered fish, a salad, and coffee.

At 7:15 Maria Egloffsberg appeared. She paused just inside the door and looked over the tables. Although her eyes did not meet his, he felt certain that she had seen him. She walked toward the opposite end of the room and sat down at an unoccupied table. He could see her plainly through the thin crowd. She was wearing a typical East German dress of no particular style or shape, and was carrying a small duffel bag that almost matched her earth-colored dress. A waitress was at her side almost immediately.

Rob ate slowly, keeping an eye on Maria. He did not want to finish too far ahead of her. He was on his third cup of coffee when he saw her getting her bill from the waitress. He rose and made his way to the door, making sure that she saw him, then sauntered around the lobby until he saw her coming out of the Moscow Room.

Going to the Reception desk, he said clearly as she drew near, "Give me the key to room 308, please." Key in hand, he proceeded to the elevator, waited for a long minute for its slow machinery to function, got in and went to the third floor. He walked down the corridor and waited near the door to his room. Five minutes passed before the elevator door opened, and Maria emerged. He opened the door to his room. She came in behind him, and he closed and locked the door.

Chapter 21

"WELL, WE MEET AGAIN," Rob said in a quiet voice with a half smile, taking her hand in both of his.

She smiled wanly. Her soulful eyes, pale green and glistening, bored into his. Each time he had seen her, she looked a bit different. The sherry-colored hair framed a face that struck him now as having a classical beauty that he had not noticed before.

"I am very glad to see you here." She spoke in a husky whisper. Her grip on his hand conveyed the same sense of desperation that he had felt in her hand in Halle.

They sat down in the two chairs near the window. There was an awkward silence.

"We should not talk about much in this room," she said in a whisper.

He nodded his head in agreement. "Perhaps it would be all right for you to tell me something about your work."

That suggestion seemed to strike a responsive chord, and it triggered a long discourse from her on the intricacies of the human eye. She went on to talk of her interest in training programs for the blind, particularly for newly blinded adults. A lot of work had been done on that subject in Germany as a result of the many thousands of war-blinded. She described the rehabilitation centers in the GDR that she had visited and then gave a detailed picture of the work done in the library at Leipzig in producing recordings for the blind.

"Blindness has two effects," she said. "One is on the blind person. The other is on other people—those with sight."

"What do you mean by the effect on other people?"

"Have you not ever noticed how a person with sight acts in the presence of a blind person?"

"I'm not sure. I have seen very few blind people."

"If you are like most people you feel uncomfortable. You do not know what to do or say. Many people freeze. They cannot move or speak."

"Why?" Rob asked.

"I believe that it is fear."

"Fear? Why should anyone be afraid of a blind person?"

"One reason is the deep human fear of darkness. It is a fear of the unknown, of a blackness cutting us off from the world."

"But why would a sighted person experience that?"

"A sighted person thinks of a blind person as being in permanent darkness, and that thought is frightening. But there is another reason for fear. The eyes are windows through which you can look into another person's thoughts and feelings, and that person can tell you much through the eyes. Do you not think that is so?"

Her green eyes were fixed on his. He could not break the connection. He felt his heart beating.

"You are looking into my eyes," she said, "and I am looking into your eyes. Is there something being communicated?"

He did not answer immediately. He was flushed with the same anxiety that he felt when Ippy Ratcliff first kissed him in the seventh grade—the sensation of being overcome by aggressive femininity. He could only murmur, "Yes, I suppose there is."

"Now close your eyes," she said.

For an instant, he wondered whether she was some kind of hypnotist because he could not break his gaze. But then, as though severing a tangible connection, he snapped his lids shut.

"Now you have cut me off. You hear my voice, but you have lost an important way of knowing what I am thinking and feeling. A sighted person is uncomfortable, or even fearful, because blinded eyes are like closed windows. The sighted person cannot see into the blind person's feelings. The sighted person also knows that the blind person cannot receive signals of that sort. I believe your word *alienation* may describe this condition. The world is divided between the blind and the sighted. There is a barrier there that is difficult to cross. The best way that some sighted people find to deal with this is to avoid contact with the blind as much as possible."

It was now almost dark. "We should leave soon," he said in a whisper. She nodded.

"I want to show you a picture of my parents," she said as she unbuttoned her bag and ran her hand inside. She pulled out a photograph the size of a postcard and handed it to him.

It was too dark for Rob to see the picture clearly. Not wanting to illuminate the room where they sat, he took the photograph into the bathroom and turned on the light. He gazed at a handsome young couple standing together in front of a garden wall. The man, tall and hatless, was dressed in a Wehrmacht officer's uniform. From his close examination of the photograph of Kurt von Egloffsberg on the table at Prinzenheim, Rob would have been prepared to testify that this was the same man. Although Maria showed no particular resemblance to him, the woman's thinnish face, the light-colored, slightly wavy hair, and slim figure were strikingly like Maria's, but his long experience in the law had taught him to be skeptical. For tonight, though, he had to go on the assumption that this willowy, attractive woman was indeed the daughter of the long-dead Kurt and granddaughter of Martina, Baroness von Egloffsberg.

After another quarter hour, they agreed to go. He had pointed out his car to her, parked near a street light halfway to the railroad station. He had left the room first and proceeded to the car. She followed in five minutes, and they were off.

Maria spoke now for the first time in a normal voice, free of apprehensions. "The van should arrive at the church at ten or shortly after."

"Yes, I was told that. How will we know that the van and its driver are genuine?"

"There is a little conversation that must take place. One of you says, 'Are you looking for Dietrich?' The answer is 'yes.' Then the other says, 'Is he at Finkenwalde?' The answer is, 'No, he is not to be found on this earth.' Do you know the significance of those names?"

"Could that be Dietrich Bonhoeffer?"

"Yes."

"What is Finkenwalde?"

"Finkenwalde is a small place near the Baltic where he ran a seminary until it was closed by the Nazis. Have you heard of the Bonhoeffer League?"

"Wolfgang mentioned it briefly when I was talking with him at Prinzenheim," Rob replied. "I gather it is an organization of church people, but I am not clear on what it does."

"It is a secret organization. I should not even be mentioning it to you. But you are now so deeply involved in this effort to get me out that you should probably know."

They drove through the wet streets of Magdeburg, heading north through the outskirts.

"Is that the organization that is behind this plan tonight?" Rob inquired.

"Yes. It is an organization of Protestants in both East and West Germany. They founded it after the GDR authorities forced a division of the churches in the late sixties. They believe that the Christian church should remain united, and they also believe strongly that Germans should be reunited as a single nation."

"It sounds as though the organization has a political purpose as well as a religious mission," said Rob.

"It probably does. At least the East and West German governments see it that way. Each is suspicious of it. Each thinks that it might be an agent of the other."

"What do you think?"

"I do not worry much about the political aspects. I agree with its ideals concerning the union of all Christians. In the kingdom of God there are no borders. The fortified border is a sin."

"Is Pastor Schreibholz involved in this organization?"

"Yes. He believes that the league is a way of pursuing the work that Bonhoeffer began. He puts Bonhoeffer just behind Jesus Christ and Martin Luther. But this is dangerous business, and I fear that one day he will be caught at something the GDR authorities consider illegal. He qualified recently as an old-age pensioner and could probably get official permission to leave for the West, but he insists that his place is with his people."

They drove on for a while without talking. The rain had resumed and was coming down in sheets. The flip-flop of the windshield wipers and the purr of the motor were the only sounds beside the pounding of rain on the car roof. They were clear of the city now, surrounded by darkness penetrated only by the car's headlights.

Maria stirred in her seat. "This is a difficult thing to do, but I believe it is the right thing."

"Do you mean it is difficult to leave the GDR?"

"After all, it is my home, the only home I have ever had. It is also the home of my parents and my ancestors."

"But all of that before you is gone, as if it never existed. It was ripped apart and destroyed forever by two world wars. The people in power here now would have no respect for your family. In fact, if your parents were still living in the GDR, they would probably be jailed."

"This regime probably considers them all to be Fascists. But home is a peculiar emotion."

"I can understand that," Rob said after a moment's silence.

"I really have little to lose by leaving. I have no close friends here. I live in a state of constant tension between my secret life in the church and my duties at work where the SED governs everything. If I do stay I believe that I will be arrested."

"Have you thought about what you will do once you are out?"

"No, not at all. I have had too much else to think about. With my training and experience, I believe I can find work in West Berlin or West Germany."

"Have you ever considered America?"

"Almost everybody thinks of America at some time. I have seen American television over the Western stations. There must be many problems there—violence, drugs, crime."

"Television shows the worst side of American life. There are parts of the country where you see little of that, and there are many fine, honest people who do not live that way."

They lapsed into silence again, watching the kilometers clicking off. Rob judged that they were almost at the turn-off. The rain had slackened to a moderate drizzle. The side road came into the range of his headlights, and he made the turn. No other cars were in sight as the lane to the church showed up in the darkness.

Rob turned off his headlights and turned into the lane, letting his eyes adjust to the blackness. He sat there, motor idling, for several minutes, reminding himself not to touch the brake pedal to avoid illuminating them and their surroundings. The blackness made it extraordinarily difficult to move. If he had not visited the site in the daylight he would have been lost.

He maneuvered as close as possible to the trees and church wall, positioning the car in order to see the road along which he had come. When he cut off the engine, a light patter of rain on the car was the only sound. For a few minutes, they sat without saying a word, awed by the darkness and the rain.

Maria's whisper broke the spell. "I need to change my clothes—put on some pants and a sweater."

Chuckling for the first time that day, Rob said, "You can change right where you are; I couldn't possibly see anything."

She half laughed. "All right."

He heard her opening her bag, followed by much squirming and rustling. Although he felt that decency required him to stare straight ahead, he did take a quick glance in her direction, but saw nothing in the darkness.

"There, I have it," she said with a sigh, laughing a bit. The sound had an unexpected charm to it.

After a few minutes, she said, "You are a brave man." The remark made Rob uncomfortable and he said nothing. "You have much to lose and nothing to gain by helping me. It is truly an unselfish act, and I want you to know that I am more grateful than I can describe."

Rob was too embarrassed to respond. He could only mutter, "I am glad I can help." Looking for a way to change the subject, he asked, "How involved is your Uncle Wolfgang in the Bonhoeffer League?"

"He was one of the founders. Somehow he is able to go back and forth between East and West more easily than anyone else I know. He works actively with the blind on both sides of the border. I have heard rumors that the West German government suspects he is a GDR agent."

"Do you think that there is any basis for such a suspicion?"

"There are also rumors that he is a West German agent." After a long pause, during which the rain picked up in intensity, she said, "As to his being a GDR agent, I must say that I myself have wondered at times."

"Are you serious?" Rob asked, surprised.

"I am very fond of Uncle Wolfgang. He has been kind to me, and we have had cordial relations. I would like for you to keep from the other family members what I am about to say, unless you think there is danger. I think I should tell you because it might be something somebody should know if anything happens to me."

Rob waited expectantly while Maria collected her thoughts.

"The facts are few," Maria continued, "but there are unusual circumstances. Within the last few weeks, two men associated with the Bonhoeffer League have been arrested by the internal security police. One was with a shipping enterprise at Rostock and assisted with importing Bibles. The other was in East Berlin. He had helped several people escape from the GDR. Very shortly before each arrest, Uncle Wolfgang had been in East Berlin."

"Of course, that could be a coincidence."

"It could. But there are other circumstances. Twice when he has been in East Berlin and had lunch with me, I have followed him afterward."

"What made you do that?"

"The first time it was just curiosity. By the second time I was beginning to have these unpleasant thoughts."

"Well, where did he go?" Rob asked curiously.

"The first time he went into the Ministry of Foreign Affairs. The second time he went into the Ministry of Internal Security, which heads the police."

"He does have a lot of interest, as you say, in the blind and the churches, so it could all be legitimate and innocent business."

"Yes it could, and I hope it is. I only mention it because if I do not get out and then get arrested, someone should know of these circumstances. He knows all the details of this plan tonight."

"He does. He discussed them with me." Rob was disturbed by Maria's suggestion. He could not bring himself to believe that Wolfgang was in cahoots with the East Germans. It was incomprehensible; but then, he scarcely knew the man.

The luminous dial on Rob's watch showed that it was nearly half past ten. He was beginning to get apprehensive. The rain had stopped, and he had rolled down his window. The air was cool, and he was glad that he had brought his trench coat. Faint insect noises and the dripping of water from the trees were the only sounds. More time passed. Neither spoke for a long while.

Finally Rob broke the silence, "The van was scheduled to be here at ten. I suppose there could have been mechanical problems, or the driver could have been delayed at the checkpoint at Helmstedt." He was trying to be optimistic.

"Yes," she whispered back, "but I fear that something else has gone wrong."

"If the plan had been discovered and we were going to be picked up, I think that something would have happened by now."

They lapsed into brooding silence. Rob could not recall such total darkness. He remembered as a child at Trepnitz Hills the dark of the countryside before REA brought electricity to places that remote. When the kerosene lamps were extinguished, it was dark; but this was a primeval void.

The words of Cardinal Newman floated through Rob's mind: "The night is dark and I am far from home."

He thought of Maria's comments on darkness and blindness. Is this how it always is for the blind—dark, isolated, out of contact? He pondered the prospect of seeing the world for the rest of his life as he saw it now, which was to say, seeing nothing at all. He had an urge to reach over and simply touch Maria in order to reassure himself of the existence of another human being. Did the blind have the same urge—a need for physical contact to take the place of visual? Blindness and the Wall have something in common, he mused. Perhaps it was not just a happenstance that Wolfgang was absorbed with the problem of a divided Germany.

"How long do you think we should stay here?" Maria asked. The same question had been on Rob's mind, but he had not wanted to mention it.

"I'm not sure. At least two or three hours, I suppose. In case there has been an accident or breakdown, we should give the driver plenty of time."

They both drifted into thought. Rob felt sleep beginning to tug at him. I must resist, he thought. He suspected that Maria was dozing at times. His eyes were heavy, and occasionally he caught himself nodding. One o'clock came, then two. There had been no passing traffic, no light, nothing. It relieved him to think that the farmer he had seen that afternoon atop the wagon was fast asleep in his bed.

Suddenly his heart leaped into high gear, thumping hard and rapidly. He heard footsteps. Or at least he heard something. His breath came in short bursts. In this blackness a man could be at his door before he could know it. Every muscle in his body was tensed, straining, but now the sound diminished. In a few minutes he could not discern it at all.

His mouth had gone dry, his heart was thumping, and his breath was coming hard. Fear was a perfectly natural emotion, he told himself; there was nothing abnormal about it. The trick was to master it, not to let it get control.

He calmed, feeling slightly embarrassed, as he thought of Maria's grim prospects and of the men and women who had faced terror that would dwarf that which was posed by this rainy and deserted countryside. After all, what did he have to lose? His father had once put his life on the line in the Argonne. Had he been afraid?

"Something has gone wrong," Maria suddenly said, her voice breaking the dark silence like a shot and making him flinch.

"It does look that way. We must give some thought as to what we do next." The sound of her husky whispery voice helped him regain his composure.

"I have one other possibility. I must take the train from Magdeburg back to Berlin. There is a lawyer there who might be able to help me. It is doubtful that he can prevent my arrest, but he may be able to delay it."

"Surely there must be something else that can be done?"

"Perhaps you do not fully understand. This country is sealed. If you attempted to go through any checkpoint into West Berlin or West Germany, this car would be searched. There is no way I can get out except secretly. And there is almost no possibility of arranging some other escape plan between now and the time I am due to report to the police." Maria's voice faltered. "It was this or nothing."

Rob realized that what she was saying was true; there was no point in disputing it.

"I think we should go back to the hotel. I would not like to be here or out on the road when daylight comes. We can rest in the room until you think you must go. That is, unless you have another suggestion."

She sighed, resigned. "No, I have nothing else to suggest. There is a train from Magdeburg at eleven in the morning. There is a telephone in the railroad station, and I will call the lawyer in Berlin from there. He represents church members all over the GDR and has been able in a few cases to work out something other than prison."

He started the motor and edged forward through the darkness down the church lane and out into the road. Switching on his headlights, he was almost blinded by the illumination.

As they drove southward toward Magdeburg, disappointment and despair filled the car like vapor. Neither said anything. The streets of the city were bereft of life. In the wetness and darkness, the drab storefronts and row houses were grim and chilling.

They pulled into the vast but sparsely occupied parking area between the hotel and the railroad station. Rob had kept his room key to avoid having to deal with someone at the reception desk at an oddly late hour. They were lucky now as they came into the front door to the lobby. No one was visible at the desk, and Maria shot ahead quickly to the elevator. Rob followed, and the door closed behind them.

They were in his room with the door locked before either spoke. "Perhaps we had better not turn on a light," Rob said. He walked over to the window and looked out on the deserted scene.

"Would it be all right," Maria asked in a tired half-whisper, "if I took a bath? I think it would make me feel better."

"Yes, of course."

She took her bag and went into the bathroom and closed the door. He turned and looked again out of the window. Gazing toward the Elbe and the hollowed out, disappeared heart of old Magdeburg, he detected the first faint hint of the coming dawn in the eastern sky.

He sat down on the side of the bed, physically and emotionally drained. He lay back on the pillow and stretched out full length on the bed, listening to the gushing, pummeling sound of water against the bottom of the tub. He closed his eyes to the darkened room and the steady roar of the water.

Chapter 22

BRIGHT DAYLIGHT FILLED the room. Robert Kirkman, momentarily disoriented, stared straight up into the ceiling overhead. His mind came into gear; he was in the hotel room in Magdeburg. He brought his watch to his eyes; it was ten past eight.

He turned his head to the left and saw Maria, stretched out full length and asleep. Now it came to him with full force where he was and what he was doing there. In another second, as he came fully awake, he caught his breath. Maria was clothed in nothing but a brassiere and a pair of underpants.

He felt a rush of blood to his face. He was simultaneously embarrassed and fascinated. He looked closely at her face. Her slow, deep breathing and slightly parted lips convinced him that she was sleeping soundly, exhausted as he had been from the previous night. Rob had not thought of himself as a prudish type, but he had a vague feeling that he would be guilty of voyeurism if he simply lay there and gazed upon this scantily clad female body. Here she was, though, right in his room on his bed, and he could hardly avoid seeing her. Moreover, she had voluntarily laid down right beside him clothed in this manner. If she were not bothered, why should he be?

What could bring her to do such an extraordinary thing? It seemed altogether out of character. Then he remembered that German women—indeed all European women—were more frank and open, and less inhibited about the human body than were American women. Maybe this was a normal thing to do; but maybe there was more to it than that. For the moment, he found himself not really caring about the explanation.

Rob was mildly surprised to discover that Maria had such a well-shaped figure. The unstylish GDR dresses not only did not reveal what lay underneath, they actually misled the observer. Her long, antelopelike legs flowed into nicely proportioned hips, which in turn curved into a narrow, flat waist, above which rose her more than adequate bosom. She stirred, turning slightly toward Rob. For a moment, he thought she was awakening.

How long he lay there, propped up on his elbow, running his eyes over her body he did not know. Inside of him uneasy impulses threatened to override his power of reason. His sense of propriety told him that he must not touch her, yet he was finding it almost impossible not to. At length, calling up all his willpower, he eased off the bed, hoping not to wake her. He stood there for a long while, unable to look away. Then, summoning all of his self-control, he grabbed his bag and went into the bathroom.

There was no shower. He turned the hot water on full force and stretched himself out as far as possible in the tub. The steamy water rising over his body calmed his inner turmoil. After soaking and soaping, he toweled vigorously, shaved, and dressed.

He came out of the bathroom to find Maria sitting in the chair by the window, wearing the brown dress she had arrived in the day before. "Did the sleep refresh you some?" he asked.

"Yes, I feel much better now. I believe that you also had some sleep."

They smiled at each other. He walked over and sat in the other chair.

"I am sorry about the way I behaved last night," she said. "I should not have been in such a state of despair."

"You have nothing to apologize for."

"But I think I lost my faith for a little while. I was so tired and upset in the dark that I forgot that whatever happens God is there." She was sitting very straight in the chair, her legs crossed; an opened book lay on her lap. "Do you know the Ninety-first Psalm?"

"Well, it so happens," Rob said, breaking into a smile, "that it was one of my father's favorite passages. I listened to him read it aloud several times."

"It is one of my favorites. I find it very comforting. May I read a portion of it to you?"

"Yes, of course."

She picked up the book from her lap and began reading slowly in German. He would have had difficulty translating it had he not been well acquainted with the lines.

> He who dwells in the shelter of the Most High, who abides in the shadow of the Almighty,
> will say to the Lord, "My refuge and my fortress; my God, in whom I trust."
> For he will deliver you from the snare of the fowler and from the deadly pestilence;
> he will cover you with his pinions, and under his wings you will find refuge;

his faithfulness is a shield and buckler.
You will not fear the terror of the night, nor the arrow that flies by day,
nor the pestilence that stalks in darkness, nor the destruction that wastes at noonday.
A thousand may fall at your side, ten thousand at your right hand; but it will not come near you.

Rob was enthralled by the soft, low voice and the rolling German cadence. "Those are powerful words," he said after a while, "but I have never been sure what they mean. They cannot, it seems to me, be saying that no physical harm will come to you."

"I believe they must be understood in a spiritual sense. God is your refuge; that much is clear. Whatever happens, we are under God's protection."

Rob heard his mother reading from the King James Bible in the small rocking chair near the window in her bedroom. The God she invoked was the same God Maria invoked in Luther's translation here in this alien hotel room. "One God, world without end." She interrupted his reverie.

"I do not really know much about you or your family, only that you are an American and a law professor. Also, I am told that you can be trusted. Will you tell me something about yourself?"

"Well, there is not much I can tell you that would be interesting. Both of my parents are dead. I have no brothers or sisters. I do have an uncle and some cousins."

"Then you and I are very much alike. We are both alone."

The statement took Rob aback. "Uh, well yes, I suppose that is so," he said slowly, feeling a bit uncomfortable under her probing look.

"Of course, you have not lost your homeland."

"My family did lose nearly all of its land. That part of the country was defeated in the Civil War. My great-grandfather was killed in the Confederate Army."

"Some day I hope to visit the estate in Pomerania—or what is left of it—where my mother grew up, and the Schloss Bachdorf where my father was born. I think that by going there and walking on the ground where they walked I would feel much closer to them."

For a long minute, neither said anything. Then Rob rose abruptly. Breaking the somber mood, he said jovially, "I'll bet that you are hungry. I am. We should get something to eat before your train. Is there a place to eat in the station?"

"I saw a cafe there."

They agreed that she would go ahead and meet him near his car. He would check out of the hotel, retrieving the all-important passport, and then they would go together to the station.

Fifteen minutes later, they were seated at a small table in the railroad station cafe. The GDR was a no-frills country, Rob had decided. Things were functional, more or less, and they were clean, but no effort was put into making them aesthetically appealing. This place was appallingly unattractive, almost unappetizing. They both ordered omelets and coffee and devoured the food when it came.

He had deliberately taken a table apart from others so that they could talk more freely. "I have been searching my mind for some move we could make other than to put you on that train for Berlin and the police station."

"There is a small possibility that the lawyer in Berlin may be able to arrange a way for me to leave. I would like to telephone him now. There are telephones near the ticket desks."

"Good," he said with reassuring emphasis. "I will wait here. Your train leaves in fifty minutes."

Maria Egloffsberg was indeed an unusual woman. He could not quite put it all together. Here was someone reared and trained in the mainstream of Marxism-Leninism, ready to cast off her past life and take great risks to escape this place. Mixed in with all of this was an unexpected sensuality that was boring its way into him. Also, he could imagine in a different time and place that she could laugh.

In his daydreams, Rob had lost track of time. She returned to the table breathlessly with only ten minutes left. Her face had brightened; it was almost cheerful. "I spoke with him. Here, I will give you his name and telephone number." On a piece of paper she scribbled Werner Schutz, followed by a number, and shoved it across the table to Rob.

"What is the plan? What can I do?"

Leaning forward and speaking in a low voice, she said, "When I arrive at the Ostbahnhof in Berlin in two hours, I will call him again. He will then tell me where to go. I will go there and get further instructions."

"Who is this lawyer and how can he help?"

"He is well known. I met him once. He devotes a lot of his time to representing church members who have trouble with the authorities. He manages to stay on good terms himself with the ruling powers, although he does run risks. The West German churches furnish him with a car. He has lots of contacts, so if anyone can help me now, he is the one."

"May I contact him to find out what happens?"

"Yes. I mentioned your name to him, so he will know who you are." She reached out and put her hand on his. "I wish you would try to call as soon as possible after you get back to Berlin. You should not try to telephone from West Berlin. You will have to go into the east side."

He glanced at his watch. "We had better get going," he said, standing up and grabbing her bag. "We should be on the platform. The train is due to leave in five minutes."

As they approached the tracks, the echoing loudspeaker was announcing that the train for Berlin Ostbahnhof was departing on Track 3 at eleven hundred. They found the track and walked along the train.

"I have a second-class ticket," Maria said as she looked for the markings that differentiated first-class from second-class cars.

"Do you mean that in this classless society there are two classes of railroad passengers?"

"More than that—you can reserve a specific seat if you pay an additional mark."

A uniformed attendant standing at the door to one of the cars verified that this was a second-class accommodation for Ostbahnhof. People were walking rapidly along the platform, getting in various cars. Rob and Maria backed away a few feet to get out of the line of pedestrian traffic. Rob put her bag down at their feet and he took her hand in both of his. They looked at each other wistfully.

"I will talk to Werner Schutz and do anything I can to help. If you should be taken into custody, I will see to it that the authorities in Bonn know about it immediately. There are releases and exchanges, as you probably know."

"Yes, I know. I feel better about everything this morning." She hesitated, then added, "Thank you again for your help. I will always remember you, whatever happens."

There was an awkward pause, their eyes fixed on each other. "Goodbye," Rob said, "and good luck."

Abruptly she threw her arms around his neck and kissed him. His arms unthinkingly went around her waist. For a few seconds they held the embrace. He felt against him the body that he had examined so closely on the hotel bed only a few hours earlier and he longed to hold on.

A loud, penetrating whistle from the locomotive broke them apart. The cars snapped at their couplings and began to move, almost imperceptibly. Rob grabbed her bag with one hand and propelled her toward the train door with the other.

"By tomorrow," she said hurriedly into his ear, "I will either be in hiding or in jail."

Rob pushed her ahead into the accelerating car and shoved her bag in behind her. The train was quickly gathering momentum. He trotted along another several yards until he could keep abreast of the open doorway no longer. He heard the locomotive's shrill, melancholy whistle. The last he saw of Maria Egloffsberg, she was standing in the doorway, receding into the distance, her hand limply raised in farewell.

Chapter 23

At five o'clock that afternoon, Rob was seated in the bar just off the main lobby of the Beroliner Hotel in East Berlin. After anguishing over what to do in the wake of Maria's departure from the Magdeburg Station, he had decided to drive straight to East Berlin and get in touch with Werner Schutz as quickly as possible. The drive had taken him by autobahn to the south of greater Berlin, skirting the western sector. On this autobahn, he calculated, within an hour he could reach the Oder River, now the Polish frontier. But he had left this road and headed north into the eastern sector of the city.

He had unexpectedly found himself passing the Ostbahnhof, the very station at which Maria should have arrived several hours before. He parked, went into the station to the public telephones, and called the lawyer. A colleague of some sort answered and told him to be at the bar in the Beroliner at five, and Schutz would appear to talk with him. Rob had given a brief description of himself—still dressed in a sport shirt, thin, sandy hair, American.

From the railroad station, Rob drove north, first along Frankfurter Allee and then Karl-Marx-Allee, the site of the first major post-war reconstruction efforts, now a relatively affluent residential boulevard dotted with shops and restaurants. In the distance, he could see Alexanderplatz. Then on his right appeared the Beroliner, one of the first Interhotels to be built by the new regime. It was the usual multistoried glass and concrete box. The lobby and the bar area were starkly and unadornedly contemporary, with much glass affording a clear view of the wide four-lane street.

Rob ordered a vodka, and that was what he was served—no ice, no vermouth, no tonic, no twist. Only two other tables some distance from him were occupied. Three men—apparently of Slavic stock, probably Romanian or Bulgarian, but not Russian—sat at one, talking volubly. At another table were two serious-faced middle-aged men, almost certainly GDR bureaucrats or enterprise managers.

Rob had been seated there for over twenty minutes, sipping the vodka sparingly, when he spotted a small man coming across the lobby, nervously surveying the bar. Reaching Rob's table the man asked quietly in German, "Are you Robert Kirkman?"

Rob nodded and pulled out a chair. Schutz sat down, they exchanged greetings, and Rob offered to buy him a drink. He ordered a beer.

Schutz was both short and thin. His dark gray suit was worn shiny and threadbare in places. His dark plastic-rimmed glasses were large for his face. His graying and thinning hair receded in a way that made his forehead seem oversized. His skin was pale, his eyes deep-set and haggard. He was a man who had worked too long out of the sun for lost causes.

Schutz apologized for the poor quality of his English. Rob assured him that he had a modest command of German. So they proceeded in that language, discussing the fine summer weather and beautiful flowers along Karl-Marx-Allee until the beer arrived.

In a much lowered voice, Schutz said, "I cannot tell you much. We must not say any names. She told me that you might be in contact with me. You are an American law professor, I believe."

"Yes," Rob said as Schutz paused and took a long swallow of his beer.

"I will tell you all that I can. That is not much." He looked at Rob with curiosity, almost suspicion, in his eyes. "We made arrangements for her to visit some people I know. They will make further arrangements."

"Does that mean that she will not be reporting to . . . for her appointment tomorrow?" Rob had taken the cue.

"That is correct," he said, sounding like a lawyer concluding a contract negotiation. "Those matters are noticed, so she may not have an easy time."

"How long will it be before we will know something?"

"Perhaps a week or two weeks or much longer. We cannot say at this time."

"Is there anything that I can do?"

"No."

"Let me ask you one more question," Rob said with a quiet deliberateness, having concluded that he would probably not get any more information. "I am not sure how I should put this, but do you think there is any chance she can get to the West?"

Schutz, obviously the veteran of many tough conversations, took a sip of beer. "You ask whether there is a chance. To that I would say yes. It could be soon, or it could be weeks or months. In these matters no one can speak with certainty." He sipped again from his beer, giving Rob the impression that his statement was at an end.

They sat in silence. Schutz quite clearly could tell him a lot more about Maria's whereabouts and the plans to get her out of the GDR, but Rob sensed that what he had just heard was all he was likely to hear.

A Polish-speaking group had just seated themselves nearby. Several men he guessed to be Mongolians had wandered through the lobby. The hotel was apparently heavily patronized by visitors from Soviet bloc countries. He couldn't decide whether this circumstance made this a safer or riskier place for an American to meet a fringe lawyer. He assumed that this man knew what he was doing but that he did not want to push his luck too far.

"I understand that you represent members of the church occasionally when they have problems," Rob said, deciding to shift the conversation to a more generalized subject.

Schutz brightened a bit and looked relieved to be able to talk about something other than Maria. "I do. I travel all over the GDR on that business. Yesterday, I was in Dresden on a case. I do so much of that work that the churches in the FRG provide me with a Volvo."

"This work does not bother the GDR authorities?"

"They watch it, of course. All lawyers are under the Minister of Justice, but the SED permits it. My work is actually a useful service to them."

"Do you handle many criminal cases?"

"Oh, yes. That is mostly what I do. I spend my time about equally in the lowest courts—the district courts—and in the higher courts—the county courts."

The tables were gradually filling up with foreigners. Rob felt that he should not detain Schutz. He had, after all, learned the crucial fact that Maria would not, for the time being at least, be in the hands of the police.

Abruptly Schutz said, "I must go. I have given you all the information that I can."

Rob extracted one of his business cards from his wallet and slid it into Schutz's hand. "May I have your address?"

"It would be better if you do not communicate with me. I know persons whom you know. They can keep you informed."

They stood up together and shook hands. "Thank you," Rob said. Schutz bowed his head slightly in acknowledgment, then he turned and walked quickly across the lobby and out the front door.

Rob resumed his seat at the table. He had time; his visa was good until midnight. His vodka was not gone, and the room was filling with an interesting collection of Eastern European characters. Here was a little slice of business-social life in the Communist world. The men seated around him drinking beer and vodka were both tough and jovial, sons of the factory and farm. Though most of those present were wearing suits and ties, they did not altogether look natural in that attire. There were in this room, Rob surmised, no scions of the German aristocracy, no one who could trace his lineage through generations of university graduates or high-ranking military officers, and it was almost a certainty that nobody here had been reared in a schloss on one of the estates in the East. These people had gone about as far as a society could in stripping away the wealthy, the educated, the landed, and the privileged. In time, education and wealth would again differentiate people. He thought of Otto sitting across from him in the Halle restaurant and the new managerial class and party leaders.

Maria rushed back into his mind: here was a flesh and blood child of the German aristocracy, one whose parents had both come from the landed classes; and yet Maria was indistinguishable from the mass of working citizens of the GDR. How many other such lost and unidentified survivors were there in this country? Maria at least had a photograph and a few fragments of information.

His lawyer's instincts nagged at him again. There was no really solid proof that Maria was in fact the daughter of Kurt von Egloffsberg. The circumstantial evidence was thin: the photograph of Kurt and his wife, the information that Maria said was given to her foster parents by the woman who had delivered the baby to them, and Maria's physical resemblance to Kurt's wife.

It was curious that Martina alone had never been persuaded as to the identity of Maria. The two had never met. There would probably never be any conclusive evidence; Martina would probably go to her grave not knowing whether she had rejected a genuine granddaughter.

There was another question that he could not quite keep out of his mind. Was Maria an East German spy? In his bones he felt that she was who she purported to be. He had to admit, however, that he was a novice at this intrigue business and unsophisticated in matters of East-West espionage. He was prepared, though, to assume her good faith. He thought that he saw in her a human being in distress, and his every instinct was to help her. Although he had always preferred women who laughed easily and—as his father used to say—had a lot of sunshine about them, there was an unusual and powerful attraction to this sad-eyed female who professed firm reliance on divine guidance. He wondered whether he was drawn to her because she reminded him ever so vaguely of his mother. At the same time, he wondered how much he was influenced by the sheer physical attractiveness of the woman, which he had had a unique opportunity to examine at close range.

Only forty-eight hours earlier, he had been captivated by Christa. Now Maria dominated his thoughts. The two were quite different in personality. How could he, he wondered, be so attracted to both at the same time? Perhaps he had been in the East too long and was losing his perspective. He felt increasingly caught in an endless series of events. He would probably never see Maria again, and his infatuation with her and Christa made no sense. Sitting in the Beroliner with twilight approaching outside the glass walls fronting Karl-Marx-Allee, Robert Kirkman decided that indeed the time had come for him to leave this tortured German soil and return to his comfortable American reality.

Once more behind the wheel of the rented Mercedes, he turned left at Alexanderplatz, crossed the slender island formed by the two arms of the Spree, drove along Leipzigerstrasse, turned left into Friedrichstrasse, and edged into the line of cars working their way through Checkpoint Charlie.

The guards seemed to be inspecting vehicles more thoroughly than usual. He saw the legs of a guard protruding horizontally from the open door of one car; he was apparently lying on the floorboards to look under the seats. After nearly an hour, Rob was finally given clearance. The gate ahead of him opened, and he drove through it into the lights of West Berlin. He felt a warm glow suffuse his body as he read the sign greeting him as he came through the Wall: You are now entering the American Sector.

Within a half hour, Rob was once again in his room at the Am Zoo. He had not eaten since the omelet in the Magdeburg station, and he was now intensely hungry. He suddenly felt tired and emotionally washed out. The loss of sleep the previous night was catching up with him. Tired and hungry as he was, he had to get in touch with Christa. He had no idea whether she and Wolfgang knew what had happened.

After letting the telephone at Christa's apartment ring a dozen times, he hung up. Where could she and Wolfgang be? It was nearly eight o'clock. He dialed her office number. Almost immediately, a female voice answered. Though he thought it was she, he proceeded to ask for Christa Schreibholz.

"Robert, is that you?" she said in English.

"Yes, I'm back."

"Good. I was getting worried. Listen," she lowered her volume, "I know what happened, at least up to a point, but we cannot discuss it here."

"Can I meet you somewhere?"

"I am very sorry, but an urgent matter has come up. That is why I am working here at the office. I must leave for Bonn early in the morning."

"How long will you be gone? When can we get together?"

"I'm afraid that I must be away for at least several days on this business. It is really too bad. How long can you stay in Germany?"

"I think I should leave tomorrow. I must be getting home. There is a lot to do before school begins." He was struck by a keen sense of disappointment.

"Oh, Robert," she said, sounding distressed, "this is just too sad. I hope that you understand that there is nothing I can do about it."

"Where is Wolfgang? Should I talk with him?"

"He has gone."

"Gone?" he asked with surprise. "Gone where?"

"He said that he had some business to attend to in Munich. He left this afternoon."

"Well, I'm sorry that I won't see him again."

"Robert, listen carefully. I must hang up. Major Catron is waiting at his quarters for you to call him. He can meet you at the hotel within fifteen minutes after you call. He wants to know about everything from your standpoint, and he can tell you all that we know. Will you call now and meet him?"

"Yes, I'll do that. Give me his number." They chatted for another minute, each expressing the hope that they would see each other again, but he thought that this was illusory. He felt slightly sick.

Shortly past nine, Robert Kirkman and Major Douglas Catron were seated in a restaurant two blocks from the Am Zoo. A shower and a bowl of soup had made Rob feel better. They were awaiting the main course.

Catron was the military man in charge. He had picked this small restaurant because he knew it well and knew that it would be uncrowded at this hour. He and the waiter were obviously acquainted. In response to a cryptic greeting and a motion of the major's hand, he had taken them to a rear table comfortably removed from the occupied tables. The illumination was a dim, pale blue, made more obscure by tobacco smoke from earlier diners and drinkers.

"We know, of course, that you did not get Maria into the van and that she is still in the GDR. Do you understand what happened?" Catron spoke with a low, official intensity.

"No, I haven't the foggiest idea as to what went wrong. All I know is that we sat at that desolate spot in the middle of nowhere until long after midnight, and nobody ever came."

"The reason that the van never showed up was not surprising, but the odds were against it happening. The driver cleared the Helmstedt checkpoint on schedule and without difficulty; but within a few kilometers, he noticed that he was being followed on the autobahn by a police car. He varied his speed from time to time, but the car stayed behind him.

Finally, he pulled over to the shoulder, got out, and lifted the hood, pretending to be checking on a motor problem. The police car pulled in and parked behind him. The two men in it came up and stood beside him, asking what was wrong. It was then clear to the driver that he was under observation. He got back in the van and got underway again. When he passed the exit to the church, the police car was still with him. He concluded, correctly in my judgment, that he had no choice but to continue on the autobahn. The police stayed with him all the way to the checkpoint into West Berlin."

"It sounds as though they had been tipped off. Isn't it too much of a coincidence?"

"Yes." Catron was wearing his most somber, official expression. "But we do not know who it would be. Also, if someone was informed about this plan, and if it were important to the GDR authorities to prevent Maria's escape, why didn't somebody pick her up at some point?"

"Maria and I were not aware of anything out of the ordinary. We had no sense that anyone was paying any attention to us. Do you know where Maria is now?"

"We have word this evening that she has dropped out of sight, apparently with some hope of getting out by other means."

Rob repeated the conversation he had with Werner Schutz.

"We know Schutz," Catron said. "He does a lot of church work—legal work—and can be relied on; but he's limited in what he can do in a situation like this. He can't afford to become implicated directly in an escape plot if he hopes to continue to function as a lawyer. I would rate Maria's chances as bleak."

The waiter appeared with their plates, large and overflowing. They shifted the conversation for a while to German food, analyzing both its quantity and its qualitative limitations. Two German couples arrived and took a table closer to them than the others but not near enough to inhibit confidential talk. They were middle-aged Berliners. Though not expensively dressed by standards here, they would have stood out in a restaurant beyond the Wall.

Rob brought the conversation back to business. "How much do you know about Wolfgang?"

"Well, something but not everything," the major said cautiously.

"This may sound ridiculous, but is there any reason why one might think that he was involved with the GDR in any of this?"

Catron continued chewing longer than was necessary; he leaned back in his chair and took a sizable sip of beer. "Let me say this," he finally murmured, speaking with unusual deliberateness, "the possibility has been considered and looked into. He is, in many respects, an admirable man who does a lot of good work. I like him personally and, after all, he is Christa's uncle. But in this part of the world we can assume nothing. He does have unusual access to East Berlin and the GDR for an ordinary West German. Beyond that, I don't think that I should say more now. People in the right places are well aware of the question you raise."

"You say that we can assume nothing in this bizarre business here, and I agree. Then what about Christa?"

Catron's eyes narrowed, and his lips tightened. Sounding a little irritated, he said, "That, I think I can say with confidence, is a known and reliable case. She has been thoroughly checked out by both the FRG and the U.S. authorities. No question has ever been raised about her from a security standpoint."

"How about from some other standpoint?" Rob was half joking, but he saw immediately that he had said the wrong thing.

"What other standpoint? What do you mean?" The major was clearly annoyed.

"Oh, nothing in particular. Perhaps character or competence." Rob was trying to back away from the subject but feared he was going deeper into it.

"I should say not," boomed the major. "She gets the highest ratings on those qualities. She's one of the finest persons I've ever met, and I've known her for quite a while."

His defense of Christa struck Rob as more vigorous than was necessary under the circumstances. The major's expression and tone of voice suggested that there was more than an ordinary professional interest. He had suspected this, but it was disheartening to be reminded of it directly.

"You two seem to hit it off quite well," Rob said, not able to drop the subject.

A sheepish grin flickered over Catron's official face. "We do seem to have a lot in common. Also if I know anything about lawyers—which I do—she is a highly competent lawyer. She wouldn't be doing the kind of sensitive, important work that she does at the Justice Office if she weren't really good."

They ate for an interval without speaking. The waiter came to clear the table, and they ordered coffee.

"While we're running through this cast of characters," Rob said, "let me ask you about Maria. What do you really know about her?"

"Probably no more than you do, and maybe less. After all, you spent the night with her, if I may put it that way." They half laughed.

"Sitting up all night in the blackness of the GDR back country is not exactly your enchanting evening. I must say that in some ways she's an appealing woman. Have you ever seen her?"

"No, I've seen snapshots of her, but GDR hairstyles and clothes don't do much for a woman. Did you learn any more about her background from her than you already knew?"

"Not really," Rob said. "She showed me the picture of the couple she says are her parents. From those who knew Kurt von Egloffsberg and have seen this picture, I gather that there's no doubt that this is Kurt."

"Yes, that's true; but there are so many possibilities for mistakes or intentional misrepresentations. In the spring of 1945, the chaos and disintegration in this society were unbelievable. Everything except this picture rests on second or thirdhand reports from people who are long dead. There are no living witnesses with firsthand knowledge of the facts to link her to Kurt. There are nothing like fingerprints or footprints or dental records that could provide indisputable proof of identity."

"True. But Christa, her parents, and Wolfgang all seem to accept her as genuine. I should add, thinking as a lawyer about the circumstantial evidence, that the physical resemblance between Maria and Kurt's wife, as shown in that photograph, is strong. That cannot be ignored, but it's not conclusive, of course."

"Actually, the only person not accepting her as Kurt's daughter is the grandmother, Martina. I think that her attitude is partly psychological. She had put the war behind her and come to grips with Kurt's death as well as the deaths of his wife and daughter. To have this resurrected may be a bit too much. At least that's my amateur theory. I've never met the baroness, but I gather from Christa that she's a strong-minded forceful woman. It's a shame, though, if this really is her granddaughter. It would be nice for them to be reunited."

"I've met the Baroness von Egloffsberg," Rob said, "and she is as you say, but she's also personable and charming. I've never been treated so hospitably and so warmly by someone I was meeting for the first time."

"Christa told me something about the unusual circumstances that brought you together. Could you give me your version?"

Rob recapped the whole story for Catron, beginning with the picture in the footlocker at Remberton. Their coffee was gone when he finished.

"That's an extraordinary story," Catron said. "This has been an unusual summer for you, to say the least. I guess you feel that the Fates have conspired either with you or against you. The coincidences along the way are almost too much to believe."

"Has Christa ever mentioned to you Pastor Schreibholz's theory about coincidences?"

"I think she did say once that he doesn't believe in them."

"That's right. I heard him speak emphatically on the point. There is no such thing, he says. What may seem to be a mere coincidence is often part of some divine plan."

"Do you believe that?"

Rob stared into space for a moment. "I can't disagree with it," he said cautiously. "The pastor is persuasive on the point, and there are many historical examples that can be cited. It's a comforting theory in any event. It gives some hope that there is a larger purpose to all this disarray around us."

"Whether you believe in the Schreibholz theory depends, I think, on whether you believe in God."

"It is unavoidable that you have to face that more fundamental question. But look, it's getting late. I've decided that I'm leaving tomorrow. I've been in Germany longer than I planned. I feel as though I've lived half a lifetime in these last three weeks. Wolfgang has gone, and Christa is leaving for several days. You're the last person I'll see."

"Well, you're right. There's nothing else to be done at this time. We'll simply have to wait and see what happens to Maria. With luck, she'll eventually surface either in West Germany or somewhere else outside the GDR; but that could be a long time off."

Rob shoved one of his cards across the table. "Here's my address. If anything significant happens, I would appreciate hearing from somebody." Rob felt forlorn. He wanted to go—to get out of Germany—but in a strange way he also wanted somehow to hang onto this place and these people into whose lives he had been so intimately and rapidly thrust. However, the time had come to return to the other world and relegate all of this to the world of dreams and memories.

Chapter 24

THE JETLINER LIFTED FROM THE runway at Tegel, heading west and climbing steeply toward its cruising altitude of just under ten thousand feet—the ceiling for all planes in the Berlin air corridors. Robert Kirkman sat in a window seat on the left side, and West Berlin sank below him. He was amazed at how much green and open space there was within this encircled half-city. Water, too, was in abundance—rivers, canals, and lakes. The Grunewald passed below, an expanse of countryside inside a metropolis; then came the strip, the high fences, and the watch towers. Now he was over the plains of East Germany with a hundred miles to cover before crossing another barren strip and line of fencing and guard towers.

Somewhere between that fortified border and the Oder River, Maria Egloffsberg was in hiding or in jail. He had a slightly uncomfortable and tingly feeling about this woman, similiar to that he had felt about Christa the night before he left for Magdeburg. Maria had seized hold of his thoughts more tenaciously. Christa was full of laughter and smiles. She was fun and stylish and alluring. There was little of this in Maria. Instead, there were sad and troubled eyes, a seriousness—almost somberness—and a concern for others. Her beauty was cool and elegant. Although Christa's early life in the East had been no bed of roses, she was now essentially Westernized. She would fit comfortably into the social scene in Frankfurt or London or Washington or wherever. Maria, on the other hand, was a total GDR product, but one who had taken the gravest of all steps. She had rejected Marx and Lenin for the God of Abraham and Isaac. She had turned from the red banners of the SED to the cross of Calvary; from Central Committee slogans to the Gospels of the New Testament. This was a woman of his own generation who had confronted the most fundamental human and spiritual divide of the times and made a decision to cross over it.

Three images flickered before him as he reclined in his seat and closed his eyes. He saw again her shapely and nearly nude body stretched on the hotel bed. Then there was the image—actually more of a raw physical sensation—of that body pressed against him in the embrace on the station platform. Finally, he saw Maria standing in the doorway of the accelerating train, her hand uplifted. He had wondered then, as he wondered now, whether he would ever see her again.

It was all unreal. He had had little association with women in recent years; he had been working too hard on law review articles. Now, within the last month, he had been caught by the differing allure of these two German women, presumably cousins. Was it possible to consider this summer a closed chapter and go back to life as usual in the States?

A thin cloud layer obscured the land. Somewhere far below was the destroyed church and cemetery where only two nights before he and Maria had waited through those fearful hours of darkness. Miles to the south lay the Thuringian Hills, the ancient seat of the von Trepnitz family. What had been a matter of intellectual and genealogical interest had become highly personal for Rob. That photograph in his father's footlocker had brought him into the midst of the twentieth-century German tragedy. He suspected that his own life had been changed forever. He was relieved to be departing this benighted land. He was weary of all the uncertainty and intrigue.

Just before leaving the Am Zoo Hotel, he had hurriedly dispatched a cable to Noble Shepperson: "Safely back in West Berlin. Leaving for London today. Home early next week."

The stopover in London was an idea that had been growing in his mind ever since Martina von Egloffsberg had told him that his father had visited the Schloss Bachdorf in 1923 with an Englishman named Harold Titheringham. Rob knew that Sir Harold Titheringham was now a Lord Justice of Appeal at the Royal Courts of Justice in London because he had written him a note in the spring telling him of Edward Kirkman's death. Sir Harold had responded promptly with a warm note of sympathy, telling Rob that if he were ever in London he should drop by for a visit. Rob was going to take him up on the invitation far sooner than he had imagined.

Rob was still struggling to absorb Martina's revelation that she had actually met his father. What made the information so startling was that his father had never mentioned the event, an experience so unusual and interesting for an Alabama boy that surely he would have told someone about it. Whether Titheringham could add anything to the facts or not, he was at least a living connection to his father's earlier years.

Seven hours after leaving Berlin, having changed planes in Frankfurt before arriving in London, Rob checked into a small hotel on Curzon Street, just off Picadilly. He had obtained a room there, despite the height of the tourist season, by calling the London hotel reservation service. He had also spoken over the telephone with the Lord Justice's clerk, who identified himself as the *clark*. He explained who he was, saying that he would like an opportunity, if possible, to talk at least briefly with Sir Harold. An hour later, the clerk called back to report that Lord Justice Titheringham would like Mr. Kirkman to join him for lunch the next day at the Middle Temple. The court would be sitting in the morning, and they should meet at one o'clock, after the court rose for the day, at the entrance to the great hall.

The next day brought unusually fine English summer weather. The sky was deep blue with few clouds. A light breeze was blowing from the direction of the Thames. Rob wanted no part of taxis, buses, or the Underground. He felt invigorated by the weather and surroundings. England always lifted his spirits. He walked along Piccadilly and on to Trafalgar Square. Hundreds of pigeons covered the ground around Nelson's column, some occasionally flapping off to perches on the National Gallery or on the column itself. Moving into the Strand, past Waterloo Bridge, past the semicircle Aldwych, he came eventually to the cavernous Victorian structure known as the Royal Courts of Justice.

Inside, the milky gray stone walls soared upward, giving a cathedral-like aura to the setting. The law and the church had been closely intertwined in earlier centuries, and this connection was manifested in the architecture here. A huge pictorial representation of the dedication ceremony in 1875 stood off to one side. There was Queen Victoria flanked by Her Majesty's judges, all in wigs and flowing robes.

This morning, barristers, clerks, and others were streaming through this great hall and into the many corridors leading off from it. The daily hearing lists for the Court of Appeal, Criminal Division showed one panel to consist of Lord Justice Titheringham and Mr. Justice Dawson and Mr. Justice Watson-Jones, both of the Queen's Bench Division of the High Court.

Rob made his way up a flight of stairs and along a corridor to the courtroom. He took a seat in the row of straight-back wooden pews just behind the row occupied by the solicitors. In front of them sat the barristers in their short gray wigs and black gowns. He had arrived at an opportune moment. One case had just concluded and another case was about to be called. There was a shuffling of papers on the bench where the three judges sat in their wigs and scarlet robes. Barristers from the previous case were leaving, along with several solicitors.

The room was square and nearly two stories high, illuminated by a skylight. Along the wood-paneled walls, bookcases filled with law reports extended upward beyond reach. The few rows of banked seating provided limited space for spectators.

The bench put the judges much higher above the floor than they would have been in an American courtroom. In front of it was a leather-covered chair on which a man in black gown and wig stood engaged in serious conversation with the three judges. As Rob learned later, the figure standing in the chair was a barrister from the office of criminal appeals, a critically important staff office assisting the judges with criminal cases. A moment later, the man was down from the chair, facing the courtroom, and calling the next case.

"M'lords," said a tall, thin man in his thirties, standing in the barristers' row. He held a sheaf of papers in his right hand, while adjusting his wig with his left.

"Mr. Harris," said Lord Justice Titheringham.

"I appear for the appellant, Michael John Putney, and my learned friend Mr. Childers appears for the Crown." The learned friend half rose and nodded his head at the judges.

The three judges, robed and wigged, were virtually indistinguishable from one another. The raiments of judicial office covered all except their eyes, noses, and mouths. The almost identical eyeglasses further blotted out any differentiating features. But this was the very point: they were the oracles of the law, not individuals. The judgments pronounced in this temple of justice were those decreed by the law, not by idiosyncratic human beings.

The Marxist-Leninist system said that all of this business about impartial justice under law was a charade. They were realists; it was the will of the working class, as determined by the Party, that was to be enforced in court. Over the past forty-eight hours, from his conversation with Werner Schutz to this English courtroom, Rob had moved across one of the fundamental jurisprudential divides—the profound difference of opinion about the nature of law. Here, at the original seat of the common law, he was unlikely to hear anything from the judges about re-educating the defendant or any inquiry about whether the defendant adequately understood the principles of democracy.

"M'lords," the thin young barrister continued, "the appellant was convicted on January tenth last at Southampton Quarter Sessions of the offense of obtaining pecuniary advantage by deception. He was sentenced by the learned Recorder to one year in prison."

Mr. Harris went on to explain the facts of the case, being interrupted sporadically by questions from the judges.

Rob had noticed that Englishmen tend to fall into one of two body types—the collie-dog type or the bulldog type. Titheringham was a collie, as was Mr. Justice Dawson, but Mr. Justice Watson-Jones was a bulldog.

"M'lords," Mr. Harris said in the Oxbridge accent that seemed to be the official tongue in the courtroom, "my submission on behalf of the appellant is that one cannot commit the offense of deception by doing and saying nothing. The transaction here was carried out entirely by those who now claim to be its victims. Mr. Putney did nothing and said nothing."

Titheringham interrupted: "But don't our holdings make it clear that a deception can be worked through one's silence?"

The bulldog spoke up. "Take the case of a customer in a public house. When he stands to depart, the publican says, 'two half-pints.' The customer says nothing, pays for two half-pints, and departs. In fact, the customer has consumed four half-pints. Is there not a deception?"

"Yes, m'lord, but in that case there was a special relationship which placed an obligation on the customer to speak up."

"Precisely so," interjected the collie, "and is that not the case here?"

Mr. Harris protested that here the defendant had been in a passive position with no obligation to convey any information. And so the exchange went for several more minutes.

Titheringham leaned over to Dawson, and they exchanged comment. He then leaned the other way to Watson-Jones with a whispered message. Silence then fell over the courtroom as each judge reached for a brown volume, fished for a certain page, and read. Only the ticking of the clock could be heard. Mr. Harris stood in his pew, glancing at the loose papers in his hand. After a long minute, the three judges looked at each other and nodded.

Titheringham spoke: "If that is your submission on that point, you may consider that you have made it and move on to other matters."

"I am much obliged, m'lord. That is my only submission."

Lord Justice Titheringham turned toward his colleague Dawson. Watson-Jones got up out of his chair and came around and leaned over between the two. Whispered comments were exchanged. Heads nodded and shook. In a moment, the judges resumed their positions.

Lord Justice Titheringham began speaking in a slow, steady, confident cadence, delivering the judgment of the court. "While there could be situations," he said, "in which a mere failure to speak could not be considered a deception, this was not one. Here reasonable persons in the presence of the defendant would have construed his silence as representing the truth of the matter at hand." After elaborating this analysis, he announced that the court had concluded that the appeal must be dismissed.

There was a flurry of activity. Barristers and solicitors rose from their pews, gathering up papers and making hurried exits. The Registrar's man was again standing in the chair, conferring with the judges. The next case was about to be called.

Rob decided to leave in order to stroll around a bit before lunch. He took a last look at the center figure on the bench, who had known his father half a century before. He tried to imagine how Sir Harold might look when he saw him face-to-face, stripped of judicial garb.

Out of the muted light of the courtroom, Rob walked into the bright summer sunshine, now with fast-moving clouds overhead. Crossing the Strand and walking down a narrow passageway, he came into the series of courtyards forming the Temple. There was Temple Church and one after another of the buildings housing barristers' chambers. Then the gardens burst into view, sweeping all the way down to the Embankment and the Thames.

For the next half hour, he walked through the grounds of the Inner Temple and the Middle Temple—two of the four Inns of Court—located side-by-side in these precincts. The green of the English grass was almost too intense to be taken for genuine.

He wandered through narrow walkways and came at length to the Middle Temple library, reputed to have the best collection of American legal material in London. He browsed the shelves for a bit; then headed out for the short walk to the Inn's fifteenth-century Hall.

He could get no closer to the womb and cradle of the common law, the direct ancestor of the American system, than he was that morning. The judge sitting in the courthouse at Remberton, some six thousand miles away, spoke essentially the same language and grappled with the same concepts as the judges sitting in the Strand. Rob was suffused with the sense of having come home to his professional roots.

He had been standing only a few minutes just inside the Hall when a tall, elderly man entered, wearing the mandatory black suit and black shoes of English barristers and judges. Rob stepped forward and asked uncertainly, "Sir Harold?"

"Ah, yes," the judge said. "You are Robert Kirkman." He spoke with warmth and enthusiasm, giving Rob the impression that no one in the world could have been more welcome. "I suspected that you were the chap I saw in court this morning—looking a bit American and having something of your father's appearance." The two shook hands vigorously. "This is indeed a surprise and pleasure. Would you care for a glass of sherry?" Not waiting for Rob's assent, he guided him into a room where a dozen men, all in the black uniform, were seated or standing and holding sherry glasses. With their glasses filled, Sir Harold and Rob sat off to the side and chatted about his trip and his work.

"I was terribly sorry to get your note about your father's death," the Englishman said. "He and I were quite good friends in our Oxford days, as you probably know. It was odd in a way, because most of the Americans didn't hit it off especially well with the English chaps. Most of the Americans were Rhodes Scholars, and they seemed to think that they were a bit special." He chuckled a little. "Your father was different in that respect. He and I lived in the same entry, and that threw us together. Both of us were reading history, and both of us had been in the war and were older than many students, so we had a lot in common. However, the main thing that I remember is that he and I could talk for hours."

"Unfortunately," Rob said, "all his letters from Oxford were destroyed by fire. I regret that he and I never talked at length about his Oxford days. He did mention you numerous times, though, and I knew that he greatly admired you."

Sir Harold rambled on for a few more minutes about Oxford in the twenties. Their sherry glasses empty, he rose and steered Rob into the dining hall. The great, high-ceilinged medieval room was filled with long wooden tables and a scattering of barristers and judges vigorously eating lunch.

"I see that we have good English fare today," Sir Harold said, motioning Rob into a chair. The waiter placed plates of roast leg of lamb, brussels sprouts, and roasted potatoes before them.

They chatted awhile about English appellate practice. Sir Harold was a master at talking almost nonstop while steadily plying food to his mouth. The fork, upside down in his left hand, and the knife in his right hand worked in a perfectly synchronized rhythm to keep feeding meat, potatoes, and brussels sprouts onto the prongs of the fork. The law talk was interesting, but Rob was anxious to get onto the subject that had caused him to stop in London.

"Sir Harold," he said, having waited for a momentary break in the conversation, "I would like to go back and ask you something about your time at Oxford with my father." The Englishman nodded his assent as he moved a portion of a potato onto his fork. "Do you happen to recall a trip the two of you took through Germany?"

"Ah, yes, indeed I do. I remember being somewhat reluctant about it at first. I had never been to Germany before, and the war had not been over for long. Frankly, I had little enthusiasm for mingling with Germans. But Ed was keen on going."

"Do you remember whether he had any special reason for wanting to go?"

"As a matter of fact, it was rather curious as I recall. Mind you, this was all some fifty years ago, so I am a bit hazy on details. My recollection is that he had a photograph of a woman and some children that he had found on the body of a dead German officer in France. He had it in his mind that he should attempt to visit this widow and inform her of the circumstances of her husband's death. I'm sure that he must have told you all about this."

"No, he didn't."

"Well, that is a bit surprising, because this was an unusual trip. Ed had located on a map the village where he thought this widow lived. I remember that we got there and found that she lived in an enormous schloss." He paused, obviously searching his mind. "You know, I cannot at the moment recall the name of the family."

"Was it von Egloffsberg?"

"Yes, that's it; but how do you know if your father never told you about this trip?"

Rob related the story of his visit to Bachdorf.

"How extraordinary," broke in Sir Harold. "I remember some beautiful gardens sloping down to the Elbe. Did you see those?"

Rob described the scene in detail, telling him of the agricultural collective and his conversation with the director.

"Ah, yes, I remember that huge front room. I can see now the uncle holding forth there about the ills abroad in Germany. I thought about that place and those people when war broke out in 1939. What was the name of the lady?"

"Martina."

"Martina," Sir Harold repeated. "Yes, of course, Martina von Egloffsberg. She was a most attractive young lady, and she was terribly hospitable to us. She insisted that we stay the night, which we did. I gather that you found no trace of her or the family there."

"Well," Rob began slowly, "as a matter of fact I did eventually find Martina von Egloffsberg."

"Extraordinary!" exclaimed Sir Harold in a show of genuine surprise. "Where on earth did you find her, and how?"

Rob picked up the account of his German wanderings, explaining how he had found Martina and how he had thought that he would be the first person to bring word of the circumstances of her husband's death.

"She has a photograph of you, Sir Harold, standing with her and my father in front of the schloss. You make a handsome threesome."

"This is indeed a remarkable experience," Sir Harold said.

"I learned something else about her. Not many months after you visited Bachdorf, she married an older man, some sort of banker in Berlin, and they had a daughter. But her husband died only two or three years later. She didn't marry again after that."

"Your telling me this reminds me of something else. Your father went back to Germany at the end of his year at Oxford.

"My father went back to Bachdorf later?"

"I am not sure that it was Bachdorf. I have a vague recollection that he may have gone to this other place—what did you say its name was?"

"Prinzenheim?" Rob said, surprised. "What makes you think he went there?"

"Well, here is what I remember. The last time I saw your father was near the Bodleian Library. I was leaving for the summer, he was scheduled to leave the next day, and we were saying good-bye. He said that he wanted to travel some more on the continent before going back to the States. He said that he and Martina had exchanged a couple of letters since our visit in the spring, and she had invited him to visit again. Your mention of Prinzenheim is what reminded me of this, because he said that she had gone to spend the summer with her family at a village not far from Frankfurt."

"Did you hear from him after that?"

"As a matter of fact, I do believe that I had a letter from him some weeks after he was back home. He reported a very pleasant trip, as I recall."

"I find it extraordinary that he never talked with me about these German ventures," Rob mused.

"It's too bad he and I did not keep up over the years; but it's possible that I may have an old letter or two somewhere. I'll take a look."

They walked together out of the Hall. The day was uncommonly beautiful. The sunlight was brilliant. The sky was cobalt blue, and the clouds were few. The breeze from the Thames was just enough to stir the Lord Justice's steel-gray hair.

Looking at his watch, Sir Harold said, "I must be getting back. This has been splendid."

They shook hands as Rob thanked him for the lunch and expressed the hope that they would see each other again. Then Titheringham turned and strode briskly toward the Strand, erect, the aging artillery officer from the First War.

Rob lingered for a while in the Middle Temple, moving slowly through the gardens and courtyards, lost in thought. He was now doubly mystified. Why had his father never talked about his German travels? And why had Martina not told him of his father's second visit? Was it possible that Sir Harold had these long-ago facts confused, and no second visit ever occurred? But what difference did it make now? Rob suddenly felt weary. He had been on the road too long, and was too deeply immersed in the past. The time had come to go home.

PART THREE
Virginia

Chapter 25

The Lawn at the University of Virginia was quiet. Despite the midday heat of late September, there was a hint of the coming autumn coolness in the air. The trees flanking the open expanse of grass were clothed in darkened, tired leaves, waiting to be turned into those glorious reds and golds.

Rob had walked up from the Corner, after having lunch there and browsing awhile in a secondhand book store. He crossed in front of the Rotunda and headed down the colonnade on West Lawn. The doors of student rooms were open, emitting music and snatches of conversation. A few students lay on the grass reading.

At Pavilion VII—the faculty's Colonnade Club—he went up two steps and entered through the solid wooden door. Passing the front parlor with its bust of Thomas Jefferson, he walked into the large rear room, which contained a large collection of the latest magazines and literary journals. After surveying the shingled rows of publications laid out on the two large tables, he picked up the *Atlantic* and slumped into one of the deep, soft chairs. Glass doors formed the entire rear wall of the room, affording a view of the grass, trees, and boxwoods of the garden, all framed by Mr. Jefferson's serpentine walls.

The academic year was now three weeks along. As a visiting professor, Rob was teaching only one course, a large section of first-year Civil Procedure. He was just now beginning to feel relaxed and settled.

He had gone directly to Remberton from London. After nearly a week there, he had gone to Tuscaloosa to turn his apartment over to his tenant for the year and to clean up some matters at the law school. Then it was on to Charlottesville with barely enough time to get set for the beginning of classes. He had had little time in which to make sense out of the events of the past summer.

At Remberton, he spent the days in the silence of his house with the ghosts of his father and mother. Again Rob found himself wrestling with those old questions about what to do with the house and what to do with his life.

"The room in the office is still there," Uncle Noble had told him again. "I know how you feel about George Wallace, but he can't last forever. If you came on back here, we could probably get you elected to the state legislature in three or four years. After that, there are other possibilities. There's the state supreme court. You've always struck me as the judicial type." He had heard all of this many times before.

Rob had spent a long evening at the Sheppersons' house, eating supper and talking on the screened porch. He told them of most of his travels and experiences, but he could not quite bring himself to tell them of Maria.

"When you were on your way to Jena, you were running parallel to my division's route. We could have gone on to Meissen or Dresden and been there before the Russians, but we were ordered to stop at the Mulde. We must have been within thirty or forty miles of where you say you crossed it."

Rob came finally to mention his brief stop in London. "Did you ever hear Daddy say much about Harold Titheringham? They knew each other during that year at Oxford."

"I don't remember that name, but I do recall that Ed mentioned every now and then that he had a good friend who had become a prominent barrister."

"Do you remember hearing Daddy say anything about his travels through Germany or trips with Titheringham?"

"Can't say that I do. He did remark that he had traveled some in Germany before coming home, but nothing specific that I can recall."

The conversation had drifted into general reminiscences. "Ed had an unusual mixture of personality traits," Noble had said. "He was a scholarly type and tended to be reclusive, but around people he was friendly. In fact, at times he could be the life of the party. But there was a private, withdrawn side to him, a part that nobody ever knew. Em's death seemed to take something out of him. There were several widows around here who had their eyes on him, but he wasn't interested. It was always your mother and nobody else."

On two of the nights that he was in Remberton, there were parties—his presence in town the occasion for both. Each night, more than twenty people were on hand, almost exactly the same guests. Indeed, it would be difficult in Remberton to have a significantly varying guest list.

They hugged and talked and laughed. Some asked questions about his trip to Germany, but there was not much interest in that subject. The talk focused on trips to the Gulf Coast and what was going on at Mary Esther and Fort Walton and Destin. There was a lot of talk also about children, which Rob found boring. Then there were the old stories of their past adventures, raucously funny or bizarre experiences which they had shared fifteen and twenty years before. The stories had been told many times, but they never failed to elicit howls of laughter, as though they were being heard for the first time. As the evenings lengthened, the noise grew, as did the level of sentimentality.

"Robby, when Mr. Noble told me the other day that you were coming, he said that he was trying to talk you into coming on back here and practicing law with him. That's what you ought to do. You know there's no better place to live anywhere than Remberton."

From another direction, a soft feminine arm went around his waist. "Robby, we've got to get you back here to stay. You've been gone long enough."

And so it went until midnight. Rob knew that these people would be here if he ever needed them. This was a place to fall back on, a safe haven from the storms and tumults of the world. They knew him inside and out, and he knew every one of them. There were few secrets here.

He pondered all this as he lay in bed in the empty, silent house on his last night in Remberton. Beyond this host of friends lay the ashes of his ancestors, there and at Trepnitz Hills. He felt again the pull of home; but he was asking himself, as he always did, what could he make of his life there.

Coming out of his reverie in the Colonnade Club, Rob quickly paged through the *Atlantic*, put it back on the table, and headed out for the law school. It was a walk of only a few hundred yards past the McIntire Amphitheater to Clark Hall. Passing under its white-columned portico, he entered the large front lobby and went into the dean's office to check his mailbox. There he found a fat envelope with British stamps affixed, bearing the return address of the Royal Courts of Justice.

A few minutes later, seated in his office, Rob anxiously opened the letter. This was the first letter from across the Atlantic that he had received since his return. He had written Martina and Christa a month earlier, but had had no answer. The lack of response from Christa was especially puzzling. He had taken pains to craft a letter to her that was warm and mildly affectionate, but still reserved. His letter, in effect, sounded her out and invited some expression of feeling. He had also asked for news of Maria.

Now he looked eagerly in the envelope from Harold Titheringham. He came first to a handwritten note on stationery of the Royal Courts of

Justice. During his recent vacation, he said, he had searched through some old boxes, and much to his pleasure he had found a letter from Ed Kirkman, which he was happy to enclose.

Rob thumbed gingerly through several pages of the enclosed document, written in a youthful version of his father's familiar hand. The ink was slightly faded, but the document was well preserved for its fifty years. It was headed Trepnitz Hills, Alabama, September 30, 1923. Rob felt as though he were receiving a communication from beyond the grave. The first few pages of the letter contained reminiscences of Old Bates, the Oxford tutor, and his father's apprehensions over settling back into Alabama small town life. Suddenly Rob's attention was riveted:

> I must report to you on my trip to Germany. You may recall that I told you as we parted that the charming Baroness of Bachdorf had invited me to pay her a visit at her family's home. Well, I took her up on the invitation. It took some effort to find my way to the village of Prinzenheim, but I made it. It is northeast of Frankfurt. Her family is named von Mensinger. The house is what I would call a large manor house, three stories high and made of dark brick. It is within a walled courtyard at the edge of a village. It is not a medieval schloss of the Bachdorf style, but it is a substantial structure. Her father is dead, but her mother lives there with one of her uncles.
>
> I am sure you remember the hospitality we received at Bachdorf. Well, this was just as warm, if not more so. They prevailed on me to stay as long as I could, and I ended up remaining there for four days. The main attraction, as you may be guessing, was Martina. You recall how we were impressed with her charms last spring. If you will double that charm, you will have some conception of what I experienced on this visit.
>
> It was my distinct impression—and I say this at the risk of seeming immodest—that if I had been in a position to stay in Germany and pursue the matter, we might have struck up quite a romance. In my fantasies since my visit, I have imagined myself settling down as a gentleman farmer at Bachdorf, managing my wife's sprawling acres along the Elbe. As I say, I believe that this was an option that was available; but I suppose the call of the home ground was too powerful.
>
> I say this not only because of the mutual attraction that we held for each other, but also because she was under some family pressure to marry a man who is some years her senior. He is a banker in Berlin. It was clear to me that she had little interest in this man and was looking for some way out. Yet the pressure on her was strong. Indeed, sad to say, I received a letter from her after getting back here saying that she was going to marry this man. I think that it was clear to both of us when we said good-bye that I would not be back. The distance was too far, the worlds too different.

> So, after this little summer fling, capping off my grand year at Oxford, I now become the county seat lawyer in Alabama, hoping that some attractive damsel will come into my life. Do let me hear from you occasionally. Many thanks again for your friendship and help over the past year.
>
> With warmest regards always,
> Ed

Rob sat for a long while gazing out of the window of his office, his eyes fixed vacantly on the low mountains to the south.

The Civil Procedure class met in West Hall, an amphitheater constructed as a wing to Clark Hall. A full-length portrait of Chief Justice John Marshall hung behind Rob as he stood at the lectern. Arrayed in front of him were 140 first-year law students, their open collars, baggy sweaters, and blue jeans constantly reminding him how much the dress had deteriorated since his student days when everyone was in coat and tie. It was hard to realize that among this disheveled group were future judges, legislators, and leaders of the bar. Yet they were surely sitting there in that room, though there was no way to know who they were.

Rob proceeded to call on one student after another—question and answer, question and answer—the student's response always leading to another inquiry from the teacher. This exercise was exhilarating. Rob was pacing back and forth on the platform as he listened to the student's comments, all the while formulating the next question. A picket fence of raised hands appeared across the room. First-year students were eager and perplexed. Rob pointed to this hand and that hand, answering some questions, turning others back on the student to pull out the point. In the midst of these fifty-minute classroom segments, during which he served alternately as lecturer and interrogator, Rob felt as though there could be nothing else in life as satisfying and as stimulating.

Here he had a magnificent setting for the exercise. Through the panes of the tall windows that flooded the room with natural light, he saw the blue of the early fall Albemarle sky and the grass and trees of Monroe Hill. There, in a small white building, James Monroe once had his law office. With that view, with John Marshall behind him and the banked and curving rows of law students in front of him, he had an unrivaled platform for pursuing the grand purposes of the law and the shortcomings of mankind that made it all necessary.

The clock hands stood at ten before the hour. Books were slamming shut all over the room, and students were struggling up from their seats. The usual clutch thronged down front around Rob with more questions and observations. This after-class session was broken up by the tide of students pouring into the room for the next class.

As Rob came out of West Hall into the lobby, edging his way through the mass of students changing classes, he was intercepted by a secretary from the dean's office.

"Mr. Kirkman, I have a message for you," she said, handing him a slip of paper. "The call came while you were in class."

"Thank you," he said, not bothering to read the message until he could thread his way through the students to the less-crowded expanse of Mural Hall.

Mural Hall was the architectural centerpiece of the building. It was a huge, open space, rising to well over two stories and covered in its entirety by a skylight. On a frieze near the top, running around all four sides, were the names of some of the legal greats of the past—Coke, Ellesmere, Marshall, Taney, and others—but the glory of the hall was its mural work. Done by Alan Cox, one of the leading American muralists, they lined both side walls. They portrayed scenes from ancient Greece. The male and female figures were life-size or larger, lightly clothed or nude. Mural Hall was often a topic of conversation, especially among new arrivals. It had long been a favorite place for law students to bring their dates to see what reactions might be forthcoming.

Here in this skylighted space, devoid of furniture, Rob paused to look at the piece of paper he had been handed. It read: "Please call Cullen Bracey." A telephone number with a Northern Virginia area code was jotted beneath the name.

Rob walked through the library reading room, past rows of reading tables and lines of bookshelves, to his office at the rear. He sat in the swivel chair behind his desk to catch his breath and unwind from the class.

Cully Bracey was one of his law school classmates. They had by chance sat together in class on the first day of their first year and had become good friends. They both ended up on the law review. Cully had seemed to Rob to be more relaxed and warmer than many of the Ivy Leaguers around the building in his student days; but they had seen little of each other since graduation. Cully went with a Washington law firm and then with the CIA.

Rob dialed the number, and Cully answered.

"Rob, it's great to hear from you. I saw in the Dean's Letter last month that you were there this fall as a visitor. I really meant to call you then to arrange to get you up here sometime. How is everything?"

Rob gave him a brief account of the law school scene and what he was doing.

"Listen, Rob, Kate and I do want you to come up for a leisurely weekend sometime, but there is a development here that has a certain urgency to it. I'm calling to ask if it is at all possible for you to come up this

Saturday, at least for a little while. I would like to have an hour or two to talk with you."

Flipping over to Saturday on his desk calendar, Rob said, "I have to be here for a dinner party at seven that evening, but I suppose I could drive up and come back in time."

"Fine. I would really appreciate it. Let me suggest this. Drive up in time to eat lunch with us, say at noon. Kate is taking the boys to an afternoon show, so we could talk at the house until you have to leave."

"That sounds fine. It'll be good to see you again. Are you still living at the same address in McLean?"

"Yes. Do you remember where it is?"

"I think so. Just off Dolley Madison?"

"That's right. We'll see you Saturday noon."

Chapter 26

The curving, tree-shaded streets in McLean, just south of Dolley Madison Boulevard, made an inviting neighborhood. The houses were of modest size, the lawns and shrubbery well tended. These were the residences of middle to upper level government officials, of youngish lawyers and other professionals, most of them probably on the way up.

Cullen Bracey's house was of modified Georgian style, with dormer windows suggesting a second floor. Rob had been here twice before, but not in a long time.

He arrived a few minutes before noon, and they sat down for lunch almost immediately. The two boys, in their early teens, ate in silence while Rob, Cully, and Kate jabbered away. Cully was slightly shorter than Rob and a bit heavier. His dark hair was combed straight back; his oval face and dark-rimmed glasses gave him an owlish look. He had matured some since Rob had last seen him. But Kate looked exactly as he remembered her—a cheerful, plumpish woman with curly auburn hair.

Cully gave a report on some of their law school classmates who were around Washington, and they talked of others they had not seen or heard of for a long time. His Washington years had not ruined his Kentucky accent. Rob regaled them with law school gossip and some of his experiences since his arrival there. He told something of his work in recent years, but avoided mentioning his German trip. That seemed too complicated for luncheon conversation.

Kate jumped up and announced that she and the boys had to leave to get to the matinee at the Kennedy Center. She and Rob hugged with assurances that they would get together again when they had more time to relax and visit.

Cully led Rob into the family room at the rear of the house. Large windows afforded a view of a small but pleasant garden with trees and shrubbery shielding it from other houses. Cully sat on the sofa, pulling an attaché case from the floor and placing it on the coffee table in front of him. He motioned Rob to a deeply cushioned armchair just off the end of the coffee table.

"I've been getting more and more into Eastern European affairs," Cully said, opening the attaché case and extracting a sheaf of papers. "A year ago, I became part of the CIA team of analysts for East Germany." Cully was paging through the papers. "All sorts of bits and pieces of information come to me out of East Germany, and I'm supposed to put the puzzle together. It's interesting work, but frustrating because it's difficult to draw very many useful conclusions."

Silence ensued for some seconds as Cully thumbed the papers, finally arriving at the one he desired. He leaned back on the sofa and pulled a legal pad over beside himself.

Nibbling lightly at a pencil eraser, Cully looked slyly at Rob. "Now you might imagine my surprise—I should say shock—when recently I was reviewing some fresh reports from our sources in East Germany and saw mention of an American named Robert Kirkman."

Rob caught his breath. "You saw my name in CIA documents?"

"You're a better lawyer than I am, so you know that one must be cautious about conclusions in the absence of evidence. I didn't say that I saw your name. I said that I saw the name of an American, and that name was Robert Kirkman." They both smiled faintly. "The reason I asked you to come here today was to ask you if you are indeed the Robert Kirkman mentioned in these reports. Have you in fact been in East Germany during this past summer? And if you have, do you think you could let me in on what in God's name you were doing there?"

Rob sat perfectly still, thinking. It had never occurred to him that the CIA—or anybody else, for that matter—would ever know of that venture. In a flash he thought of Major Douglas Catron; he was in official communication with Washington. But were there other sources in the GDR? It was unnerving to think that his movements there might have been under observation. As to why in God's name he was there, he didn't know, but he thought of telling Cully to contact Pastor Schreibholz.

"As a matter of fact, I was there, in and out twice in July."

"Were you at any time in Halle or Magdeburg?"

"Yes, I was." Rob suddenly felt he was under interrogation. He wondered uneasily whether something ominous lay behind what he had been assuming was an informal conversation between old friends.

"This is the most extraordinary piece of information I've come across since I have been at the CIA. Here is my old classmate, the scholarly and mild-mannered Rob Kirkman, gallivanting around Communist East Germany and getting involved in an escape plot. I'm not sure how much I can tell you about what we know of all this and its ramifications, but I would surely be interested to hear all about it from you."

"Do you want the short or the long version?"

"I'd like to hear everything. I've set aside the whole afternoon."

"Well, I'll begin at the beginning and give you all the details. If I'm telling you more than you want to know, just say so."

Robert Kirkman began with the death of his father and recapped the whole saga, from the footlocker to his last evening with Major Catron. He talked for nearly an hour while Cullen Bracey took notes on the yellow legal pad.

"That in essence," Rob said, leaning back in the well-cushioned chair and stretching his legs out, "is the story of my summer in Germany. My guess is that you would like to crossexamine the witness."

"There are just a few points. You mentioned that you met Wolfgang at Prinzenheim and in West Berlin and that you saw him on the streets in East Berlin. How much do you know about what he does?"

"Not much. He is something of a mystery. He seems to have three major interests—the blind, the church, and the reunification of Germany. In fact, his involvements with the blind and the church cut across both Germanys. The notion of one Germany apparently dominates his thinking." Rob went on to relate the concern that Maria had voiced about Wolfgang. "Do you people know anything about him?"

"I'm not trying to play coy with you or to act like a spook in a B-movie; but you can understand that I am not at liberty to tell you everything we have in our files. Let me say this: this man is not unknown to us. As you have said, he does appear to have an extraordinary ease of movement across the East-West border."

"Maybe I've been reading too many espionage stories, but a question has arisen in my mind. Is there a possibility that Wolfgang could be a double agent?"

"Well, that's a possibility. But what can a blind man do? So what if he is shuttling back and forth across the border?"

"I wouldn't underestimate him on account of blindness. He is highly mobile and goes everywhere alone. His memory and sense of sound and direction are unusually sharp. He's a keen-minded fellow, and I wouldn't assume that he's not fully capable of doing anything."

Cully pursed his lips and put the legal pad on the sofa beside him. "How about a beer?" he said, standing up.

"That's not a bad idea." Rob followed him into the kitchen.

When they were seated again, a can of beer in front of each on the coffee table, Cully said, "I have another question. Did you, at any point along the way, hear any mention of something called the Bonhoeffer League?"

"Yes."

"Well," drawled Cully, giving the impression that he knew more about all of this than he was saying, "how about telling me what you heard on the subject."

"All I know is what I was told by Pastor Schreibholz and Maria. Apparently it was started by a few men who had known Dietrich Bonhoeffer. To understand them and their motives, you probably have to know something about Bonhoeffer. Are you familiar with him?"

"I have read of his activities in the thirties with the so-called Confessing Church in opposition to Nazi policies."

"Do you know that he was arrested and eventually put to death?"

Again a silent nod came from Cully.

"As I understand it, those who are in the Bonhoeffer League today want to reunite the church in West and East. I'm not sure what else they are after. The organization smacks of an underground group." Rob described the curious password he was instructed to use with the driver of the van assigned to take Maria out.

"Your hunch is not far off the mark. The Bonhoeffer League is a group of members of the German Protestant Church who believe that the present regime in the GDR is essentially no different from the Nazi regime. Both regimes are basically antireligious. So those in the Bonhoeffer League hold that they are continuing in the spirit of Dietrich Bonhoeffer by vigorously propagating Christian doctrine in a repressive state. You can see that such a stance can easily be perceived by the authorities as one of political opposition, which, of course, cannot be tolerated in a Marxist-Leninist state any more than in a Nazi state. But to make matters even more ticklish in this case, the Bonhoeffer League is mixed up in the notion that the two German states should be reunited."

"But the GDR hardly favors reunion."

"Correct. But there's more to it than that."

"West Germany, as I understand it, holds the reuniting of Germany to be a matter of basic national policy."

"Correct again. But the unspoken truth is that the Western allies do not really want to see Germany reunited."

"But," Rob interrupted, "all American presidents have decried the division, saying what a blotch on civilization the Wall is."

"I know. We openly take it for granted in this country that a divided Germany is a tragic aberration—one that must be overcome. But what I'm telling you is that this is not the position of our European allies, and it is not in reality the American position either."

"Are you saying that the American presidents have all been deliberately misstating our policy?"

"No. They believe what they are saying, but they haven't had to face the question in anything other than an abstract way. If we were faced with the practical likelihood of reunion, we would probably come to the realization that the European allies are right."

"Well, I'm shocked by the thought that all we think and say about the dehumanizing features of the division would be forgotten if a reunion were a serious prospect."

"I've talked to Europeans about this. If you heard them you could understand their view. Three wars in Europe in the last hundred years have been caused by a united Germany. Some of them say that if you merged the two German states now, the first thing you know they would be talking about adjusting the border with Poland or reclaiming Koenigsberg, the romanticized seat of the Teutonic Knights."

"So West Germany stands alone in really wanting reunion?"

"That's about right. And most people there may not actually desire it. So, to get back to the Bonhoeffer League, to the extent that it is a force in Germany bent on promoting reunion, the Western powers have some concern about its activities."

"Do you mean to say that in relation to this organization, the GDR and the Western allies have a common position?"

"You can put it that way. Mind you, we have the greatest sympathy for these people in the league and for much of what they stand for and do; but they are closely watched on this reunion point."

"Ironic, isn't it?" Rob said slowly, lost in thought. "Here is a group of courageous men and women resisting this Godless state in the way we now applaud Bonhoeffer for doing, and yet we side against them."

"Wait a minute," Cully said, sitting up on the sofa. "We offer them as much support as we can and wish them well in their opposition to Communism. We only get edgy when they start talking reunion."

"This brings us back to Wolfgang. Do you suppose he's a spy for the West, a spy for the East, or neither?"

"We don't know—or I should say that, in any event, I can't say."

"What about Maria Egloffsberg? Do you have anything on her?"

"Only that she has disappeared. She could be dead or she could be in hiding. She could be in custody, but that's unlikely because we usually know who is officially detained for any substantial length of time." Cully broke into a smile. "Do I sense correctly that these two gals—Christa and Maria—have attracted your attention to a more-than-average degree?"

Rob took the last swallow from his beer, then he too smiled. "That's probably a fair statement."

Cully laughed. "This is probably the most fascinating aspect of this summer venture. Here is Robert Kirkman, with an amply demonstrated ability to fend off women, a semiconfirmed bachelor, who goes for a few weeks to Germany and finds two attractive women—one in the East and one in the West—and gets all aflutter over both. It's almost too much to believe."

"It is odd," Rob commented meekly.

"Which do you prefer, or is this all fantasy anyway?"

"You've probably hit it on the head—fantasy. But it's pleasant fantasy. They're quite different. Each is appealing, but in a different way." He tried to describe them.

"If we get anything on Maria, I'll let you know. I gather from what you said that the grandmother, Martina, doesn't acknowledge the relationship."

"She seems to want some uncontrovertible evidence. Who knows? She may be right. In that *Alice-in-Wonderland* world over there, Maria could be a spy. But all of my instincts tell me she's not. If I turn out to be wrong on that, you can remind me how bad my judgment of women is."

"Perhaps I'm not going out of bounds," Cully said, "by telling you that Schreibholz is under close scrutiny by the GDR internal security police. For his own sake, he should leave. He could probably get out. The GDR is happy to have the West Germans pick up the old-age pension payments on its citizens."

"He's committed to the people there and to his ministry. But now I find myself—despite my instincts—with some disquieting thoughts about Maria. Do you suppose she could have been part of an effort to set up Schreibholz? That whole escape scheme and the way it fell through always seemed curious to me."

"That possibility cannot be eliminated. But my information suggests that it's unlikely."

The shadows were growing long in the Braceys' garden. "I ought to be running along to make this dinner party tonight. You remember Harry Edmonds—he taught us torts? He and his wife are having a group over to their house. They've just moved out to Ivy and want people to see their new place."

"He gave me my lowest grade in the first year," Cully said, but he did put on a good show, so I don't hold it against him. Tell him I said hello." Cully promised to keep Rob informed if anything new came his way, and Rob promised the same.

Two weeks passed. The tints of autumn were everywhere—on the trees lining the Lawn, around the university grounds, and splashed on the sides of the low-lying mountains surrounding Charlottesville. Dusk was coming earlier, and along with it a chill that had not been there before. The smell of wood smoke was in the air along West Range as Rob walked homeward in the evenings.

He came out of his civil procedure class one morning and picked up his mail in the dean's office. In his box was a letter bearing a West German postage stamp. The return address read C. Schreibholz, with a Charlottenburg apartment number. He wanted to tear the letter open on the spot and devour the contents, but he resisted, denying his almost overwhelming curiosity until he could reach the uninterrupted privacy of his office.

He passed through the cavernous skylit space of Mural Hall, beneath the names of the Anglo-American legal greats, beneath the nude and seminude Greeks. Coffee was a near necessity after the exhausting fifty minutes of a class, so he rapidly took the steps up to the Faculty Lounge. He would deprive himself of the tantalizing communication for another quarter hour.

Back in his office, Rob sat down in the swivel chair at his desk and carefully tore open the envelope. He read the letter all the way through rapidly and then reread it slowly.

> My dear Robert,
>
> Many times I have thought of you and have intended to write you since you were here—especially since I received your lovely letter. I have been very busy, but the real reason I have not written is that each day I have hoped that I would have some news to report to you about Maria. There has been none until yesterday.
>
> Now I am sad to tell you that we have just learned that Maria has been arrested by the police in the GDR. Actually, she may have been arrested a week or more ago, but we have just now learned these facts. She will probably be charged with attempting to leave the GDR unlawfully and unlawfully importing goods that are prohibited. She will almost certainly be convicted. Werner Schutz is representing her. If he can get a sentence of no more than two years for her, he will be doing quite well.
>
> The West German government does make deals with the GDR for the release of prisoners, so we are contacting officials who handle such matters in Bonn. We hope that Wolfgang's connections will be helpful.
>
> If my Grandmother were convinced that Maria is really her grandchild she could be helpful because she knows people who in turn know high-ranking officials in Bonn. As you may recall, she has been unwilling to believe that Maria is Kurt's child in the absence of some positive proof.
>
> I have thought of you many times since you were here last summer. I remember fondly the evening you came to dinner in my apartment. I was very sorry that we were not able to get together after you

came back from your mission. I admired your courage and unselfishness.

It is sad that we are so far apart. I do not know when, if ever, we will see each other again. Is there any possibility that you may be coming to Germany in the near future?

I will inform you of any news that we receive about Maria. In the meantime, I would enjoy hearing from you again.

With love,
Christa

Chapter 27

AUTUMN WAS DEEPENING. The leaves were falling now, covering the ground with their brown and withered shapes. The night chill had forced Rob into a top coat. The coolness and the advancing autumn brought a heightened clarity to the evening sky. The stars emerged with special sharpness, and the half-bare branches of the denuding trees stood out in bony relief along the colonnades of the Lawn.

Having eaten a quick supper at the Corner, Rob walked along the arcade of West Range. He passed Edgar Allen Poe's room, seeing through its opened door furniture of the 1820s and the black scrawling on the wall: Nevermore. The wind stirred the leaves under the arcade.

The Jefferson Society, a literary and debating organization about as old as the university, was holding its monthly meeting. Some law students had gotten word of Rob's trip of the previous summer and had asked him to speak on the subject of Germany, East and West, with emphasis on the East. A trip of three weeks, he smiled to himself, had qualified him to expound as an authority on the topic. He had recently read a couple of books in the Alderman Library on contemporary social and economic life in the GDR, and that gave him more confidence.

Jefferson Hall, midway along West Range, resembled a small mid-nineteenth-century courtroom. Seats for some sixty spectators faced a table with chairs behind a wooden railing. Fading photographs of bygone members lined the walls. Woodrow Wilson had a prominent spot. His room was only steps down the arcade, the bronze plaque beside the door making it a target for tourists and life for its current student occupant one of constant interruption by the curious.

Jefferson Hall was rapidly filling. Beer was being dispensed. The president, a tousled-haired fourth-year college student, approached Rob and introduced himself. In ten minutes, all chairs were filled, and a few students were sitting on the floor along the walls.

Rob began by outlining the contributions of Germany in the late nineteenth century. He was convinced that the two world wars had obscured that chapter in German history, particularly the influence of the German universities on American higher education. He then described the division after 1945 and the differences he saw between the Marxist-Leninist society in the East and the parliamentary democracy in the West. He tried to convey some of the flavor of Weimar, Jena, Leipzig, and Halle.

The floor was thrown open for questions. A hand shot up in the back.

"Mr. Kirkman, does East Germany have any redeeming features? Is there any way in which it is better than West Germany?"

"This may surprise you," Rob said, choosing his words carefully, "but there are several. Indeed there is much to be said for it. For example, there is a low crime rate. You can walk safely along the darkest and most deserted streets late at night. There is no litter. The streets are clean. There is little or no drug problem. Everyone is guaranteed a job. There is no unemployment. Medical care is free. Schooling is free. There is a sense of community." He was surprised to find himself talking like the SED's propaganda minister.

Another student hand went up. "But isn't there a striking contrast between West Berlin and East Berlin?"

"Yes. Materially, the West Berliners are much better off. The goods in the stores in the West are just not there in the East. But the winos and broken liquor bottles on the steps of the Kaiser Wilhelm Memorial Church also do not exist in the East. I saw no drunks or rowdy groups in the East, but I saw plenty in the West."

Continuing to surprise himself, he went on in that vein. "Playing the devil's advocate, I could easily point out that in the West we have crime, drugs, unemployment, and poverty. Contrast that with low crime, housing, full employment, and free medical care in the East. What you give up in the East is a certain kind of freedom, which they consider illusory anyway. It's hard to imagine anyone walking across Alexanderplatz carrying a sign reading Erich Honneker must go."

"What about the churches?"

"Church attendance is down in both Germanys," Rob explained. "The destructive experience of the war is seen by many as evidence that there is no God. But a crucial difference," Rob continued, "is that in the East the government and ruling party are officially atheistic. No member of the church, so far as I could determine, held a high or even moderately high public office."

Rob went on fielding questions for another quarter-hour. The president of the society announced that time had run out and that he would exercise the prerogative of the chair and ask the last question.

"Taking everything into account and boiling it all down," he said to Rob, "what is the one most impressive facet about East German life or government, good or bad?"

Rob hesitated, although he didn't really need to think long. "I think that it's the unwillingness of the authorities to let their own people out of the country. They are psychotic on this point." He elaborated on the sealed border, the Wall, and the assault he saw on the values of Western Civilization.

Rob paused. The room was quite still. He was aware that all eyes were fixed on him. He was tempted to continue, but his better judgment told him to stop.

"Mr. President," he said, with a slightly apologetic smile, "I'm afraid that I gave you more of an answer than you wanted. But your question was an excellent one on which to conclude." He thanked the society for the invitation to join them for the evening, and the meeting was adjourned.

As Rob came out of the stuffy hall into the fresh night air, he suddenly decided to walk to his apartment by way of the Lawn. He felt no urgency to get back to his quarters, and the Lawn at night was always a moving experience. He walked southward along West Range.

He had been in an emotional reversion to the German scene since the day before, when he had at last received a letter from Martina von Egloffsberg. Except for the address, the stationery was identical to that on which she had written her last communication to her husband in 1918. It had rekindled his memories of last summer.

It was a long letter, mentioning the family members Rob had met. She expressed particular regret that he had not met Helga. She explained that she had not written earlier because she had gone on a month-long trip through Italy shortly after his visit and that since returning home she had not been feeling well. Her doctor had told her that if she did not improve, she should go to Frankfurt for tests. Rob was touched by her references to him and his father:

> Your visit brought back happy and long-buried memories. The moment I saw you, I knew that you must be Ed Kirkman's son. Your expressions, especially the smiles, are very much like his. Your father's visit brought the first real joy to me since my husband's death. He was also the first American I had ever met, and he gave me a warm feeling for your country that has remained with me.

He remembered especially the references to Christa and Maria:

> Christa told me about your daring, and perhaps foolish, trip to assist the young woman named Maria to escape. She could be my granddaughter, and if she really is, I want to know her. But I have

> always had doubts. As you may have heard from Christa, Maria is in jail awaiting trial in East Berlin.
>
> Christa and an American army officer appear to be seriously interested in each other. My impression is that this could lead to marriage.

The letter concluded with Martina's saying that she hoped to see him again and that he would always be welcome in Prinzenheim.

Rob reached the end of the arcade and saw a man coming from the direction of the law school, lighted cigarette in hand, walking with a familiar rapid and slouching gait.

"Alex," Rob called out, taking pleasure in the privilege of addressing this legendary personage by his first name—something unimaginable in his student days.

"Uh, yes, hello," Dean Pembroke responded, sounding lost in thought. "Oh, is that you, Rob?"

"Yes. I gather you've been working a bit late."

"Trying to catch up on some paperwork. What brings you this way at this hour?"

"The Jefferson Society asked me to give a little talk, and we've just broken up. I thought I'd take a swing around the Lawn for some fresh air before heading home."

They walked along the edge of the Amphitheater, the dean grousing about his problems in getting the university administration to provide more money for the law library. As they crossed in front of the statue of Homer, Rob saw a sliver of a moon through the bare limbs of the trees. Ahead in the shadows he made out the life-size figure of George Washington standing on his pedestal, looking forever across the Lawn at the seated Thomas Jefferson.

"Say, Rob, if you're not in a hurry, why don't you come on in for a chat? Mary is spending the night with her sister in Richmond."

After protesting mildly that the hour might be too late, Rob agreed. The two entered the Dean's Pavilion on East Lawn, Pembroke leading the way into his large, high-ceilinged study, lined with crowded bookshelves. He waved Rob into a leather wing chair.

"How about a highball?"

"Well, if you're going to have one, I'll join you."

"I certainly am going to have one. Those budget papers will drive a man to drink. What will you have?"

"Bourbon and water will be fine."

Having given Rob a glass filled with ice, Virginia Gentleman, and too little water, Alex Pembroke dropped wearily into the high-backed swivel chair behind his broad mahogany desk, which was mounded with papers and opened casebooks and volumes of the *U.S. Reports.* He pushed aside a fluorescent light extending over the desk in order to get an unobstructed view of Rob.

"Cheers," Alex said as he motioned his glass toward Rob and took a sip. Rob reflexively repeated the gesture and took a swallow.

The dean seemed to have the law library on his mind, and he wandered on about its problems. Then he straightened up, leaned forward in his chair, and looked intently at Rob.

"It's quite a stroke of luck that we ran into each other this evening," he said in an accent reminiscent of nineteenth-century Virginia. "For several days, I've been wanting to get with you to talk about a very important matter concerning you and the law school."

Rob shifted uneasily in his chair. He wondered whether there had been student complaints about the way his classes were going. He recurrently doubted that what he did in class was effective. He said nothing, and the dean continued.

"As you may recall, when we asked you to come up here for the year, it was to fill a temporary gap in the curriculum. Well, it turns out that we are being authorized a couple of new positions. The faculty has not taken action yet to fill these slots, and, of course, I can't speak officially on what the faculty might want to do."

He paused and sipped. Rob did likewise.

"But speaking for myself—and I know for some others—I would like to think that you might be interested in staying on with us. We need another procedure man. The reports on your class have been excellent. Billy was just telling me that your draft paper comparing the converging trends in German and American courts is first-rate. I think that the chances of your being tendered an appointment are very good."

"Thank you, sir," Rob said, slightly embarrassed. "It's always reassuring to learn that I haven't bombed out." Rob was interested to hear the dean say that Billy Gilbert had commented on his paper. Rob had given him a copy two weeks earlier, but had heard nothing from him about it.

"I'm mentioning this now so that you can think about it. I would be delighted to have you come on board here, but I would rather not present the proposition to the whole faculty if you're not interested. So, I suggest you turn it over in your mind and then let's talk again in a few days."

"Well, I can say now that even the suggestion is a great honor. I do appreciate your thoughts. However, there are some considerations that I should brood over."

"Yes, I can imagine. I know that you have always been attached to Alabama."

"That is so," Rob said reflectively, "but times and moods do change."

"I've come to think more and more that a man needs to ask himself what he wants to look back on," the dean said.

"There's no question that the university and the law school have a strong pull on me. I feel very much at home here. Sometimes when I am in the midst of a lively class or I am walking along the Lawn or out at somebody's party with the Blue Ridge in the background, I think that I could stay here for the rest of my days."

Alex Pembroke smiled and leaned back in his chair. They both sipped on their drinks for a moment. A group of students passed near the half-open window, laughing and talking as they walked down the alley toward East Range. The dean lapsed into recollections of life in Albemarle County in the thirties when he came on the faculty. Rob listened, laughed, and made occasional noises to indicate that he was listening. He heard faintly in the distance the carillon in the University Chapel clanging eleven.

"I'm afraid it's later than I realized," Rob said, standing up. "I must run along. Thanks for the drink and for your thoughts about the future. I'll be turning it over in my mind."

Alex followed him to the front door. They shook hands, and Rob was once more out in the chilly air, walking along the colonnade toward the lighted portico of the Rotunda.

Reaching the top of the colonnade, he ascended the flight of wide marble steps leading to the portico. Standing between the great white columns, he turned and looked down the Lawn. The two parallel lines of one-story columns stretched away in the distance, interspersed with the five two-story pavilions on each side. The architectural genius of Thomas Jefferson was nowhere more evident than in the spacing of these pavilions; they appeared to be the same distance apart, but in fact they were placed progressively farther apart in order to create just that illusion as they were seen from the Rotunda.

Since his first days as a student here, Rob had carried this scene in his mind. Here the Pantheon from Rome, slightly reworked, had been placed on this ridge of land against the backdrop of the Blue Ridge.

The two great bronze plaques flanking the tall double doors leading into the circular building were impressive evidence of the devastating effects of 1861-65. Here were the names of over five hundred university alumni who died in the service of the Confederate States of America. An entire generation of potential leadership was listed on this wall, reminding Rob of those long lists of names on the walls at Oxford and Cambridge, those who did not survive 1914-18. He thought also of those names on the monument in Prinzenheim, men gone in another lost cause. He saw again in the dim illumination of the portico the lettering he had looked at so often in his student days: Trepnitz, Henry, Ala. 1864.

Rob sat down on the top step. The enveloping quiet was broken only by muffled voices of students far down the way, passing near Homer. His great-grandfather, sitting on this very step in the 1850s, would have been looking at essentially the same scene. His mind drifted to Remberton.

He was standing beside the open graves, first of his mother and then of his father. He heard those mystical words being intoned—words he had never fully understood but always assumed to hold some ultimate truth that someday, somewhere would be revealed to him: "In my Father's house are many rooms. . . . He that believeth in me, though he were dead, yet shall he live."

Where? And how? Where are the five hundred named on the wall here, his parents, and all his forebears, back and back through the generations? Maybe Thomas Wolfe was right: you can't go home again—right for the reason that home isn't there. Home is always somewhere else. Or perhaps it is nowhere here on this earth, other than in the mind. And yet there remained the powerful pull of place—not just any place, but special stretches of earth and houses and sky that lived in his thoughts and caused his heart to beat faster.

The chapel chimes struck eleven-thirty. Rob rose from the Rotunda steps and made his way homeward, walking along Rugby Road in a half-dream. Alex Pembroke's suggestion jostled in his thoughts with Martina's letter. The idea that Christa might be marrying Douglas Catron had shaken him. He had actually been toying with the notion of a quick trip to Germany when classes ended; but the only motive for such, he had to admit, was to see Christa and just possibly to see Maria if she could be gotten out of East Germany.

He was more puzzled than ever at the failure of Martina to mention his father's visit to Prinzenheim. Thinking like a lawyer, he wondered whether he should send her a copy of Titheringham's letter to see what she would say; but what would be the point at this late date? Then there was her disbelief in Maria, the most provocative, enigmatic figure in that strange cast of characters that he had encountered. Maria had surfaced and resurfaced in his mind. Many times since summer, he had seen the Magdeburg hotel room, the Magdeburg station platform, and the nearly desperate embrace.

Ten minutes after he entered his apartment, the telephone rang. He was brushing his teeth and was about ready to plop into bed. It was nearly midnight.

"Hello," Rob said, trying not to sound irritated over a call at this hour.

"Is that Mr. Robert Kirkman?" asked a man speaking slowly in a strong German accent.

"Yes, this is he."

"This is Wolfgang von Egloffsberg. You may remember me from Prinzenheim and Berlin last summer."

Rob would hardly have been more surprised if the caller had said that he was the president of the United States. "Yes, yes. Of course, I remember. Where are you calling from?"

"I am in Washington. I am sorry to call so late in the night. Several times earlier I have called and had no answer."

"I've been out for several hours and have just come in. I'm glad to hear from you again. How long will you be in Washington?"

"Not long. I leave in two days. Is there a possibility that you could come to Washington tomorrow?"

Rob mentally ran through the next day's schedule. He had a class in the morning but no other fixed appointments. He had planned to spend the afternoon in the library, but he knew that he could not pass up this chance to hear what Wolfgang had to say.

"Yes, I can get up there in the afternoon. Is that all right?"

"Yes. Is two o'clock agreeable? I am staying at the Dupont Plaza Hotel on Dupont Circle. Could we meet there?"

"That's fine. If you'll wait in your room, I'll call you from the lobby when I arrive."

Chapter 28

SHORTLY PAST TWO the next afternoon, Rob was seated on a sofa in Wolfgang's room at the Dupont Plaza. The room was large with a queen-sized bed. Wolfgang sat in one of the two chairs flanking the coffee table and the sofa.

He was in shirtsleeves with his collar open. His coat and tie lay on the bed alongside his long white cane. Rob had forgotten how large a man he was. His dark, graying hair was combed straight back from the pronounced widow's peak. The scar tissue and misshapen face struck Rob anew. He had forgotten the extent to which the marks of war had been laid on this man.

"I am sorry that I do not have anything here to offer you. This is a short and busy trip. May I order something for you? Perhaps a gin or a vodka?"

"No, thank you. I've just had lunch." There was no point in revealing the menu—a hamburger and milkshake picked up in Warrenton and eaten on the road.

Wolfgang explained that he had come to the States on short notice to confer with representatives of blind organizations about an international conference being planned in Germany. "I met with one group yesterday and another this morning. East Germans as well as West Germans will have major parts. We do not want any difficulties with the Americans or others about that point. I have an appointment at your State Department later today."

"Do your activities on both sides of the line give you any trouble?"

"They do not give me trouble, but they do bother the authorities."

"The blind people and the church people seem to be the only ones who function across the border," Rob said. "Is that correct?"

"Yes. And you have made a very important observation. I work on both of these fronts, as the military men say. Being blind gives me an enormous advantage."

"I never thought of blindness as being an advantage."

"In this work it is. You see, people assume that a blind man can do nothing. They even assume that he cannot hear or speak for himself. Have you noticed that when someone speaks to a blind person he raises his voice, as though the blind man is deaf as well? And then if I am with someone, others will ask me questions through that person. Sometimes in airports I am asked whether I would like a wheel chair. Can you imagine that—a wheel chair?" he laughed derisively. "Actually, the simple presence of a blind person causes people to become nervous, to stop talking, and behave in many strange ways. They often freeze."

"I've probably been guilty of some of that myself. But if anyone were around you for long, he would soon realize that a lot of those assumptions are wrong."

"That may be, but the authorities do not see me much. So they assume that I must be harmless and cannot function."

"Do you mind telling me what you do that would trouble them?"

"You have heard of the Bonhoeffer League, yes?"

"You mentioned it at Prinzenheim, but tell me more about it."

"It is probably what is called an underground organization. It wants to preserve unity between the churches in the GDR and the FRG. Some of its members would also like to bring about a political reunion of the two German states, and that is where it has the most trouble. Because I am blind, I can go back and forth, serving as a messenger or communications system, as the army says."

"Have the authorities on either side ever looked into your activities?"

"They have on both sides. It is actually amusing. The West thinks I may be an agent for the East, and the East thinks I may be a Western agent. In Bonn, my mother's family and the long military record in my father's family give me protection. But in the East all that counts for nothing. Indeed it makes them more suspicious."

"I take it that you do not consider yourself an agent for either."

"Correct," Wolfgang said emphatically. "I am independent of all that. I am a German, not an East or West German. No adjectives, I say. The church, of course, has a higher allegiance. I think of the blind the same way. There is an international communion among them that runs across all manmade boundaries. I met a Russian some years after the war who had been blinded in action against Germans, as I had been in action against Russians; but we were instant friends."

Wolfgang talked for several more minutes about his theories of the gospel and blindness as twin forces for peace and union. As interesting as this was, Rob was anxious to hear of some other matters. At the first pause, he shifted the subject.

"How is your mother? I had a letter from her recently and she said that she was not feeling well."

"She is not well. She is not eating properly, and she has lost weight. When I return from this trip, I will take her to a large hospital in Frankfurt for a complete examination. One reason I called you to meet with me is to tell you that she wants you to come back to visit her. I think she believes that she may not have long to live. Another visit with you seems to be on her mind."

"I'm certainly sorry to hear of her condition. I would enjoy seeing her again, but it won't be easy to arrange." Rob was somewhat uncomfortable in saying this, as he had actually been considering another run in that direction, but with Christa in mind. "Incidentally, how is Christa?"

"I have not seen Christa for several weeks. She is all right, as far as I know."

"Your mother's letter mentioned that she and an American army officer might be getting married. Do you know anything about that?"

"She and Major Douglas Catron do see each other a lot; but I know nothing of their plans."

"And what about Maria?"

"That is a sad story. She will be brought to trial, I think very soon. The East Germans may release her to the West later; but I think that they consider it important to convict and sentence her first. This is the kind of person that they do not want to lose—a well-trained professional in medicine, intelligent and young. That is what they need."

Wolfgang was walking up and down, apparently full of nervous energy. "It is nearly two hours before my appointment at the State Department. I think I should order drinks. You will join me, *ja*?"

"If you'd like. I'll just have a short one. Before long I must start back for Charlottesville."

"Good. I will order vodka. It is the only good thing to come out of Russia." Wolfgang was maneuvering around the bed to the telephone. "No, that is not right. The Russian novelists are magnificent. I mean, of course, the novelists of the Czarist period. Solzhenitzen has something of their power, but there is not much else there in this century." He picked up the receiver and ordered vodka and ice.

"How long do you think it will be before the West German government can arrange to get Maria out?" Rob asked.

"At best, a month or two, but possibly three months, four months, or possibly never. There is no way to say. I have a friend who was with me in the army on the eastern front, who is now a member of the Bundestag. He knew Kurt. He is putting pressure on the right officials in Bonn. It will cost the government some money, but they have often shown that they are ready to spend it for such purposes. It must be handled quietly. Werner Schutz is good at this work. We are lucky to have him helping us."

"What do you think that Maria would do if she were released into the West?"

"She and I talked about that once. She would like to continue with her medical work in the field of eyes. I believe she also would like to marry and have children."

"I'm surprised that she has not gotten married."

"She told me something similar to what Christa once said. She said the men she had met did not appeal to her because they were too impressed with themselves and too selfish. Christa could compare German men with Americans, and she thought the Americans came out better. Maria has had no one to compare, but I think their views of German men must be similar. They may be right. Of course, I never married. What woman is going to get involved with a blind man? There have been two or three who showed some interest in me, but my mother was convinced that they were mainly interested in living in the schloss and enjoying life as a Baroness von Egloffsberg. They did not have much warmth, and I believe she was right, but it has been lonesome. I have been lucky to have Mother and Olga and my work."

Rob answered a knock at the door and directed the waiter to place the tray on the coffee table. He insisted on paying and then on pouring. Vodka on the rocks was not his preferred drink, but he said nothing as he splashed a light jigger's worth over the ice.

"No ice, please," Wolfgang said. "I ordered ice for you, in honor of being in the United States."

Rob handed Wolfgang a glass, somewhat heavier on vodka than his own. He sat back on the sofa.

"I hope that you do not mind my saying so, but you do not act blind."

"What's acting blind? I received mobility training at your American center for blinded veterans at Hinds, Illinois. I was fortunate to go there." Wolfgang paused, pensively sipping his vodka. "Blindness robs a man of more than sight. It robs him of much of his past. You don't realize how much of your memory is dependent on your looking at pictures and books. What you think you remember about people, places, and events is constantly refreshed and kept alive by use of sight. For example, my mother looks at photographs of Bachdorf and of the family. That fuels her memory. I must depend entirely on what was imbedded in my mind thirty and more years ago."

"I hadn't thought of it that way. It's a wonder that depression doesn't set in."

"Oh, I think it does, but it comes and goes. For the first year, I did not want to live. I remember wanting to give up my life in some heroic cause, in some act that would benefit others, on the theory that my life was not worth living in a blinded state."

"Do you still have such thoughts?"

"Yes. For years, I have not cared whether I live or die. By my assessment, my life is cut in half in its value because of blindness, so I am already halfway to the grave. I have become impatient with those who are worried about dying. That is in part because I have less to lose, but it is also because I have come to know that this earthly passage is but a flick of time on the way to eternity. Do you know Dietrich Bonhoeffer's poem on the stations to freedom?"

"No, I don't. Has it been published?"

"It has just recently come out in the collection of his writings called *Letters and Papers from Prison.*"

"Oh, yes. Pastor Schreibholz had a copy at Halle."

"It has appeared in an English language edition. You should get a copy."

"What do East Germans think of Bonhoeffer today?"

"Many believe that if he could stand up to the Nazis, people in our time can stand up to the Communist party. Having him as a hero in the East puts the authorities there on the spot. You may not have noticed this, but he is the only non-Communist whose name appears on any monument in East Berlin erected by the Marxist-Leninists." Wolfgang paused and sipped.

"Where is that?"

"On a tablet in the rear of the main building at Humboldt University. He is listed with several Communists as having been murdered by the Nazis. There is also a street named for him in East Berlin. So the state is reluctant to criticize anyone for admiring him. That is one reason the Bonhoeffer League bothers them. They are concerned that it is involved in spying of some sort, but the name of Bonhoeffer gives the group a certain protective cover."

"I gather that Pastor Schreibholz is much involved with that organization."

"He is, and I fear that he may be in some danger. He has earned sainthood, in my opinion, by staying in the East to serve the people there, when he could easily have left years ago. He is something like Bonhoeffer in that respect. When Bonhoeffer was in New York in 1939, friends urged him to stay. But he thought his place was in Germany, and he went back to his death."

"Have you kept up with Helga? She is your half-sister, right?"

"Correct. I was very fond of her when we were growing up. Of course, I was several years older. I looked on her as my baby sister. I can remember many times at Bachdorf when we went riding together. She had a pony, and I had a horse. We would ride along the Elbe. I have always felt close to her. My mother and I hope that they will come to live with us at Prinzenheim."

"Do you think that they will make such a move?"

"If it looks as though he will be arrested, I think he will. Otherwise, I am not sure."

"I am sorry that I did not meet Helga when I was in Halle."

"Yes, I am too. She is similar to Christa—full of energy, cheerful, interested in helping others. I am told that they look alike too."

Wolfgang excused himself and went to the bathroom. Rob looked at his watch. It was nearing time to start back to Charlottesville. He stared out of the window at the thickening traffic on New Hampshire Avenue, four floors below. To his right he could see the three lanes of automobiles arcing around Dupont Circle in the graying November afternoon. Why had Wolfgang called him for this meeting? Nothing startling had come out of this conversation.

Wolfgang returned and seated himself in the chair at the end of the coffee table. He resumed sipping his vodka. He looked at Rob as though he could see. "I would like for you to tell me exactly what happened when you and Maria went to the church near the autobahn."

Rob was on guard. He had not forgotten Maria's disquieting comment about Wolfgang and the fact that Wolfgang was not there when he got back to Berlin from the failed mission. He had questions for Wolfgang, but he didn't know quite how to ask them. He saw no harm in telling of that dark and harrowing night; he had already described it to Major Catron, who had undoubtedly passed the story along to Christa, so Rob recounted the events from the Magdeburg hotel to the deserted church. Then he abruptly put a question to Wolfgang.

"Were you told that the van driver could not get off the autobahn to pick up Maria because the GDR police were following him?"

"Yes, that is what he reported later."

"Do you think that someone could have informed the police of this escape plan?" Rob asked cautiously.

Wolfgang took a deep breath and exhaled. "No, I think that is unlikely. If the police had known of the plan, they would probably have taken Maria into custody in Magdeburg or even during that night in the country. In that case, my friend, you would have been in some trouble yourself."

"I have tried to think of everyone who knew of this plan. There was Pastor Schreibholz and probably Helga. Then there were you, Christa, the van driver, and me. Major Catron knew, I assume. Were there any others?"

"Probably a few—those who were necessary in coordinating the arrangements—but I do not know who they were."

"What about the people at the cathedral in Magdeburg?

"They would have known only that they would receive Bibles."

"So I guess that we must say it was just a coincidence that the police followed that particular van on that particular night." Rob laughed, catching himself. "Do you know Pastor Schreibholz's notion about coincidences?"

"He does not believe in them."

"That's what he told me in Halle. I have some trouble with that theory, but it is provocative to contemplate. If that event that night were not a coincidence, and no one tipped off the GDR authorities, what does it mean?"

"Ah, if we knew the answer to that question we would be possessed of divine power. We can, of course, amuse ourselves by speculating, and that may not be useless. I have found that there is sometimes a message in what seems to be a coincidence."

Rob described the sermon in Halle and Schreibholz's theory that God may have brought him to East Germany, implying that it was to help Maria escape. "It seems to me," Rob added reflectively, "that the failure of the plan shows this theory to be wrong. In other words, the happenstance of my being there at that time was a mere coincidence, and there was no divine element in it." Rob announced this with the joyful note of one who has conclusively rebutted an argument.

"Wait just a minute," Wolfgang shot back. "The fact that this escape plan failed does not show that it was not all part of some larger divine purpose. Because you and I cannot see or understand what the purpose is does not mean that there is no purpose."

These words hung in the air. Neither man spoke. Traffic on New Hampshire Avenue was a steady roar. Rob drained the last watery swallow from his glass. Wolfgang's right hand went to his left sleeve and pushed up the cuff, revealing a wrist watch. His forefinger flipped open the crystal cover and ran quickly over the dial. "Representatives from the blind organization will arrive here very soon. They have a driver and are picking me up to go to our appointment."

"I must be going myself," Rob said, rising from the sofa. "I am sorry that we must part, I feel as though we could talk for a long time. There is much more that I would like to discuss with you." He found himself drawn to this gruff, blind German, despite the uneasiness planted by Maria's suspicions.

"I agree. We must visit again. I thank you for meeting me today. My mother will be glad to learn that I talked with you. Please keep in mind that she would like to see you at Prinzenheim again."

"Yes, I will. Say hello to her and Christa for me. I hope that she is soon feeling better. Have them send news about Maria when they learn anything."

They shook hands. Rob looked into the dark eyes that were fastened intently on him in focused concentration as though their possessor could see.

"One last word," Wolfgang said as he held onto Rob's hand, "I want to tell you that what you did that night in Magdeburg was a courageous and loving act. There was every reason for you not to do it. I am sure that it was noted in the place where it counts."

Tears almost welled into Rob's eyes. "*Auf wiedersehen,*" was all that he could say.

Reaching the hotel lobby, Rob walked around the corner to the public telephones. The area was deserted. He went to a telephone and leaned against the wall beside it for several minutes, pondering his next move. He was torn as to the right thing to do. Should he pick up the receiver and place the call, or should he go on down to the hotel garage, get in his car, and be on his way to Charlottesville?

Five minutes passed as he stood there lost in this internal debate. Then he took the receiver off the hook, dropped his money into the slot, and dialed Cullen Bracey's number at the CIA.

Chapter 29

For Robert Kirkman, the days and weeks following the meeting with Wolfgang von Egloffsberg were a mixture of hard work, emotional buffeting, odd dreams, and sleepless nights. Teaching classes continued to dominate his days. He had another talk with Dean Pembroke about his future, and the dean reported strong faculty support for offering him a permanent position. He also said that Rob could take until mid-January to decide, a concession that greatly relieved him, at least temporarily.

The meeting with Wolfgang had been upsetting. It brought back in full force the mental entanglements of the German summer at a time when they had begun to recede a bit. He found himself torn between wanting to go back and wanting to forget the whole thing.

He had been invited to Alex Pembroke's house for Thanksgiving dinner, and it turned out to be a grand occasion. The day was chilly, overcast, and rainy. The crackling, oak log fire in the main parlor gave just the right touch of warmth and hospitality as they stood around it with sherry and Bloody Marys before dinner. Mary Pembroke played her usual role as superb hostess. Alex himself enthusiastically carved the turkey for the dozen guests seated around the dining room table. Once again, Rob felt creeping over him that sense of home and of belonging, causing him to wonder how he could ever leave.

The most interesting guest, Rob thought, was Sir Edward Shaw-Phillips, a Cambridge history professor who was at the university as a visiting professor for the fall semester. His wife was also present, a chubby, cheerful, rosy-cheeked English woman. They were both full of conviviality and light-hearted banter. Rob had observed that an Englishman was a prized ornament at dinner parties around Charlottesville and Albemarle County.

Sir Edward's field was Europe since Waterloo. A man of about seventy years, he had spent much time in Germany between the wars.

"What are the prospects for German reunion?" Rob asked him at a momentary lull in the conversation.

"It is important psychologically to many in West Germany, especially those who came from the East, but it is probably an unrealizable illusion. I think it would be right to say that the French really are not keen on the idea. I daresay that you and I might have the same attitude if we had been overrun three times by the Germans, as they have. The French can imagine that a united Germany would again be looking longingly at Strasbourg and Metz."

"And what is the view in England on the German question?" interjected the young man sitting next to Lady Shaw-Phillips. He had been introduced as Bennett Chisholm from Georgia, a graduate student who lived in the room next to the Pembroke's Pavilion.

"I should say that it is not greatly different from that in France," Sir Edward replied, as he worked a piece of turkey breast onto the upside-down fork in his left hand. "We've also had our share of united German energies. There is a mystique in Germany about those Eastern lands. Poland is sitting on top of a lot of former German territory. As you know, Poland is what got us into the mess in 1939."

Lady Shaw-Phillips spoke up. "Edward gave a perfectly marvelous paper several years ago on the irony of all that."

"What irony did you address?" asked Alex Pembroke. "There have been a great many."

"In that paper," Sir Edward said, stopping the knife-work with his right hand, "I dealt with one of history's supreme ironies, that Britain went to war in September 1939, as did France, to preserve the independence and freedom of Poland, and the result of our action was to deliver Poland into the clutches of the Soviet Union and a Communist regime."

The dinner was the finest Rob had experienced in a long time. The conversation ranged over contemporary European affairs, history, current goings-on in the History Department, and Washington political gossip. They had gathered at one in the afternoon, and when they rose from the table the grim, rainy day had turned into darkness.

The day after Thanksgiving a letter from Martina arrived. It was on the baroness's same elegant stationery, but the handwriting was shakier.

> My dear Robert,
>
> I am glad that you and Wolfgang had an opportunity to see each other again. When he came home from that trip he took me to Frankfurt for medical tests.
>
> The news from these examinations is not favorable. The doctors say that I have cancer. It seems to be in the pancreas and the liver. They say that they could perform surgery, but that it is doubtful that anything they could do would give me more than a few months more

to live. So I have decided against it. For one, at my age it seems foolish to try to hang on to life for a few months, as though life on this earth is all that we have. What all this means is that I do not expect to see the spring.

It is not easy to think of one's own death, even when one has confidence, as I do, that it is but a step on the road to another and better world. I want very much to see you again at Prinzenheim. I know that this is asking much, but can you possibly come here before long? There is not much time, I fear. After the middle of January we cannot say what the situation will be. Please let me hear from you.

With love,
Martina

Rob had come to the faculty lounge on the top floor of Clark Hall to read the letter. With the law school in recess for Thanksgiving, the place was quiet and almost deserted. The library was open, but only a handful of students were scattered around the reading room. Rob sat alone in the lounge, cup of instant coffee in hand, looking absently through the glass doors toward Brown's Mountain and Monticello. The rain had stopped, but the day was sunless and somber. Autumn was passing; the stripped trees, damp chill, and ever-shortening days signaled the approach of winter.

He was stunned by Martina's letter. The prospect of death unsettled him. The letter, lying open beside him on the sofa, had in a flash radically altered his thoughts about the coming weeks.

His eyes fell on the engraved words: Martina Freifrau von Egloffsberg, Schloss Prinzenheim. He was overwhelmed with images of the walled courtyard, the red brick manor, the antlered stairway and corridor, and the great hall with its sanctified display of generations of Mensingers and Egloffsbergs. He saw again the poignant photographs on the table in that high-ceilinged, tapestried room. The realization that his father had set foot in those very places fifty years before continued to tantalize him beyond any rational reason. Something was telling him that he must return to Prinzenheim to see this dying woman.

However, Christmas would soon be at hand, followed by examinations in January with the avalanche of blue books to be laboriously read and graded. A trip to Europe, especially with winter setting in, did not fit comfortably into that schedule.

"Where are you going for the holidays?" Mary Pembroke had asked him at dinner the day before.

"Home, I imagine," he had said.

"And where do you call home these days?"

The question put him off balance. "Well, what I mean to say is that I'll go back to the town in Alabama where I grew up."

Uncle Noble and Aunt Nan had invited him to have Christmas dinner with them. The invitation was natural. Ever since Rob was a boy, after the house at Treptnitz Hills burned, the Kirkmans and the Sheppersons had spent Christmas Day together, alternating between their houses from one year to the next. After Rob's mother died, he and his father always went to the Sheppersons'. This year, for the first time, he would be going alone.

Sitting by himself in the upper reaches of the deserted law school this day after Thanksgiving, he was suddenly overcome with a sense of loneliness greater than he had felt for a long time. He supposed it was the prospect of the coming Yuletide with no one in the empty, old house in Remberton to greet him. His friends there were all married, with children to consume much of their interest. Perhaps he should have married long ago. He had been pretty picky and demanding about the female traits he wanted, and had been consumed with teaching and writing. Christa was the most attractive woman he had met in a long while, but he sensed no romantic inclination in that direction. Fingering the letter from Martina, he perceived that it was not life but impending death that beckoned him back to Germany.

Over the next several days, Rob settled his plans. He wrote Martina expressing distress at the news of her condition, and accepted her invitation to visit. He would go to Remberton for Christmas and would leave for Germany immediately after New Year's Day. At the same time, he wrote Christa, telling her of his intention to go to Prinzenheim. He suggested he could come to Berlin to see her.

He did not hear from Christa until a few days before Christmas when he was on the brink of leaving for Remberton. Christa thanked him for his thoughtfulness in coming back to see her grandmother again. The latest report from the doctor gave her only about two more months. Officials in Bonn were still negotiating for Maria's release, she reported. Wolfgang had prevailed on the president of the blind association in the GDR to speak on Maria's behalf to the Procurator General. This should help, Christa thought, because the blind association president was a member of the SED.

Rob was not altogether surprised at what he came to next in Christa's letter:

> I now have some important news to tell you about myself. Doug Catron and I have decided to marry. We had originally planned to have the ceremony in the spring, but my grandmother's condition has caused us to change that. We have decided to have the ceremony two days after Christmas in the church at Prinzenheim.

The letter went on to say that her father and mother had obtained permission from the GDR authorities to leave temporarily for two reasons—

the terminal illness of Helga's mother and the wedding of her daughter. They had also decided to apply to leave permanently, and their application was pending. Thus Pastor Schreibholz would perform her wedding ceremony. The letter concluded:

> My dear Robert, I want you to know that I admire you and value your friendship. Marrying an American means that I will at some time come to live in the States, so Doug and I hope to continue our friendship with you in the future.
>
> You have come to be thought of as a member of this family. The only one of us you have not met is my mother, but perhaps she will still be at Prinzenheim when you are there. I thank you again for all you did for us last summer and for visiting Grandmother before she passes on.
>
> Love always,
> Christa

Inexplicably he felt a slight twinge of loss. Here was another closed chapter to be added to his mental collection of interesting women he had known.

Two days before heading south from Charlottesville, Rob dispatched a cable to Christa in Berlin. It was a bare bones message: "Congratulations to you and Doug. Best wishes for many years of happiness. Robert Kirkman."

That evening, as he was packing his bags, the telephone rang. "This is Peter von Reumann," the German-accented voice said. "How are you?"

"Fine," Rob said, struggling to get Peter von Reumann back in focus. "I called your number several times earlier in the fall but got no answer."

"I was in Europe for three months. I just returned last week."

"I want to tell you that I found some members of the von Egloffsberg family. You may recall that you were good enough to give me some genealogical information."

"Yes," said von Reumann, "and I would be interested to hear about them. I am calling now to let you know that I have found some information about the von Trepnitz family. Last summer you mentioned that you would like to have that too."

Rob was silent for a moment. He had indeed said that he wanted whatever this German genealogist could find on that subject; but that was last July. His world had turned over since then. He had uncovered more in Germany than he ever reckoned on. He was not ready for any new discoveries.

"Why yes, that is very good of you. I would be interested in seeing what you have, but you've caught me just as I'm leaving for Christmas. Perhaps when I'm back in January I could call you."

"I am sorry," replied the gruff German voice, "but I will be leaving for Barbados immediately after Christmas, and will not be back for three months."

Thinking that he had better catch the elusive German while he could, Rob agreed unenthusiastically to be at his house the next afternoon at three.

Von Reumann's house was positioned on a hill a mile west of St. Paul's Church in Ivy. Rob sat in the wood-paneled library, holding photocopied pages filled with archaic German print. Through the tall narrow windows he had a spectacular view of the Blue Ridge, standing out starkly against the sky on this clear, cold December afternoon. Oak logs simmered in the fireplace. The slight, bespectacled figure of von Reumann was seated at a table nearby, with papers spread out in front of him.

"These charts do not go all the way back to the beginning," von Reumann said in his heavy accent. "I have the earlier history here, but I have not copied it all. What I have given you goes back only to the time of Frederick the Great."

Straining his eyes to decipher the elaborate and crowded print, Rob identified Friedrich Karl Hans, Baron von Trepnitz, born 1735. No date of death was given, but there was the terse notation: "Founder of the American family." The genealogist who prepared this book obviously had no interest in the American scene. That line of the family simply ended here with Karl and his two sons.

"Although you cannot trace your line down in America by this chart," von Reumann was saying, "you are able to see the descendants of your ancestor's other son. You had told me that one son was left behind in Germany. This book shows that to be correct."

Rob examined the generations fanning out below the son who had been left behind. The gulf between these Germans and the unlisted American descendants widened with each generation. Rob felt far removed from those who may have been born in the twentieth century, if there were any.

"You notice," von Reumann said, "that the latest year of birth is 1890. The book was published a few years after that."

"That's too bad," Rob said. "It would be interesting to know what descendants there are, if any, in more recent times."

"Ah, there I have some information." Von Reumann spoke with solemnity in a tone of mixed expectancy and sadness.

"Do you mean that you know something more up-to-date about the members of the Trepnitz family in Germany?"

"That is correct. I have learned of this during my recent visit to Germany."

All of Rob's senses quickened. "What did you learn?" The summer's experiences had made him wary about prying into another German Pandora's box.

"It is quite a coincidence how I found this information. I had the name *Trepnitz* in mind since I talked with you last summer. In October, I stayed with an old friend of mine in Dusseldorf. He is a retired banker there. He is interested in German history and German families. He has helped me in the past to find some of the books I have here now. I mentioned the Trepnitz name to him. To my surprise, he said that he had known Rudolph von Trepnitz."

"Rudolph von Trepnitz?" Rob repeated. "I have never heard that name. Is he related to those listed here?"

"In fact, he is the son of the last man listed, the one born in 1890."

"So that makes him some kind of cousin of mine—maybe sixth or seventh or eighth cousin?"

"Oh, yes, you would definitely be related to him, though, as you say, it would be distant."

"Well, what's the story?" Rob asked, his curiosity rising.

"My Dusseldorf friend knew Rudolph von Trepnitz in the banking business there in the fifties and sixties. But first let me go back. The man shown on your page there—Gerhard Hans von Trepnitz—was the father of this Rudolph. He became a history professor at Goettingen. Because of poor eyesight, he was not in the military service during the first war. Rudolph was born during that war, and he became a chemical engineer. He held an important position with I. G. Farben."

"I thought you said he was a banker."

"Ah, that was later, some years after the second war. It was during that time that my Dusseldorf friend came to know him and to learn about his family and his experiences."

Von Reumann had leaned back in his chair. His inscrutable German countenance seemed to be focused for a moment on the Blue Ridge. Then he resumed.

"Professor Kirkman, from what you have told me I believe that you know much more about Germany than most Americans, so you know that the thirties and forties were unusual times. What men did then and the circumstances they faced were judged at a later time and place, under quite different circumstances." He paused, gazing again toward the distant blue line sharply delineated against the western sky. "And they were made to look very bad. That is not to say, of course, that much of what happened was not bad, very bad."

"But what about Rudolph von Trepnitz?" Rob said with rising unease.

"In the confusion that was everywhere in the summer and autumn of 1945, hundreds, thousands, of Germans were taken into custody or put under investigation. All adult males who held any kind of responsible position seemed to be under suspicion by the Allies. So, according to what my Dusseldorf friend tells me, he learned later, this man—shall I say your cousin Rudolph—was charged with crimes against humanity, or war crimes—I am not sure which—for his work at I. G. Farben."

Von Reumann shifted in his chair. Rob looked vacantly across the room at a wall of books and beyond them through the window to the open sky, where a jet was in a long, gradual line of ascent from the airport north of town. The only sound was the sizzling of the logs in the fireplace.

Rob heard himself saying quietly, "Do you know specifically what he was accused of doing?"

"Not precisely. Apparently it had something to do with the manufacture of gas. Also, I believe there were allegations of the use of foreigners as so-called slave labor in factories."

"You say there were allegations. Were any of these charges ever proved?"

"I do not know how much you have read of the many proceedings at Nuremberg after the war. Many persons were convicted there of charges like these. Some were acquitted. Officers from most of Germany's largest and most respected concerns—Krupp, Thyssen, Siemens, as well as I. G. Farben—were involved. Who can say with certainty who was really guilty of what?"

"But what was the decision of the court in this case?"

"They found him guilty. This was not one of the main trials. I hope that you will not take it as an insult if I say that your kinsman was not one of the major figures among the defendants at Nuremberg."

Rob ignored his momentary and odd resentment at the remark. "What happened to him?"

"He received a sentence of five years imprisonment, but he was released two years later. You may recall that many of those convicted and given sentences of this sort were released earlier. The economy needed their talents, and one could not really say that they were ordinary criminals.

"What did Rudolph do then?"

"That is when he came to Dusseldorf and entered the banking business. He became an official in one of the large banks there."

"Is he still living?"

"No. He died in the middle of the sixties."

"Did he marry and have children?"

"Yes. My friend told me that he believed his widow to be living in Stuttgart, which is where she came from. They had a son and a daughter who are now married and living also somewhere near Stuttgart. I should add that Rudolph von Trepnitz was considered a leading citizen of Dusseldorf at the time of his death. My friend tells me that his memorial service was attended by the mayor and other city officials."

His car packed, Rob headed southward from Virginia, through the Carolinas—Greensboro, Charlotte, Spartanburg, Greenville—then Atlanta and the smaller Georgia towns—Newnan and La Grange. As the miles and the hours passed, Rob's mind roamed over his perplexing experiences of the last six months. He would shortly be going back to Germany, but he was not really looking forward to the trip. He was now concerned about his own future, whether he should remain in Virginia. Beyond all this, von Reumann's news of his remote von Trepnitz relatives had opened a new well of troubling thoughts.

He crossed the Chattahoochee and pressed on westward. Ahead in the gathering darkness lay the great crescent of the Black Belt, spreading west and north into Mississippi, with its network of rivers—the Alabama, the Cahaba, the Black Warrior, the Tombigbee—their yellow-brown waters flowing inexorably southward to Mobile and the Gulf. He would soon be home in the house of his childhood, the house of his father, his mother, and his Grandfather Shepperson, the house where no one now lived, the house occupied only by memories and artifacts of the past. Yet it was tangible, existing. The great house at Trepnitz Hills was embedded forever in his psyche, but it was gone, disappeared, wiped from the face of the earth. But Remberton and the house surrounded by his father's camellias were still there. When he was not there it was home—that most magic of all words which would forever in his mind mean primarily and perhaps only that one little spot toward which he was now headed in the darkening gloom of the December evening.

PART FOUR
Prinzenheim

Chapter 30

A LIGHT DUSTING OF SNOW lay over the German countryside, but the roads were clear and dry. Robert Kirkman headed northeast out of the Frankfurt autobahn network in his rented Volkswagen. He had arrived the previous day and had spent the night at an airport motel to recover from the jet lag. This January day was clear and cold, with the temperature right at the freezing point. The lush green of summer, stretching across the valleys and hills on both sides of the road, was now a thin white carpet.

For days, he had been amidst the trappings of his own past, where most of the friends of his youth still lived. He had made his obligatory call at the cemeteries. The camellias were blooming—the Pink Perfections, the Professor Sargents, and the Alba Plenas—shedding their pink and red and white petals on the graves of his ancestors.

At least he did not have to worry about the house in Remberton for a while. That problem had been solved for him out of the blue a couple of days after Christmas. He had stopped at the Texaco station on Center Street.

"Well, I'll be a son-of-a-bitch if it ain't Robby Kirkman," boomed the six-foot-tall, two-hundred-pound attendant emerging from the station as Rob was getting out of the car.

"Leroy, how in the world are you?" It was Leroy Simmons—pronounced *Lee-roy*, with emphasis on the first syllable. He and Rob had been high school classmates. Leroy had played tackle on the football team, and he looked it, but he was now sporting considerably more stomach; the shirt with the Texaco emblem on its pocket bulged over his belt. It was one of those unseasonably warm days in late December that put men into shirtsleeves in that part of the country.

Leroy shoved the nozzle into Rob's gas tank; the numbers behind the glass on the pump whirred, racking up gallons and dollars and cents by the second. "You missed the last class reunion. Where in the hell have you been?"

"Hiding out in Tuscaloosa and Virginia."

"Virginia? That's a damn long way from here!" Rob's tank was full, but Leroy was continuing to inject spurts of gas, jerking the cents forward on the pump to round the total charge up to seven dollars. "This son-of-a-bitch was nearly empty," he muttered.

Tires screeched in the street; a car backed up and nosed hurriedly into the station. Dr. Clif Edwards jumped out. He had been a year ahead of Rob in school, one of those confident, long-range planners who began saying in the fifth grade that he would be a doctor.

"Hey, Leroy," he waved to the attendant who was ambling toward the station door to get change for the twenty-dollar bill Rob had given him.

"Howdy, Doc," Leroy called back.

"Say, Robby," the doctor said as he walked up to him. "I'm glad I caught you here. I've got some good news. Can't stay but a minute now. I'm running late on getting back to my office."

They had already had a long visit. Clif and his wife Susie had invited Rob to their house for a Christmas afternoon party. Susie came from Jackson and was a student at Sophie Newcomb when Clif met her. They had married by the time he finished medical school at Tulane. She was a voracious reader, especially strong on the bestsellers. To Rob, she was one of the most interesting people currently residing in Remberton; but anybody from elsewhere, unless positively repulsive, added sparkle to the town.

"Well, what's the big news?" Rob asked.

"At the Rotary Club today they said the glove plant was getting a new manager the middle of next month. They said he wants to rent a furnished house for at least six months. So there, I figured, is the answer to your house problem. I was going to call you about it tonight."

Rob nodded. "That does sound good. Who is this fellow?

"He's coming down from Massachussetts. A Yankee, I'm sure, but most of them they've sent down have been just fine. One time, though, they had one who didn't like Remberton and he left. Can you imagine anyone not liking Remberton? Folks here always did think there was something funny about him."

Before he left town, Rob had enlisted Uncle Noble to follow up; and Mr. and Mrs. Steven Barinski of Springfield, Massachussetts, were now scheduled to arrive with their fifteen-year-old son in the middle of January to take up residence in the house on Morgan Street.

Now, seven thousand miles to the east, he was moving into a different past. He heard the rounded English tones of Sir Harold Titheringham's voice saying, "Your father went back for another visit." And he had in his briefcase his father's report of that visit.

On top of that perplexing report, something new, dark, and troubling was smoldering within him. He could not rid himself of it. Von Reumann's announcement had opened a trapdoor through which Rob now peered into the abyss of German history, circa 1933-1945. Disclosure of the simple fact that Rudolph von Trepnitz had existed had probably altered for all time Rob's image of himself and his German connections. He had to face the reality that they had been part of one of civilization's worst hours.

He had not been content to rely on the mere assertion of von Reumann. As busy as he was, preparing to depart for Christmas, Rob felt compelled to look into the matter. He plunged into the lower stack levels at the Law Library and found the hundred volumes of the proceedings of the International Military Tribunal. In the list of industrialists brought to trial on charges of using foreigners as forced labor appeared the name of Rudolph von Trepnitz. It leaped from the page as though it had been in flashing neon lights—*von Trepnitz*, a name among those of the ancient and noble families of Germany and a name among the first families of the Alabama Black Belt. His mind had difficulty comprehending what his eyes saw—his own name among the defendants in the dock at Nuremberg.

Though he had been across the ocean from it all, had no part in it, knew nothing of it, he now felt linked to it all through blood in a way that could not be severed. If he felt this way from his remote position, how must those feel who were right here in the midst of it? Was it possible that the von Egloffsbergs' involvement had been more than he had been led to think? And how many more members of the von Trepnitz family—his kinsmen—were still out there? What had they been doing in those years before 1945? He was not sure that he wanted to know.

He entered the village, driving along its bending central street. He saw the church to his left and the stone slab recording the long list of young men the place had given to two lost causes: "All in God's hand." As the road began its slight ascent, he saw ahead around the curve the high wall surrounding the schloss.

As he turned the car into the gateway, he was almost as apprehensive as he had been the day he first entered that courtyard six months before. He had no idea then what he would find, and he had little idea now. It had been three weeks since the last communication from Germany had been dispatched to him. In this family, much could have happened since then.

The Volkswagen rumbled across the cobblestones of the courtyard and stopped on the far side, well away from the entrance steps to the dark red facade of the manor house. Rob got out and extracted his suitcase and briefcase from the rear seat. The place was deserted and quiet. His shoes crunched through the thin snow overlaying the cobblestones. Mounting the steps, he paused to collect his thoughts before rapping on the thick wooden door.

A minute or more passed. He heard no sound. He knocked again, louder this time. In a few seconds, he thought he caught a sound from within. Then he heard a bolt turning. The door swung inward, and there he saw Olga, still the sturdy, somewhat stocky woman he remembered from the previous summer.

"Herr Kirkman," she said with no expression, "we have been expecting you." He recalled that she spoke no English.

He greeted her, and she asked him in, taking his suitcase. She led the way up the dark wooden stairs lined with the headgear of countless stags, down the long corridor, its paneled walls blackened with age. She led him at length up another flight of stairs, darker and narrower than the first, into the large bedroom where he had stayed on his summer visit. He had forgotten how massive German furniture could be. The huge posts at the corners of the bed rose well above his head. The table, chest of drawers, and chair were similarly proportioned.

"This is your room," she said, placing his suitcase on the floor by the table. Olga, he recalled, was not the talkative type. "Dinner will be served at seven."

"Tell me, please, how is Freifrau von Egloffsberg?" Rob found it awkward to get back into German, so he spoke with an artificial deliberateness.

"She is very sick. Some days are better than others. Some days she walks around and sits in chairs. On other days she stays in bed. Yesterday was not good. Today has been better."

"When do you think that I can talk with her?"

"She expects to be at dinner tonight. She asked me to tell you that she will see you then. She also wants to talk with you tomorrow. You will remain here at least two nights, *ja*?"

"If that is convenient, I will."

Olga withdrew from the room, closing the door behind her, before he remembered to ask her who else was here. The place was so quiet that it occurred to him that perhaps no one was on hand but himself and Martina.

Rob stood at the tall window and looked out over the wall and the rooftops of the village to the undulating fields and hills on the far horizon. When he had looked from this window in July, the scene was quite different. Now all was whiteness, but the white blanket showed patches of ground here and there. Obviously there had been no heavy snow recently. It was just past three o'clock. He knew nothing to do except to relax until it was time to bathe and dress for dinner.

After hanging some shirts and a couple of suits in the corner wardrobe, he pulled out of his briefcase a copy of the book from which Pastor Ernst Schreibholz had read in Halle and which Wolfgang had mentioned in Washington—a collection of letters, essays, and poems written by Dietrich Bonhoeffer while in prison. Just before Christmas he had finally located a copy. He had been reading it in snatches and had spent most of his flight over absorbed in it. He was overwhelmed at the pathos of such a man imprisoned. What a waste of talent and energy, he thought at first; but then it occurred to him that those months were not wasted at all, because they resulted in this profoundly significant volume.

Rob came to a poem that especially arrested his attention. It was written in July 1944, more than a year after the Gestapo had taken Bonhoeffer into custody, and nine months before he was put to death. The title was "Stations on the Road to Freedom." He suddenly recalled that Wolfgang had mentioned this poem at the Dupont Plaza Hotel.

The poem was constructed in four stanzas, one for each of the stations: discipline, action, suffering, death. Rob surmised that Bonhoeffer saw these in autobiographical terms, the progression of his own life through these four stations, with the last yet to come, yet probably not far away. It was the last that riveted itself in Rob's mind: "Death—Come now, thou greatest of feasts on the journey to freedom eternal." The man actually seemed to view death as a celebration, a joyous feast coming as the culmination of discipline, action, and suffering, and as the last step to freedom: "At last we may see that which here remains hidden."

Somewhere down these gloomy corridors lay a woman scheduled to die before the snow cleared and the grass grew green again. Coming up the dark and creaking stairs to this room, he had felt the aura of death hovering in the air. He remembered when his mother was dying, day after day, night after night, a peculiar quietness, muffled conversation, a smell of medicine. It had never occurred to him that he was attending the greatest of feasts.

Rob was standing again at the window. An early dusk was setting in. The short days of winter were even shorter at this latitude. A few lights were already twinkling in some of the village houses.

Directly below him, the snow-covered courtyard extended to the long, high wall, shutting off from view the public road on the other side. He ran his eyes along the wall to the gateway at the far end. Through this gap in the wall he could see in the thickening dusk the road leading northward out of the village. Just as he was about to turn away, he saw a slim figure come through the gateway from the road. She was wearing a long coat, a wool cap, and boots that came almost to her knees. She walked rapidly along the drive that passed by the end of the schloss and led to its rear. Her hat was pulled over her ears, and the collar of her coat was turned up, leaving only her face exposed. Goose bumps suddenly flashed over Rob. In the dim and fading light just before the figure disappeared from sight, he believed he recognized Maria Egloffsberg.

An hour later, Rob had emerged from the bathroom and was finishing dressing when a knock came on the door. He opened it and found Olga standing there. Martina was not feeling well enough to come to dinner, Olga reported, but she requested that Rob come to her room now for a few minutes. He quickly put on his tie and coat and followed her down the long corridor.

"Have you received any news about Maria Egloffsberg?" Rob asked as they walked through the semidarkness.

"Yes. She was released by the East Germans. She is here. She came at Christmas."

Rob put his hand on Olga's elbow and pulled her to a stop. "Is she staying here in the schloss right now?" Rob was leaning close to Olga's face and speaking in a low voice. When Olga nodded, he continued. "I had heard that the baroness did not believe that she was really Kurt's daughter. Is that true? What does she think now?"

"She believes now that Maria is actually her granddaughter."

"How does she know?"

"Perhaps she can explain it to you."

They came first into a relatively small but fashionably furnished sitting room. Here there was none of the heavy German flavor. The sofa and chairs could all have been in a contemporary apartment in New York or Paris. There was a modern coffee table in the center and a writing desk in the corner. Olga told Rob to wait there, and she went through a door at the far side.

In a moment Olga reappeared and motioned to Rob. He followed her through the door and found himself in a room three times the size of the sitting room. Only the bed, with its tall heavy posts, was Germanic; the rest of the furnishings were in an elegant modern style. In the middle of the great expanse of bed, propped up against pillows, wearing a rose-colored bed jacket, was the thin and aged Martina.

As he walked across the room toward her, she said in English, "My dear Robert, it is good of you to come this distance to see me, especially in this cold winter weather."

Her voice was soft and low, lacking the vibrancy it had when he last heard it. Had he not known who she was, he would hardly have recognized her. Her face was thinner and more wrinkled, her skin a chalky gray. The specter of death hung over her.

Rob took her hand in his and bent over and kissed her cheek. She smiled, seemingly with effort. He struggled for the appropriate thing to say. "I'm glad that I could arrange to come."

She motioned him to pull a chair up to the bed. "I am sorry that you have found me this way; but we must be honest about the situation. I do not have a great while longer. At this last stage I see the divine plan at work. I can explain the events of the past month in no other way. Christa was married, and I was able to be at her wedding in the church here. My daughter, Helga, and her husband—I believe you met Ernst—were allowed to leave the East and now at last have come here to live. Then, perhaps a miracle, Maria was released into the West, and I am convinced now that she is indeed my granddaughter."

She paused, as though the emotional and physical energy necessary to convey this information had fatigued her.

"Those are extraordinary developments to come in so short a time. It is wonderful that they have all happened—" Rob almost finished his sentence, "while you are here," but he caught himself. "Did you say that Pastor Schreibholz and his wife are here now?"

"Yes. They will be at dinner. I am glad that you will meet Helga. I believe you missed her when you were in Halle last summer."

Rob nodded his head.

"To have her back under my roof—and especially out of the East—does me more good than anything else could."

"Is Wolfgang here?"

"No. He is away on a trip. We expect him either tomorrow or the next day. That brings me to a question. Can you remain here for two more nights?"

The pathetic sight before him prevented Rob from giving anything but an affirmative answer. "I didn't make a specific reservation for my return flight, so I could stay."

She took a deep breath and let out a long sigh. "I ask you for two reasons. One is that I want you and Wolfgang to have an opportunity to visit, and I am not certain that he will return tomorrow. The other is that I want to have time to talk with you, and there are not many hours in the day when I feel well enough to engage in conversation."

"I understand."

"The mornings are my best time. Could you come back at ten tomorrow morning? I will feel better then, and we can have a good talk."

He sensed that she did not wish to prolong this meeting. He rose from the chair and again took her thin hand in his. "Yes, certainly. I'll be here at ten."

"I regret that I will not be able to enjoy dinner with you tonight. But you will have the occasion to get to know Helga and to renew your acquaintance with Ernst and Maria.

Rob leaned over and kissed her again. "I will see you at ten in the morning. Do rest well." He left the room with tears welling up in his eyes.

Stepping from Martina's comfortably heated apartment into the chilly corridor was almost like stepping outside. Rob stopped to pull out his handkerchief and dab his eyes and blow his nose. Olga suddenly came around the corner, startling and embarrassing him.

"The others want you to join them for a drink before dinner. They will be in the large room where you were on your last visit at half after six."

He made his way back to his room to await the appointed hour. It was completely dark now. He slumped down in the chair. Although he knew that Martina was seriously ill, seeing her face-to-face had brought the fact home with special impact. He revised his intentions. He could hardly bring up the subject of his father's visit here, as he had planned. It was too late. He would let the past stay buried.

At half past six he walked down the corridor toward the room he remembered so well—the tall windows with their draperies, the tapestries of medieval knights, and the assortment of framed photographs on the large table. He did not quite know what to expect. His pulse rate, he noticed, was slightly elevated. In the last half hour, sitting quietly in his darkened room, thoughts of Maria had flooded his mind. He had trouble grasping that she was here in this house. He found the prospect of seeing her again to be highly pleasurable.

He paused at the carved wooden door with his hand on the leverlike handle, took a deep breath, and entered.

Pastor Schreibholz was sitting in one of the wing chairs surrounding the cloth-covered table with his face buried in a magazine. He looked up with a smile, and then rose.

He came around the edge of the table, moving with the familiar limp, and extended his hand. "Herr Kirkman," he said in German, "it is a pleasure and honor to see you again."

They shook hands. The rough, firm grip matched the huge frame, the rugged face, and the steel gray hair. Rob reciprocated the greeting, and they sat down.

The pastor recounted his experiences of the past month. They had finally decided to leave the GDR for several reasons—age, the tightening suspicion of him because of his activities in the Bonhoeffer League, Christa, and Martina's condition. It is surprising, he said, how few material possessions one accumulates in that society. There is little money, few goods, and no room to put them. They gave what furniture and belongings they had to the church. Parting with his congregation in Halle was not easy. They stayed through Christmas Day to conduct his last services there and then left. It was a tearful occasion, a break with the homeland after a lifetime. While they were thankful to have this place to come to, he would always have the people of Halle and the East close to his heart.

Schreibholz went on without stopping, as though he had been waiting for some moment when he could pour it all out. Rob listened with fascination to this man torn by the fragmentation of family and friends. He was eventually interrupted by the click of the door handle. Rob turned in his chair to see an attractive, plainly dressed woman of medium height standing in the half-opened door.

The pastor was on his feet. "Ah, here at last is my Helga." He went toward her, taking her hand. "And here, Helga, is Herr Robert Kirkman from the United States."

She and Rob advanced to meet each other. "How do you do, Mr. Kirkman," she said in English with a strong German accent.

"It is grand to meet you," Rob responded.

The three sat down in chairs surrounding the table. Rob examined Helga carefully. She was an older version of Christa; the mother-daughter resemblance was quite evident. He had not noticed it so much from the photographs he had seen, but he now saw before him Christa's blond hair, tinged with gray, and similar facial features, though weathered by a life not too easy. Both Helga and Ernst were still dressed in what could be described as GDR clothes—garments adequate but without style.

"Mr. Kirkman," Helga began, "I regret that I was not in Halle to greet you last July. I have heard much about you since then." She had an appealing smile strongly reminiscent of Christa's. "May I, perhaps, call you Robert? All other members of this family seem to do so."

Rob smiled and nodded his head. "Yes, of course. And may I call you Helga?"

"And you must call me Ernst," the pastor interjected.

Rob asked about Christa's wedding. Helga took the lead in describing it. It was a small ceremony in the church in Prinzenheim, but it was beautiful, with candlelight and flowers. Several American army officers were present, friends of the groom. They were all wearing dress-blue uniforms and looked impressive. Several young women from West Berlin who were Christa's friends came, as well as family friends from Frankfurt and Munich. There was a reception afterward in the great hall in the schloss. Although they had not met Major Catron until the day before the wedding, they agreed that he seemed to be a fine man and they liked him. The couple had gone for a wedding trip to the Canary Islands and were not returning for several more days.

"Christa's marriage would, of course, have been a special occasion at any time," Helga said, "but three things made it unusually special. One is that Mother could be there. That meant much to all of us. Another is that the ceremony could be performed by Ernst." She looked at her husband and smiled. He was sitting quietly with a wistful expression, slightly nodding his head.

"The last very special thing," Helga continued, "was the unexpected appearance of Maria. She was suddenly released three days before Christmas—quite a present for us. She was able to be here for Christmas Day and the wedding. A month ago, no one would have predicted that either Maria or we would be in Prinzenheim. It is an unbelievable series of happenings."

"You wouldn't say that they were coincidences, would you?" Rob asked Ernst Schreibholz, smiling impishly.

"No, no, of course not," shot back the pastor. Turning to Helga, he said, "Robert and I have had a previous discussion about coincidences."

"I can imagine," Helga said, "I have heard about the subject for years."

"It is all really extraordinary," Rob said. "I am happy for all of you—that is, of course, except for your mother's illness. But she seems to be dealing with it sensibly and realistically."

"Yes, she is. We are trying to keep up a cheerful appearance; but it is sad, and we know that she will not be with us much longer. She seems to look forward to talking with you, and we are grateful to you for coming so far to visit."

"I gather that she now accepts Maria as her granddaughter."

"I am indeed happy about that," Helga said. "It would have been sad for her to pass on without that being settled."

"Excuse me," Ernst interrupted, "would you like some wine, or perhaps some of the von Mensinger family liqueur?" Two bottles of white wine and a bottle of the von Mensinger schnapps stood in the center of the table. They each took a glass of wine, poured by Ernst.

With a clanking of its handle, the door from the corridor swung open. Rob, mildly startled, turned in his chair. There, closing the door, was Maria Egloffsberg.

She walked toward Rob, the closest person to her. He rose to greet her. A light-headedness gripped him; he caught his breath. This was the woman he had last seen in a forlorn farewell on the station platform at Magdeburg. He would have recognized her anywhere, but the overall image was strikingly different. Gone were the GDR clothes. She was wearing a high-fashion cocktail dress in a deep rose red. Her sherry-colored hair, coming nearly to her shoulders, was brushed and shiny.

Their eyes were fastened on each other as they converged. She had an almost sardonic smile, as if she were saying, "Well, here I am. Aren't you surprised?"

Rob extended his hand, expecting to shake, but she ignored it and ran her arms around his neck, pressing her cheek against his and giving him a firm hug. Rob resisted the impulse to run his arms around her in the presence of the Schreibholz couple. He detected a nose-tingling perfume. She backed away and took his hand, continuing to look into his eyes.

"This must be a dream," she said the English words in the soft, almost husky German accent, suddenly flooding his memory with that long night and morning at Magdeburg. "I really did not believe that I would ever see you again."

Rob was having difficulty formulating anything appropriate to say. He simply blurted out, "It did seem very unlikely, but," he laughed nervously, "stranger things have happened."

Turning and leading her to the table, he said, as if making an announcement, "And here, Pastor Schreibholz, we have no mere coincidence, right?"

They all laughed and sat down. Ernst poured a glass of wine and handed it to Maria.

Helga spoke up. "Maria, we were just telling Robert how thankful we are to have you here."

Rob joined in. "I imagine that since I saw you at the Magdeburg Station you have been through an ordeal that you would like to forget. I would be interested, though, to hear a little about what happened and how you got here, if you don't mind."

Maria sat impassively. Though her face wore a faint smile, it was the face of one who had known sorrow, disappointment, and loneliness. The shape of the face, the cheek bones, and the hair were Martina's; but the eyes were different, suggesting harrowing experiences, rather than the sadness of advanced years.

After a moment, Maria began to talk softly and steadily. "I do not mind telling you what happened. It is something I will never forget."

When she reached the Ostbahnhof in East Berlin after leaving Rob in Magdeburg, she was met by the lawyer, Werner Schutz, who took her to some friends who were members of the Bonhoeffer League. They took her to the house of some other members near Oranienburg, north of Berlin, where she stayed in hiding for several weeks. The plan was to smuggle her out of the port of Rostock in a crate of goods bound for Sweden; but the internal security police came one day and picked her up. She never learned how the police knew of her whereabouts. She was put in jail in East Berlin. Werner Schutz came to see her, and he represented her from then on. She was charged with attempting to leave the GDR unlawfully and with antisocialist activity. She realized that she had been indiscreet in her comments during the past year among her fellow workers, because two of them testified at her trial and repeated her statements.

The evidence of her attempted flight was all circumstantial. She was surprised that the police had learned of her trip to Magdeburg and of a plan for her to be picked up on the autobahn. When she was convicted, she was sentenced to two years in a prison near Cottbus where political prisoners are held. She was not badly mistreated, but she found prison to be a grim and humiliating place.

She knew nothing of negotiations for her release until a guard came to get her a few days before Christmas. She was moved back to East Berlin and was told that she might be released to the West. Three days before Christmas, she was taken to a checkpoint. There she walked into West Berlin, free.

The room was absolutely quiet. "When you came into West Berlin, what did you do?" Rob asked in a low voice.

"Werner Schutz had sent word to Christa, giving her the place and time of my crossing. She was there waiting for me. I do not remember ever having a moment of such happiness." Maria smiled a genuine smile, and her eyes flickered into life. "She took me to shops to buy clothes, shops such as I had never seen before. She gave me this dress for a Christmas present. Wolfgang had given her money to get other clothes for me. It was a fairyland day. I spent the night at Christa's apartment. Two days later, which was Christmas Eve, we flew to Frankfurt, and then came here to Prinzenheim. I have been here ever since."

Olga appeared and announced that dinner was ready.

When the four of them were seated in the heavy, high-backed chairs around the large dining room table, Pastor Schreibholz invoked the blessings of Almighty God on the house and all within it; he gave thanks for the safe arrival of Maria, of Helga, and of himself in this free land. He concluded by asking for a painless passage of the Baroness von Egloffsberg into eternal life.

Conversation was desultory throughout the meal. The reminder that Martina lay close by with a terminal illness had cast a pall over the group.

At one point Maria turned to Ernst and said, "While I was in prison, I thought often of Christ's words on the cross: 'Father, forgive them for they know not what they do.' I said to myself that these people do know what they are doing, so they should not be forgiven. Was I right?"

"We are not God," he said, "and that is why it is hard for us to forgive. But the message to us is clear. We should forgive our enemies. When we find ourselves unable to do so, all we can do is to ask God's forgiveness for our own failure."

They talked of Martina. Helga said that one of the regrets of her life was that she had seen little of her mother for the last twenty years. Since Christa's wedding the two of them had spent hours talking together, trying to make up now for all that lost time. Maria described the strange sensation of learning, long after she was grown, that she had a living grandmother. The experience of meeting her for the first time only two weeks earlier was one of the most memorable she ever expected to have.

"Mother has looked forward to your visit," Helga said to Rob. "You made a strong impression on her last summer."

"I saw her briefly this afternoon, and we agreed to meet at ten tomorrow morning."

Olga's methodical service had brought them to some heavy pastries for dessert. Helga reminisced over her childhood with her mother at Bachdorf. She did not remember her father at all, because he died when she was two. There were no longer such places as Schloss Bachdorf in the GDR, she said. If Schloss Prinzenheim had been a hundred kilometers farther east, it would be today the offices of a state enterprise or the headquarters for an agricultural collective.

With the meal over, Helga and Ernst said that it was their bedtime. They would see Rob tomorrow, perhaps at lunch. Rob shook hands with Ernst warmly. Helga gave him a quick hug.

"I took a long walk this afternoon," Maria said, "so I am a little tired. I think that perhaps I too should go to bed."

"I will be with Martina in the morning. Could we take a walk together in the afternoon?"

Rob had come around to Maria's side of the table. She had risen and was standing beside her chair. They looked into each other's eyes.

"That would be nice," she said. "There are some pretty walks along the roads into the country."

They stopped in the cold corridor outside the dining room. Rob took her hand, leaned forward, and kissed her lightly on the cheek. "Good night," they both said, almost simultaneously. She turned and went toward the family apartments, and he headed in the opposite direction down the long antlered corridor toward the guest room.

Chapter 31

For robert kirkman this night was not restful. It was punctuated by intermittent sleep and wakefulness. The clouds had cleared, and a nearly full moon was in the sky. Its light, magnified by the snow's whiteness, filled the bedroom with an eerie illumination.

He lay awake for a long while brooding over Wolfgang. What did he really do? Maria said that she and Werner Schutz never knew how the East Germans learned of her escape attempt through Magdeburg. Wolfgang, of course, knew all about it, but others did also.

Rob had talked with Cullen Bracey a week after Wolfgang was in Washington. Cullen had come down to Charlottesville for a football game. After the game, he and Rob had met at the Farmington Country Club. While Kate Bracey played tennis, Rob and Cullen sat in a quiet corner of the front parlor and talked.

"I checked out the meeting in the State Department," Cullen had said. "This blind conference in Germany seems legitimate. The fact that it involves the East Germans is not bothering anybody. In fact, it is now part of our policy to promote East-West interchange. We are supposedly coming into an era of better relations. The in word now for all this is *detente*. Our friends in Bonn are suspicious of Wolfgang, but they don't seem to be able to get a line on him. He comes from an old and distinguished family in Germany. That still carries weight in the West, so they are reluctant to do much.

"The Bonhoeffer League has them worried in Bonn. They get a kick out of seeing the East Germans nettled by that crowd, but on the other hand they're secretly worried by too aggressive a movement there toward reunion, especially if it comes with a Marxist, Soviet-type coloration. We also have reports that the GDR is cracking down on the Bonhoeffer League. Some arrests there will not be surprising. Your pastor friend would be well advised to get out."

They speculated over possibilities. It was indeed possible that Wolfgang was a GDR spy. The CIA and West German intelligence simply did not know.

Rob eventually fell into a sound sleep. It was full daylight when he was awakened by a knock on his bedroom door. Olga stuck her head in and asked if he wished any breakfast. He said that coffee would do, and Olga brought it to his room.

He shaved and dressed without haste, sipping coffee all along. His thoughts were fastened on his upcoming conversation with Martina. It would probably be one of his last. He recalled the fragmented exchanges with his mother during her final days; there was no moment then when he could say that this was the last. Here, however, he could say with certainty that when he left he would not see Martina again.

In the distance, muffled by the closed window, he heard the church clock bonging ten. He pulled himself together and headed toward Martina's apartment.

When he entered, he found her seated on the sofa in her sitting room. He was surprised to see her there and not in bed.

"Come in, Robert," she said in a stronger voice than the previous afternoon. "Olga is just arranging coffee for us."

Rob took a chair across the table from the sofa. Olga was placing a pot of coffee in position, along with two cups. She poured them both a cup and then left the room.

"Come over here, Robert," Martina said. "If you sit beside me on the sofa I can speak more quietly with less strain."

Rob moved over beside her, and she continued talking. She said again how wonderful it was that her daughter and son-in-law had at last left the East and come home, although she realized that to them this place was not really home. She elaborated on her great joy in accepting Maria as Kurt's daughter. In her, she felt that she had a living link with her long-dead son, who, like his father, lay in an unknown grave on foreign soil.

"Maria, as you probably know," she said, "is a medical doctor. That makes it possible for her to be of special help to me these days. She knows all about the medicines I am taking, and she understands my pains and problems. She talks with the doctor when he comes by to see me, and she can explain what he says to me. It is really a godsend for me and Olga to have her now. And, of course, Helga is a great comfort and help, too."

"You are certainly well taken care of. In spite of your condition and all that has happened over the years, you have a lot to be thankful for."

"Yes, I do. My lawyer came here recently, and we revised the documents relating to all of this property after I am gone. The ownership of the schloss and the land that goes with it will be divided three ways. One-third will go to Wolfgang, one-third to Helga and Ernst and then to Christa after they are gone, and one-third will go to Maria. They should all be in comfortable circumstances; there are bank deposits and investments that will be divided the same way."

She paused, let out a sigh, and then picked up the coffee cup and sipped. Up close, Rob saw the ravages of this disease that he had not seen since his mother's death over fifteen years before. Martina's ashen skin had shrunk down to her bones, as though there were no flesh between skin and bone. Her hair was a dull, mousy color. She seemed to be drained of all energy. Rob could not think of anything appropriate to say, so he too sipped coffee.

In a minute, Martina resumed. "Maria will need to make a completely new start. She should have enough money to take some training in the latest medical developments concerning eyes. Her future in the West should be bright. I am worried about Wolfgang, though."

Martina paused again, so Rob spoke up. "I do not understand what he does."

"I must say that I do not know what he does. Men I do not know come here sometimes to pick him up, and they go away. I know he is in West Berlin frequently because he stays in Christa's apartment. An old friend of our family called me from Bonn several months ago to say that Wolfgang was under suspicion there for being too friendly with the East Germans. I asked Wolfgang about that, and he said that his work involved blind people and church groups in the East."

"That sounds admirable."

"This divided country is a terrible thing, Robert. No one outside Germany can really understand it—the splitting of families and homeland. The new generation senses it less. Perhaps if it lasts long enough, it will be accepted as the normal arrangement. But Wolfgang is unwilling to accept the division."

"Have you heard of the Bonhoeffer League?"

"Oh, yes, many times. I have known of Dietrich Bonhoeffer for nearly forty years. The first time I ever heard his name was when Wolfgang came home once from Berlin and described a lecture Bonhoeffer had given. I heard much more about him later. He was a courageous man of deep convictions. I can understand why Wolfgang and Ernst admire him. I remember that several months after the war I heard of Dietrich Bonhoeffer's death at Flossenberg camp only days before the Americans arrived."

Perhaps here, Rob thought, was a point where he could raise one of his questions. "Can you tell me," he said, speaking softly and slowly, "what it was like in Germany during the thirties?"

"It was a strange time." She spoke without hesitation. "We went from depression and confusion to prosperity and war in six years. The Nazi Party has put a black mark on the name of Germany that will not be erased for generations, if ever. They were looked on as a bunch of ruffians by my family and my friends. The tragic thing is that nobody took Hitler seriously for a long while. The circles in which I moved were composed of the old families with strong allegiance to the German nation. They included army officers and public servants who had no reason to be attracted to Hitler. Kurt was in the army before Hitler came to power, and he simply remained as an officer out of loyalty to his country. I remember that he told me once that he and some other officers deeply resented the substitution of the swastika for the official flag. The unfortunate result was that every German soldier appeared to be a Nazi. Of course, that is ridiculous. Neither of my sons was a Party member, and I had very few friends who were. I would say, Robert, that no one who was not himself a German can understand the position Germans were in during that time. It is easy for those in the rest of the world to shake their heads and say that the Germans should have stood up to Hitler, but that view is far too simple. They do not understand."

She wearily leaned back against the sofa. She closed her eyes and sat quite still. Rob thought it best to let her rest, so he sat silently.

In a few moments, she sat up and spoke again. "Robert, have you had an opportunity to talk with Helga?"

"Only last night at dinner. She is a friendly and bright woman. She and Christa look alike."

"Yes, I agree." She had turned toward him and was regarding him intently. "For several months, there has been a burden on my mind. I have been uncertain of what to do about it. Although I am not as deeply religious as my children seem to be, I have prayed many times, hoping for guidance on this problem, and I have now decided what to do."

Rob felt slightly uncomfortable. She continued to stare at him with her sunken eyes and drawn features. She seemed to be hesitating and groping for just the right words. Her bony, fleshless hand moved over and clasped his.

"I have decided to tell you something that I resolved years ago to tell no one. No other person—either living or dead—knows what I am about to tell you. I had long thought that I would take it to the grave with me, but now that I see the grave looming ahead, I want to unburden myself to you."

After pausing a few seconds, she resumed. "First, though, I want you to make a promise to me. I must believe that I can trust you absolutely. Before I say more, I must have your word of honor that you will not disclose to any living person what I am about to tell you as long as I am alive. I leave it to your judgment as to whether to tell anyone after I am gone."

They sat looking into each other's eyes, less than a foot apart. Her request posed no problem for Rob. He would as soon commit a murder as breach a confidence, but he was perplexed as to why this woman, to whom he was a stranger until six months ago, was about to impart to him alone something of such apparent importance.

"You have my word of honor," he said. "I will not reveal what you tell me as long as you live."

"Let me begin, then, by saying that I did not tell you the full story of your father's contact with me and my family. When you were here in the summer, I told you that he and the young Englishman came to Bachdorf. I showed you a photograph that was taken of the three of us." Rob nodded, and she continued. "We had an enjoyable time. What I did not tell you is that your father wrote me after he returned to Oxford, expressing his appreciation for the hospitality at Bachdorf, and his desire to come back at his next vacation. I had found your father to be a refreshing contrast to the German men that were around, so I answered his letter. We exchanged several letters after that. He was finishing his year at Oxford in late summer. At that time, I would be here at Prinzenheim visiting my family, so I invited him here, and he came."

Rob felt compelled to simulate total surprise. "My father actually came to this very place?" he asked more-or-less rhetorically.

"He did, and he remained several days. My mother was here at the time, and she thought him quite engaging. But there was a problem. My family was trying to persuade me to marry a man from Berlin. I did not really love this man, but the family made a strong argument that he could provide security and, with the shortage of eligible men, he was not a bad choice. So my mother was not enthusiastic about your father's visit, although she was polite to him."

Martina leaned her head against the back of the sofa and closed her eyes. It was not clear whether she was tired or whether she was lost in nostalgia. Rob felt a bit let down. Is this all that she had to say? A half-century-old visit hardly seemed to be information worthy of an oath of secrecy.

In a moment, she came erect. "It became clear to me after your father had been here for two days that I was in love with him. It sounds silly now, but we took long walks in the country and sat up late at night talking about all sorts of things. I was exhilarated as I had not been since before the war." She tightened her hand over Rob's. "He was staying in the guest room on the top floor, the room where you are staying. On the last night of his visit, we talked until a late hour in the parlor. When we said good night there, he took both of my hands in his. We stood there for a long while. Then, for the first time, he leaned over and kissed me, just quickly. Then we parted."

Fatigue was now overtaking Martina. She leaned back again. "Would you like another cup of coffee?" Rob asked.

"No, thank you," she answered in a whisper. In a moment she roused herself, still holding his hand firmly.

"I went to my bedroom, but I felt restless, excited, and unable to sleep." She hesitated, searching for words. She seemed almost to be talking to herself. "I put on my robe and went down that long corridor and up the stairs to his room. I knocked on the door, and he said, 'Come in.' I entered and saw him standing by the window in the darkness. Even now, I find it difficult to relate what happened. All I can say is that it was nearly daylight when I left your father's room."

Rob sat immobile, his countenance devoid of expression, struggling to suppress all signs of surprise, shock, and amazement.

"I will go right to the point," she said. "Helga is your father's daughter."

Chapter 32

The cloud-covered sky and the snow-sprinkled ground enshrouded the earth in a gray-whiteness on this cold January morning; the sky, hills, and fields blended into an inhospitable scene. Robert Kirkman sat in the chair in the guest room facing the window. He had not moved since returning from Martina's sitting room half an hour earlier. He felt sick, incapable of movement.

Information transmitted to the brain by the eyes or ears is not always absorbed immediately. Time is sometimes required for facts to be processed and assimilated. His father—he was fixed on that figure—Robert Edward Kirkman, his own father had been here in this room where he now sat, in this monstrous German bed, where he slept. His father was the father also of a daughter—the father of Helga, father of a descendant of the von Mensinger family of Prinzenheim. Helga was his half-sister. He thought he had no sisters or brothers. Now Helga was his halfsister. . . . and Christa, his niece?

These disturbed ramblings were interrupted by a knock at the door. "Come in," Rob said reflexively, as though shaken out of sleep. He did not move. Olga peered through a crack in the door and said that lunch would be served in fifteen minutes.

He did not want to go to the dining room. He was not hungry. He wanted to be alone with his thoughts, but he could think of no good excuse. "All right, thank you," he mumbled.

Having splashed cold water in his face and revived somewhat, he entered the dining room. The same threesome of the night before were gathered there, standing by the window. They all sat down after greeting Rob. Ernst again invoked divine blessings, and Olga began serving the soup.

Rob found himself staring at Helga, who sat to his right, as though she was a different woman from the one who was at dinner the evening before. This woman was bone of his bone, flesh of his flesh—part Kirkman, part Trepnitz, just as he was. Those German genes, rooted in Thuringia and carried across the Atlantic nearly two centuries before, had been brought back to the Fatherland. He felt eyes upon him and turned his head to see Maria looking at him from directly across the table. She quickly diverted her gaze to her soup.

They conversed about the weather, with Rob doing as little talking as possible. It was unseasonably mild, the Germans agreed. It had been colder, and it would get much colder, and there would surely be more snow.

As the talk rambled on about Prinzenheim, the surrounding countryside, and how it differed from the country where they had lived in the East, Rob tried to study Helga without being conspicuous. Do we resemble each other, he wondered. She must be about six years older, he reckoned, born long before Ed Kirkman had met Emily Shepperson.

To avoid having to talk much, Rob groped for a question to keep someone else going. Turning to Ernst, he asked, "Could you tell me a bit more about Dietrich Bonhoeffer? How well did you know him? What kind of man was he?"

It was instantly apparent that Rob had picked a good subject. "Ah, yes," Ernst responded enthusiastically. "You must remember our talk at Halle."

"I certainly do. I have even obtained my own copy of *Letters and Papers from Prison.*"

"Good. That is the later Bonhoeffer—the man and theologian in his last stage. Some of the views he expressed there have puzzled students. He wrote of the church in the 'world come of age.' It is a point of endless fascination to wonder what he meant by that and what he would have thought in the postwar world."

Ernst reminisced about some of the Bonhoeffer seminars in the thirties. Then he added, "He later became caught up in the Confessing Church movement, the wing of the Protestant church that went into active opposition to the Nazis. I did not become an ordained pastor before the war, so I did not come into contact with him after my student days, but I read his books."

Ernst Schreibholz talked on about the Confessing Church and its seminary at Finkenwalde, near the Baltic coast, and explained the uncertainties that he had about entering the ministry. As it was, he was not ordained until the war was over. By that time, he said, he had taken unto himself what his friends called a child bride. He looked amusingly at Helga, who laughed. "As you may know, Robert, I am some years older than my sweet wife. But I have not minded a bit."

"No," chimed in Helga, smiling kittenishly, "I have found it nice to be married to an older man."

Much to Rob's relief, Ernst and Helga reminisced through the rest of the meal about their lives in the GDR when Christa was growing up. Maria said almost nothing. Occasionally she and Rob exchanged awkward glances. Rob was too distracted by the information that had been unloaded on him that morning to be an interested listener.

They had finished eating and were on the verge of rising when Maria looked at Rob and said, "Would you still like to take a walk?"

In his disconcerted state, Rob had forgotten that they had agreed the night before to go for a walk after lunch. "Yes, of course," he said haltingly. "Yes, that would be invigorating."

As they were leaving the dining room, Helga and Rob came close together in the doorway. "Mother told me just before lunch," she said, "that she appreciated your visit with her this morning."

He was within inches of her face, a rather well-preserved face for a woman of fifty. He resisted the urge to take her hand or her arm or to hug her—to hold this daughter of his father.

Maria Egloffsberg and Robert Kirkman walked side-by-side, striding briskly down the sloping street toward the center of the village. The air was clear, clean, and cold; the temperature was just above freezing. The solid cloud cover had broken, and the sun cast a thin sporadic light through openings in the moving clouds. Only an occasional automobile or pedestrian marred the solitude of their outing. They turned and walked along the street, passing in front of the church and the stone monument listing the war dead of Prinzenheim.

"Here is where Christa was married," Maria said.

"What did you think of the occasion?"

"It was beautiful, but simple. I have never been around so many Americans before."

"What is your impression of them?"

"They laugh and joke a lot. Some of them must be serious, but they do not act that way."

"Is that the way that I appear?" Rob ventured.

Maria hesitated and then looked at him with a slight smile. "No. That is . . . well, I do not quite know how to answer. You do not behave in a silly fashion the way some of those Americans did."

They had now left the village behind. The narrow road wound through low, rolling, open land, probably pasture covered with snow.

"This road circles around," she said, "and joins another road that leads back to the schloss. It is a nice walk. I have taken it several times. No one seems to come along here."

The West, she said in response to his inquiry, was something of a shock to her. The traffic in the cities was overwhelming. People were disorderly and loud. Advertising was unsightly. There were drunks, and she had read about crime and drugs. There was great freedom too, and she could hardly believe the volume of magazines and newspapers. Life in the GDR was less hectic, more organized, and more dull. Having passed through West Berlin and Frankfurt, she was glad to be in the quiet of Prinzenheim. She needed time to adjust.

"What do you plan to do in the future?" Rob asked.

"I want very much to go back to my work. It has been many months since I have been in a hospital or any medical office. The day before I met you in Magdeburg was the last day I worked. But I need new training. The West is ahead of the GDR in medical technology."

"Do you have any idea where you might go to get the training?"

"The doctor who comes here to see my grandmother has talked to me about it. He knows eye doctors in a large Frankfurt hospital, and he believes that they would take me for training. But I have decided not to begin anything like that as long as my grandmother is alive. She and Helga and all the others have been so good to me that I feel obligated to help here."

"What do you think the outlook is for Martina?"

"From what her doctor says and what I know, I would say a month, perhaps two."

They moved along in silence for a few minutes in contemplation of that impending event. The exercise and winter air had refreshed Rob, but the morning's revelation had not left him. It flashed through his mind at intervals like the quickly appearing and disappearing light of a rotating beacon. "Helga is Daddy's daughter, my half-sister," it would say.

Maria broke the silence. "This may surprise you, but I have even thought of going to America."

Rob snapped his head toward her. "America! From the GDR to the States? If you have found West Germany hectic and confusing, I don't know what you would think of America."

The road was rising now, and their breath was coming faster. They had kept up a rapid pace and covered a couple of miles. Icy patches spread across the road where it had been shaded by a clump of trees. They slowed and moved cautiously. Maria's foot slipped, and Rob instinctively shot his hand out to grab her arm. He held on to her elbow until they reached dry surface a few yards farther on. His gloved hand slid down and encircled hers as they resumed their brisk pace.

The gray, grim cloud canopy of the morning had shifted eastward. The heavens above were now a deepening blue. The winter sun of late afternoon, sinking at their backs, threw their lengthening shadows ahead of them. They passed a farmhouse, the red brick cluster of low buildings forming an inner courtyard. The mixed aroma of hay and manure was strong. A dog barked somewhere to the rear.

They walked briskly onward. In the afternoon stillness, their boots rapped loudly on the road's asphalt surface. Rob heard their clump, clump, clump as Helga, Helga, Helga. How strange it was, he mused, that a single fact communicated to him in a single sentence by a dying woman could instantly alter his view of the world forever—the way he thought of himself, of his father, of this whole group of Germans, and even of Germany itself.

"We are coming just ahead to an intersection," Maria said, slightly breathless from the long slope they had just ascended. "We will turn right onto a road that runs back to the schloss. There is an old cemetery along the way where members of the von Mensinger family are buried."

Rob asked whether she had had opportunities to talk with Wolfgang since she arrived. What was her view of him now?

"I find him difficult to understand," she replied. "At times, he sounds harsh and abrupt. But I believe that at bottom he is a kind man with an enormous concern for his fellow human beings. He has given much of his life to improving conditions for the blind in the GDR as well as in the West. He has nothing to gain personally from these efforts. In the East he is helping people with whom he has little in common."

"Since being here," Maria said, shifting the subject, "I have learned some of the history of my mother's family in Pomerania. They were Junkers and had huge land holdings. My great-uncle was a general who was killed in the First World War, and there are several other generals going back before the time of Frederick the Great. The seat of the family in Pomerania is now in Poland. If the schloss was not destroyed in the war, it is probably now occupied by twenty families or a Polish state-owned enterprise. All the names there have been changed from German into Polish, so the place cannot be located on a map today."

"Wolfgang and Martina knew your mother, at least for a little while. Have you ever talked with them about her?"

"Yes. I am curious to know more about her. They remember her as a beautiful woman."

"Resembling you?" Rob laughingly interrupted.

"Now that you mention it, they have said that," she said with an amused twinkle in her eyes that he had not noticed before. "But they seem to have thought of her as aloof and not especially warm toward the von Egloffsberg family. You would not think of me in that way, would you?"

The question caught Rob off guard. "Why . . . no; I think of you as a compassionate person with love for this family." He was embarrassed by the trite comment, so he looked straight ahead as he spoke.

"They did not really know my mother well because my father was killed soon after they were married. My mother remained in Berlin, where she had friends. Isn't it odd," she asked, after having fallen silent for some seconds, "that the homes of both my father and mother are cut off from me forever? How very fortunate my grandmother was to have a home in the West, a place to come to when the Red Army overran Bachdorf. Thousands, even millions, of others had nowhere to go. They simply moved westward and began again with nothing."

A dark stone wall about waist high began on their left and ran for some distance ahead, parallel with the road. "Here is the cemetery," she said.

A small driveway passed through a pair of stone gateposts. The cemetery was long but not deep. Leafless trees, the large diameters of their trunks testifying to their age, lined the inside of the stone wall and the drive that looped through the graves. Lichens and moss covered the weathered headstones.

"The von Mensinger family plot is down here," Maria said as they walked along the narrow drive. They came to a square area delineated by a low stone border running about forty feet in each direction. Inside, the von Mensinger name appeared everywhere. There were two massive upright markers, several smaller ones, and numerous flat gravestones.

"Four generations are buried here," she said. "Here are my grandmother Martina's parents, my great-grandparents." They were gazing down at two flat gray granite headstones. "And you can follow each generation back into the eighteenth century." The largest monument was that of the General von Mensinger who achieved modest fame in the Franco-Prussian War.

"When I arrived here," Maria resumed, "my grandmother was still able to get out of the house. The day after Christa's wedding, she brought me here and told me about these people. She said that it was important that I know my family, that there was a danger in these times of forgetting the great German families of the past and what they had contributed to the country and the world." Maria pointed to one of the few remaining open spaces in the plot. "Here, she told me, is where she will be buried. It is next to her parents."

"What is this?" Rob asked, indicating a granite slab next to the open space that Martina had designated for herself.

"That is a memorial stone to my father and grandfather. She told me that since they had no known graves, she wanted some record of their existence. So she put this stone here after the war."

Rob bent over the stone and brushed away the rotting leaves and snow. Translating the German, he read:

To the Honor and Memory of

Bruno Karl Hans von Egloffsberg
Born 13 March 1895
Fell 19 October 1918

Kurt Bruno Gottlieb von Egloffsberg
Born 4 February 1915
Fell 10 January 1943

Lo, I am with you always,
even to the end of the world.

"There is room here also for Wolfgang," Maria said. "Then, it seems to me, that the entire plot will be filled. What does that mean? When a family's burial place for generations is filled, what happens? It may mean here that this family, like the Germany to which they belonged, is at an end."

Rob took her questions to be rhetorical and said nothing, but continued looking at the array of graves. On a low wall bordering one side of the plot, he sat down. She came over and perched beside him.

It felt good to sit after the long walk. A truck in need of a muffler roared by on the road, its raucous noise dying away as it passed into the countryside. Near total silence enveloped them. Lost in thought, they sat for some time, their eyes surveying the last resting places of the numerous von Mensingers whose lives had been centered in the venerable schloss just down the road.

"These families," Maria said after a while, almost dreamily, "those of my father and my mother—in Pomerania and along the Elbe—are the types I was taught to think of as Fascist. Ever since I started school, I have heard that those families, who lived in houses like the schloss here and who owned large amounts of land, were the enemies of the working class. They were imperialists, exploiters, the people's enemies. I grew up like everybody else in the GDR—not knowing anything different. I had difficulty adjusting my thinking when I learned who I really was. It is natural not to believe evil things about one's own ancestors. I still have doubts because that early training was deeply implanted. It is really hard to believe, though, that my grandmother and Wolfgang and Helga were ever Fascists. They are all kind and considerate people. I have come to love them, although I have doubts about Wolfgang's activities."

She turned to Rob and asked plaintively, "Do you think that the members of these families were Fascists?"

"Hmmm . . ." murmured Rob, wanting to take his time in answering. He thought of Rudolph von Trepnitz, the I.G. Farben engineer. "I doubt that there is a simple answer to that question," he said finally. "First, I certainly do not think that those friendly and gracious people in the schloss here are or were Fascists, but they are the only members of these families I know. Part of the problem is defining the word *Fascist.* What the Russians and East Germans would call a Fascist I might not. We surely cannot assume that all the families living in large houses and owning a lot of land were Fascists; many of them were not. So unless you have some clear evidence otherwise, I think that you should not assume that your relatives were Fascists. Not everyone serving in the German army during the Second World War was a Nazi or a Fascist; many of them were just soldiers. I can easily imagine that your father, who had already entered the professional army by the time Hitler came to power, considered that he was just doing his professional duty."

"I am glad to hear you say that. This has been a hard adjustment, and I still feel uncomfortable."

"My observation is that in the GDR if you do not subscribe to Marxism-Leninism you are considered a Fascist. In their view, there is no third choice. They do not understand that there can be such a thing as a real democracy that is neither Fascist nor Communist."

"Yes, I agree," she said softly. "Church members are looked at in almost the same way. They are thought to be disloyal and untrustworthy because they have allegiance to a god other than the Party and the state. The SED borrowed one of the Ten Commandments and put it to its own use—'Thou shalt not have any other Gods before me'—*me* meaning the SED."

Rob was enthralled by the cemetery. He had long been fascinated with cemeteries. He must have visited hundreds from Alabama through the Carolinas to Virginia and in England, Scotland, France, and Germany, ranging from a handful of graves deep in the countryside to poignant military cemeteries. They were typically quiet and deserted, peaceful, and redolent of the past. They were good places to contemplate the vicissitudes of the human condition and the mortality of man.

The similarity to Trepnitz Hills suddenly struck him. He thought of the graves there stretching out behind the church, the granite and marble stones tracing the generations of the Trepnitz family. Take away the village here, he said to himself, and you essentially have Trepnitz Hills. A hundred years ago, the likeness would have been striking indeed, except for one difference—here the people farming the place would have been white, while those at Trepnitz Hills would have been black. For a fleeting moment last summer, he had felt at home as he stood at the window of his bedroom in the schloss. That feeling now came over him again.

The shadows were deepening as Maria and Robert rose from the wall and walked through the stone gateway into the road.

"The schloss is only a kilometer ahead," she said.

The road curved gently. To the west the snow-covered fields sloped away gradually, and faded far away into the low hills on the horizon. The sun was just touching earth. A light pink cast was flung across the sky overhead, but as they watched, it darkened gradually into an orange-red. The scattered islands of clouds reflected the sun's brighter rays. The sun itself was a large orange disk, sinking almost visibly by the second.

Rob and Maria had stopped as if by command to watch this magnificent show. They stood at the edge of the road, looking westward, saying nothing.

In the dusky solitude left in the sunset's aftermath, they turned and faced each other. Neither spoke. Their eyes were locked together. Rob felt blood throbbing in his temples. He knew what he wanted to do. His instincts were to grab this woman around the waist, pull her tightly against him, and kiss her. But he held back. He felt awkward, embarrassed. He had always been clumsy with women, unsure of himself in situations like this.

Long seconds passed. His breath quickened. He then heard himself saying, "It will be dark shortly. We should get on back to the schloss."

Chapter 33

AT DINNER THAT EVENING the same foursome gathered. Wolfgang had not returned. Martina was still not feeling up to coming to the dining room. Rob picked at his food. He felt tired and uninterested in conversation. He yearned for bedtime, solitude, and for time to sort out his thoughts.

He studied Helga again, trying not to be obvious about it. He was now beginning to question the facts. His lawyer's instinct was taking hold. Could Martina possibly be mistaken? She had married shortly after his father's last visit. How could she be certain that Helga was his daughter? He had perhaps too readily accepted Martina's unsupported assertion of this fact.

As the meal concluded, Rob announced that he felt tired and would retire for the evening. They all rose. Helga and Ernst said good night and left. Rob and Maria paused at the door as they had done the night before.

She smiled and said, "May we take another walk tomorrow afternoon?"

"I would enjoy that," he said, smiling wearily back at her. "I will visit Martina in the morning, so we can go after lunch."

"Wolfgang should be here by dinner tomorrow."

"Good," said Rob, "I will be glad to see him again."

They were in the penetrating chill of the corridor. "I do feel quite weary," Rob said. "The jet lag and that walk must have caught up with me."

"That walk today was one of the most pleasant experiences I have had in a long, long time," Maria said.

"We'll do it again tomorrow." He leaned forward and kissed her on the cheek. "I really must get to bed," Rob murmured in a whisper. "I will see you tomorrow."

After knocking softly on Martina's apartment door the next morning,

Rob waited but heard nothing. He knocked again. All was quiet. He cracked the door and looked into the sitting room. No one was there. He went to the bedroom door and knocked. In a moment, Olga's face appeared. "Please have a seat," she said. "She will be with you in a few minutes."

For Rob, the world seemed brighter and better than it had last night. Overnight, with sleep, his body and mind had begun to absorb and adjust to Martina's revelation. He felt more at ease now with the startling news, but not quite willing to accept it.

The door from the bedroom opened, and Martina came toward him, followed by Olga. On her feet, she appeared more frail and pinched than ever. The faint smile seemed forced.

"Good morning, Robert," she said, extending her hand and taking his. "I hope you rested well."

"I did, and I hope you had a good night."

Martina began explaining how her condition varied from day to day. "But enough of my problems," she interjected suddenly. "Maria tells me that the two of you went for a long walk yesterday. I hope you found the countryside pretty. I have walked all over it for many kilometers in all directions, and I have never tired of the scenery and fresh air."

"It is beautiful, and I was glad to have an opportunity to visit with Maria."

"I feel as if I have known her all her life. Christa is more vivacious and cheerful, but I think that Maria is perhaps more sensitive and serious."

Rob nodded, anxious to get to the subject foremost in his mind. He was about to ask a question when Olga came in with coffee. After she had poured them both a cup and left, he moved in with his inquiry.

"What you told me yesterday about Helga came as a shock. I wonder whether you would mind my asking you a question about it."

"No. Please ask whatever you would like."

"Well, this is a bit awkward for me to ask, but I will do so anyway. You told me that you were married to an older gentleman from Berlin shortly after my father's visit here." Martina nodded her head but said nothing. "What I cannot help wondering is how . . . that is, how can you . . ." His embarrassment kept him from framing the question.

She came to his rescue. "I know what you are trying to ask. It is a perfectly reasonable question. You want to know how I can be sure that Helga is your father's child and not that of the man I married. Is that correct?"

"Yes, that's right."

"In the usual situation there might be a serious doubt on that point. But here there can be no doubt whatsoever, and I will tell you why. The man I married turned out to be completely impotent."

Having made that announcement—one almost as startling as that of the previous morning—she picked up her coffee cup, leaned back on the sofa, and sipped. Rob sat forward in his chair, looking blankly at the table. He had not imagined that a single sentence could so absolutely and finally settle this matter. There was nothing to be said, but she seemed moved to elaborate.

Putting her coffee cup down and again leaning back, she said, "You may be wondering what an impotent husband thought when he discovered that his wife was pregnant." Rob sat motionless, not speaking. "That was one of the most tormented moments of my life. I had thought that I would be clever and pretend that the pregnancy occurred after we were married and later that the baby was born a little prematurely. But, of course, that plan vanished when I learned of his impotency. And, as you can imagine, I was not long in learning that."

Rob squirmed uneasily in his chair. He was not accustomed to such conversations with women, especially with one of his mother's age. But Martina was evidently determined to give him the whole story.

"I felt dirty and shabby," she continued. "In my whole life, I have never felt that I had so clearly sinned. I was in a panic. I considered going to our pastor and telling him the facts, confessing all, and seeking his help and prayers. But then I made a decision that I have held to ever since—that is, until yesterday. That decision was that no one but me and my husband would ever know the facts. I remembered my Lutheran training—the priesthood of all believers, the doctrine that one does not need a priest to intercede. So I prayed for forgiveness and for guidance. That gave me added strength to face my husband."

She sat still, as if to ponder what she had done those many years ago.

Rob spoke up. "May I ask what your husband did when he learned that you were pregnant?"

"I will never forget the day that I told him. We were upstairs in his house in Berlin. It was a quiet Sunday afternoon. I had tried to pick an unhurried time. When I said that I was pregnant, he was obviously hurt and his eyes told me that he suffered an immense disappointment in me. After a long silence, his face brightened and he exclaimed, 'Well, we will have a child after all.' I believe that after the first shock he was glad. As the days passed, it became clear that he was truly happy to be seen by others as the father of a child. We agreed that we would forever treat the baby as his, and that was that. When Helga was born, he could not have been a better father."

"Did you ever tell him who the real father was?"

"No. I simply told him that it was a friend who had gone out of my life. I assured him that there would never be any contact between me and the father again. He seemed to accept that."

"Did you ever inform my father of the situation?"

"No. He never knew about it. I wrote him only once after that last visit, and that was to tell him that I was getting married. He had written me just after he returned home. We never wrote each other again."

"So for all these years," Rob mumbled almost inaudibly, "my father never knew that he had a daughter in Germany."

"It is just as well. I have considered that episode as my worst sin, one that I fervently hope the Lord has forgiven. I suppose it will not be long before I find out. Helga has been a wonderful daughter. Having her come home to me at this time is a blessing beyond calculation. I like to look on this as a sign that God has forgiven me and is demonstrating that by sending Helga here—and Maria too, not to mention you. It is extraordinary, don't you think?"

"It is. . . . It truly is." That was all that Rob could bring himself to say.

Moments passed before either spoke again. Then Rob said, "I will not tell anyone of this as long as you are alive. But there may come a time when I feel the need to tell someone. Then I will have only my own word. Would you be willing to write out and sign a statement?"

Martina gave a tired sigh and thought for some seconds, then rose slowly and unsteadily and went to her desk. Laying a piece of writing paper on the desk, she took pen in hand and scribbled. She handed the paper to Rob. "Do you think this is adequate?"

Rob looked at the paper. It was the familiar stationery with her name and address engraved at the top. In her shaky and scrawling handwriting, the following appeared:

> This is to certify that Edward Kirkman is the father of my daughter, Helga, born 2 June 1924.
>
> Martina von Egloffsberg

"That seems fine. You might put today's date at the bottom."

Martina took the paper back and scribbled under her signature, "5 January 1974."

The clock in the church tower was clanging two as Rob and Maria came out of the courtyard into the public road.

"Let's go another way today," she said. "There is a small road leading south that winds around into the hills and forests. The scenery is different there."

They struck out at a fast pace. The day was clearer than the day before. Overhead was a deep blue canopy. The air was cold, and they could see their breath. The road ran for a while through open fields covered lightly with snow, then curved and began an ascent toward wooded hills. The floor of the forest was dank and moss-covered. The snow had hardly penetrated through the branches of the trees.

Rob asked her about growing up in East Germany. It was not unduly grim, she said, but it was dull and highly controlled. First, she joined the Young Pioneers, as almost every child did. They were drilled on the virtues of socialism and what it could do for humanity. When she was fourteen, she joined the Free German Youth, as almost everyone did. They regularly scheduled functions on Sunday mornings directly in conflict with church services and church youth functions. That didn't make any difference to her then because she didn't know anything about the church.

"I was reared as a good Communist, a model Marxist-Leninist youth. There was no one around to question anything. It was only when I went to the University in Berlin and began to see Western television and hear some of the students quietly criticizing the authorities that I began to wonder."

"The couple that reared you—were they really dedicated Party people?"

"No, not at all. They were not SED members, and they did not seem interested in politics or government. They had rather ordinary jobs and lived fairly comfortably, and that seemed to be the most important thing to them. They constantly told me that a new day had come and that all of us had to cooperate in building the country. The odd thing is that I suspect they thought and acted the same under the Nazis. I was once going through a drawer in an old wardrobe, and I came across a framed picture of Hitler and several pamphlets published by the Nazis praising the new National Socialist regime. Most of the people in the GDR are that way, I think. They will go along with whomever is in power, as long as there is adequate food and shelter."

"It is hard to imagine the radical change of mind you must have undergone after years in that environment."

"It was quite a shift. I had begun to have serious doubts about the whole system by the time I graduated from medical school. The turning point came when I met Ernst in the Charité Hospital. He and Helga opened up the world of the church to me. I did not go through one of those instantaneous conversions. It was a gradual process, but it came steadily and surely, and I wondered how I could ever have lived without faith in God and the hope and assurances that Christianity offers the world. I also came to believe that the GDR could not last because a country that wars against God cannot survive."

The trees were thick on both sides of the road. Their topmost branches almost touched each other overhead, forming a latticework arch against the blue sky. In the summer, Rob imagined, this must be a fairylike tunnel of greenery.

"But I do not think the West is all good," Maria said after some moments of silence. "In fact, it may be on a course of self-destruction. There can be nothing good in the crime, the drugs, the pornography, and the general decline in public behavior and morality. There are some good things in the GDR. If we could adopt them without all the rest of that system, we might have the best of both worlds."

"What features would you like to copy?"

"There is a certain sense of community there. People tend to cooperate with each other. Although it is somewhat forced and sometimes artificial, there is still a spirit of working together for the common good that I do not sense in the West. Here it is everyone for himself. Making money seems to be the most important point of life for many people. There, it is less materialistic, less worry about money. Children are better disciplined. I was never afraid to walk on any street in any city late at night. I am told that I should never go alone in some parts of West German and American cities."

The road emerged from the woods and curved around the side of a hill. The countryside opened up to view and the entire village of Prinzenheim was spread out below them, about a mile in the distance. Rob was surprised that they had gained such altitude. The major landmarks were clearly visible—the main road, the church, and the schloss.

"Let's sit here and rest a bit," Rob said, gesturing to a low stone wall along the edge of the road.

"Do you see the land that lies behind the schloss?" Maria asked, pointing to the north. "That is the land that still belongs to the family. It runs to the base of those hills there." She swung her arm to outline the terrain. "Grandmother described it to me. She also said that when she was a little girl almost all the land around the village belonged to the von Mensinger family. That is gone now, some sold off and some lost in the twenties and thirties."

"Has your grandmother told you what her plans are for this property?"

"Yes. She says she has now arranged for it to be divided into three parts—one-third to Wolfgang, one-third to Helga and Ernst, and one-third to me. At Wolfgang's death his share will be split between Helga, or Christa if Helga is not living, and me. Christa, of course, will eventually get the share going to Helga and Ernst."

"In other words, you and Christa will one day own the whole place together."

"Yes. That seems to be the plan. For me, it is like a fairy tale. I cannot believe it."

"If you consider who your parents were, it is not really surprising; but if you think of the circumstances in which you were reared, it is truly astounding."

"I do not know how it all fits into my future life. As I told you, I do want to go back to work in medicine, and there is no way to do that here. There is plenty of room here for all of us to live. Each of us has a separate apartment now. I could come and go, but most of the time I would need to live somewhere else."

For some moments, they sat in silence on the wall, taking in the view. They could see for several miles over the rolling snow-covered land. Another village lay in the far distance.

"It is so peaceful and beautiful here," Maria murmured. "I think it is my favorite spot around Prinzenheim. Several times since Christmas I have walked here alone just to think."

"What do you think about here?"

"Oh, my whole life and where I go from here."

"Yesterday, you said something about America. Have you thought much about that?"

"More in the last two days than I had before." She smiled coyly.

"It may be worth looking into. There are many hospitals and medical schools, and I would think that you could work out an arrangement somewhere. As a matter of fact, if you are really interested, I would be glad to make inquiry at the medical school at the University of Virginia. A couple of months ago, I met the head of the Department of Opthalmology at a party. He seemed to be a nice fellow. I could speak to him."

She suddenly put her arm around his and snuggled up to his side. "Do you really think that you could do that?"

He looked into her faintly brightened but still sad eyes. Her arm held them tightly together as they sat on the wall.

"Yes, I think so," Rob said weakly, almost inaudibly. Their eyes were now fixed on each other. Seconds passed, maybe more. Rob felt his heart thumping, his breath quickening. Their faces moved slowly toward each other, and their lips touched, lightly and briefly. Their faces separated, ever so little, nose almost touching nose. In an instant, mouths were rejoined. The cold had numbed skin and lips, but the warmth that now flowed made that irrelevant.

Rob pulled away. They sat silently gazing over the valley bathed in the weakening sunlight, their arms clasped together.

At length she spoke, barely above a whisper. "Do you remember the first time we ever saw each other?"

"I surely do. It was in the dining room of the Interhotel in Leipzig."

"Yes. I have a confession to make." She gave him a sly smile.

"What is it?"

"I thought to myself as we sat at the table that you were a handsome man. Even on that brief meeting, you appealed to me."

Rob was embarrassed and ill at ease, not knowing if she was simply flattering him.

"That is surprising. I'll tell you what I thought at that time."

"What?" She snuggled more tightly against him.

"I had two impressions. First, I said to myself that this is the typical new woman of a Communist state, a serious, trained technician, a dedicated Marxist-Leninist. I remember one of the first things you said. You asked, 'What do you think of our country?' "

"That is a standard question that everyone in the GDR asks of Westerners. What was your other thought?"

"I watched you walk out of the dining room, and it came to me that you were somebody I would like to know better. Of course, I assumed that it was a momentary encounter and that you had gone forever."

The sun was nearing the horizon, and the chill was beginning to penetrate their bulky winter coats. They stood up, and Rob stamped his feet and swung his arms to warm himself.

"Now, I have a small confession to make," he said, taking both of her gloved hands in his.

"All right, what is it?" Her face showed a radiance that he had not previously seen.

"Do you remember when I came up to your table in that cafe on Unter den Linden?"

"Yes, I had stopped there to have some coffee. I must say that I was astonished to see you."

"Well, my confession is that I had followed you there."

She was genuinely surprised. "You had followed me?" she exclaimed. "From where?"

"I saw you and Wolfgang walking along Clara-Zetkin-Strasse. I had already met Wolfgang on my visit here at Prinzenheim, and I recognized you from the Leipzig hotel. I was absolutely stunned to see the two of you together, so I fell in a little way behind you to see where you were going. He took a taxi at the Friedrichstrasse Station, so I simply kept on in your wake."

"Well, you are a clever man," she said, laughing a bit.

"You may imagine how I was startled again when you gave me your name. I had never heard that the family which I had just come to know had any relatives in the East, other than Helga and Ernst."

A rosy tint was suffusing earth and sky. "It looks as though we have another spectacular sunset this evening," Rob said.

They looked westward, watching the changing colors as the moments passed. In the reddish glow, the schloss was accentuated on its high ground, dominating the village. This sunset, Rob thought, brought the frail woman lying there in her bed one day nearer to her departure. It suddenly occurred to him that the end of this day brought all of them one day closer to that "highest of feasts."

Could his father have once stood on this spot? Yes, of course. Why not? Ed Kirkman and Martina von Egloffsberg in their days of walking these environs must surely have come this way and paused here together to survey this peaceful scene. There were more houses in the village now, but the schloss, the church, and the encircling fields and hills spread out below him had all been there in 1923. Martina's devastating news had forever altered his view of his father. Why should an apparently youthful and impulsive act of indiscretion a half-century ago have shaken him so badly? Was it because it seemed so irresponsible? Was it because it was so inconsistent with the solid family man, the leading citizen and lawyer of Remberton? Was there some element of deceit here in not disclosing to his only son the fact that he had been in Prinzenheim? His feeling was ridiculous, he kept telling himself. His father was still the man he had known from birth—a good man who loved his wife, his son, and his community. Nothing could change that, he said to himself; but Schloss Prinzenheim seemed to have done so.

Her voice roused him from his brooding. "I shouldn't say this, but I cannot hold it back." She hesitated. They were still holding hands, facing each other by the side of the deserted road. "It's . . . it's this. I think that I am falling in love with you."

Rob did not know how to respond. The situation was getting out of control. What was he doing here anyway, thousands of miles from home with a woman he scarcely knew? He thought of the plane leaving for the States the next day. He would be on it, removed from this scene. He yearned for that moment to come. And yet . . . yet . . . he felt powerfully drawn to this unusual woman.

He kissed her again lightly and said, "It's getting cold and late. We better be getting back for dinner." He was acutely aware that he had made no response to her dramatic pronouncement. He was too confused to say anything.

Chapter 34

THE OAK LOGS BLAZED high behind the andirons in the mammoth fireplace in the great hall. The fire threw out a circle of heat for a dozen feet around, but beyond that the air was chilled. The scene triggered childhood memories for Rob of winter evenings in the front parlor at Trepnitz Hills, where half the room was left in the cold, as though an invisible curtain had been drawn in a semicircle around the fireplace. Here in that chilly region beyond the light from the fire and lamps Rob could see the shadowy portraits of three centuries of Mensingers and the few Egloffsbergs that Martina had brought on her westward exodus.

The group had assembled in this baronial space at the suggestion of Martina, who wanted an especially festive evening to mark the return of Wolfgang and the departure of Rob. But there was an underlying melancholy to the occasion, for, though unstated, it seemed likely that this might very well be among the last evenings that Martina herself would emerge for dinner. She was gaunt and pale, her flesh drained of color. She was obviously here only through gargantuan effort.

They were now gathered within the cluster of chairs and sofas flanking the fireplace. Wolfgang was unusually animated, even agitated at times. He had been delivered late that afternoon, so Olga reported to Rob, by a strange man driving a black Mercedes. The man deposited Wolfgang at the steps and departed immediately.

Martina was seated on the sofa with Helga on one side and Maria on the other. The three men stood in front of the fire. On a table to the side were vodka, scotch, wine, and the ever-present von Mensinger liqueur. The women and Ernst were having wine. Wolfgang had announced with gusto that he was taking vodka. Rob joined him.

"I was at Marburg a few days ago," boomed Wolfgang, "at the headquarters of our association of blind intellectuals. The name does not translate well into English. The association includes teachers, lawyers, judges, and government workers. Our international conference will be in Leipzig this spring; that is why I was in Washington in November."

Helga spoke up. "Wolfgang, how is it that you can go and come so freely in the GDR? I have never understood. Other people have asked us about it, and we have never known what to say."

As Helga was talking, Wolfgang was at the table seeking out the vodka bottle with his hand. Having located it, he poured a hefty quantity into his glass. There was no ice or mixer.

"You should know by this time that I have had special arrangements. There is nothing secret or illegal about it. However, I am not free to tell you the details."

"Now that we are all out of the GDR, I thought that you could tell us more," Helga said.

"This may sound arrogant, but I would say that these arrangements have benefited all Germans. For some purposes, I make no distinction between East and West. In fact, look at those in this room. We are all East Germans, and so is your daughter, Christa. We were all born on the territory of what is now the GDR, except mother, who married an East German and lived there for years. I will not let this cruel happenstance of history control my thoughts and actions." His voice rose as he warmed to the subject. "If I wanted to sound even more arrogant, I would say that my work benefits all mankind, because what happens in this divided Germany will affect the entire world for better or worse."

Martina's weakened voice intruded. "I want to say that I am very proud of what my son is doing. Whatever it is—and I know little about it—I believe that it is all for the good."

"Thank you, Mother," he said in a much-lowered voice. "It is comforting to know that there is at least one person among all the suspicious persons in this world with confidence that I am doing the right thing."

"Also," Martina continued, "I want to say that I am very proud of all my children and grandchildren and, of course, of Ernst. To have you here tonight is the finest blessing I could have." Her eyes were glistening with tears. Helga gave her a hug. "I am only sorry that Christa is not here."

"She will be here in a few days," Helga said.

Wolfgang spoke up in a more somber tone. "Helga, you have asked me about my special arrangements. I had not intended to give you this news tonight. It is bad news that I must report. The GDR authorities are moving against the Bonhoeffer League. I was summoned to the Ministry of Foreign Affairs in East Berlin while I was there three days ago. I was informed that my travel privileges were being terminated. They said that they had evidence that I had engaged in activity against the interest of the state. They were not going to arrest me, they said, but they were cutting off my access to the GDR. Worse than that, I learned that the police are beginning to arrest church members who are active in the Bonhoeffer League. So far, no pastors have been arrested—they seem reluctant to move directly against the church—but some members have been taken into custody for investigation."

Wolfgang pulled a folded piece of paper from his coat pocket. "Here," he said, extending the paper toward Pastor Schreibholz, "see if you know any of these. Some, I believe, are from Halle."

Schreibholz rose from the chair in which he had seated himself, took the paper, and sagged back down. He unfolded the paper and examined it intently. His expression told the story. "This is very bad, Helga," he said, looking toward his wife. "There are three of our members on the list. You remember Martin Bucholt, I am sure." Helga nodded. "Also Inga Schuler and Hans Niemeyer."

"Oh, I cannot believe it," exclaimed Helga with great anguish.

"They are also, unfortunately for them, members of the Bonhoeffer League."

"What is going on here," Wolfgang said, "as I understand it, is that the GDR has determined to put the Bonhoeffer League out of business. At the same time, they do not want to upset the slightly warming relations with the West. I think it is very good that you left when you did, Ernst. And Maria, it might be more difficult now to negotiate your release."

Wolfgang's news cast a somber pall over the group. Helga seemed pained over the plight of their former church members. Ernst was lost in thought behind his metal-rimmed eyeglasses. Maria held Martina's hand in hers. Wolfgang inhaled a long swallow from his glass of vodka. Rob shifted uneasily, not knowing what to say.

The moody silence was broken by the appearance of Olga to announce that dinner was ready. "Well," Martina said, "as sad as this news is, we must not let it ruin our dinner. We have much to be thankful for in having you here instead of there."

Helga helped Martina to her feet, and they moved toward the hallway leading to the dining room. Wolfgang and Ernst followed.

For a few moments, Maria and Rob were left alone in the great hall. The fire bathed them in its crackling glow. Maria was wearing a blue silk cocktail dress, another of her Christmas presents from West Berlin. Rob felt warm inside from the vodka. He had just finished his second glass. She took his hand, and they smiled warmly at each other.

"That is indeed bad news for a lot of people, but I agree that we must not let it spoil our evening," she said. "This is a night that I do not want to end."

"It's not nearly over yet," Rob said.

They walked toward the door, still holding hands. "I think that Wolfgang is having too much to drink," she said. "Before you arrived, he had already taken a full glass of vodka, and now he has had two more."

"I think he is upset by this news and by what has happened to his travel privileges into the GDR, but I wouldn't worry about him tonight. After all, he is in his own house."

Martina sat at one end of the table, Wolfgang at the other. Helga and Ernst were seated along one side, with Maria and Rob on the opposite. Martina asked Ernst to say a blessing. Out of the corner of his eye, Rob saw Olga standing behind Martina's high-backed chair, bowing her head.

Pastor Schreibholz invoked divine blessings in the same resounding tones that Rob had heard coming from Martin Luther's pulpit in Halle. Rob marveled at the length of the blessing; it was a small sermon. It occurred to him that the pastor might miss the opportunity he had always had of holding forth every Sunday before a congregation.

Olga began serving food and wine with great efficiency. Martina lifted her glass, "I want to toast our American visitor. He has come a long way in cold weather. He has almost become a member of our family in a short time, and though I may not be here, I hope that he will return to Prinzenheim."

They all lifted glasses and drank. Rob felt a blush spring to his face.

"Thank you," he said with an embarrassed smile. "You have indeed made me feel at home." He involuntarily glanced at Helga. She was looking at him with a benign smile. "I do hope that I can return at some time."

They all ate vigorously. The conversation turned to the weather. Snow was predicted for the next afternoon. From such beautiful sunshine one day to snow the next, Martina commented, was hard to believe, but the weather there could change rapidly.

"Perhaps you will get out ahead of the snow," Wolfgang announced.

"My flight is due to leave Frankfurt at noon, so I should make it," Rob said.

Apparently not paying much attention to Rob's response, Wolfgang boomed out again, "Ernst, I have a theory, a theological theory, or perhaps a mixed political and theological theory, and I am wondering whether you would consider it blasphemous." Rob watched Wolfgang empty his second glass of wine.

"Well, what is it?" Ernst asked. "I should say to Robert here that Wolfgang is a man with many theories. Some are very good, others are, should I say, debatable."

"I am not a theologian. I consider myself a man of action." Wolfgang was even more animated now than he had been before dinner. "You remember, Ernst, Bonhoeffer's poem on the four stations to freedom. Right after discipline he put action."

Rob felt an inner satisfaction in having actually read that poem. Did Wolfgang consider himself to be in the action stage, with suffering yet to come? He thought of asking, but decided against it. He was apprehensive over what Wolfgang might say through the growing haze of alcohol.

"What is this theory of yours?" Ernst asked.

"We are told that Christ on the cross symbolized the broken and sinful world, that he was there to pay the price for our sins. Could it be that in our time, in this fragmented and sinful century, Germany is God's symbol?"

"Are you suggesting that Germany is paying the price for the sins of mankind?" Helga asked.

"I am asking whether that is not a sound theory. Think of it this way. What better people or nation to be called upon to bear that burden as Christ bore it?" Olga filled the wine glasses again, including Wolfgang's, but he hardly paused. "To begin with, we have the Jewish difficulty. I will never forget the theology student in Berlin who told me in the late thirties that he knew Hitler was doomed the minute he moved against the Jews. The Nazis had touched the apple of God's eye, he said, and that was fatal. He was right. He spoke of the Nazis, but he should have spoken of Germany as a whole, that the nation was doomed. Beyond the Jews, there was the inhumane aggression wreaked on many countries. I myself reserve judgment on the campaign against the Soviet Union. There is the antichrist; but putting that aside, Germany had to pay for its sins—the good Germans along with the bad. What better way for God to exhibit to the world the wages of sin than to bring destruction on German cities, slaughter its people, and divide the land. Yes," he took a long breath and exhaled, "we have been chosen by divine power to show God's judgment to the world in this century." He took a drink from his wine glass and leaned back in his chair.

Wolfgang had been speaking so loudly that when he stopped, the silence was almost startling. Rob took another swallow of wine, although he was beginning to think that he too might be having too much to drink. However, no one at the table seemed to be refusing refills by Olga.

"That is an interesting theory," said Maria, who had been relatively quiet so far. "I have never heard it all put that way before."

"Interesting it is," Ernst said, "but we must remember one point: for Christians, all the world is in a state of sin and fragmentation; and human beings are powerless alone to overcome that condition. Germany is just the most dramatic example. We will not find a healed world free of sin on this side of the grave."

Rob couldn't decide whether Wolfgang was drunk, was trying to be clever and provocative, or was really serious. Ernst's mention of the grave made him wince. He thought that the word must hit Martina with a special impact.

"We should turn to less somber subjects," Martina said, mustering a smile. "Maria has told me that she is thinking of going to America for further training. Has she mentioned that to you, Robert?"

"Yes, and I have told her that I will inquire into the possibility at the University of Virginia Medical School. I have met the head of the Department of Ophthalmology there."

"That would be wonderful," Martina said. "What do you think of that, Maria?"

"It sounds like an excellent idea; but, of course, it is only a suggestion at this point. I am sure that it is not easy for a foreigner, especially one educated in the GDR, to be admitted to training in an American hospital."

"I suppose," Helga said, addressing Rob, "that since Christa is now married to an American, she will eventually be over there. Perhaps you will have occasion to see them in future years in your country."

Before Rob could respond, Martina interrupted. "That is true, but I hope that she will keep her connections with Germany. After all, she will own a part of this schloss some day. German and American blood have intermingled for a long time. Actually, it is more accurate to say that American blood is German blood to a great extent. Look at Robert. The blood of Thuringia runs in his veins. Isn't it strange that fifty years ago his father and I met in Germany and here is the son back again?"

Rob shifted uneasily in his chair. He looked at Helga, but she was focusing on her mother. This talk of mingling German and American blood and of his father's visit brought them to the edge of the powerful biological fact known only to Martina and himself. There was something enormously discomforting in Helga's ignorance of the matter. At this moment, he felt that he would be driven to reveal the fact to Helga when Martina was gone.

"I must now retire to my room," Martina said. "I have not been up this late for a long time, and I am quite tired. All of you should go back to the fire in the great hall. I will see you in the morning."

"I have one more toast I want to make," announced Wolfgang. He lifted his half-empty wine glass and looked straight down the table at Martina. "Here is to the finest mother," he always called her *Mutti*. "No family ever had a better mother."

They all voiced approval, laughed, and raised their glasses.

"Thank you," Martina said. "No mother ever had a finer family. We are a remnant of what we should have been and once were, but I hope that there will be descendants. My hope is that Christa and Maria will have children who will carry on, even though at least some of them may be Americans. And, Ernst, am I right that we will all ultimately be together again?"

"That is what I believe—in the world to come."

For an instant silence enveloped the room. Then Martina struggled to her feet. "I must say good night."

Helga jumped up and hurried around to her chair. "I will go with you to your room."

When the two had gone, the others walked back to the great hall. The fire had been freshly piled with logs, and it was crackling anew.

"Robert, I recall that you liked the von Mensinger brand of schnapps. Would you join me in a glass?" Wolfgang seemed a bit unsteady on his feet. A blind man already had enough problems, Rob thought, without getting drunk.

"Yes, I believe I will," Rob heard himself saying without thinking. "But I will help myself."

He turned to Maria, who had seated herself on the sofa. "Would you like some of the local produce?"

"I think I will have some," she said to his surprise. Ernst had taken a chair and shook his head, indicating that he did not care for anything.

Rob handed Maria a glass filled with the colorless, fiery liquid. He sat down beside her on the sofa. Wolfgang took a chair near the fire. They sat silently, satiated with food and drink.

As if he felt it necessary to start a conversation, Ernst said, "Wolfgang, we were talking about your work. I want to say that in my judgment of all that you do, your efforts on behalf of the blind are probably the most important."

"Yes, the blind," Wolfgang repeated slowly, and then launched into a meandering soliloquy. Rob was now convinced that the man was inebriated; but he himself was also not far from that state.

"The blind have certain advantages," Wolfgang said in a half-mocking tone. "They do not have to see all the unsightly and tawdry buildings, people, and clutter. For me, the world looks exactly as it did in 1942. Imagine that! Thirty years later, Unter den Linden still looks the same to me. I do not have to see all the rubble and gaping spaces where buildings used to be. Of course, I know that if I try to find the Adlon Hotel, I will come into a parking lot. And if I am trying to enter the Imperial Palace, I will go into the Palast der Republik instead. But at least I do not see the depressing scene. Now the other side of that is that I do want to know what some things look like, and for that I am entirely dependent on the descriptive power of the person I happen to be with. You probably do not realize how much people vary in their ability to describe even a simple structure or how another person appears—features, hair, shape of face, and so on." He took a hefty swallow of the schnapps, pausing to let the internal fire subside. "In fact, I grow terribly weary of having to do almost everything through someone else. The frustration can be immense. One of these days, I may crack and in a moment of total rage grab someone by the throat! Don't worry. I am not at that point tonight." He half laughed and sat quietly for some seconds. Only the simmering flames broke the silence.

"Well, I can certainly understand the frustration," Ernst said.

"You probably cannot," Wolfgang said sternly. "I believe it is impossible to grasp the situation without being in it. Think of a bird in a cage with a black cloth draped over it. Imagine that someone carries the cage everywhere—on the streets, on trains, on airplanes, in buildings, the theater, around the house. The bird can hear and smell everything but is cut off from any contact, sees nothing, is separated, trapped. He is there in the midst of it all, but is not really part of it. A large gathering is the worst. People are all around talking, the noise grows. It is impossible to know who is next to you. I came to understand for the first time what happened to Samson. He was standing next to that pillar with the huge crowd all around. I can hear the noise now, the babbling roar of that multitude. He was in it, but, as always, not part of it. Finally Samson said to hell with it and pulled the whole thing down."

A stillness came over the room, interrupted by the opening of the large wooden door. Helga came in, saying that her mother had gone to bed very tired, but glad that she had been at dinner. She wanted them all to be reminded that she wished them to come to her room in the morning for a special service.

"I think that it is our bedtime too," Ernst said. Helga agreed, so they said good night.

"I too believe that it is time for me to go to sleep," Wolfgang said, his speech slightly slurred. As he stood up unsteadily, he raised his glass and said, "Here's to the sunflowers of the Ukraine."

Rob and Maria remained seated on the sofa alone in the somber, half-illuminated, half-heated hall. The fire was dying. Their glasses were empty.

Rob moved his hand over on top of hers. "It's getting late," he said softly. "I suppose that I also ought to retire. I need to be up fresh in the morning. I must be presentable when I appear in Martina's room for this service she has planned."

"Yes," she whispered.

As if his limbs were those of a puppet being controlled on strings by someone else, Rob's arm went around her shoulder. The other went across her waist. He pulled her toward him, and she did not resist.

Between kisses, she murmured, "Do you remember what I told you this afternoon?"

"Yes."

"I am even surer of it now."

Again, Rob made no response. He found this woman alluring, fascinating, and appealing beyond any woman he had known. It was even possible that he was falling in love with her, but his sense of honesty would not let him say those magic words until he could do so with complete truthfulness. He held back, hanging on to at least some measure of self-control despite the evening's lavish flow of vodka, wine, and schnapps.

He stood up and pulled her to her feet. They embraced for an indefinite time, sealed together in one long kiss.

"We must say good night," he said, taking her hand and heading for the door.

At the junction of the corridors, where one led to the family apartments and the other led down the length of the schloss toward the guest room, they kissed again and parted.

Moonlight illuminated Rob's bedroom. He stood at the window, gazing at the eerie snow-reflected light making the whole landscape visible. He had brushed his teeth, splashed cold water on his face, and put on his pajamas. It was clear to him that he would be better off if he had taken at least two less glasses of wine and no schnapps. He was unsteady on his feet, and his mind was whirring over past and present, but he felt peculiarly alive, charged with the drama of the circumstances in which he found himself.

The far hills were bathed in the strange light. It came back to him that Martina and the sightless Wolfgang had stood here in April of 1945, listening to the rising, awesome sound of tank engines—American tanks. Had they remained at Bachdorf and been looking eastward, they would have been listening instead to Red Army tanks. In his imagination, he saw the courtyard below this window filling with American soldiers, armed and suspicious Americans milling around the front steps confronting Martina and her blinded son, as white flags flapped overhead.

His mind went back to the first war, that fundamental catastrophe of the twentieth century. The walls of the missing at the Menin Gate, mile after mile of British cemeteries stretching from Ypres through the Somme, the macabre environs of Verdun, the Marne, the Argonne—the slaughter fields of a generation, perhaps of a civilization.

Except for the Great War of 1914 to 1918, he mused with semicoherence, he would not be standing here in Schloss Prinzenheim at the moment. It was that alone that brought together for a few fleeting moments

Edward Kirkman of Trepnitz Hills on the Alabama and Bruno von Egloffsberg from Bachdorf on the Elbe.

His mind was still wrestling with the fact that his father had slept in this very room where he was now standing in this moonlit midnight. Slept here, yes, but not alone. That one night in this room left behind something of which his father never knew, something that was now a fifty-year-old woman named Helga, sleeping at this very hour less than a hundred yards away.

The sudden revelation that Helga was his half-sister was enough mental trauma for a lifetime. Beyond that, he was still troubled by the revelation that one Rudolph von Trepnitz, direct descendent of his own ancestor, had stood in the dock at Nuremburg. And now there was Maria. Was this a momentary infatuation that would fade as soon as he was on that plane over the Atlantic at thirty-seven thousand feet? Suppose she should come to Charlottesville?

And what of his own career decision? He had to say very soon whether he would remain at Virginia beyond June. With his father gone, perhaps the time had come to move on to another phase in his career—not deserting the house of the fathers, as Professor George Marks Wilton would have put it, but simply moving to another room in it.

So ran the intoxicated thoughts of Robert Kirkman as he leaned against the large window soaking in the moon-bathed village of Prinzenheim. But his mental meanderings were broken off by a faint noise, a soft tapping on his door. His heartbeat quickened. This room was far removed from the family apartments, down long, dark, antlered corridors and up an even darker flight of stairs. He went quietly in his bare feet to the door.

"Who is there?" Rob asked in German.

"It's Maria," came the response in a stage whisper.

He opened the door, and she stepped in, wearing a woolen bathrobe. He closed the door behind her to keep out the chill.

"What are you doing wandering around these cold corridors at this hour?"

"I could not sleep. I feel too awake, too . . . too . . . what do you say . . . excited to sleep." She looked toward the window. "How bright this room is! The moonlight here is much stronger than it is in my room on the other side of the house."

Rob walked over to the window and stood beside her. "Oh, it is truly beautiful!" she exclaimed. "You can see the whole village and even the fields and hills on the other side."

They faced each other. "I had to see you again. I hope you are not angry with me."

She ran her arms around his waist and laid her head on his shoulder. He felt her soft hair against his cheek. His nose caught the faint and provocative scent of her perfume.

"No, I was not asleep either."

Maria raised her head from his shoulder and placed her hands on his face, holding it in a soft vise as she kissed him.

"Oh, Robert," she said, backing up a bit, "I will miss you so much when you leave. I cannot bear to think of tomorrow. It is now past midnight, so it is actually today that you go."

The loose sash that had held her bathrobe together had come undone, letting the robe fall open. Rob saw with startled amazement that she was wearing nothing underneath.

She moved forward, putting her arms around his neck and kissing him. He pulled her closer with his arms around her back. He now sensed warm, soft flesh firmly pressing against his thin pajamas. The pounding of his heart was audible. Blood pulsated in his temples.

She stood back, her hands on his face. The moonlight illumined her white skin between the open folds of the robe.

They embraced again, the warm, feminine flesh—the body he had carried vividly in his mind from Magdeburg—crushed against him. Rob now felt out of control, no longer standing on solid ground.

The moon had waned, roosters had crowed in the distance, and a faint hint of approaching dawn had touched the sky when she left the room and he fell asleep.

Chapter 35

"LORD THOU HAST BEEN our dwelling place in all generations. Before the mountains were brought forth or ever thou hadst formed the earth in the world, from everlasting to everlasting thou art God." Pastor Ernst Schreibholz was intoning the Ninetieth Psalm in his best pulpit German. He was once more in clerical garb—black coat, vest, and trousers, with white collar.

They were gathered at Martina's bedside. Wolfgang stood beside Ernst, his eyes fixed straight ahead. On the opposite side of the bed, facing Ernst and Wolfgang over the thin, propped-up body of Martina, Rob stood between Helga and Maria. Olga was at the foot of the bed, her eyes resting on the woman she had accompanied and served for thirty years.

"She had wanted to be dressed and here in this room," Olga had said to Rob when he entered the sitting room a few minutes earlier. "But I think that the last two days have been too much for her, so the service will be at her bed." Rob had walked on into the inner room to find all the others already gathered.

Rob had scarcely spoken to any of them before the readings had begun. He and Maria had exchanged sheepish glances. The pastoral cadence and the rolling words of the psalmist mingled with Rob's thoughts.

"Thou hast set our iniquities before thee, our secret sins in the light of thy countenance. For all our days pass away under thy wrath. . . ." The words aggravated his sense of embarrassment and guilt, intensifying the queasiness in his stomach. Despite the coolness of the room, he was breaking out in a thin sweat. With only a couple of hours of sleep and a headache from too much to drink, he was not in good shape at this moment.

Helga slid her hand into his and clasped it firmly. As though triggered mechanically, Rob's other hand moved over and took Maria's.

"The years of our life are three score and ten, or even by reason of strength, fourscore. Yet their span is but toil and trouble. They are soon gone. . . ." She had been given her allotted span, Rob's befogged mind noted—this last link to two German families of the golden age before the Great War brought down the curtain. Flanked here by the remnants of those families, this dying woman was linked also and forever to Robert by that most basic and intimate of all relationships, the living flesh and blood evidence of which was standing beside him, the two clasping hands, Kirkman blood pulsating against Kirkman blood.

"Yea though I walk through the valley of the shadow of death, I will fear no evil, for thou art with me. . . ." Everyone in the room was perfectly still and expressionless. The only sound was the deep-timbered voice reading the ancient assurances.

That voice emitting from the gray-haired, rugged figure with the metal-rimmed eyeglasses took Rob's thoughts back to the sermon in Halle. He remembered Saul's search for the lost donkeys, the seemingly inconsequential task that was God's device for bringing him to Samuel.

"In my father's house are many rooms . . . I go to prepare a place for you. . . ." It suddenly hit him that this was essentially a funeral service, an anticipatory service, with its subject lying in front of them, still very much alive but within sight of the grave. He began to sense the formation of tears. Waves of hot and cold perspiration broke out on his forehead. He dared not look to his left or right, but only straight ahead.

In his mind's eye, Rob saw the coming picture of the group at the cemetery just up the road, the casket resting over the open grave next to the memorial tablet recording the long-ago existence of husband and son. Old familiar words filled the air—the hope of resurrection . . . into the everlasting arms . . . the last day . . . the peace that passeth all understanding.

The pastor had closed the Bible and begun a prayer, expressing thanks for the life of this woman now afflicted and sick, for all those who had gone before and entered into eternal life. The lines from Bonhoeffer's poem came back to Rob: "Death . . . the highest of feasts on the journey to freedom eternal." This then was a celebration, or should be, Rob thought, not an occasion for sadness. The prayer was concluding, the pastoral voice calling down the blessings of Almighty God on all of them, including "our friend, Robert Kirkman."

First, Ernst bent over and kissed Martina on the forehead, then Wolfgang did the same, followed by Helga and Maria. Rob moved forward and took her skeletal hand. She spoke aloud for the first time. "I would like to have a visit with Robert alone for a few minutes."

Helga said, "We will say good-bye to you on the front steps."

"All right," Rob said. "I must leave in a quarter-hour."

The door closed, and Rob and Martina were left alone. He saw now that her eyes were moist with tears, as were his.

Pointing with her free hand, she said, "Go to the top drawer there. You will find a brown envelope. Bring it here and open it."

Rob returned to the bed with the envelope. He pulled out two photographs. The one on top he recognized from last summer when she had showed it to him. He looked again into the smiling and youthful faces of his father, Martina, and Harold Titheringham in front of the gray medieval schloss.

The second he had not seen. This, he recognized immediately, was the clinching proof of his father's return visit. In this picture, his father, still as young but smiling less, and Martina were standing in the front courtyard of this very house. The vine-covered brick walls looked almost exactly as they did now. Martina, scrubbed-looking and vibrant, had her arm looped through his father's.

"The second photograph was taken as your father was leaving. Five minutes after it was taken, he was gone, and I never saw him again. You may have both of these."

"Thank you," Rob said, as he put them back into the envelope and shoved it into his side coat pocket. "I'll keep them always." He sat on the edge of the bed and took her hand in both of his. "I must be going."

"Robert," she said, a tear trickling down her cheek, "You are so like your father. He had vanished from my life as a dream from my youth, then you came last summer. You must remember that fifty years had gone by. It was as though he himself had returned. I was so overcome by this that I decided that I must share with you the secret that I had promised to myself never to tell anyone. I leave it with you. It is yours to do with as you please after I am gone. But whatever you do about that, I do hope that you will remember Helga and stay in contact with her."

Rob slowly nodded his head, finding no suitable words. Now he felt the warm track of a tear down his own cheek. She struggled to prop herself up higher against the pillows. She winced with pain.

"The last two days have meant much to me," she said after a moment, with a labored effort, "but physically and emotionally they have put me lower. It will not be long now. . . ."

Her voice trailed off. For a long moment, they were silent. Her gaze went to the tall window. Outside, clouds were forming into a gray canopy over the wintry landscape. Her words replayed in Rob's mind. "You are so like your father." Like his father . . . yes, like his father. He suddenly realized that the sense of mixed anger and deceit he had felt toward his father in the wake of Martina's revelation had vanished. Events since midnight had stripped him of any basis for such feelings.

Martina spoke softly: "We will not see each other again on this side." He could say nothing. "When I am half sleeping and half dreaming—I take a lot of morphine to hold down the pain—I think of the coming days. I wonder when and where I will see Bruno. Will he be young? What will he look like? Will I see Kurt and all of my family from childhood and all those people from Bachdorf?"

"I doubt that anyone, even Ernst, can answer those questions," Rob said.

Tears were coursing down his cheeks. He was surprised that he was not embarrassed and he did nothing to hide the tears. "The time has come for me to start for Frankfurt. It has been an honor to know you." He leaned over and kissed her on her sunken cheek.

She squeezed his hand tightly. "Good-bye," she whispered, "and thank you. Take care of Maria, if you can."

He paused at the door, raised his hand in a faint farewell gesture, smiling wistfully, and then closed the door gently.

Olga was standing at the top of the main stairway. She had already put his bags in the car. He thanked her for all of her attention and pressed two hundred-mark bills into her hand.

Helga, Ernst, and Maria were waiting for him at the bottom of the stairway beneath the forest of antlers. They walked together out onto the curved front steps of the schloss.

"I think that the prediction of snow today will be correct," Ernst said, lifting his face toward the graying sky. "But you will probably get to the airport before it begins."

The air was noticeably colder. The entire mood of the landscape had changed. All was now a colorless smudge. The cold air striking Rob in the face was refreshing. He felt his lungs and mind clearing.

"We would like to take some pictures," Helga said. She was carrying a small camera. "I will take the three of you," she said, as she motioned Ernst, Maria, and Rob together at the bottom of the steps.

The heavy wooden door was pulled open, and Wolfgang emerged, white cane swinging from side to side ahead of him. "Wolfgang, you are just in time for the picture. Come down straight ahead and stand beside Robert."

"I notice that your cane tip is quieter in the snow," Rob said as Wolfgang reached his side.

"It is indeed, and that is a real problem. People in my condition navigate by sound, and snow deadens sound. Snow is the blind man's fog."

Helga snapped the picture. "Now, Ernst, you take all of us."

After Ernst duly complied, Rob spoke up. "May I have you take a picture of me and Helga and then one of me and Maria?"

Rob and Helga stood together, while Ernst located them in the viewfinder. On impulse, Rob slid his arm through hers and pulled her close against him just before the shutter clicked.

"Now, Maria," Ernst said, "it is your turn." Maria and Helga exchanged places. Rob took her arm in the same way. Ernst clicked the shutter.

"Take another," Maria said in an unexpectedly assertive tone. "That one might not be clear."

"All right," Ernst said, adjusting the camera again. "Now, smile."

Rob felt Maria's arm slide around his back. In reflex action, he put his arm around her shoulders. "Good," exclaimed Ernst as he clicked the shutter.

They were all saying good-bye to Rob. He shook hands with Wolfgang. Helga came up, and they hugged.

"You must come back to see us," she said. "Even though mother will not be here, you will always be welcome."

Ernst came up. Rob grasped his large, rough hand. "*Auf wiedersehen*," the pastor said.

"Remember," Rob said laughingly, "there are no coincidences."

Ernst broke into a broad smile, slapping Rob on the arm with his left hand. "Ah, you remember the lost donkeys."

Helga, Ernst, and Wolfgang turned to go up the steps. Looking at Rob, Maria said, "I will walk to the car with you."

They crunched across the snow-covered cobblestones to the rented Volkswagen. The massive front door to the schloss banged shut behind the others. Maria and Rob were alone in the courtyard. They stood beside the car, facing each other.

"I want to apologize for last night," she said.

"If any apology is due, it is mine for the way I acted. I'm afraid I didn't behave in a very gentlemanly manner."

"That is absurd." Her eyes were brighter than he had ever noticed. "I am the one who came to your room." She smiled slyly and took both of his hands in hers.

Rob's face brightened. "You have some interesting freckles."

"You are certainly a close observer."

"I had already had a good look at them in Magdeburg."

"Magdeburg!" she exclaimed. "You should be ashamed."

"What was I to do when you put them on display right in front of me?"

She sighed. "Oh, what a night that was. I was so depressed and tired. All of that now seems like a nightmare. It belongs to another world. The memory I want to carry of it is your courage." She squeezed his hands.

"I know that you want to stay here as long as Martina is alive—"

"Yes," she interrupted, "and that will not be long. The doctor was here earlier this morning, and I talked with him."

"Will you consider coming to the States then?"

"Yes. I have decided that that is what I want to do."

"I will try to make arrangements for you at the hospital and medical school in Virginia."

She slipped her arms around his neck; he encircled her waist. Despite the bracing effect of the cold air, Rob's head still ached from his overindulgence, and he was thirsty. But his pulse was now up, and all the curious stirrings inside him were aroused again. The clock in the church tower finished striking. They kissed, and the only sound was their breathing.

"I love you," she whispered.

In response, Rob's voice, detached from him, uncontrolled by him, whispered those words he had not been able to say to this woman: "I love you."

The car door was open. As he stepped inside, his eyes swept the vine-covered bricks of the schloss. High up on the top floor at the far end was the tall window of his bedroom. His room and his father's room. Whatever this place had meant to his father, Rob's life, he sensed, was forever changed by Schloss Prinzenheim.

There was a faint hint of sleet in the air and as he eased the car forward across the cobblestones, moving through the gateway, Robert Kirkman glanced back an instant before the wall shut off his view of the courtyard and the schloss. In his last fleeting glimpse, he saw, standing alone in the middle of that deserted space, the tall, slim figure of Maria Egloffsberg, hand uplifted and smiling sadly, just as he remembered her in the Magdeburg Station.

The clouds were low and dense and the snow flurries were thickening as the huge jet lifted smoothly off the runway at Frankfurt. The ground disappeared immediately as the plane was enveloped in the impenetrable mist. It climbed upward sharply and steadily, through five thousand feet, ten thousand feet, and broke into the clear sunshine. From his window seat, Rob could see only the blue dome overhead and the undulating white cloud floor below.

Climbing to thirty-nine thousand feet, so the pilot had announced, the plane was heading northwest over Germany, over Europe, over the Atlantic, to the New World and home. Passing far below was the tortured terrain of a thousand years of European conflict. Crecy and Agincourt were down there, as well as the Somme and the Ardennes. Once more, he felt that sense of release at being above it, out of it, heading west.

With the seat back in its fully reclined position, his head nestled in a pillow between the seat and window, Rob was stretched out full-length. He pulled the photographs from his coat pocket. He gazed at his father locked arm-in-arm with Martina fifty years ago in front of the vine-covered wall where he himself had stood with Maria three hours earlier. Exhaustion was overtaking him. His mind flickered with jumbled images—Maria in her blue cocktail dress seated on the sofa, Maria in the red glow of sunset on the road above Prinzenheim, Maria in the moonlit window of his bedroom.

Half-dreaming, he was sucked into history. War was the dominant experience of the human race. Everything about their lives was the result of wars. The moments of high purpose, of cruelty, of sorrow and joy—all of these were at their keenest in war. War was paradoxical. It was the rejection of civilization but the savior of civilization.

In the swirling cordite and whining machine-gun fire of the Argonne, he saw the young Lieutenant Kirkman kneeling over the dead officer in field gray, another name to be added to those long lists weathering years later on village monuments. Then it was another war, a quarter-century later, dust churning from the tanks' clanking metal treads, the unearthly roar of their engines blotting out all else, on their sides the white stars, the swastikas, and the red stars. Then back and back in time, the black, red, and gold banners were flapping in the breeze as lines of Prussian cavalry passed through the Brandenburg Gate, bands blaring and hooves clattering on the Unter den Linden. Then jarring forward into the twentieth century, the black crooked cross on white and red hanging on the front of the new Reich Chancellery. Rubble, block after block of rubble, then the Wall—high concrete, barbed wire, guard towers and automatic weapons—slicing through the city.

Other men in gray flickered and swirled around him, not field gray, but the gray of a different time and place, long lines of dusty, gray-clad soldiers moving behind the starred St. Andrew's cross, flapping in the Virginia summer breeze. There was Lt. Col. Henry Trepnitz, with the blood of Thuringia and Saxony in his veins, moving on to his doom with the thousands of others from the river bottoms and hill country of the South who would find graves in the Virginia woodlands and fields.

Now he was back in Remberton in the Victorian house of his youth. His mother was sitting by the window reading in the soft light of an autumn afternoon. His father was in his study cleaning his shotgun, the sweet odor of Hoppes No. 9 drifting into the hall. Then it was a hot summer afternoon. On the screened porch, sitting by the opened footlocker, he was looking at the mysterious picture of a young woman and two infants. Thunder was rumbling in the distance, growing ever louder, signaling an approaching thunderstorm.

Then it was late afternoon of another summer day, years earlier. He was at Trepnitz Hills, riding his Welsh pony along dirt lanes through cotton fields, where the blooms had just opened. Thunder in the west had begun murmuring ominously and was now growing louder and closer. He prodded the pony into a gentle gallop, heading into the road for home. They would be wondering where he was. Supper would soon be ready. The aroma of frying chicken, he imagined, was already emitting from the kitchen behind the house.

The sky had gone to a slate gray. The thunder was now rolling almost overhead, the wind was rising, trees were swaying. His pony was now at a full run. The wind, suddenly cool before the advancing rain, was strong in his face as he and the pony came up the long, last slope toward the big house. The first large rain drops began to splatter around him. He heard the roar of the wind and the rain moving like a wall of water as it approached through the swaying pecan trees. They would be waiting for him there—Mr. Ed and Miss Em, Grandmother Clarissa, Uncle Charles—they would all be there, forever there.

He was bent over the pony's neck, swatting her on the flanks with the end of the reins, but she was already at her top speed. His nostrils filled with the odor of saddle leather and sweaty horseflesh. He saw the wall of water coming at him along the road and through the trees. It broke over him in torrents. Lightning was flashing in bright sheets and thunder crashed overhead in an ear-splitting cacophony as the pony, needing no guidance, turned at the great columned house for the hundred-yard dash to the brick barn at the rear.

Epilogue

THE MINISTER OF JUSTICE of the Federal Republic of Germany strode briskly across the lobby of the Hotel Esplanade. Flanked by black-suited aides, he nodded greetings to other black-suited men. The group filed into a small conference room just off the lobby. One of the aides called the little assemblage to order, and the minister came to the podium.

"As you know," he began, "we are here to receive your reports on progress in unifying the administration of justice in the five new states and to discuss what remains to be done."

One by one the justice ministers of the new eastern states rose and reported. The state names were redolent of the Germany of old: Mecklenburg-West Pomerania, Brandenburg, Saxony-Anhalt, Thuringia, Saxony—all now back in the fold. Their ministers all had the same message. The investigations of the former GDR judges and prosecutors had gone more slowly than anticipated. The Stasi files were immense. The involvements of the courts with political persecutions had been far more extensive than had been known. Germany had been criticized last time, they said, for being too lax in letting Nazis remain as judges; they must not make the same mistake this time with the Marxists-Leninists. Despite the difficulties, however, they expected all investigations to be completed by the end of 1991. It was unlikely that many judges and prosecutors would be cleared, so for the next several years large numbers of jurists must be sent in from the West.

It was nearly noon when the reports were concluded and the federal minister took the podium again. "We have some important guests here today," he said. "The American Ambassador in Bonn requested permission to send a delegation to observe these proceedings. As you know, there is much interest in the United States and throughout the whole world in our reunification process. I want to recognize the chairman of the distinguished American delegation, Professor Robert Kirkman of the University of Virginia law faculty."

In the rear of the room, Rob rose to his feet, his lean frame clad in a black suit, deliberately chosen to match what he knew would be the universal dress for the occasion. The somber attire was in stark contrast to the almost luminescent quality of his silver gray hair. He thanked the group for the privilege of listening to the great efforts being made to revamp the entire legal order in the East. From what he had learned on this trip, he said, the world could be assured that government under law would prevail in the reunified Germany.

With the meeting over, Rob walked through the lobby surveying the crowd for his wife's face. He heard the familiar voice calling over the noisy babble: "Rob, over here!" He turned and saw Maria motioning to him from beyond the reception desk.

"Come on girls. Here's Dad," she said as he approached, turning toward two teenage girls animatedly talking to each other.

"Well, Emily," Rob asked the older one as she came up to him, "What have you been doing all morning?"

"Just wandering in some stores." She had closely cropped, light brown hair, much like Maria's, but her face showed more traces of Rob.

"What do you have there, Martina?" Rob asked the younger and smaller of the two.

"A Berlin bear," she said, giggling and holding up a brown, furry object.

Rob laughed and pinched the bear's nose. "All right," he announced, "we're going to see where your mama used to work."

Outside they piled into a taxi. "Charité Hospital," Rob directed the driver.

"Drive through the Potsdamer Platz," Maria said, assuming a German command voice, "so we can see from there how it is now open to the East."

"It is all Berlin now," the driver remarked with a touch of sarcasm.

Emily spoke up, "Mom, will this hospital look like the hospital where you work at home?"

"I expect not," Maria said. "These people have had a very hard time. But give them a few years. . . ."

Rob said, "One of the Justice Minister's assistants pulled me aside in there this morning to say that they had just obtained information from the Stasi files about Wolfgang."

"Oh, what is it?" Maria asked, instantly alive with interest. For years, they had not been able to learn the circumstances of Wolfgang's death. He had left Prinzenheim shortly after Martina died, saying that his place was now in the East. Despite protestations of the family that he was surely courting trouble since he had been officially barred from the GDR, he left and was never heard from again. Months later, they got word that he had died in the Cottbus prison.

"According to the Stasi files," Rob said, "he crossed the GDR border on forged papers and went to Leipzig. Apparently they had been watching him for years." Rob went on to relate what he had just been told. A Stasi informant's report said that Wolfgang was trying to organize Bonhoeffer League members into a militant organization to mount protests against the GDR. He had said that the Communists were no better than the Nazis and must be resisted. He was also working with the blind organization in Leipzig, but the Stasi viewed that as a cover. They listed him as an enemy of the state.

"Now here is a fascinating point," Rob continued. "One of the Bonhoeffer League members in Leipzig had a car, and Wolfgang hired him to drive him to Bachdorf."

"What? Bachdorf? Why would he do that?" Maria looked perplexed.

"I suppose he had an urge to go home again, back to his point of origin. I detected that in our conversations. Anyway, Stasi agents followed the car to Bachdorf, and they arrested Wolfgang there in the schloss. But he didn't go quietly. The arrest report says that he exhibited antisocial behavior by standing on the stairway swinging a white cane at the agents and shouting that he was in the house of his fathers where they had no right to be and that the day of judgment was coming for these atheistic impostors just as it had for the Nazis."

They sat silently for a few moments. The taxi moved in fits and starts through snorting buses and a sea of cars. Maria, her face blank, pondered this revelation. "I had a feeling," she said slowly, "that on that last night you were with him at Prinzenheim he was approaching a ragged edge, so I am not really surprised to hear this." After a pause, she added, as though talking to herself, "Well I am happy that at least he did see Bachdorf again, but I guess *see* is not quite the right word."

"They took him from there to the prison. There is no record of any trial. The report says that he died in prison of a heart attack on April 9, 1975. As you know though, reports about causes of death in these circumstances are highly suspect."

"Poor Uncle Wolfi," murmured Maria, her eyes glistening. "We'll probably never know exactly what happened to him."

The taxi broke out of the traffic into Potsdamer Platz. "There it is," exclaimed the driver. Ahead they looked eastward into the broad expanse of Leipzigerstrasse, a view that had been obscured from a long generation. No Wall, no guard towers. Daylight had come, and the nightmare was gone.

"I did not think I would ever see this sight again," Maria said in a half-whisper as the taxi moved along through a point that had been impenetrable for nearly three decades.

"In twenty years, a new generation will not believe that it was ever there," Rob said.

At the intersection of Friedrichstrasse and Unter den Linden, the taxi bogged down in traffic. Mercedes were everywhere, punctuated by an occasional Trabant, its two-stroke engine emitting its lawnmower clatter above the surrounding noise.

"Let's get out here and have some lunch," Rob said. "Then we can walk to the hospital."

The four stood on the sidewalk absorbing the scene. Far down to their left were the massive columns of the Brandenburg Gate. Gone was the concrete wall stretching across its base.

"I have just realized an extraordinary fact about Wolfgang," Maria said. "He died on exactly the thirtieth anniversary of Dietrich Bonhoeffer's death. He several times mentioned that Bonhoeffer had been executed at Flossenberg on April 9, 1945. The date seemed to be burned into his mind."

Rob wondered but said nothing. Another coincidence? Maybe not. Then he asked, "Do you think if he were here now he would say that Germany had been redeemed, having paid for its sins?"

"No, I am inclined to think that he would say that this is the undeserved grace of God bestowed on an unworthy world."

They gazed around for several minutes, having difficulty assimilating the reality. A short distance to their right, Frederick the Great astride his horse rose high above the crawling traffic, now indistinguishable from the traffic in the West.

"Do you recognize that cafe?" Rob asked as he took Maria's hand and pointed a little way up the street.

Maria looked at him impishly. "At least there was one day when the coffee there was excellent."

"Well, let's see how it is now for lunch."

They took seats at a table in the rear, near the window opening onto a small patio. "Has it really been eighteen years?" Rob asked rhetorically.

"No doubt about it," Maria said, smiling broadly. "Here are two pieces of living evidence to prove it." She jostled Martina's head playfully. "Oh," she said, suddenly looking back at Rob, "I meant to tell you that I talked with Helga over the phone this morning. She is really looking forward to our visit. She says we will be the first guests at Prinzenheim since Ernst's funeral."

"Will anybody else be at Aunt Helga's?" asked Martina. Her hair was cut like Emily's. The girls were almost twins in appearance, though two years apart in age.

"No," said Maria, "Christa and Doug had hoped to come, but they have to stay in Omaha because of his business."

They finished lunch and came out into the sunshine of a magnificent June day. "All right, everybody," Rob announced, "let's strike out for the Charité."

Rob and Maria set out energetically through the midday pedestrian throng along Unter den Linden. Emily and Martina trotted along behind. The dark, U-shaped facade of Humboldt University appeared across the wide boulevard. Maria slipped her arm under Rob's.

"Have you decided whether you will tell Helga?"

Would he tell Helga? That question had bedeviled him for years. He had debated it agonizingly over and over. He had eventually told Maria, feeling an overwhelming need to share the fact—a fact possessed by him alone among all living beings. Helga was nearing seventy. Why should he at this late date inject into her life such a potentially traumatic revelation? But did he have any moral right to withhold it?

He was oblivious now to the crowds through which they were passing. He was in Remberton, in his father's house, pulling the photograph of the young woman and her two small sons from the opened footlocker. Then he saw the dying woman at Prinzenheim, clutching his hand and entrusting to him the secret known only to herself. Remberton and Prinzenheim . . . how extraordinary . . . Edward Kirkman and Martina von Egloffsberg.

At long last, he had made up his mind. His course of action had become clear. He would close the circle, finish the unfinished business.

Looking into Maria's eyes, he spoke as though he were pronouncing the last judgment. "Yes, I will tell her."

The bells on the cathedral were sounding, deep bonging intermingling with higher pitched clanging. "Give me your hands, girls. This is a busy street to cross." Rob grasped hands with Emily and Martina, one on each side.

They crossed near the Spree. The Cathedral dome loomed against the blue sky of early summer. Rob's eyes lifted and caught the inscription high above the portal of that great Hohenzollern edifice, an inscription that had survived Nazis and Communists: Lo, I am with you always, even to the end of the world.